Susanna Det...

from: Mary Beth
for my 18th Birthday

Jamie MacLeod
HIGHLAND LASS

Jamie MacLeod
HIGHLAND LASS

MICHAEL PHILLIPS
JUDITH PELLA

BETHANY HOUSE PUBLISHERS
MINNEAPOLIS, MINNESOTA 55438
A Division of Bethany Fellowship, Inc.

Published by Bethany House Publishers
A Division of Bethany Fellowship, Inc.
6820 Auto Club Road, Minneapolis, Minnesota 55438

Printed in the United States of America

Library of Congress Cataloging-in-Publication Data

Phillips, Michael R., 1946-
  Jamie MacLeod, highland lass.

  I. Pella, Judith. II. Title.
PS3566.H492J3   1987   813'.54   86-33377
ISBN 0-87123-918-3 (pbk.)

DEDICATION

to
Jeannie Pella Storbakken
Our Mutual Friend and Sister Whom We Both Love

THE STONEWYCKE TRILOGY

The Heather Hills of Stonewycke
Flight from Stonewycke
Lady of Stonewycke

THE STONEWYCKE LEGACY

Stranger at Stonewycke
Shadows Over Stonewycke

THE HIGHLAND COLLECTION

Jamie MacLeod: Highland Lass
Robbie Taggart: Highland Sailor

THE AUTHORS

The PHILLIPS/PELLA writing team had its beginning in the longstanding friendship of Michael and Judy Phillips with Judith Pella. Michael Phillips, who began his writing career with a number of non-fiction books, chanced upon a half-completed sheet in the typewriter in the Pella's home. Inspecting it closer, he asked their friend, "Do you write?" After many discussions of common literary interests and plots, collaboration began on a series of novels.

Judith Pella holds a nursing degree and BA in Social Sciences. Her background as a writer stems from her avid reading and researching in historical, adventure, and geographical venues. Pella, with her two sons, resides in Eureka, California. Michael Phillips, who holds a degree in several fields from Humboldt State University and continues his studies in history, is a businessman who owns and operates Christian bookstores on the West Coast. He is the editor of the bestselling George MacDonald Classic Reprint Series and is also MacDonald's biographer. The Phillips also live in Eureka with their three sons.

CONTENTS

Introduction

Part I—Gilbert MacLeod

1 / Evening Vigil   15
2 / A Dream of More   18
3 / The Ebony Stallion   27
4 / Lundie's Proposal   33
5 / Parting   40

Part II—Finlay MacLeod

6 / The Shepherd   51
7 / Sunset   55
8 / The Old Trunk   61
9 / The Lass of the Mountain   68
10 / Another Farewell   72
11 / Winter   81
12 / The Sailor   89
13 / Rescue   94

Part III—Aberdeen

14 / Sadie Malone   103
15 / First Days in the City   108
16 / A Row on Hogmanay   116
17 / Broken Dreams   125
18 / The Vicar's Wife   131
19 / Lessons   140
20 / Another Change   152

Part IV—Aviemere

21 / A New Home   161
22 / The Master of Aviemere   167
23 / An Afternoon's Excursion   171
24 / Edward Graystone   180
25 / Guests   189
26 / Two Conversations   193
27 / A Midnight Intruder   200
28 / Father and Son   208
29 / The First Flowers of Spring   213
30 / Candice Montrose   222
31 / A Journey into the Past   227
32 / An Unexpected Visitor   237
33 / Brotherly Strife   241
34 / Midnight Encounter   247
35 / Rumors   257

Part V—Robbie Taggart

36 / The Sailor Returns   269
37 / The Call of Love   274
38 / Dreams   283
39 / Andrew   288
40 / Thoughts   293
41 / A Surprise Visit   298
42 / The Laird and the Sailor   302

Part VI—Jamie MacLeod

43 / Pledges   309
44 / A Piece of the Puzzle   316
45 / Donachie   319
46 / The Laird of the Mountain   326
47 / The Unmasking   331
48 / Family Secrets   339
49 / Derek Graystone   346
50 / The Final Return   347

INTRODUCTION

This story of a Scottish shepherd lass growing up on a wild but beautiful, untamed but silent Highland mountain called Donachie typifies all men and women. As Jamie MacLeod (pronounced MacLoud) grows, she begins to look into the distance, scanning the horizon for what life can offer. The only hope she knows of to validate her own existence is to fulfill her father's dying dream—that somehow she rise from her humble beginnings, the poverty and restrictions of her upbringing, to become a lady, to *be* someone in the world.

Jamie's quest is a universal one. We have all climbed to the top of our own mountains, gazed into the distance, and wondered, "What's out there?" We all long to "make something" of ourselves. Shackled by muddled notions of what constitutes a fulfilled life, our roving eyes scan the horizon for the distant sunrise, for the greener grass on the other side of some ethereal fence.

But the tragic fact is that we often seek the roots of our own identity, our own personhood, outside the one place where true personhood begins.

Equipped for a joyful life of communion with God—with His creativity built into our natures, with His love and goodness surrounding us in the world He made, and with the peace of His Son available to our souls—we yet spend fruitless years looking elsewhere for that which we think will satisfy this deep longing.

Our eyes look "out there" for something which can be found only by turning upward and inward. In vain we pursue the meaningless search for things that can never be, when all the time true *life* is before us, around us, and within us—life from God himself! We try to make ourselves men and women of stature in the world's eyes, failing to understand that the only stature of real and eternal value is to grow in wisdom and to find "favor with God."

He is not as concerned with the horizons of "over there" as He is with nurturing and maturing our characters right where we stand. When we come to the end of the search and grasp at last where it has led us, the question is: are we willing to "lay down our arms" and surrender to the One whose hand has been guiding, urging, encouraging our steps all along? The search is not one which can find an answer in the streets and byways of the world or in a pot of gold at the end of the rainbow in Aberdeen. Only in listening to that "still, small voice" of God in our hearts will we discover the fulfillment of our heart's dream.

This, then, is the tale of Jamie's quest for ladyhood, a journey leading from the land of her beginnings to the city of dreams, and then back to the source from whence it all had sprung. The lure of adventure and romance tug at her, but in the end Jamie finds true love, the peace of the God of her fathers, and the essence of her own personhood where she least expects it.

This first book in "The Highland Collection" is a story of true personhood as revealed through the eyes of God, not of men. The complete picture of personhood will be seen in this series of books through the three essential ingredients which comprise it: manhood, womanhood, and sonship. Personhood—the relationship of God's created beings to himself as Creator and to themselves—cannot be grasped one-dimensionally, but only as manhood, womanhood, and sonship are clearly understood in their relationship to their Maker. Book One, *Jamie MacLeod: Highland Lass*, asks, "What is *true* womanhood? What does it mean to stand before the God who made me as the complete woman He created me to be?"

As you walk by Jamie's side, enjoying the mystical beauties of Scotland's mountains and valleys, look through her eyes as she searches the horizons of life for her own true person. But as she comes to the end of her quest, look through her eyes into your own heart. There you may be surprised to discover, as she did, that the meaning to life for which you have been searching has been in your heart from the very beginning; that for which you have longed has been within reach.

Jamie's granddaddy read to her from his Book, "Seek and ye shall find. . . . If any man hear my voice and open the door, I will come in to him. . . ." By looking too far into the distance, our eyes will be out of focus to see His ever-near presence on our own personal Donachie—right beside us.

The door to being a fulfilled person is inside, not on distant horizons. As Jamie discovers, womanhood before God is the most intimate discovery a woman created in the image of God can make in the quiet of her own heart. For He promises, "Lo, I am with you always."

Michael Phillips
Judith Pella
1707 E Street
Eureka, CA 95501

SCOTLAND

Cullen

Fraserburg

Nairn

Peterhead

Inverness

Skye

Donachie

Aviemere

Gilbert MacLeod's farm

Aberdeen

The Village

Moor

Mull

Perth

Sterling

Glasgow

Edinburgh

Scotland

England

Ireland

Miles

0   50

PART I

Gilbert MacLeod

CHAPTER ONE

Evening Vigil

The thin moon inched its way toward the top of the night. The silvery hues from its reflected brilliance cast ghostly shadows over the moorland below. Later in the month it would shine out boldly upon this lonely land, but in its first quarter it could barely illuminate the humble cottage standing silently in the ethereal glow, as if awaiting some change which was at hand. But even the light of a new moon was sufficient to reveal the stout stone walls and massive chimney and the cobbled pathway leading to the sturdy oaken door. It was hardly the home of a gentleman squire, yet there was an air of substance to the place— if it did not exactly emulate affluence, at least there had been a brave, though perhaps faltering, step in that direction.

Inside, the cottage seemed to show its truer face. All was simple and coarse, even by the standards of the 1860s, but it was tidy and clean. A dark-haired girl was alternately stirring and blowing at the struggling peat fire on the hearth, encouraging the fading embers once more to life and warmth. Her pure face and wide, innocent eyes, seen in the flickering dance of an occasional flame, would have given a stranger the impression that she was no more than four. Yet she carried herself about the place as if she were twelve; in reality she was seven. Rising from the fire, she returned to her wooden stool and, with her elbows propped on the rough pine table, rested her chin in her tiny hands. After a few moments her eyes drooped, but she quickly jarred herself awake, refusing to fail in her evening vigil.

Many nights she would sit thus, alternately tending the fire, dozing off, staring, entranced, into the red-orange glow of the single candle in the room, and glancing out the window at every sound—waiting ever for that *one* sound which would light her lips with a smile and her emerald green eyes with a sparkle more radiant than the combined efforts of fire and candle. Though small for her age, with thin, frail-looking limbs and pale skin, there was a certain upward tilt of her chin, a firmness about her lips that spoke of strength and determination well beyond her tender years.

It was difficult for any amount of tenacity and pluck to keep a child awake so late, however. Her day had begun before dawn, and a steady flow of necessary chores had followed. After milking came the preparation of a hearty Scottish breakfast of oatmeal porridge with cream. Then had come washing up and sweeping out the cottage. The cows had to be taken out to pasture, and today had also been laundry day. The day had been warm, so she had been able to hang the garments outside, and had only just retrieved them as the purple-pink dusk gave way to the descending night.

Suddenly she heard a sound outside.

She jumped up and hurried to the window, pressing her warm face against the clear pane. But all was still and quiet.

The girl sighed. It must have been only the breeze through the birch tree sending the tips of some of its branches against the window.

She shuffled back to the fire to have a peep inside the kettle perched on its three-legged stand. The simple barley stew had boiled away into an almost tasteless, gooey mass. She gave it a deft stir, hoping it would not cook away to nothing. The biscuits she had so lovingly prepared were already cold, but they could be salvaged with a few moments over the coals of the fire.

She never thought of complaining, never questioned her lot, knew no other life but this. The smile on her lips and the sparkle in her eyes came from her heart, for it was a heart full of love. Though her life may have been a hard one, she did not consider it so. If she went to sleep tired each night, she also went to sleep content, for the object of her youthful ministrations was one she loved. Was he not her own?

She returned again to the stool and her endless waiting. Had she known how to read, the hours may have passed more quickly. But she could not read, and there were no books in the cottage. There was mending to be done. But she was tired, and it could wait.

So she waited in the light of the peat fire, as the cottage wherein she sat waited in the pale northern moonlight—waited for something which seemed to be at hand. But neither she nor the cottage knew what was to come, for neither was aware of the true object of that waiting.

Though she was content, there had been many times in those long, lonely hours when she had recalled with longing the way it used to be. She could just vaguely remember when Mama had been there, but she sensed, with more of an ache in her heart rather than a recollection in her brain, that those had been sweet days of joy. Maybe it was the laughter from Papa's mouth she remembered. He didn't laugh like that anymore. They were happy, the two of them. But there were long hours of being alone, too. And even when they were together, she sometimes saw loneliness in her papa's eyes.

She certainly did not begrudge him the hours she spent alone. It was not her father's fault that he must work so hard. Winter was coming, and the harvest had been poor. The girl knew very little about the value of a farthing or a shilling, but she could tell that the cupboards were emptier than when Mama had been alive, and emptier now than they were a year ago. She knew her father sometimes had but one biscuit at mealtime in order to spare the rest for later. He could not hide his hunger, though he tried to make light of it. And although it took far less to feed the furnace of her tiny body, she could feel her own hunger at times as well.

But Papa said things would get better! And she knew he must be right because he was the wisest person she ever knew. He said she would have fine dresses and be a lady. Their house would have furnishings befitting its stalwart exterior—perhaps they would even have a new house, larger, more stately, with servants.

They were landowners, after all! He had said so many times. They should live up to their station. The child did not know what her station meant, and gave the matter little thought. But once in a while she did think of pretty dresses and a soft bed. She knew these things would make her father happy, so they must be good; they must be important. Thus, she wanted them too—because they would make Papa happy.

All at once she heard another sound outside. She went quickly to the door and listened. Then she heard the footfall on the wooden step, and her heart leaped inside her tiny chest. The long-awaited moment had finally come!

CHAPTER TWO

A Dream of More

"Ah, Jamie, my darling bairn!" exclaimed the man as he gathered the petite child into his arms.

He was so tall he had to duck to enter the cottage, his gaunt frame accentuated all the more because of his dark, deep-set eyes and well-pronounced cheekbones. And by this time of the day the tiredness clearly evident in his countenance added still more to that look. When he smiled at his little daughter, the smile seemed too large for his face, a strange contrast with the sad drooping of his weary eyes. But Gilbert MacLeod did smile, and that was all young Jamie saw, or cared about.

"Papa, how tired ye must be!" the girl said, snuggling her head into his shoulder.

"Tired, indeed," he sighed heavily and the edges of his smile faded. "Tired mostly of havin' to leave ye all to yourself."

"I dinna mind, Papa."

"Tired of havin' nothin' to show for a whole day's livin'," he continued as if he had not heard her. "Tired . . . but from all the wrong things."

"Supper's ready fer ye, Papa!" said Jamie, doing her best to sound cheerful.

"Ah, ye dear child! What would I do without ye?"

She slipped from his arm and went about the task of laying his supper out before him on the coarse old table. She smiled all the while under the sweet balm of his praise. She served him like the handmaiden she was, anticipating his every need before he asked, making sure he never wanted for anything. As the last swallow of tea disappeared, she was there immediately to refill his cup, watching all the while that he ate each of the three biscuits she set on his plate. She forgot all her previous drowsiness.

When the meal was finished, Gilbert pushed back his chair, the only highbacked one in the cottage, stretched out his long legs, and occupied himself with the complex process of cleaning and lighting his pipe. Stopping what she was doing, Jamie watched the procedure with fascination, absorbed in the deep look of concentration in her father's eyes, which seemed to reach its climax in the knitting together of his bushy black brows. Before long Gilbert MacLeod was puffing away contentedly. And then came the most delightful moment of all for Jamie—for Gilbert could execute the most perfect smoke rings in the village and Jamie never grew tired of following them upward till they lost their shape in the accumulated haze which hung near the roof.

The father took the daughter's hand and drew her to him. "Come here, Jamie, my dear," he said, lifting her onto his lap. "Tonight ye can leave the washin' up till the morrow."

She made no protest and relaxed in his arms.

"I'm glad ye are young, child," he went on. "Too young to understand how things are. Or do ye, lass?"

He gazed deeply into her eyes as if he sought there to discover the answer to his own question. But the only reply reflected was the simplicity of love and admiration.

"I wonder if too much has been put upon ye, child. The moon is fully risen, and 'tis the dark of night, and ye should be in bed asleep. But here ye are layin' out a supper for me."

She clung still closer to him, saying by her mere presence and the extra squeeze of her loving arms that to be with him was enough. She needed to understand nothing beyond that.

"But I swear, my bairn, things will be different—they will! Ye'll have the things ye deserve, the things I should be providin' for ye. I only wish your mama could have been able to see that day. But you will see it, lass. I feel it's comin', Jamie! I've been savin' the best news of the day for the last." Here a smile crept onto his face, and a mischievous glint lingered in his eyes for a moment.

"A surprise, Papa?"

"Aye—a surprise—and I nearly forgot; there are two surprises!" He reached into his shirt pocket and pulled out a stick of the reddest candy Jamie had ever seen.

She reached up slowly, almost reverently, for it. "Oh, thank ye, Papa," she said as her tiny fingers closed around the treasure. She took it from him, but did not eat it, or even take a bite right then. It was too special and pretty. She would lay it by her pillow as she slept, and perhaps tomorrow take a small bite, making its goodness linger as long as possible.

"And for my other surprise," Gilbert said, "I'll begin by telling ye why I know things are sure to be changin'. I met a fellow today who was on his way to the big city—going all the way to Aberdeen, he was."

"Where's that, Papa?"

"It would take three, maybe four whole days to walk there. 'Tis by the sea, lass."

Jamie's mouth fell open. To her young mind such a distance was more than she could fathom. The very words *the sea* evoked a sense of awe, wonder at the great unknown.

"This man," her father went on, "works in a big factory there. He said that no man who is willing to work need sit idle in the city. There is work a-plenty. He said with my knowledge of figures, I could get clerical work. The pay would be good, too. Would ye like to go to the city, Jamie?"

"I dinna know, Papa," she answered with some uncertainty. "What aboot oor cottage here?"

"Ah, the house . . ." he replied thoughtfully. "It always seemed so important because it was *ours*. But what good be a piece of land when there's no food in the cupboards? We worked hard to keep it, yer mother and I, Jamie. But I must face the facts, lass. I just can't hang on to this place and this barren scrap of land, not if it means starvin'."

"I can work harder, Papa!" pleaded Jamie. "We dinna have t' go!"

"Oh, my bairn!"

His lips trembled and his eyes filled, but he blinked back the tears so Jamie would not see.

"No need for ye to work in Aberdeen," he said, making an attempt at a laugh. "I'll work hard and bring in plenty. Why, before ye know, we'll have another house, finer than this one. And ye'll ride in a carriage with two sleek white horses. Ye'll have a bonnie pink bonnet and a dress to match with lace all over. Ye'll *be* somebody, Jamie! Ah, Aberdeen—"

Abruptly he stopped. For a moment his shoulders shook with a repressed fit of coughing.

"Papa, ye'll be sick again!"

"No, child," he replied, tenderly brushing a hand over her silky dark locks. "It's just come to be a habit these days. But now 'tis time for you to be in bed. Ye can dream of Aberdeen tonight, lass. Where the air is filled with the tangy smell of salt water and the great ships come and go every day. Aberdeen is where we should have gone long ago. I'll find what I'm looking for there—I know it!"

Jamie said no more, the effects of the long day finally stealing over her weary body. Her father picked her up and carried her to the straw mattress tucked away in a warm corner of the cottage. With a sleepy smile she kissed her father's cheek as he laid her between the blankets. And indeed, in the dark hours which followed she did dream of that faraway city of her father's visions, where the streets in her imagination were no less than paved with pure gold.

Gilbert MacLeod shuffled back to his chair where he continued to sit for some time, puffing quietly on his pipe, gazing at the far wall but clearly not focusing on it; his thoughts were far beyond, over the hills, toward the sea. Every now and then a cough rose to his lips, but he took pains to muffle it with a handkerchief so as not to disturb the child. Slowly the blaze in the hearth began to die into orange embers, which threw dark and forlorn shadows about the cottage. Gilbert made no attempt to rekindle it; the night was not overly cold and the child would be warm enough under the heavy wool blankets. As for himself, he took little thought for his own comfort; the cold or the heat mattered but little to him of late. Acutely aware of the meager quality of their life, this frustration had pressed upon him so that he had had room to think of little else. Only Gilbert's intense love for his daughter forced him to at least care for her needs, though casual observers might think he had even failed at this.

"It will be better," he murmured. "It *will* be better!" The words were the litany to the only religion he had heart to embrace these days.

He often recalled the faith he had learned from his father; perhaps he even longed for the peace and comfort it offered. But Gilbert MacLeod was a proud man—too proud to turn to a religion he had walked away from in his youth, at least not until he could turn to it with head held high. How could he now, in his hour of desolation, ask consolation from a God whose help he had long ago spurned?

In the deepening gloom of the cottage his mind wandered,

as it had many times before, to that day on which he had walked away from his father's house. The single-room, sod-walled dwelling with thatched roof, surrounded by the rugged bluffs inundated with bracken and yellow broom and heather would always remain vivid in his memory. The very name of the grand mountain where he grew up, with its verdant yet rugged beauty and treacherous paths, spoke worlds to him—*Donachie*. There his father had been a herder of sheep, and there he too would have followed in his footsteps, except that he had not been able to stay. Donachie's awesome allure was not enough to hold him. He had had to find his own way, he had to prove . . .

What was it—now, so many years later—that he had to prove? At the time it had burned like a passion within him. Yet lately things had grown muddled. The passion, the drive, the energy of his youth had faded. Had he been a fool to leave? But there was Jamie. She had been given him as a result. How then could he look upon his decision as anything but providential?

His father had been a good man. It took the maturing of Gilbert's own manhood to allow him to see that his father had, indeed, been unique. In his boyhood, Gilbert wanted to be like him; in his youth, to make him proud. In the turbulence of his eighteen-year-old mind he thought the only way to do this was to better his station in life. Though he loved Donachie and revered his father, he yet disdained the poverty of their shepherd's existence, barely able to eke out a living from their sheep and other animals, and the few vegetables they were able to grow in the stubborn soil. Even the ground whose every feature he and his father knew better than the back of their own hands was not their own. *Nothing* was their own, nor would it be so long as he remained on Donachie. He had to get away, to move up in life, to have something—to be somebody!

The old man was torn with grief at his son's decision to leave. Begging him to stay, he told Gilbert he belonged on the mountain, that he would be happy nowhere else, that it was folly to search for some elusive dream when he had been born to a herdsman's and crofting life.

But the father's fervent and loving entreaty was taken by the son as a challenge.

"I'll show ye!" he had said. "When I come back, I'll be a great man!"

Three days later he marched with determination down the grassy fellside, and had never since laid eyes of flesh on Donachie again.

His father groaned within himself, knowing what a mistake he had made, though Gilbert would never realize his father's grief. The tears he wept for the following week, with none to share his anguish but the dumb sheep under his care, were rooted in the fear that he would never see his son again.

If Gilbert had shared any such fears, he hid them well. Every night in the quietude of his own soul he dreamed of his grand return to Donachie. The vision of meeting his father's challenge, of bettering himself, of making his mark in the world carried him through many a prodigal son's hardship, until gradually the circumstances of his life did begin to improve. He was hired by the owner of a shop in a small village in the valley to take deliveries around with his wagon, and occasionally to clerk in the store. The pay was nominal, but it provided him a roof over his head and regular meals.

The shopkeeper's daughter Alice, though the eldest of several children, was pale and sickly, with few prospects for marriage. The other sons and daughters had married and gone, and only Alice remained at home. Drawn to her soft-spoken gentleness, Gilbert came to love her, and she him. The storekeeper had cherished the hope of a better match for his daughter. But as this seemed the only match likely to come along, he gave his consent. They would be poor, no doubt, but he and his wife had been happy with the shop, and so would Gilbert and Alice after he was gone, for his wife had died two years prior to Gilbert's coming. He had, however, all but forgotten his wife's cousin—unmarried, childless, with no near relations, and ailing.

Within two years of their marriage, Alice had to face the death of her father, followed shortly by the unexpected communication that a cousin of whom she knew nothing had passed on, leaving no heir, and had left the whole of his inheritance to Alice. It encompassed a small parcel of land, some fifty acres, a few miles from the village—nothing by the standards of men of means, but an unbelievable windfall for a hapless shepherd-turned-shopkeeper like Gilbert. It was a fertile strip of acreage despite the fact that it ran along the arid heath; a few years' honest labor would make it green and profitable, and for Gilbert it represented the fulfillment of all his dreams.

To be a landowner!

It was more—much more!—than he could have hoped for so soon in his life. The gleam of pride and enthusiasm in her husband's eye swelled Alice's heart with satisfaction, and she agreed to sell the shop in the village in order to finance Gilbert's dream. Nurtured by his newfound confidence, the land seemed to prosper. But more land was needed, he could see that clearly. More land would double his yield, as well as his profit, and would strengthen his position among the other local landowners. His would be an estate to be reckoned with, and he a man of means and influence in the county!

With the proceeds from the sale of the shop, Gilbert set his eye on a piece of land adjacent to his own. Over-zealous, with little business instinct, he did not stop to consider why Mackenzie Graystone, laird of the nearby powerful estate of Aviemere and owner of most of the valley, would let this particular parcel go so easily. He concluded the deal, unable to pay more than a scant third of the total with his available cash, but optimistic that his payments to Graystone would come easily once his operation was in full production. It was his now! All his! And as is often the case when enthusiasm outstrips means, his dream did not bow to the practical.

Jamie's birth brought a joyous time. Yet the thunderclouds of grief soon appeared on the distant horizon. The hardship of bearing a child visibly drained the strength from Alice's frail body. In and out of bed for the next four years, one chill autumn morning she finally breathed her last.

The sought-after piece of land did not prove to be the boon Gilbert had anticipated. So eager had he been to increase his holdings, he had not seen that no amount of wealth or land could make one such as he accepted by the local gentry. He was, after all, of peasant stock, and they would never forget that no gentle blood flowed through his veins. As a shopkeeper he had been in his place, but now they treated him worse than before, looking upon him with scorn and contempt for trying to be something he never could become.

Nor were these developments lost on Graystone himself, a shrewd, some said a cunning man. He had known from the beginning how it would turn out. He knew that after Gilbert extended himself beyond his means, it would only be a matter of time, one burden added on top of another till the load became unbearable, before the struggling farmer toppled. And was that not precisely what he wanted, why he had sold the land in the first place? He loathed the idea of this peasant, this lowly shopkeeper, making airs, posing as one of *them*, setting himself up as a sort of would-be laird on the fringes of his own estate.

He would not have it! By giving a little now, by selling off a small parcel temporarily, he would soon be able to step in and not only take back what was his own but lay claim to the whole lot and completely dispossess the usurper. His solicitor had so drawn up the papers that it was only a matter of time. MacLeod was a fool, and he, Mackenzie Graystone, would reap the rewards of his folly!

One calamity after another played into Graystone's hands. Alice's death was followed by two unseasonably dry springs and summers, with a long harsh winter with unpredictable frost between them which destroyed much of the severely needed spring planting.

Fool that he had been—even Gilbert himself now recognized that fact—he was not a stupid man. He saw that he could not hope to hold on to his dear land much longer. He was now so buried in debt that even should he sell the land at a market price, he would barely be capable of paying the severest of his obligations. He also knew that a struggling farmer gathers the vultures as readily as a rotting carcass of highland deer, and he could already sense the circling of the nearby landowners. They were anxious to get rid of him—to squeeze his tiny hope for a better life into the dirt under their feet. Getting market price for his land was an illusion! He would be lucky to get half what he paid Graystone for the whole of both parcels! He would lose everything! And who would be there to pick up the pieces, with a cruel smile on his evil lips, but Mackenzie Graystone himself!

The news of Aberdeen could not have come at a more fortuitous time. This was the hope he needed, the hope he *had* to have in order to dull the heartbreaking reality of the inevitable decision facing him.

Gilbert MacLeod had to hope. He had to hope or admit failure—and that he could not bear to do.

Gilbert slowly rose to his feet. He knocked his pipe against the stone hearth, emptying its contents into the cold fire, then quietly walked to where Jamie lay sound asleep, full of her own dreams. He bent over and kissed her cheek.

"Ah, lass," he sighed softly, "yer dreams are all ahead of ye, while mine are past—and never to be."

He turned from the bed, took his woolen coat from the peg where it hung, pulled it around him, and left the cottage. A cool breeze blew into his face as he directed his steps westward toward the arid moor on the edges of his land. He often walked here at night when the solace of sleep eluded him. The barren desolation suited his mood, and the harsh elements turned his feelings, if not his thoughts, toward forces larger than the achings within his own heart.

CHAPTER THREE

The Ebony Stallion

The sky was only beginning to shake its black shroud when Jamie awoke.

The cottage consisted of four rooms, a couple of them good-sized, and it had at one time been no mean dwelling. But only the large front room and another small sleeping quarters adjacent to it were in use these days. The other rooms were cold and damp and it was difficult and costly to keep them heated, so the father and daughter had contented themselves with the present arrangement. Jamie had her small straw-filled bed in a corner of the large room where it was warmest, and Gilbert occupied the other. From this room Jamie could now hear her father's steady breathing. She had no idea he had been asleep only two or three hours, but she tiptoed quietly about her tasks nonetheless.

By the time she had rekindled the peat fire and set the kettle to boil, streaks of amber and pink were coloring the sky. Notwithstanding the old nautical limerick about sailors taking warning from morning red skies, Jamie hoped there would be at least a couple more fine days before winter settled upon them in earnest.

While the kettle heated, she slipped into her coat and, gathering up the milking pail, crept softly outside. One look around told her that winter was approaching rapidly; a thick hoarfrost covered the ground about the cottage and out onto the fields beyond. She shivered in the early morning cold, slipping once on the ice as she made her way toward the byre.

It was no warmer inside. The byre had been constructed to accommodate up to fifteen cows, but only two now remained— a somewhat scrawny roan and a black and white, both still good milkers. Jamie caught up a little wooden stool and walked up to the roan.

"Mornin', Gracie," she said as she set the stool into position and slipped the pail beneath Gracie's swelling udder. She sat down and began coaxing milk from the animal. Her fingers were cold and awkward at first, but soon warmed to the task, and the creamy yellow milk flowed out readily.

"Well, Gracie," said the girl, "Papa says we'll be goin' t' Aberdeen soon. Winter's comin' an' maybe it'll be warm there. 'Tis near the sea. I hope ye an' Callie'll be comin' wi' us. But I dinna ken much aboot it noo. 'Tis a big city, he says. I wonder where they keep the bo's there? Ye are sich braw friends, I jist know Papa will fin' ye a home there wi' us."

She rubbed the cow's great flank, then moved over to Callie's stall where she began a like procedure until the pail was filled.

"Dinna ye worry noo," she said as she left the byre. "We winna be leavin' ye behin'. They got t' need milk in Aberdeen, too."

She loved the two cows. She felt no deprivation for having no brothers or sisters or children-friends; besides her father she had these two silent but loving companions. She had taken special pleasure in them in the last several months when they had fallen completely under her care. She milked them each morning, took them out to pasture, and cleaned their stalls. To her, such activities were hardly chores but more like recreation, she so thoroughly enjoyed the company of these living creatures. There had at one time been more animals about the place—chickens, a horse or two, and a fine collie dog—and, of course, sheep. Most of the other animals had long since been sold out of necessity, and the chickens and sheep were more than young Jamie could tend alone. As there were no neighbors nearby, Gracie and Callie were usually the only company the girl had. Her childlike concern for the two animals on this day went deeper than her young mind could even fathom. Her own fears were wrapped up in her anxiety for her two bovine friends—her fear of the unknown, of the mystical place they called Aberdeen that was supposed to fulfill all their dreams.

Back inside the cottage again, she began preparing the morning's porridge. She poured water from the kettle into a great iron pot, then slowly added handful after handful of oatmeal, stirring with her left hand, until it was creamy and thick. This would be their breakfast as well as her own lunch. She went about each

job meticulously, with confidence, as if she had been at it forever—and in reality, that was very nearly the truth. When her
mother died, Jamie had been but four. Gilbert hired a crofter's
daughter to help with the child for a while, but it soon became
apparent that he could not afford the cost. By the time she was
five, Jamie was almost completely self-sufficient. And it was not
long before the entire little household, including her father, was
completely in her competent care. Gilbert took it all rather in
stride, never quite realizing just how well managed the affairs
of his home were, considering the tender years of its mistress.
He accepted food and drink gratefully, obliviously living day
after day as if the whole proceeding was the most usual thing in
the world. Yet deep inside, perhaps below the level of his conscious thought, he knew what a prize he possessed in his daughter. He rarely expressed even a hint that he knew she was invested with extraordinary gifts of ministration. But unmindful
though he might have been of her unusual nature, she nevertheless meant the world to him. And so Jamie basked contentedly in love, if not in praise.

The rich aroma of porridge caused Gilbert to stir; then the
hissing of the bubbling teakettle brought him fully awake. He
stretched his long body and rubbed his hands over his face. His
eyes were dry and still weary—the short sleep had not been
altogether refreshing. He coughed several times, while in the
other room Jamie listened with concern.

He pulled his suspenders up and over his shoulders as he
came out into the front room. He smiled at his daughter, but her
heart quivered at the sight of his haggard face.

"Papa, are ye sure ye're not sick?"

"Aye, child, I'm sure," he replied carelessly. "Well, ye have
breakfast all ready!" he went on, acting both surprised and
pleased as if that very occurrence had not been the routine for
months on end. "Ye're a dear one, my Jamie!"

They partook of their humble fare in silence for some time.
At length Gilbert spoke.

"I'll be goin' to the village this morning for a spell."

He paused and ate several more spoonfuls of porridge.

"Shall I take Gracie an' Callie oot t' pasture, Papa?" Jamie
asked.

"My business won't take me long, and I must come back by
here on my way to work at the mill. So I was thinkin' ye might
want to come to the village with me."

"Really, Papa?"

"Ye'd like that, would ye?"

Her sparkling eyes answered for her.

"Then," he said, "ye can put on your prettiest dress, and we'll be off."

As soon as the breakfast things were cleared away, Jamie scurried off to the chest where her clothes were neatly kept. There was only one suitable dress, a pale blue linen with a bit of white lace at the neck. It had been mended only two or three times, and she thought it was still pretty. She found a blue ribbon and attempted to tie it in her hair. The bow was twisted and clumsy, so she went to her father and asked him to fix it as best he could.

Gilbert held her out at arms' length. *What a beautiful child she is!* he thought. With alabaster skin framed by silky dark locks, and her large green eyes looking almost as if they had been painted on, she resembled an expensive china doll. But his proud heart ached as he noted the mended places covering the tears in her dress. Would she always have to remain such a poor raga-muffin because of him? She was fit for better things! Maybe if *he* was not meant to have them, *she* could. If his life had been a disappointment, there was no reason why hers would have to be!

The village was an hour's walk away. They went but seldom together; Jamie could recall only two or three visits to the valley since her mother died. The village itself, set on the edge of the valley, was composed of two intersecting lanes, themselves so hilly that the stone buildings gave the appearance of being set haphazardly into position. On the topmost hill sat the ancient parish church, its thick stone walls covered with dark green moss and ivy. The cross on the steeple stood proudly as the very crown of the village. With wonder Jamie gazed upward at it as they passed, wanting more than anything to see inside the grand building with its pretty colored windows. Gilbert promised they would do just that when he finished his business.

The pair trudged along the main street beyond the church and up a steep hill toward the other side of the small town until it leveled off and they found themselves in front of a building where Gilbert stopped. On a wooden placard was carved a pic-ture of a black rearing pony. Jamie could not read the words beneath the pony, but they read: *The Ebony Stallion*. It was the only public house for miles in either direction.

Looking now in one direction, now in the other, Gilbert loitered about outside the inn for some time while Jamie stood quietly at his side. There were few others about on the streets, and no one came in or out of the great oak door. Neither was there much activity in the shop across the way, which Jamie watched until she became bored. She had no idea why her father had come to town.

Suddenly she sensed movement in her father's frame. Following his gaze down the road at the foot of the hill, she could hear a sound of approaching horses. A carriage came into view, sleek and black, drawn by two lively chestnuts. She did not take her eyes off it during its entire ascent to the top of the hill, and finally to her amazement it came to a spirited stop before the very spot where she and her father stood, the horses snorting and pawing as if they would charge off again if given half a chance. She felt as if the fairy-tale carriage had been sent for *them*, and had Jamie been older and read romance stories she might have expected the driver to jump down from his high perch and offer her his hand.

Self-consciously she stepped back behind her father. But no one was paying the slightest attention to her. There would be no hands offered this young princess in peasant's clothing today. Instead, a man stepped from the enclosure of the coach and called up brusquely to the driver, "Wait here, Adams. I'll not be long!"

He was of medium height, not so tall as MacLeod, who stood nervously awaiting him. His thickset frame, while far from fat, was nonetheless dignified, and was made even more so by the black cape that fluttered out behind him. He wore a black silk hat, and his stern face was clean-shaven except for a thin moustache. Strands of gray hair peeked timidly from under the edges of the hat, but they were the only timid features about the man. He was altogether an imposing man—in voice, in stature, in the total authority which his carriage commanded.

"Lord Graystone," Gilbert said rather hesitantly as he stepped forward slowly.

"Yes," the man replied with a hint of condescension. Because of Gilbert's height, it was physically impossible for Graystone to look *down* on him, yet he somehow managed to convey that impression.

"I'm Gilbert MacLeod. We—uh—had an appointment."

"Quite so, MacLeod," Graystone replied. "Of course, that's why I'm here."

"Would ye—would *you* be wantin' to come into the inn? The ale is none too bad, and I'd be glad to buy."

Graystone glanced disdainfully toward the building. "Would you now?" were his only words as he swept past Gilbert into The Ebony Stallion.

"Wait here, Jamie," Gilbert said, then turned and followed the laird of Aviemere.

The following thirty-minute wait passed quickly for Jamie, for she now had the carriage and the horses to keep her active mind occupied. Graystone's coachman, while obviously not accustomed to children and hardly comfortable with the nursemaid's role which had been thrust upon him, nevertheless allowed her to pet the team with many stern injunctions he needn't have given; Jamie was well-used to such creatures. The horses were the finest animals she had ever seen, and her eyes studied them intently as they continued to prance with impatience.

Jamie imagined what it would be like to ride in such a carriage. If it were hers, she would tell the coachman to give the chestnuts every inch of freedom they desired, and she would feel herself fly down the road, looking out the curtained window as the countryside whizzed past.

Engrossed in such childish fancies, Jamie hardly noticed the passing of time. Before she knew it, Graystone strode out of the inn. He looked considerably pleased; the sternness she had felt from him before now seemed to have changed into a smug look of triumph. His man helped him into the carriage, then jumped back up onto his seat and whipped the reins into action; the horses lurched down the hill. They quickly reached full stride, and within a minute they moved out of sight in the same way they had come.

It was several minutes before her father exited. The relief that the carriage was gone showed clearly on his face. He mumbled something under his breath that if he must pay for the brew, he wasn't going to let it go to waste. But he said nothing more and Jamie could feel the cloud that hung over him; he remained sullen all the way home, saying hardly a word.

They did not stop at the church, nor pay a visit to the store where Jamie had secretly hoped another treat might await her. She tried hard not to be disappointed.

CHAPTER FOUR

Lundie's Proposal

It was dark when Gilbert came again to the inn. His mood had changed little despite a hard day's work, and he had not yet been home. He had carried out what work was to be done at the mill, and the few other odd jobs he had hired himself out for on that day. But when the time came to return home, he could not bear it.

It would never be his home again!

The bargain had been sealed that morning between him and Mackenzie Graystone with a cold handshake. That was all there was to it; a lifetime of hopes and dreams were suddenly washed away in a flood of grim necessity.

Ah, yes, there were other dreams, and Gilbert clung to them with the tenacity of a drowning man hanging on to a thin hunk of driftwood. Yet somehow they were more difficult to conjure up at this moment. Now, all he could feel was loss—hollow and inevitable loss; the emptiness of dreams that would never be.

He felt dirty, too, as if he had deceived poor, dead Alice. If he had come away with something it might have been different. But as he had guessed, his arrangement with Graystone barely left him with his debts paid and twenty pounds to his name.

Twenty pounds!

It might seem wealth untold to most of the peasants around him. But he had been a landowner! Now his land was gone and he had nothing to show for it.

He should probably have considered himself fortunate. Graystone could have waited and simply repossessed the land by default. At least this way he had something. But the mere memory of the laird's pompous face when he made his brutal offer was enough to enrage Gilbert. ''I'm doing you a favor, MacLeod, by offering you this much," the laird had sneered. "I could just wait you out—so take it or leave it." Gilbert had seen in the man's eyes the faint hope that he would turn it down. What could make a man so eager to prey upon his fellows?

Twenty pounds! thought Gilbert again. *'Tis an outrage!*

Well, at least a couple of shillings from it would be spent tonight—trying to forget.

The pub was dark, and the glow from the hearth provided nearly the only light. It revealed several men standing about, others seated at the rough tables—and all holding pints of cheap ale. Some preferred to drink in solitude; others sat in tightly knit groups discussing everything from the weather to their livestock. Gilbert bought a pint from the barman and carried it to an empty table in a lonely corner of the place. He sipped the dark beer slowly, for he was not a drinking man, though it was true that many of his daughter's sleepless nights had been spent waiting while he sought what courage was to be found within the dank walls of The Ebony Stallion. If no courage was to be had from its brew, at least there was a certain amount of companionship there. It prolonged the moment when he must trudge home and dulled somewhat the daily reminder of the raw pain of his failure.

Tonight he was not long to remain alone, for soon after he settled into his seat, a man arose from one of the groups at the far end of the large room and ambled toward him. He set his glass on the table and slid onto the bench opposite Gilbert without a word. It was not until after he took a long swallow of beer that he spoke.

"Evenin', MacLeod."

"Evenin', Lundie."

Both men drank deeply.

"I heard ye sold yer property t'day," Lundie said.

" 'Tis true."

The conversation between the two men had been subdued; neither had been that intimate with the other previously. But suddenly Lundie's glass slammed down on the table.

" 'Tis a blasted shame!" he said passionately.

All eyes in the place turned momentarily toward him, to which he replied with a fierce sneer. Gradually all resumed their previous activities and took no further notice of the pair.

" 'Tis true," repeated Gilbert mildly, revealing none of the churning emotions within him. "But that's life. She's a cruel mistress, sometimes."

"Ha!" returned Lundie. "'Tis that slimy snake Mackenzie Graystone."

"I know we're friends, Frederick, an' have drunk a pint or twa together upon occasion, but I've never heard ye speak out before against the laird."

"That's because the scum had not quit me o' my job before!"

Frederick Lundie, a compact, muscular man in his forties, had been until two days earlier the factor at Aviemere. He was considered by some hot-blooded, quick-tempered, quick-witted, and just as quick to befriend any man who treated him fairly. He had come to Aviemere from Lord Michalton's estate near Perth, with extremely high credentials. He was a good man, and Graystone had hired him immediately. That was ten years ago.

"What do ye mean?" Gilbert asked.

"Hae ye gane deaf, MacLeod? Ten years o' perfect service o'er—ended! That's what I'm meanin'. Told me t' get oot. No notice. Nothin'!"

"He gave ye no reason?"

"Reason!" Lundie spat on the floor. "I killed his horse, he's sayin'. But it's a lie!"

"What happened?"

"I took the horse oot fer his usual paces—'twas his prize stallion. When I brocht him back t' the stable he was sound an' whole. I dinna ken *what* happened. That evenin' when the laird went oot t' hae a look at him, there he lay on the straw, leg broken—'twas an awful sicht!"

"He didna believe ye?"

"In ten years I ne'er once lied t' the man! I'll tell ye what happened. That weasel o' a son o' his took the horse oot an' rode him to his death."

"Do ye know that of a certain?"

"I know fer certain that the blaggart more'n once took the animal oot to impress his friends, wi'oot his father knowin' a thing aboot it. I looked the ither way, I did. He's a rum 'un t' hae on yer back. An' in the laird's eyes the boy can do no wrong. But I'll show 'em. I'll show 'em all!"

They were silent for some time while they finished what remained in their glasses and began fresh ones. At length Lundie broke the silence.

"They treated me like scum fer ten years," he said, as if the previous conversation had never ended. "I gave 'em the best years 'o my life. I stayed because good jobs are hard t' find. An' they were payin' me more'n I could hope t' git anywhere else. I had my family t' think of. Then one mistake—an' it weren't e'en *my* mistake!—an' see what becomes o' me!"

" 'Tis a sorry pass," Gilbert sympathized. "I'm sorry."

"Ye should ken more'n anyone what I mean."

Gilbert had temporarily forgotten his own plight, and now, reminded of it again, said nothing but stared into his glass.

"Come now, man!" Lundie went on. "The vermin has done the same t' ye!"

"I—I don't understand," said Gilbert looking up.

"Ye dinna think he bought yer land oot o' the kindness o' his heart, do ye?"

Gilbert looked down again. Of course Lundie was right! That very thing had fueled his own anger and brought him here this very night.

"I'll answer fer ye!" Lundie went on. "The man has no heart! How much profit did ye make on the sale?"

Gilbert remained silent for a long, tense moment. He knew he had been, if not swindled directly, certainly exploited by Graystone. But he had been taught to guard his words, and one could never tell where the laird's ears might be.

"Enough to make a new start in Aberdeen," he said at length.

"Start like paupers, I'll warrant!"

Gilbert offered no response.

"Everyone knows ye got less than half what ye paid Graystone himself fer the land!"

"It's over and done with now."

"He's been eyein' yer plot o' land fer years," Lundie continued; "since e'en before yer wife inherited it. He was jist waitin' fer the right moment, jist waitin' fer the right circumstances that would send ye under. He hated the likes o' a common man—meanin' no disrespect, MacLeod—tryin' t' better himsel'!"

"It's over, I said!" repeated Gilbert, his voice rising. "I did the best I could—but it wasn't enough!" The color in his face flushed, but then his voice fell once more to a toneless whisper. "It's over."

"It doesna hae t' be, Gilbert, my friend."

"I'm leavin' for Aberdeen. My child and I. We'll make a good life there. I'll be startin' over."

"Fine! Go yer way t' Aberdeen. Hae yer good life!" Lundie

drew close to his companion, and his voice dropped to a barely audible whisper. "But dinna go wi' yer pockets empty."

"You're speakin' in riddles, Frederick. You've had too much to drink."

"I'm thinkin' more clearly than maybe I hae fer years!" returned Lundie. " 'Tis oor chance, MacLeod. Don't ye see? Oor chance t' prove t' them Graystones that they aren't the only ones wi' power."

He paused and took a slow drink as if waiting for the impact of his words to sink in. But Gilbert continued to stare at him, bewildered.

"I found oot a valuable piece o' somethin', Gilbert, aboot them blaggarts," Lundie continued; "somethin' they'll be wantin' t' keep quiet. An' that old jackal'll pay a heap t' keep it from bein' known, too. He couldna afford not t' pay once he knows what I know."

"Frederick, ye've drunk too much of this ale."

"I'm not drunk, man." Lundie's voice was steady, unflinching. Almost lethal.

"Then ye're crazy!"

"I'll get my due from 'em, an' there's nothin' more sane than that!"

"Ye're talkin' about bleedin' a rich an' powerful man, Frederick. Men have killed for less. Ye can't be serious!"

"That's why we must work t'gither," Lundie reasoned. "They wouldna dare kill me if they knew there was someone oot there t' blab the minute somethin' was t' happen t' me. Wi' two o' us, there'd be no danger. 'Tis a perfect setup, an' no risk fer ye because they won't e'en ken who ye are."

"Then why use me at all?" asked Gilbert. "It only matters that they *think* someone else knows."

"Them cursed Graystones are too wily fer that. They'd know. I'd hae t' hae proof t' protect mysel'. An' besides, what do ye hae against makin' yersel' some fast loot, an' bringin' the rat doon in the process?"

"I'll not make my money that way," Gilbert replied. "I have no taste for such revenge. I just want to take my daughter and get far away from here."

"I ne'er took ye fer a 'holier than thou'!"

"Ye'll not intimidate me, Lundie."

"I meant t' do none o' that," Lundie said. "Maybe I hae had a wee bit too much o' the ale. But I'm dead serious aboot everythin' else. I need yer help, because if somethin' was t' happen t' me, I'd need someone I could trust to speak oot fer me—fer my family's sake. Someone I would know wouldn't take Graystone's side."

"For your family's sake, then, give up this foolishness."

"I canna. Graystone swore I'd ne'er hae another job in these parts again. I hae no choice."

Gilbert leaned back heavily against the stone wall. "I'm sorry, my friend, but I cannot have any part in such a thing."

"I've always respected ye, MacLeod," Lundie said, seeming at last to give up on his plan. "Ye've had a rough time o' it, but ye kept t' yer principles. Where e'er ye go an' what e'er ye do, ye can always be prood o' that."

Pride!

How Gilbert had longed for it! Somehow he did not feel very proud of anything at the moment. The word from Lundie's lips seemed to jolt him back to the reality of his desperate situation. For a moment he forgot everything else.

When he glanced across the table, he realized his companion had continued talking but that he had heard nothing more. As he tuned his ears again to the sound of his voice, it was only in time to hear his final words.

"I'll go it alone, then," concluded the factor solemnly.

That night Gilbert walked slowly home across the moor. It was dark and cold, the air full of the approaching winter. A breeze whispered dismal sayings over the boggy ground, and in its peculiar way seemed to clear Gilbert's mind.

He had managed to depart The Ebony Stallion with his integrity intact, but out there on the cold, unrelenting heath, he began to wonder if he would regret his decision. How different his honorable notions might seem if he heard of Lundie's sudden wealth and good fortune! Would he then consider himself a fool for his decision of this night?

He had made many honorable decisions in his life, and they had done little for him. In fact, it seemed he had not moved forward at all, but rather backward, far back. Graystone would no doubt be willing enough to pay to protect his secret if it was as serious as Lundie indicated. More willing to pay than shed another's blood, certainly. He could afford the money. Yet how was a man's pride to be anticipated? Graystone would be sure to seek revenge on anyone trying to extort money from him.

But on the other hand, wouldn't it be a harmless enough ruse? Did he not deserve something more from his efforts than a mere twenty pounds?

Gilbert was not a man of faith, but from somewhere higher than the peat moor, like the very breath of Donachie—the mountain he could almost have seen in the distance had it been daylight—he heard a new whisper. He heard the quiet words of his father, the finest man he had ever known—words of honor. And he could not shake them from his mind; he *would* not shake them.

Honor was all he had left.

CHAPTER FIVE

Parting

The cold increased over the next several days. A chill wind raced down from Donachie and the highlands beyond, stripping the leaves from the trees and leaving the valley as stark and gray as the blossomless, scraggly heather shrubs.

Gilbert went to the mill no more, but spent most of his time shambling about his property. With a mournful sense of loss, he looked upon each dear thing that surrounded him. "Will it be the last time I walk out to the wall on the upper pasture?" he would murmur. Or, "How many times have I mucked out this byre? Well, this will be the last."

He had scarcely thought of it before, but now he realized how deeply a part of him all these places were, all the sheds and walls and stalls and fences he had either built or repaired. Memories of Alice flooded his mind wherever he went; for this had, after all, been *her* land, not his. And he had now lost it all! Silent tears filled his eyes with each remembrance of her pale, sad eyes.

Graystone had given him only two weeks to sever the ties and clear out. It was scarcely enough time. But there was no choice. And would any amount of time be enough to sever the dreams of a lifetime?

The day Graystone's stockman came to lead Gracie and Callie away, Jamie burst into tears.

"Papa," she cried, "I promised them they'd come wi' us!"

"I'm sorry, child," he replied, his heart breaking for sorrow at what he had been forced to do.

He rubbed the back of his sleeve across his eyes, took Jamie's hand, and led her to the cottage. "We'll not be needin' a bo in the city," he said cheerfully, through eyes that had grown red of late. "Why, a man'll bring us our milk right to our door fresh

40

every mornin'. No more milkin' for you, Jamie. Ye'll be goin' to school and to fancy parties instead!"

"I want t' stay here, Papa!"

"Come now. We'll be makin' a lady of ye. Remember?"

Jamie sniffed back her tears and tried to match her father's bravado. How could she know how false his cheerful face was? What child is ever capable of comprehending his parent's silent pain?

With a portion of his money Gilbert bought a tired old mare to hitch to his cart. They would pack what would fit onto the cart and thus carry their possessions to the city, there to make what he hoped would be a successful new beginning. The animal served to cheer Jamie considerably, not taking the place of her two friends, but at least helping to console her at their loss. And it helped, too, that her papa promised she could ride upon the cart whenever she grew tired of walking—just like a princess, he said.

With two days of their tenure left, as night drew down around them, Gilbert tucked Jamie into place on her bed, and the moment she was asleep he kissed her gently and slipped into his coat. He would take one last late-night walk upon the moor and bid goodbye to the place that had occasionally served to comfort him.

Though the moon was up, giving him ample light to walk by, the wind was blowing at full force and would not be kind to the cough deep in his lungs. It had grown worse in the last weeks. He looked toward the sky and saw, in the moonlight, heavy, dark clouds rolling in. It would surely rain before morning had dawned. He tried not to think that they might have to travel in such weather.

He made his way west over the lowland pasture. It was still green and would remain so at least until the snows fell. But it had never been green enough to sustain more than a few sheep. Sheep needed space, more of it than he had. That was why he had tried to invest in crops. Oats and barley had flourished elsewhere around him, but Gilbert's timing had been poor. Those last few seasons had been difficult for everyone, but especially for someone like himself, starting new. He glanced to the south, toward the field where he had planted his oats. It looked only a little more barren now than it had at harvesttime.

"I'm just not a farmer by nature," he said to himself as he walked along. "Just wait till I get to the city—that's where I belong!" He had said the words so many times he had almost begun to believe them.

He climbed the rocky incline to the upper pasture. Here the wind was even more persistent, and he had to hold his hat on with his left hand. It was only a short distance further to the "dry stane dyke" that divided the heath from the pasture. The wall of dry stones had been a futile attempt to keep out the arid bog; like everything else he set his hand to, it was a failure. The bracken and brush had pushed some distance into the pasture, and in many places the wall itself had crumbled as if in silent defeat.

He paused a moment before attempting to climb over the wall. The wind whistled in his ears, and his shoulders jerked as his lungs contracted in a painful spasm of coughing. A certain heavy disquietude crept under his skin.

He shivered.

Was it only the wind he heard?

He shrugged and made a vain attempt to laugh. " 'Tis only the spell of the moor," he said aloud. Then he climbed over the wall. In years past he had leaped over it in a single bound, but that strength was far gone now.

As his feet touched the ground, another involuntary shiver trembled through his body.

Ah, this is an evil place! he thought. *Why do I come here?*

He labored on until ahead in the eerie darkness loomed the dark shapes of the craggy granite boulders that dotted the moor with irregular symmetry. The constant howling of the wind now knifed painfully into his ears, and his breathing came in short wheezing gasps. He turned toward one of the huge rocks where he could crouch down at its back and find a few moments respite from the savage elements.

He was only two or three paces from the rocks when something shot out from the darkness toward him. Before he had time to react, he was caught in a vise-like grip. In the darkness he could see no face and the voice was muffled by the whining of the increasing wind. He struggled desperately until he saw the gleam of a razor-sharp skean-dhu flash in the moonlight.

"What—what d'ye want?" he gasped. "I have no money!"

"Money!" spat the voice of his attacker. "You'll be lucky, you broken old man if that's all I take from you!"

He loosened his grip on Gilbert, but before he could escape the man flung his hand with a sickening blow into Gilbert's face.

Gilbert stumbled backward and, tripping over some loose rock, crumbled to the ground. He could already feel the warm blood oozing from a cut under his right eye.

"That'll teach you to try to blacken my name, you miserable scum!" The man stood glowering over Gilbert, still brandishing the gleaming dirk.

"I dinna ken yer meanin'!" shouted Gilbert, in his terror forgetting his speech he had worked so hard to polish as a landowner.

"Blackmail, you lout!" shouted his assailant over the wail of the wind.

" 'Tisn't true."

Even in the darkness Gilbert could see this man was not Mackenzie Graystone, although there was a certain similarity in the timbre of the voice. He had never seen either of Graystone's two sons, but he had little time to ponder who else it might be, for the evil laugh of his attacker forced his mind to the single question of survival.

The man had grabbed him by the collar and yanked him up to his feet, only to beat him down again. Gilbert was in little condition to offer much resistance.

"You'll learn to keep your mouth shut or the same will happen to you as happened to your dirty accomplice. You're lucky I have no more taste for blood tonight."

"What d' ye mean? I have no accomplice. I swear t' ye—"

"And you think I believe what you'd say, you bounder! The factor's dead, and so will you be if ever you breathe a word of what you know."

"I—I dinna ken a thing—he ne'er told me what it was!"

"Ha! I've heard from the tenants how the two of you blighters were thick as thieves. They said you were up to no good, but only I know what it was about."

" 'Tis not true!"

For his only answer the man kicked Gilbert in the soft of his belly, sending a sharp throb of pain from his ribs. As the poor man staggered backward, the younger man sheathed his knife and began thrashing him about the head with his fists. Struggling with what little strength remained within his worn frame, Gilbert tried to resist, knowing now that if he didn't, he could well be a dead man before morning—dead like his friend Frederick Lundie.

The ominous hand was raised one more time against him

when Gilbert reached up and grabbed weakly at it. He caught only the sleeve before it was jerked away from him. He fell back again, his fingers clutched around something cold and hard. The fight had torn from him his last remnant of strength and he reeled back and slumped unconscious, to the dry stony ground.

The assailant kicked him once more, and when the limp body made no response he spat upon it.

"I'll let the moor finish my work for me, you cur!" he said, then turned and strode away across the heath in the direction from which he had come.

The wind did not once let up, even to succor the hapless victim that lay exposed to its vicious blight. Gilbert lay unmoving for hours until the cold sting of falling rain later in the night finally brought him to the edge of his senses. But he could barely move, for his limbs were numb with cold and pain, and the pain in his chest was enough to send him into a fresh faint. In the delirium of his fevered brain, he knew it was his destiny to die out there on the lonely moor, with the rain beating down upon his wasted corpse.

He thought of the jaunty lad who had confidently left his father's home, promising to return as a great man. What would he have done then if he had been able to see himself as he lay now? Oh, he had been such a fool! This was no prodigal-son tale in which his father would kill the fatted calf for the feast upon his return. If only he could see his father again! But it was not to be. He had left the home of his father as a young fool, bent on a dream that never was, to become a man he never could have been! He had wallowed about, feeding upon the husks thrown to the pigs by the laird of Aviemere, sinking deeper and deeper into the mire himself, until now. And here he would die!

If only he had not left, this nightmare would never have been!

Suddenly he thought of Jamie. If he had not left Donachie, she would never have been either.

"Oh, Jamie, my bairn!" he moaned.

The thought of his child, alone in the cottage waiting for him, stirred some dormant strength within his pain-racked body. He forced his legs to move, then grasping clumsily at the wet rock next to him with one hand, he pulled himself to his knees, and at last to his feet. He realized now that his other hand still clutched rigidly to something. He opened his hand, covered with blood where the sharp edges of the object had punctured his flesh. It sparkled golden in the moonlight and he saw flashes of gems. What was it? A button or a cufflink? He closed his hand upon it again, not thinking to drop it into his pocket, then he stumbled forward on his last trek across his moor.

Half walking, half stumbling, sometimes crawling, he made his way at last to the fine cottage that had once been his. He had scarcely the strength to turn the latch, but he managed to do so somehow, then fell into the room, feebly calling his daughter's name.

Jamie had been dreaming.

The rain pounding down outside had intruded into her sleep, though it made only a dull sound as it fell onto the soft thatch of the roof, and she dreamed that hundreds of tiny pebbles were being hurled toward her. Alone and weeping, there was no one in her dream to help her. She had tried to run, but always the torrent of pebbles pursued her. She screamed, but her voice would utter no sound, and her papa was far away and couldn't hear. Her legs were heavy and couldn't run. At length she fell, and then the pebbles caught up to her at last. Just when she was certain she was about to die from the deluge, she heard him. He called her name, distant and soft at first, then it grew louder and louder . . .

The blast of freezing air from the open door finally awoke her from her nightmare. But she continued to hear her name. Was she still dreaming?

Suddenly her eyes opened and she saw her father lying senseless on the floor, the wind howling through the open door behind him, threatening to make an end of what little fire was left on the hearth.

"Papa!" she cried, flying from her bed toward him.

"My little bairn," he managed to whisper through his unconsciousness.

It was *he* who had needed rescuing all along, for the pebbles had been aimed at him, not her! He was so bruised and battered, with dried blood about his face and coming from between his fingers that well she might have imagined he had been caught in a shower of stones.

She ran to the door and slammed it shut so nothing else could hurt her dear papa. Managing to rouse him, she led him to her own bed in its warm corner by the hearth. She peeled from him as much of the wet clothing as would yield to her efforts, then covered him with all the blankets she could find in the place.

But even after she had stirred the fire into a roaring blaze, he continued to shake violently with combined cold and shock from the beating and exposure. She made tea and tried to make him drink, but he choked and gagged on the hot liquid.

At length Jamie contented herself with sitting by her sleeping father's side with his hand between her two soft palms. Then the golden cufflink fell onto the floor. She had never seen it before and knew it could be nothing her papa had ever worn. She didn't even know what a cufflink was. Could it have been meant as a gift for her? She wiped away the dried blood from its edges to examine it more closely. But it wasn't any use, for tears filled her eyes.

"Oh, Papa!" she sobbed as she absently tucked it into her pocket.

"Jamie, it belongs to . . . it belongs . . ." He tried to speak, but his coughing prevented him from finishing. "Doesn't matter . . ." he finally breathed.

Throughout the following day she nursed him as best she could, but the elements had exacted their toll from his already weakened body. His fever raged and his breathing grew more and more labored.

When night came, he made one last effort to speak to his daughter—knowing it was to say goodbye.

"Jamie," he whispered, "ye have been a sweet bairn . . ."

"Thank ye, Papa. But jist rest noo."

"Ye should o' had mair . . . I've not been a good—"

"No, Papa! Ye been so good t' me an' Mama. I love ye!"

"Ah, my bairn . . . my bairn. If only—if only I hadna failed, ye would hae been a gran' lady someday—if only—"

"Ye ne'er failed, Papa!" said Jamie, crying now. "I'll be a lady fer ye yet. I will, Papa!"

But Gilbert MacLeod had not heard his daughter's sobbing outburst, for even as he uttered his final words, the sounds about him grew faint and the life ebbed from his tired body.

Jamie threw herself upon him weeping, feeling none of the mystery, but certainly much of the loneliness of death. That he was dead she somehow instinctively knew, even though she tried to persuade herself he was but sleeping again. He looked more peaceful than she ever remembered seeing him.

Then four words from the past tumbled into her mind. How she could have recalled them she did not know, but she had heard them after her mother died. A woman who had come to visit had spoken them. "She looked so peaceful," the woman had said. With the memory and the look on her father's face, at last the full truth broke upon Jamie: her father was gone from her forever, just as her mother had been taken earlier.

She lay her head again upon his chest and sobbed.

Graystone's agent found her in the morning curled up asleep on the floor next to the bed where her father's cold body lay.

The ensuing several days became a mournful blur to the orphaned child. She was carried off to the home of the miller. She remembered the kind and gentle voice of the miller's wife. Snatches of the horrible procession with a cart carrying a box shrouded in black would now and then invade her memory, but they seemed like pages out of a picture book rather than like anything she herself had witnessed. The picture was not of their old mare, or their cart, or their things on their way to Aberdeen. This cart stopped at the churchyard and the box was put into a big hole in the ground and people threw handfuls of dirt on it, and someone—but not the miller's wife—made her throw a handful of dirt, too. She still didn't get to see inside the church. Some people were crying and she cried too, because she was alone and she wanted to see Papa again. But then she remembered that Papa had looked so peaceful, and he was gone—and she would never see him again.

Some days later the miller packed Jamie's belongings into the old trunk where she had always kept her few dresses, and loaded it onto his cart. His wife tucked Jamie into a corner of the cart and kissed her tenderly. There were tears in the kind woman's eyes as she wondered what the future held for the poor, homeless child.

"I wish we could keep ye," she said. "But it wouldn't be right when ye got someone who's family."

"Am I gaein' t' Aberdeen?" Jamie asked, her eyes widening. Maybe Papa was there already.

"No, child. Yer gran'father'll be wantin' ye noo."

The cart pulled away with a jerky motion, and the miller's wife faded into the distance, taking her kind smile with her.

Jamie slept most of the way. Late in the afternoon she turned around and saw the great mountain looming large ahead of them, and terrible-looking. Almost immediately their way grew steeper, and before she knew it the mountain seemed to surround them in its mists—gray and stark and cold, for its beauty was now hidden beneath the mask of approaching winter.

Jamie was afraid. She hoped the cart would find the valley again. But the cart continued steeply up the hillside, and when it finally stopped, Jamie found herself in the very heart of Donachie.

PART II

Finlay MacLeod

CHAPTER SIX

The Shepherd

The quiet bleating of sheep was the only sound in the craggy mountain canyon. An old man followed them without a word, occasionally prodding an errant lamb with his staff. He had been over this path countless times, and even his failing vision did not daunt his sure-footed stride. His feet struck the rocky earth with a firmness that belied his seventy years.

The picturesque procession climbed over a rise and began a slow descent into a sheltered dell where the grass was green and lush from recent summer rains. Soon the sounds of the sheep were mingled with the musical bubbling of a small burn winding its way between the rocks and through many hidden glens and pools, then gradually down the side of the majestic mountain called Donachie.

The white-haired shepherd led his charges to the edge of the burn where it tumbled into a deep still brown pool, and while they drank eagerly of the topaz-brown, peat-stained cool water and helped themselves to mouthfuls of the rich grass which grew down to its side, he knelt down and had a drink himself.

He sighed contentedly and murmured, "Thank ye, Lord. Ye always lead me beside yer still waters, jist like yer son David said."

He set himself near a small cluster of medium-sized rocks, leaning against one of the larger ones; from this vantagepoint on the edge of the small herd he kept a watchful eye on his sheep. Occasionally his lips broke out in an unconscious quiet tune, but mostly he simply watched the activity of the animals in front of him as if it were the most satisfying task in the world.

After some time his attention was drawn toward an old scots fir where he had noted some rustling in the branches and occasional flickers of color. All at once the object of his gaze winged out of the tree in a flash of dark blue and black. He was not surprised to see the great peregrine falcon, for he had been following its nesting activities for many days now. The great animal swooped gracefully toward the burn, and then for the first time the shepherd spotted its prey—a small brown curlew. With instinctive response the small bird, alerted to its danger, immediately dove into the water. Not to be deterred so easily, the falcon hovered above the water until the curlew reappeared. Then the drama was played out again. This occurred several more times until the falcon finally grew weary of its sport and flew off in search of a simpler meal.

As the falcon crested the rise over which the shepherd had entered the dell, the insistent bleating of a lamb suddenly broke in upon the man's thoughts, diverting his attention.

"Ah, Finlay!" he muttered. "Ye haena been at yer job!"

An adventuresome lamb, whose frisky tendencies had more than once given the man trouble, had wandered up the opposite craggy wall of the dell, and getting so high, found he could not come down again. There he stood, helpless, bleating a demand for someone to come rescue him. The shepherd pulled himself to his feet, bracing his stiff body on his staff for a few seconds until he could fully straighten up. Then he strode across the grassy meadow and was just starting up the steep incline when a voice called out to him from above, hidden from his view by the sunlight coming over the rocks.

"Gran'daddy!"

He looked up, shielded his eyes from the sun, and returned the grin peering radiantly down upon him from the ridge above. His broad smile brought the hundreds of wrinkles on his brown and weathered face to life. The figure perched among the rocks may not have been as clear in the focus of his ancient eyes as it once would have been, but the voice was music to his old ears and brought a song to his heart.

"A lamb be caught," he called.

"I see him," the voice replied. "Dinna move. I'll get him frae here."

The youth was about seventeen years old and slight of frame and limb with a shock of short-cropped dark hair tucked beneath a ragged wide-brimmed hat which was in perfect keeping with the drab oft-patched breeches and homespun tunic. But the lanky body was lithe and agile and descended over the rocks

and through the thorny mountain brush with the ease of a highland roe.

The lamb was within reach in a matter of moments, and
stopped its clamor the instant the hands of the rescuer grasped
its white woolly coat. Tucked safely in the young shepherd's
arms, the animal seemed almost to sigh contentedly, and the
two continued over the rocks to the grassy carpet below.

The old man walked up to the pair and first looked sternly
at the lamb and scolded it gently. "Ye're a troublesome one. Noo,
be off t' yer mither!"

Then turning to the youth, he smiled and said, "Ye saved my
auld banes some wear. What would I do wi' oot ye, Jamie, lass?"

But for boy's clothing and a tanned, smudged face, in some
respects Gilbert MacLeod's daughter had changed little in ten
years' time. Though cropped short, her hair was still rich and
lustrous, and her emerald eyes still sparkled when she laughed.
Indeed, many mistook Jamie for a boy upon first glance. Though
her body had rounded and shaped itself slowly, womanhood
had stolen upon this child of the mountain by such gradual degrees that she was hardly aware of it herself. Her grandfather
saw it but said little; he did not want to lose another young one
to the passage of time.

But there was little danger of that. Though her body teetered
wonderfully and precariously between childhood and womanhood, in Jamie's eyes still flashed the exhilaration of innocent
youth. Though her slight frame often did not betray her years,
the inner vitality exuding from within it revealed a strength far
beyond her years.

She threw back her head and laughed wholesomely and fully.
" 'Twill be the day when ye're needin' my help, Gran'daddy!"

"What's bringin' ye oot t' the meadow this time o' the day?"

"Ye haena forgotten? I was bringin' ye supper. But in the
excitement wi' the lamb, I left it upo' the ridge. I'll be richt back!"

She sprang across the grass in the direction she had come
and, foregoing the path which wound some way eastward before
making the gradual ascent, she scurried up the rocky face where
the animal had been trapped. Finlay MacLeod watched with
delight; the girl never failed to stir within him a deep well of
pride and joy. From the moment she came into his home ten
years ago, she had brought with her something that had long
been missing—a stirring, invigorating purpose.

Yes, Finlay knew where all purpose originated. He had always been content with the life the Creator had marked out for him. But when the child came, it was as if God had added a special gem to His glorious purpose—replacing with his granddaughter the son he had lost to the valley some twenty years before.

Finlay had deeply mourned the death of his son. How his heart ached that Gilbert had never been able—or willing—to return to his home on the mountain! It was more than mere luck that brought them together and allowed Finlay to share his mourning with his granddaughter. Together they wept, together they comforted one another, and together they grew strong again in the healing that follows the winter. In this way the relationship that might otherwise have been awkward and difficult grew quite naturally over the years into a bond even deeper than the common blood that flowed through their veins. As the years had passed, the memory of Gilbert gradually gave way in Finlay's mind to the reality of his relationship with Jamie. Without loving his son the less, he was able to pour himself into his granddaughter in a way his own son could never permit. But knowing the pride and ambition that had ultimately killed his son, he could not suppress the hidden fear that the same thing might lure Jamie away from Donachie when she came of age and began to feel the tug of the world.

But perhaps his fears were unfounded. She was a lass, after all, and lasses were different from lads.

But there were times he'd come upon her without her knowing he was watching, when, catching her unaware, he'd see a far-off gaze in those emerald eyes—the same look Gilbert had evinced before he walked away from Donachie. He had left and never returned. It was natural, then, that old Finlay clung with a certain possessiveness to his granddaughter.

But now as he watched Jamie descend the bluff, he almost laughed within himself at his fears. She loved the mountain, too, and knew it almost as well as he did who had spent his entire life there. If occasionally she seemed distant, he also saw in her eyes a love and a oneness with the wild place that had become her home.

CHAPTER SEVEN

Sunset

If Jamie had been conscious of fears that first day on Donachie, they were now only a distant memory of the past. Sometimes those early years in what her grandfather called the lowlands—which were really not the lowlands at all—were but a vague glimmer of another life that hardly seemed her own. Yet she tried to keep those memories alive and dear, and to hold a sharp and clear picture of her father in her heart. But it was difficult when she knew how painful it was for her grandfather to speak of him. He never became angry with her inquiries, but each time a wall as impenetrable as stone shot up between them which forced her to silence.

Lately the frequency of her questions, and with them an undefined sense of disquiet, seemed to be growing. Perhaps it was a natural outgrowth of maturity. But whatever the cause, forces from beyond the mountain were nagging at her more and more. Last night she had had a terrible dream. She had been walking over a familiar path contentedly breathing in the lovely fragrance of the mountain, filled with the happy delight of her surroundings. Suddenly her father appeared over the next rise in front of her. She knew it was he, for he called to her in the way she always remembered—"Jamie, my bairn," he said. His hand was stretched out to her and she ran toward him joyfully. But when she looked up into his face, the joy vanished and she screamed out in terror—the form had no face!

She awoke in a sweat, crying out, "Papa! . . . Papa!" If Finlay heard her on the other side of the single-room cottage, he made no attempt to come to her and comfort her. It was likely he was praying for her in the silence of his own bed. But it was also likely he could not bear to comfort her longings for her father.

Now lying on the grass with the peace of the mountain all about her, listening to the sheep and the bubbling burn, she tried to understand. Had she loved him less, she might have been an easy prey to a growing root of bitterness in her heart at his seeming obstinacy to let her know her own father, even if only in memory. But she *did* love him, and she knew he was only trying to protect her from the same pitfalls, and protect himself from the pain of his own broken relationship with his son. The dear old man had taken her in and cared for her and taught her all the wonders of Donachie. Whatever she knew of life and God's creation, she had learned from him. She could not resent him if he withheld a small part of his heart from her. She realized she could repay him, not with confrontive and painful questions about her father, but by accepting things as they were.

Still, new forces were rising within her. In her purity and innocence she could hardly realize their implications. But maturity and adulthood were sprouting inside, and would soon blossom in earnest. Womanhood, which was yet only a hint, a suggestion, was rapidly on its way too. Things were changing for young Jamie. Though she could not see where these forces were taking her, she could feel the stirrings in some deep vault of her being.

And through it all, the fact remained that the aspiring blood of Gilbert MacLeod coursed through her veins. Even from the grave, his own yearnings reached out and turned her eyes to the horizons of life, engendering in her a shadowy discontent to remain satisfied with only what was under her feet. She had loved her father with a totality only a motherless single child could. She did not want to forget him! And the realization that the memory of her father was indeed fading slowly into the recesses of her mind was heartbreaking. He was becoming, as the terrifying dream so graphically depicted, a frightening, faceless apparition.

She was therefore torn both ways—toward two men she loved with all her heart. Could she have them both? Could she cling to the present and the dear love of her beloved grandfather and still keep alive within her own soul the dreams her father had passed on to her?

"Look, Jamie!" Finlay's old voice interrupted her thoughts. "The auld falcon's comin' home. He didna get the curlew, but he's got dinner all the same."

For a few moments she watched the falcon, its prey tucked

securely in its powerful beak; but the introspective mood in which she had uncharacteristically found herself could not so easily be shaken. Soon her eyes and mind had wandered again to other things.

The sun had sunk low in the western sky. In another hour it would drop below the rise and leave the little dell washed in the color and shadows of the summer gloaming. Something about the sun slipping from sight simultaneously disturbed her and sent a thrill of excitement and anticipation surging through her body.

"Gran'daddy," she asked quietly some time later, "whaur the sun be goin' noo?"

"I dinna ken, lass."

"Will it be risin' on some ither land, someplace else, far awa?"

"Aye. I s'pose ye're right."

"What are they like, Gran'daddy, those ither lands?"

"The mountain's the only place that matters, Jamie," Finlay replied, and his voice seemed to have caught a sudden chill from the sunless dell.

"Didna God make them all, Gran'daddy?"

"Aye, He did."

"Then the ither lands must be important, too."

"Aye, important t' them that's there. But not t' us. What does any ither place matter when we hae the best o' His creation?"

"I dinna ken," she said as she followed the fading sun with a distant gaze in her eyes. " 'Tis jist that Papa wanted t' see them I think, an' I canna help mysel' wonderin' what's oot there."

Finlay was silent a long while, then inched his way to his feet.

"Time t' be bringin' the flock in," he said, and then began whistling and calling the sheep together.

Jamie jumped to her feet, and in the solace of the activity of getting the stubborn animals down the hill, her thoughts did not wander down melancholy paths again. Instead, her eyes once more reflected the laughter and sparkle which had been old Finlay's sustenance these past several years.

Soon the sheep were snug in their pen and the two shepherds walked toward home. It was a small cottage—one room was all Finlay had ever needed—built of rough granite, as rugged as its surroundings, it gave the impression that it had almost grown up where it stood as part of the mountain itself. One look showed it to be sturdy enough to withstand the most violent of highland storms. But the rugged exterior was balanced inside with a warmth which was able to hold out even the icy blasts coming down from the peak of Donachie. To the windward side there were no windows, and the stone wall was thickly packed with a solid layer of turf as further insulation against the elements. In the center of the single large room was dug a pit where the fire burned, sending warmth to every corner of the room. A table and two chairs and a few shelves for cooking utensils stood against one wall, and a straw-covered cot for Finlay was against the adjacent one. The opposite corner had been partially partitioned off for Jamie's own straw bed. It was an eminently comfortable home, completed by a medium-sized byre and a shed for storing their peat fuel. Their tastes being simple, the two never wanted for anything.

Periodically Finlay made his trek down to the estate of Aviemere to make an accounting of his small croft to the laird who owned Donachie and most of the valley besides, and to pick up supplies. In recent years the factor had made it a practice to come up to Donachie himself three times yearly to check on the old sheepherder. Finlay did not like to bow to the concession because of his age, yet he was nevertheless thankful for the factor's consideration. In recent times it had grown more and more difficult to keep Jamie at home when he went down the mountain. A gnawing uneasiness made him fear her setting foot on the lowland paths, even if it was with him. But as they had little reason to leave Donachie, they had been content there to remain. And as Jamie grew older, he more often let the factor come to him.

Jamie stirred the fire and prepared their evening meal. When they had finished the steaming bowl of potatoes, oatcakes, and hearty brown bread, Finlay picked up his worn leather Bible and thumbed through it for a moment. At length the pages ceased their fluttering and the open book lay on the table. Jamie knew he had found his place and was ready to read. For a moment all became very quiet, then the old voice began, taking on a dignified resonance:

"Them that beirs the yoke o' slaverie maun haud their maisters worthy o' all respeck, that the name o' God aŋ oor doctrine binna ill spoken. Slaves o' believin' maisters maunna lichtlie them because they are brethren in Christ: raither, they maun sair them the better. . . ." *

Jamie loved this time of day best of all. She never tired of

---

* 1 Timothy 6:1, 2.

hearing the words from her grandfather's book in his thick brogue. Since she had never heard the sayings from God's Word in any other way, she had no reason to believe that God himself, as well as Moses and all the prophets, did not speak with a thoroughly highland tongue. And he read each word with such deep belief and assurance that she could not help but believe everything also. The very sound of his voice, and the soothing, melodic lilt of his voice, which would occasionally break out into phrases from the ancient Gaelic that she could not understand seemed to cover her with a sense of peaceful and holy security. The whole setting each night imbued her with a sense of God's presence among them. As she watched her grandfather sitting across the rough table reading from his treasured book, she detected in his eyes the glinting of a deeper thrill than even the mountain could stir within him. Yet he so often said that the mountain was but one more reflection of the character of God as revealed in His Word.

Suddenly Jamie started, for she realized she had missed some of the reading. What pulled back her attention she could not tell. Had the timbre of her grandfather's voice altered, rising slightly? She now began to listen more intently than ever.

". . . gudeliness wi' oot seekin' nae mair nor a man needs is gret gain. We brocht naething intil the warld, an' we canna tak onything out o' it. Sae, gin we hae wir bit an' sup, an wantna for cleadin' an a bield, we s' een haud us wi' that. Them at seeks walth falls intil the girns o' temptation laid by the de'il; owre they whummle intil a flowe o' the fuilitch an' scaithfu desires in whilk men sinks doun tae ruin an' perdition. Fainness for siller is the ruit o' all ills, an' there is them that has gaen agley wi' ettlin tae mak rich, an' brocht on themsel's a vast o' sorrow. But ye, man o' God, maun haud awa frae a that an ettle at richteousness, gudeliness, faith, luve, patience, douceness o' hairt. Kemp awa i the noble kemp o' faith; cleik hauds o' iverlestin' life, tae whilk ye war caa'd."*

Finlay closed the book and bowed his head in silent prayer for a long moment. Then he broke out in the Lord's Prayer and Jamie joined in with him:

"Oor Faither in heiven," they prayed, "hallowt be thy name; thy Kingdom come; thy will be dune on the yird, as in heiven. Gie us oor breid for this incomin' day; forgie us the wrangs we hae wrocht, as we hae forgien the wrangs we had dree'd; as sey-

*1 Timothy 6:6–12.

us-na sairlie, but sauf us frae the Ill Ane."

When they had finished he looked up at Jamie.

"Do ye unnerstan' the words I read frae the book, lass?"

"I—I think sae, Gran'daddy."

"They be important words fer ye."

"Why?"

"Ye dinna want t' be fallin' intil a snare, do ye, lass?"

"No, Gran'daddy. But how cud I do that wi' ye here t' protect me?"

"Oh, lass . . . dear lass!" said Finlay, rubbing his hands across his face.

The two were silent a moment.

"I'm afraid ye'll ne'er unnerstan'," Finlay continued. "An' how cud ye?"

He sat for some time gazing into the fire without another word. At length, lost in his own thoughts, his lips began to move again. "But she is her father's daughter," he murmured, ". . . she must unnerstan'." He no longer seemed to be aware that Jamie was even in the room.

Jamie did not know what he was thinking, and somehow she knew she could not ask. Perhaps someday he would tell her. Perhaps someday she *would* understand. But for now, maybe that's what the book meant by being content. She would just have to wait—though she was not sure what she was waiting for.

She stretched and yawned, rose, kissed her grandfather goodnight, and went to her bed.

CHAPTER EIGHT

The Old Trunk

Three days later it dawned dark and cloudy.

When Jamie awoke she thought it must still be nighttime, for there was no sign of the sun anywhere in the eastern sky.

Looking about she saw that Finlay's bed was empty, and she heard nothing of him anywhere. He had awakened early and left without a word. Perhaps even in his sleep he had sensed the approaching storm and wanted to be sure the sheep had a chance to graze before it broke.

Jamie rose, tended to the fire, then pulled on her coat and walked out into the chill, dank morning. The air was stuffy, full of the moisture which the sky would soon loose. She walked to the byre, found the pail, and began milking their one old cow. It was a job she had done, as far as she could remember, every day of her life. She had lost none of her affection for animals, but though she remembered them fondly, she had forgotten the names of the two cows she had tended as a child on her father's land. And still she talked casually to the cow as she milked, on this particular day chiding her grandfather to the animal for not letting her take the sheep out on such a day.

During the wet and stormy days of autumn, and the raw, chilly days of spring, Jamie took charge of the sheep most of the time. But as soon as summer broke out upon the highlands in earnest, Finlay insisted upon carrying the bulk of the shepherding once more himself. Even then Jamie was constantly at his side. In the last two or three years, his age had begun to tell more definitely upon him. His abiding love for the mountain, and his familiarity with its ways, had kept him going long past the age when most men turn their tasks over to those younger than themselves. But then, old Finlay MacLeod had nowhere

else to go. The mountain was not only his love, it was his home—
the only home he had ever known.

When Jamie finished milking, the pail was less than half full.
"Ah, Missy," she said, "ye'll be gettin' auld yersel', aren't ye
noo? Weel, we willna be needin' sae much milk onyway." She
took up the pail and carried it back into the cottage.

The black clouds were rolling thickly across the sky. The rain
could not hold back much longer. It seemed impossible her
grandfather would be back before the storm broke. *The sheep could
have remained where they were for one day*, she thought.

A rumble of thunder startled her.

She hurried to the window and looked out. There was no
evidence of the approaching flock. Patience had never been easy
for her if she thought there was the slightest chance her grandfather might be in danger. Today she sensed a particular urgency.

Without waiting a moment longer, she reached again for her
coat. But she had taken it off in the byre and left it there, so she
hurried outside and down the path without it.

From signs along the trail she saw that her grandfather had
not taken the sheep to the dell nor to any of the lower places.
She made her way north, and there she could see evidence that
he had gone instead to the high pasture. It was closer at hand,
and part of it was protected from the north winds by a huge
projecting cliff that shot out and up from Donachie's mighty west
flank. But the climb to the high pasture was steep and taxing,
for man as well as beast, and Finlay had not gone there alone in
nearly two years. *He must have decided to take the shorter path*, she
thought, *thinking he could outrun the storm*.

But even as Jamie's sure feet ran up the steep ascent, pellets
of rain began to fall. Halfway up she was soaked to the skin,
bringing her to a slippery half walk. Her climb was cut short,
however, for she looked up and saw Finlay approaching.

"Gran'daddy!" she cried. "Ye're a stubborn ane, ye are! leaving wi' oot me!" A hint of anger was mingled in her tone of
concern. "We'll both be catchin' oor daiths, we will!"

"The storm'll be lastin' two or three days," he replied. "The
lads an' lassies needed t' get oot, an' they'll be fine up there."
He pointed up the hill from where he had come.

His final words were drowned in a blustery gust of wind that
almost blew him off his feet.

Jamie sighed in frustration.

"Weel, come on! Let's get doon an' oot o' this wind an' rain!"

The descent was tricky over the rain-slick rocks; the muddy path had already become a creekbed. Every now and then a brilliant flash of lightning lit up the dark silhouette of Donachie's massive north face, followed almost instantly by deafening cracks of thunder. This was no distant storm: this one was their very own!

At length they were back inside the shelter of the cottage. A large segment of the packed earthen floor had puddled into mud before they were able to get themselves into fresh shirts and trousers. But even dry clothes did not seem to bring warmth to Finlay as he stood shivering convulsively before the fire.

"Ye're chilled, Gran'daddy," said Jamie as if she were a parent rebuking a child. "Ye're goin' t' yer bed."

" 'Tis but the middle o' the mornin'!" protested Finlay.

"That makes nae difference," insisted Jamie, taking him by his arm and leading him to the corner where he slept.

He continued to shake with the cold, and Jamie pulled the heavy wool blankets from her own bed and laid them tenderly on top of him. All the while a horrible, undefined knot had been forming in the pit of her stomach.

Why was she suddenly filled with such fear? Her grandfather had been sick at other times. He had merely caught a chill from being too long out in the rain. He was a hardy old man. He would recover. He always did.

Yet seeing him tremble so, it was as if—

Suddenly she remembered!

Her father had come in out of the rain, too—trembling with cold and pain. There had been blood on him! She had laid him in bed also. She had made him tea and tried to nurse him.

But it had been of no use.

Her father had died despite her efforts!

Was she destined to fail her grandfather in the same way? But she could not stand idly by and do nothing.

"I dinna need all these blankets," Finlay continued to argue. "What'll ye be usin' fer yersel'?" For he could see that she was trembling now too. But he did not know it was something other than the cold which shook Jamie's body.

"Don't ye worry aboot me, Gran'daddy," she replied, trying to put a cheerful note into her voice. "I'm yoong an' strong. An' I'm not sae cauld as ye are yersel'. Ye jist get yersel' t' sleep!"

"Jist look at ye!" he went on. "Ye're shiverin' too."

"The fire's warmin' me. An' I'll brew us some tea."

Finlay was asleep before the kettle began to steam, much to Jamie's relief. She set the tea to steep, and since the rain had let up for a moment, went out to the byre to retrieve her coat. She found it on the peg where she had left it that morning and gradually slipped her arms into it. Glancing around for some additional blankets to take inside, she walked to the driest wall of the place, which was attached to the cottage itself. Along the wall was stored, in addition to a stack of blankets used to keep ailing animals warm, a vast assortment of miscellaneous paraphernalia. Here had been collected over the years an assortment of items almost never used but kept around just in case—pails, ropes, cooking gear, rusted wool-shears, and an old mackintosh, at which Jamie shook her head and sighed, "Ye're doin' a great good here, ye are!"

Moving the accumulated junk aside to get to the blankets, Jamie worked her way toward the wall. As she picked up the stack from the large black trunk on which they were resting, she suddenly realized it had been in that very spot for years without her so much as noticing. It was the trunk that had come to Donachie with her as a child. She had not given it a thought in years. And now—or was it merely her imagination?—it almost seemed as if the bottommost blanket of the stack had been carefully draped over the trunk so as to hide it from view.

Surely the trunk must have long since been emptied. If her grandfather had not wanted her to discover it, and was so reluctant to talk about the past, he would never have left . . .

Rational arguments notwithstanding, perhaps nothing is more naturally compelling than the curiosity that urges one to open an old trunk. Jamie stepped forward, turned the latch, and lifted the great black lid.

Far from being empty, the trunk contained most of the items that had come with Jamie ten years before. Though she had not thought of them in years, she instantly recognized nearly everything she laid eyes upon. In ten years she had worn no dress, nor had she had any thought to wear one. Gently her hands reached down and pulled out a soft blue dress, badly faded and mended many times. She replaced it and held up another—pale pink with a red ribbon around its middle. Another was white, slightly yellowed, trimmed in delicate lace with pearl buttons. As a child she had never noticed the many places mended with the unskillful touch of a man's hand, or the hems that had been let down to accommodate her growth through the years.

These were the dresses of a little lady—not of the unpolished shepherd girl named Jamie MacLeod.

Next to the dresses lay a book, brown and hardbound, with goldleaf lettering on the front and spine. As she lifted it up she trembled again, but this time with a kind of awe. She did not know how to read, and her grandfather had not cared to teach her, so the words were a mystery to her. But that did not matter. She somehow felt—holding the book—very close to her father: it must be his book!

Struggling to light her own memory, she could only recall that there had been no books in their house. Her father had never read as her grandfather did. But . . . but . . . yes, she remembered now! He had always kept *this* book. Now she could see it as she pictured that little cottage down in the valley!

Could it—just maybe—have been her mother's?

She opened it slowly. There was a handwritten message on the flyleaf. The writing was too lovely to be any man's. Absent-mindedly she traced her finger over the elegant script. She closed her eyes as she had done countless times before, and tried to imagine what Alice MacLeod was like. The picture in her mind was more vivid than any real picture could have been, for she did not have to draw upon a faulty memory. She had no visual memory at all to blur her mind's eye.

As she stood there she saw a beautiful lady with dancing eyes and a merry smile, dressed in velvet and ruffled lace. And she was always sitting in a shiny black coach drawn by two sprightly chestnuts.

"Mama, I wish I could ha' known ye," Jamie murmured.

She turned the pages of the book and gazed intently at them, as if she might, by staring, unlock the bonds of her illiteracy. The words must have meant something to her mama, she thought. If only she knew what they said!

Was her mama a lady?

Was that why her papa always wanted *her* to be a lady? For if Jamie forgot everything else, she would never forget her father's last words to her: *"If only I hadna failed, ye would ha' been a gran' lady some day . . . ."*

Tears rose in Jamie's eyes. "Oh, Papa, an' I canna e'en read Mama's book! I'm sorry, Papa!"

She snapped the book shut in despair and laid it back in the trunk. As she did so her eyes fell upon another object. An involuntary shiver ran up her spine but then passed just as quickly.

It was the last gift her father had given her; she had forgotten all about it. Such a strange gift it was! She knew it was some kind of jewelry, but what it was remained a mystery to her—it could be neither a brooch nor a ring. It looked valuable, studded with gems. But what could it be used for? As a gift from her father she should have treasured it. But there was something about it she didn't like, though she could not explain what.

"Lass!" rang out a familiar voice behind her.

Jamie spun around as if she had been caught in some evil deed. Her face flushed.

"Gran'daddy," she said, her voice trembling. "Ye . . . ye should be in bed."

"I'm warmed noo, too," Finlay replied. "But I was worryin' fer ye."

"I—I came lookin' fer blankets."

"Aye, but ye found somethin' else."

There was no anger in her grandfather's voice, and Jamie relaxed. She reached back into the trunk and lifted out the book.

"Was this my papa's?" she asked.

"It was with yer things when ye came t' me," he answered.

"Can ye read t' me what's written here?"

She held the book out to him, open to the handwritten message.

Finlay made no move to take it. After a long, tense moment, he spoke. "Jamie, yer papa is gone noo. 'Tis best fer ye t' ferget. 'Tis nae use fer ye t' try t' remember. 'Twill only bring ye pain. Please, lass, ye maun try t' trust me."

"But Gran'daddy, hoo can it bring me pain when forgettin' hurts too? I loved him, Gran'daddy. It jist wouldna be doin' right by him t' forget him."

"Do ye believe that he wanted only the best fer ye?"

Jamie nodded, and Finlay continued.

"Then believe me, child, that t' forget is the best fer ye, an' would noo be what he would hae wanted."

"No!" Jamie cried. "That canna be! What can be wrong wi' rememberin'? All I'm askin' is fer ye t' show me how t' read these words."

Hardly realizing that he was in danger of making the same mistake with his granddaughter that had so grieved him with his own son, and looking suddenly weak and old, Finlay replied, "I canna."

"I know ye hate him!" Jamie shouted in her despair and frustration. "But I willna. I loved him, no matter what ye say!"

With the words she dropped the book into the trunk and ran past him out into the rain.

"Jamie—lass!" Finlay called after her. But she was already gone out of sight.

CHAPTER NINE

The Lass of the Mountain

The pounding rain washed over Jamie as if it were trying to clean away her anger and confusion and pain. But she was hardly aware of the storm despite the crackling thunder or the dazzling flashes of lightning.

From the cottage she ran north, taking a path even the sheep could not tread to its end. Steep and narrow, it led upward—always upward. She had set her sights on the very crown of Donachie. It was there she hoped to get as far away from the source of her trouble as possible, or perhaps get closer to the answer.

The rocks were slippery, but her bare feet knew them well and traversed them without a thought of their imminent treachery. She not only knew this country, this path, these rocks, she understood them. In a way, they had been kind to her. They had opened up to her and let her love them, and in return had been a comfort to her. She had roamed every inch of this mountain at one time or another. But she had always taken the mountain for granted because, first and foremost, she had her grandfather. Suddenly now it seemed Donachie was all she knew and understood. But was it enough?

Why did this have to happen? She wanted only to love the mountain and her grandfather and have no other cares in the world. But she could not deny the feelings stirring within her. And more than anything, she could not deny her father! Why he had this day suddenly come to life, as from the very grave, she didn't know. Something inside her told her he had departed this world leaving something unfinished. And now the path lay before her, his daughter.

But what was it? *What did she have to do?*

The path ahead of Jamie began to disintegrate until it was no path at all. Most climbers did not go beyond this point, but Jamie persisted stubbornly toward her goal—ever higher. She knew the way. Protruding rocks and thorny overgrowth did not daunt her. The rain was coming down in sheets, and the higher she climbed the greater became its angle against her, for she was ascending into the very heart of the wind. The lightning and thunder had now abated and given way to the full outpouring from the black clouds, the very source of all the trouble.

After an hour, her clothing tight against her skin, her soaked hair pasted against her uncovered head, Jamie emerged upon a broad plateau from which she could go no higher. Not a tree, not a single piece of scrubby brown heather was to be seen— only granite. This was the top of Jamie's world!

She climbed onto her favorite boulder, fighting the fierce wind to keep her balance. When the skies were clear, she could from this vantage point see many, many miles in every direction. It had been said that one with exceptional eyesight could see the ocean in the distance, but Jamie could not. And such days were rare indeed. For about Donachie, as though it were a Scottish Sinai, there always seemed to hang a shroud of mist, obscuring its heights from observers below.

Here, at the very pinnacle of her world, the Mount Sinai of her own spirit, it seemed natural to pray. She had come here many times before to think, to meditate, to talk to God. But now her prayers all seemed to end in agonizing questions that had no answers.

Where was the faith she had learned from her grandfather? Where was the peace the Book told her she should have?

Was it true, then? Would she in the end have to choose between her father and her grandfather?

Why should such a choice have to be made?

Why, why, why?

"Why?" Jamie shouted as loud as she could, but the echo was muted in the blast of the storm. The word seemed visibly to crumble into nothingness, like the vague emptiness of her soul.

A fierce howl of wind whipped itself upon the girl who dared to challenge the power of the elements at the height of their madness. A crackle of thunder followed away eastward where the storm was heading into the depths of the Cairngorm highlands.

Are there no answers to the questions which have suddenly come to haunt me? Jamie wondered.

If there were answers, would she have to leave Donachie to find them?

Leave?

"Dear God, I cud ne'er leave this place," she said aloud. "I couldna leave my ain gran'daddy. I love him too much, an' I need him too. Ah, it would hurt him fer me t' leave."

Her own father had left Donachie. Perhaps he had been to the top of the mountain, too, and stood on this very spot. Perhaps *he* had seen the sea, and it had called him away from this, his home, called him to the better life he sought but never found.

But his leaving had grieved his father. Had it even made him hate his own son? She couldn't bear for him ever to feel that way toward her!

Yet she still *had* to know what was out there for her to see, to discover, to learn. Was she destined to try to fulfill her father's dream?

Dear Lord, what would ye hae me t' do?

But she heard no answer. The only sound all around her was the pounding rain and the ferocious wind trying to blow her off the top of this wild and untamed mountain.

Two hours later Jamie returned to the old cottage once more. Her emotions had settled, as had the fury of the storm. She was now left with just a hollow feeling inside and a bit of apprehension about facing her grandfather again.

Slowly she pulled the latch of the door and slipped inside. The warmth that met her felt comfortable on her wind-reddened face. Finlay sat at the table, his open Bible before him. He looked up, and she smiled awkwardly as if to reassure him that the angry words had been left outside.

"Ye're wet clean through," he said.

"Aye," she replied.

She removed her coat and hung it on a hook near the fire, and went to her own corner and changed her clothes. She slipped on the clothes she had worn that very morning, now dry. What a long time ago it seemed when she had gone out in search of her grandfather before the storm!

Jamie was thankful for the diversion of changing her clothes. It gave her and her grandfather the opportunity to get used to one another's presence once again without the awkwardness of stumbling over words. When she came back out into the big room, she laid her wet things about the fires and set about making supper.

It was Finlay who broke the long silence.

"Will ye nae be speakin' t' me onymore, lass?" he asked.

"Ye maunna think that, Gran'daddy," she answered, her voice choked with emotion. "I'm sorry."

"I been tryin' t' unnerstan' hoo ye're feelin'," he went on. "I been prayin' that I would learn an' that ye'd be patient wi' me."

"Oh, I will, Gran'daddy!" she exclaimed, "I will." She ran to him, putting her arms round his shoulders and kissing his wrinkled cheek. Renewed tears streamed down her face and she felt the wet from Finlay's own tears on her lips. "An' ye maun be patient wi' me!"

"Sit ye doon, here, lass," he said, pulling the other chair up next to his. "I'll try t' teach ye some o' the words in the Book."

Jamie sat down with a radiant smile on her face. Though it was the words in the other book in the trunk that she really wanted to read, this would be a start.

"I canna keep ye frae learnin' the truth fer yersel' fere'er," he said. "An' jist maybe, lass, if ye learn these words, 'twill help ye t' unnerstan' more aboot yer ain father. An' help ye t' see why I tried t' protect ye so."

"Thank ye, Gran'daddy! I'll try my hardest t' understand."

As Jamie began her first lesson, she did not allow all the questions that had plagued her on the mountaintop to crowd out the happiness she felt at that moment. This *was* a start! Perhaps this was the beginning of the answer to everything else. Her relationship with her beloved grandfather restored, perhaps the other anxieties would also soon begin to dispel.

But for a girl of seventeen, *soon* does not carry the same meaning as it does for the Master of all Time. For her questions to be answered, for her vision to extend to the sea, young Jamie MacLeod had many more Donachies yet to climb.

CHAPTER TEN

Another Farewell

It was autumn again.

This was not a season she loved, for winter always followed close behind, forcing her indoors. Without being able to roam freely on the mountain, Jamie could never feel altogether whole.

But this year the season contained a new and exciting element: longer hours indoors meant more time for her lessons. Jamie proved a quick learner, and the only thing hampering her progress was the fact that old Finlay was no teacher. He tried his best, but the process was slow. And Finlay could perhaps be forgiven if this did not grieve him as much as it did Jamie. He knew what the end of his teaching would bring. In his brittle old bones, he knew that Jamie would eventually have to leave Donachie.

Jamie herself never faced the inevitable squarely. Though there were times her gaze turned toward the distant horizon and the questions returned, her grandfather's home was the very core of life's meaning, and she never asked herself what would become of her once he was gone. However, no one could have failed to note how her face brightened on the day when the factor from Aviemere came up the mountain.

"Welcome t' ye, Mr. Ellice," said Finlay, as the visitor entered the cottage.

"Thank you, Finlay," replied the factor. "And that is always what I feel when I come here."

George Ellice was of middle-age, with thin, graying hair. Slight of frame and quiet of personality, he stood in direct contrast to his predecessor, Frederick Lundie, whom he had replaced ten years earlier.

"My gran'daughter'll fix some tea fer us, an' ye can bide a

wee. 'Tis a mighty long walk up the mountain frae the estate."

"Aye, it is," agreed Ellice. "But you know I love making the walk and always look forward to my visits."

" 'Tis the only reason I let ye do it fer me."

Ellice laughed. "That I know."

"But I'm thinkin'," Finlay continued, "that next year I'll be sendin' my gran'daughter doon t' min' my business. She'll be comin' o' age noo, ye ken."

Ellice smiled warmly at Jamie. "Yes, she is. And so I suppose I'll have to find another excuse to come up your mountain."

"Ye'll be needin' nae excuse; ye're welcome onytime."

Jamie could hardly concentrate on serving the men tea. All she could think to do was to throw her arms around her dear old grandfather. And she could not keep the broad smile off her face. Finlay saw it, and knew what his words had meant to this granddaughter he had finally come to trust, even more than he had his own son.

Jamie knew Finlay's words were an act of faith on his part. It meant that evenings poring over the old black Bible were not wasted. She must be achieving the understanding he wanted for her. And it meant, too, that the time could not be far away when he would tell her about her father, and let her read the book tucked away in the trunk, which had not been touched since that rainy day several months before.

The days now passed swiftly and joyfully for Jamie. Hardly aware of the chill, the intermittent rains, and the heavy skies, she looked forward more than ever to each moment spent with her grandfather at the table. Though he said little, she felt her progress must be pleasing to him. In later years she would never forget these evenings in the warm cottage, with the wind whistling in a frenzy outside, as she sat listening to her grandfather's voice and trying to understand the simple gems of wisdom he offered as he taught her to read and comprehend the book opened on the table in front of them.

"Do ye ken what the Maister said aboot sheep an' shepherds, Jamie?" he asked one evening.

"No, Gran'daddy. Ye never read me that."

"Aye. We'v' read it, child. 'Tis one o' my favorite passages. It's like He's talking jist t' the likes o' us that tend His sheep. But we haena read it fer some time noo. But tonight, I want fer ye t' try't yersel'."

He turned the big Bible to the tenth chapter of St. John.

Pointing to the page, he said, "There ye be. Try't Jamie."

"The—"

"*Thief*."

"The *thief* comesna for ocht but tae—steal—an fell—an des—"

"*Destroy*—ye're doin' fine, child!"

"Oh, Gran'daddy, couldna ye read it all t' me, so I cud hear all aboot the sheep in yer ain voice? I'd so like t' hear ye read it all t' me!"

Needing no further encouragement, the old man pulled the book close, and began the beloved passage again.

"The thief comesna for ocht but tae steal an fell an destroy: I am come at they may hae life—ay, an rowth, an mair, o it! I am the guid shepherd. The guid shepherd lays doun his life for the sheep. The hireman, at is nae shepherd, an isna aucht the sheep himsel, forleits the sheep, whaniver he sees the wouf comin, an scours awa, laein the wouf tae herrie an skail the hirsel. He rins awa, because he is a fee'd man, an cares nocht for the sheep. I am the guid shepherd; I ken my sheep, an my sheep kens me, een as the Faither kens me, and I ken the Faither; an I am tae lay doun my life for the sheep. But I hae ither sheep, forbye thir, at belangsna this fauld, at I maun bring in, tae. They will tent my caa, an syne there will be au hirsel, an ae shepherd."*

He closed the book and the only sound was the low burning fire and the wind outside.

"Ne're forget, Jamie, my bairn," the old man said at length, "that Jesus is *yer* shepherd, jist like we are t' the sheep. When *we* get stuck on a rock an' can't fin' oor way an' can't get doon, *He's* the shepherd that saves us. Ye'll remember that, won't ye, Jamie?"

"Aye, Gran'daddy," she replied softly, "I'll remember."

The next morning Jamie awoke and was surprised to find Finlay still asleep. Even in winter such a thing was highly uncharacteristic. And when he did wake some time later, his movements appeared to Jamie slower and his speech imperceptibly dulled. She said nothing, only served him with the greater tenderness. For the rest of the week he seemed tired and scarcely left the cottage. When evening came, he was too weary to read and they had no lessons.

Then came a morning which dawned particularly chill and damp. Winter had come and was everywhere! Icicles hung from

---

*John 10:10–16

all the eaves of the cottage and the ground was frozen as hard as iron. Finlay was up at dawn, and when Jamie rose she could immediately see that a great change had come upon him. He was restless and fidgety. He had already been outside twice, walking across the yard, looking this way and that, standing for moments facing the north face of Donachie, breathing deeply with nostrils distended, as if waiting some sign from the high country above him. Then he would turn again into the cottage to continue his ministration to the morning fire, only to drop it and again walk out into the cold, this time focusing his attention in the other direction. To Jamie's questions he returned odd and evasive answers—still restless, anxious, waiting as if for something at hand. After breakfast he began to dress in his finest set of clothes, and no amount of exhortation on the part of Jamie could dissuade him, nor could she make the least sense of his explanations. He had someplace to go, he said, but where he would not say.

Thus it went for some time as he all the while grew more agitated. He ate little, despite Jamie's urgings.

"Too late fer food, my bairn," he said. "Time t' be goin' t' the high pasture."

"Ye'll do no such thing, Gran'daddy!"

" 'Tis time, child . . .'tis time. I *maun* go!"

"Ye're stayin' right here, Gran'daddy. I'll take the sheep oot today—an' *not* t' the high pasture. Today's nae day fer that!"

"I maun go!" insisted the old man. " 'Tis time, I tell ye! I can smell it in the air. 'Tis time. It's comin'."

"I know, Gran'daddy. I can feel the winter too. An' that's why I'm takin' oot the sheep today. Ye stay here an' rest."

"Too late fer rest, child . . . too late. I wasna speakin' o' the winter!"

"I'm takin' the sheep oot, Gran'daddy," Jamie insisted as she pulled on her coat and walked to the door. "I was hopin' t' be alone t' study today; I hae a surprise fer ye."

"Do ye noo?" he said, but his voice sounded distracted. "An' can ye nae study jist as well here?"

" 'Tis better ootside in the cauld air."

With the words she closed the door behind her and hurried off before he could argue any further. She had grown worried about him and wanted him out of the cold. Glancing back toward the cottage, she saw him standing in the doorway. He was not watching her, but again was looking to the mountain high above her, peering into the distance. She followed his gaze, then shook her head and said to herself, "He's nae doobt right. Snow's a-comin'! I can feel it too." She pulled her coat the more tightly around her shoulders and quickened her pace.

Despite the cold, the day was clear and bright. The clouds that would bring the snows to the highlands were not visible to the eye, only to the senses. The bluffs surrounding the dell to which she took the sheep seemed sharper and crisper and more real and beautiful than ever. Even the grass, struggling now against the harsh northern elements, looked greener and richer. Jamie found it hard to believe that within a short time—a few days, perhaps hours—it would all be covered with a thick blanket of white snow.

She settled herself down in a dry spot sheltered from the cool breeze and opened Finlay's Bible which she had sneaked out of the house without his noticing. With some effort she opened it to Psalm 121. For the last weeks, since her lessons had begun in earnest, she had been spending every spare moment poring over this passage. She knew it was her grandfather's favorite; he had read it countless times to her. Now she wanted to surprise him by reading it for herself!

The process was slow and difficult, for the words she knew by sight were still few. But she was familiar enough with the gist of the passage, that, with the words she knew and the sounds of the letters which she painstakingly applied to those she didn't, she had, after several weeks, learned the entire psalm. She hoped he would approve, even though she would surely sound more *English* as she said it than his Scottish ears would like her to.

"I will lift up mine een t' the hills, frae whence help comes . . ."

She tingled with excitement!

Tonight when she and her grandfather sat down at the old table, she would open the book and actually read it to him! It would be the most precious gift she had ever given him. It would be her way of thanking him, not only for teaching her to read, but also for the deep trust in her it had represented.

The days were growing shorter, and it did not seem long before the shadows on the bluffs began to lengthen and the sun began to slip away into the valley of the west. Jamie drove the sheep back to their pen, and if she drove them a little too quickly, they did not mind.

The cottage was still quiet as she turned the latch. No sounds came from within as she stepped across the threshold.

It was chilly inside.

"Gran'daddy," she called softly.

There was no reply.

Quickly she glanced around. A hunk of cheese sat on the table. He had brought it in from the byre—probably for her.

The fire was cold.

Frantically she looked about, then to her astonishment saw that Finlay was lying on his bed—motionless.

With heart pounding she ran toward him. He would never take to his bed so early in the day unless something was dreadfully wrong.

Fearfully she knelt down. One arm dangled over the side of the bed and she reached out to lift it into place. But the moment she grasped the beloved hand she dropped it in dread.

It was cold—icy cold.

"Gran'daddy!" she said, her voice trembling.

"Gran'daddy!" she shouted. "Gran'daddy!"

But he did not stir. There was no flutter even of his eyelids. She sank to her knees next to him and wept. She knew he was not asleep.

Whatever he had felt in the air had come before the winter's snows. He had gone to the high country.

Jamie's tears did not stay with her long. As the deeper grief assailed her, it seemed to dry the wellsprings of emotion for a time. The sense of loss was too great to be contented with tears, although they would come in their season. But for the rest of the day she could not cry, she could not speak, she could not pray. All was numb. As she knelt beside him she could not fathom the thought that her grandfather would never more answer the questions of a growing girl, that she would never again hear that gentle, wise, tender old voice. Perhaps something deep within her subconscious remembered the futile tearful cries of a young child long ago over a dead father. Those tears had not helped then.

And now, as the child had done so many years ago, Jamie fell asleep next to her dead grandfather. He had gone to where all true waking begins, but she must remain, and must therefore dull the pain of life with sleep.

In the morning she awoke wondering why she was lying on

the floor. She shivered involuntarily.

The cottage was freezing.

Then she remembered, and the dull ache returned to her heart.

She did not look toward her grandfather's bed again. She knew something must be done, and this time there was no one to come and take her away. She was alone.

It did not occur to Jamie to seek help from the estate. Aviemere was to her as remote a world as Aberdeen had been to the wide-eyed young child of seven. She and her grandfather had always taken care of their own needs. Except for the infrequent appearance of the factor, the estate might as well never have existed. She had learned early in life to stand on her own and to make difficult decisions. She had gained a confidence beyond her years, which would as her life progressed quicken the maturity necessary to cope with change.

She had been around animals long enough to understand the rudiments of what must be done with the dead. Her grandfather had always taught her that life was something more than the body which houses it, and now that her practical nature went about the necessary preparations, she told herself that he was more alive now than ever and that the body which lay cold and stiff in the cottage was no longer him. But the lonely mind rarely finds much comfort in such eternal truths.

Jamie went to the byre, found a shovel and a pick, and then walked out in search of the right place to lay her grandfather's body to rest. She chose a spot several hundred feet from the cottage. Now, under a clouded sky, it was a dull and dismal place. But in the summer, with the green elder standing over it, it was peaceful and bathed in warmth from the sun. This is where her grandfather would want to stay.

The surface of the icy ground was hard as rock. Jamie loosened the sod with the pick before beginning to dig deeper. It took most of the morning, and when the grave was finally dug she returned to the byre, pulled out the rickety old cart, and with it transported Finlay's body to the site. It seemed her small frame would collapse under the weight of the burdens she bore—but necessity added to the strength which in Jamie went far deeper than bone and sinew.

As she scattered the dirt over her grandfather, covering him forever from her sight, at last the terrible pain in her heart burst to the surface.

How alone she was!

The only person who loved her was gone—the only person after her own father and mother she had loved. All about her was desolation.

I should say something . . . do something . . . pray something, she thought as she stood beside the fresh grave. Something was called for at a moment like this. She was no longer a child. The weight of life now rested upon her own shoulders and no one else's.

Then she remembered the surprise she had prepared for her grandfather!

Perhaps it was for this very moment she had prepared it. Perhaps it would give him more joy now than it could have before. What more fitting eulogy could she give the man who had taught her everything!

But not here—there was only one place fit to receive her sacrifice of love for the man who lay at her feet!

An hour later, hot with the climb, the cold air piercing her lungs, Jamie scaled the summit of Donachie to stand once again on its peak. The clouds which had been hanging overhead had drifted away westward and all was clear in the rest of the sky. The winter's sun was bright but pale. Jamie's breath stood out from her face in bursts of white warmth in the bitter cold air.

Quickly she glanced around, then turned her eyes down the hill in the direction from which she had come. She could just barely make out the cottage below her.

"This is fer ye t' remember me by, Gran'daddy," she said softly. Then she lifted her voice and repeated the words which would be imprinted forever in her memory:

> *I will lift up mine een t' the hills, frae whence comes my help.*
> *My help comes frae the Lord, who made haiven an' earth.*
> *He will nae suffer yer fut t' be moved; he that keeps ye willna sleep.*
> *He that keeps Israel sall neither slumber nor sleep.*
> *The Lord is yer keeper: the Lord is the shade upo' yer right han'.*
> *The sun sall nae smite ye by day, nor the moon by nicht.*
> *The Lord sall preser ye frae all ill; he sall preser yer soul.*
> *The Lord sall preser yer gaein' an' yer comin' frae noo till all time,*
>   *an' fer e'ermore.*

As Jamie spoke the words of the psalm, the tears of grief began to flow once again. The words her grandfather loved opened the gates and the tears streamed uncontrolled down her face. As she finished speaking, the words seemed to go on and on, but now spoken in Finlay's raspy voice and thick brogue. As she looked about her, upon the mountain that had been his life, and heard the words echoed, *"I will lift up mine een t' the hills, frae whence comes my help,"* her heartbroken soul was not able to fully grasp their significance.

But her spirit stored them up, along with the memory of the face from whose mouth the very words seemed to emanate. Not only was this her own eulogy to her grandfather, this psalm had been her grandfather's final prayer for her as he had collapsed upon his bed. And now, through the book that had been his life, he reached across the bonds of death to touch her spirit indelibly and forever.

At length, drying her eyes and drawing in a deep breath of the cold mountain air, Jamie sent her gaze far off toward the distant horizon.

Could she just make out the blue of the sea? Or was the sky playing tricks upon her eye?

"What is oot there?" she wondered to herself. "I maun find out, Gran'daddy," she said, this time aloud. "I hope noo ye can understan'. There's somethin' oot beyon' these hills that's beckonin' t' me."

Slowly she turned her sights all about her. The snow was already visible to the southwest on the distant highland mountains of Grampian. To the south the valley of the Dee wound from the sea inland to its origins west of Braemar. To the north and out of her sight, the valley of Strathbogie lived on as if unconcerned with the vicious snows that fell in the higher regions.

But always her gaze returned eastward toward the sea.

The blood of Gilbert MacLeod flowed warm in his daughter on this cold winter's day. And in her eyes could be seen Gilbert's far-off gaze toward the horizon—the unknown land of dreams.

CHAPTER ELEVEN

Winter

Time now passed slowly for Jamie.

Had it been spring or summer it might have been different. She could then have roamed about the mountain with the sheep. But as the first snows began to make their appearance, she was confined more and more to the environs of the cottage. The peat for the winter had already been cut, dried, and stored. The sheep required little attention beyond an hour or two on some days, and there was little to keep her occupied.

For a time even her interest in reading was gone; it reminded her too painfully of the happy evenings with her grandfather—a close bond between them that now seemed to have come too late. The unrest which had occasioned her outburst the day of the storm when she had climbed Donachie in the rain began to take sharper focus, although she could still not isolate any course of action she was to follow.

She lay down in her bed one night, her mind full of the conflicts of trying to decide what to do. As she drifted off, her sleep was fitful and agitated. She dreamed she was standing on the mountain, but she could not recognize the place. It was early in summer and all was green and lovely. As before, Gilbert stood at some distance before her beckoning her to come. His face remained a blur, but it was not frightening as it had been the last time.

She turned, and saw her grandfather, far away, also entreating her to come to him. From one to the other she stared in utter confusion. The silent battle seemed to last an eternity. And she stood in the very center. The battle was in her will—which direction would she go?

At length Finlay drew his hands slowly back to himself,

smiled, and then she thought she saw him slowly nod his head. As she looked he began to fade from sight. At the same time, turning in the other direction, the previously blank features of her father were taking fuzzy and undefined shape. Finlay was almost gone from her vision now, and she could not bear it. She screamed out for him to help her, but no voice would come. Her father was now walking toward her, his face distinct and younger-looking than she ever remembered seeing it—and happy and peaceful, too. She began walking toward him, then started to run. She looked back over her shoulder again. Her grandfather had almost completely disappeared. Again she tried to call out to him . . .

Suddenly she was awake, in her own bed, alone, in the cottage. Her perspiring body trembled, and her raw throat told her she had indeed been screaming out in the night.

Jamie crawled from the bed and rekindled the dying fire. It was early morning. Dawn would not break for an hour or more, but despite the darkness she knew a return to sleep would be hopeless. Had it been June she would already have been out on the hills in the full light of morning. But in the dead of winter's cold, the days were short.

Aimlessly she wandered about the cottage in search for something to occupy her. Unconsciously she put on the kettle, but neither breakfast nor any household chores seemed important at such a time. At last she pulled on her winter boots and heavy coat and trudged out to the byre. Missy would be awake by now and in need of milking.

Missy turned as she approached, gave a lazy half-moo deep in her throat and whisked her tail back and forth as if to acknowledge the presence of her young mistress. Arranging the pail and stool, Jamie began the task her fingers could have carried out in her sleep. As she sat there her idle mind wandered back to the dream. Had her grandfather been yielding, giving his permission for her to follow her father? Is that what the fading of the one face and the growing reality of the other was to signify?

If that were true, she should have felt a wonderful release! Instead, she could not escape the awful desolation that had stolen over her at the fading of her grandfather's form. Yet, there was something in her father's eyes she had to follow, something he had wanted her to do she had to fulfill. But her grandfather had been her life, her rock. He had taught her everything. He had prepared her to stand alone. He had taught her about life, about the mountain, about God. She could never leave all that—even to follow the path her father set before her!

Was there no way to fulfill her life in the eyes of both men whom she knew must still love her? Was there no way to follow her father's dream, to follow his distant gaze to far horizons, to fulfill his hopes, to be the lady he had always wanted her to be, and yet still live the life of godly simplicity which had been the essence of her grandfather's existence? Did the one form have to fade while the other grew clearer? Could they not both look down on her with smiles on their faces, pleased with what they saw?

Jamie's stomach churned and she shook her head as if to shake free of the confusion which was so intent on hounding her. She set down the pail and looked aimlessly about the byre. Without being aware that she had even turned in that direction, suddenly she realized her eyes were resting on the old trunk still sitting against the wall. She had not touched it since that first day when her grandfather had come upon her. She had always planned on opening it again, with him, when he deemed the time right.

When the time was right . . .

The vision of her dream came again into her mind. She saw old Finlay again as she had in the dream, quietly and contentedly nodding his head.

Could this be the time? What had he been trying to tell her?

"Oh, Gran'daddy!" she sighed.

At that moment he had again become closer to her than any other distant figures out of the past—even her father. How she missed him! But he had been trying to tell her something. He had been—she was sure of it!—releasing her to follow her father. During his lifetime he had so staunchly tried to keep her from the world which had lured her father away. Now it seemed he had told her to go. Was this God's answer to the cries of her heart?

Slowly she rose. With even a greater awe than before, she approached the old black trunk. Whatever answers there were for her must lie inside.

She opened it. Nothing had changed; all was exactly as she had left it.

Again her hand reached out toward the faded, homely little dresses. One after another she held them up to the light of the lantern.

She could almost hear her father's voice now, smiling as he turned his little girl around looking her over approvingly from head to toe.

"You'll soon be a lady, you will, Jamie, my bairn, and be goin' to fancy balls in the city, and wearin' even prettier dresses! But you're a pretty one now, you are!"

A lady!

Did he really mean it?

Surely these pretty little dresses had been worn by no ragamuffin little urchin, but by a little lady, just as her father said.

"If only I hadna failed ye, Jamie, my bairn . . . ye would hae been a gran' lady someday!" Her father's dying words tumbled back into her mind across the years.

"Ye didna fail, Papa!" she cried, the tears beginning to flow down her cheeks. At that moment Jamie knew nothing of lost property or bad investments or dreams that would never be. How could she understand the heartaches of a broken man?

He was her papa!

What else could matter alongside that? As she knelt on the dirt floor of her grandfather's byre, she was seven years old again in mind and emotions. Her father represented only the highest qualities of achievement. He had been the world to her, and could never be a failure!

She would prove it!

She would prove that her father's word had meaning, that he had not died in vain, that his final words would not go unfulfilled.

"Ye didna fail, Papa!" she repeated, sobbing in earnest now. "Oh, Papa . . . I will—*I will be a lady fer ye, Papa!* Ye'll see!"

Without her knowing, all at once the angst of unrest which had been plaguing her soul for months suddenly crystallized into purpose.

This was the thing that had been unfinished. It had been so important to him that he had spent his last words on it. This had been her father's dream—to *be* somebody in the world! His distant gaze had always been searching the horizons of life for something more. Even as he died they had been preparing to follow his gaze to Aberdeen, to the sea, where his dreams awaited fulfillment.

She would follow that dream!

She would give meaning to her father's life by doing what his life had been cut too short to do. She would go to Aberdeen!

She would find what he had been looking for! *She would be the lady he had wanted her to be!*

With mounting joy she recalled her grandfather's smiling face. Of course, he knew all about it too! No longer did she have to lose his approval. He had released her to do what she now could see she had always been compelled to do.

Suddenly Jamie came back to herself, and to the present.

She looked down at herself, kneeling on a dirt floor in a broken-down highland byre, dressed in ragged boy's garb.

She was no lady!

She was no longer the sweet seven-year-old child who had worn these dresses, either. She was nothing but a shepherd, a backward mountain waif who could hardly read and knew about nothing but animals and mountains.

How could she ever hope to be a lady?

Was it a dream like those of her father, destined to remain only in the eye of her mind, unfulfilled to the end of her days?

With a sigh she laid the dresses back into the trunk. In the semidarkness her hand fell upon the book. She clutched it and drew it out. With a deep breath she opened it and peered at the inside cover in the faint light of the growing dawn. If she thought her halting lessons would make everything intelligible, she was greatly disappointed. Printed letters she could recognize, but this handwritten script was altogether different than anything she had seen. Occasionally something looked familiar, but she could make nothing of the content of the personal inscription. Of only one thing she was certain—at the end of the message was signed the single name *Alice*.

Again Jamie began to weep. If only she could read it!

She closed the trunk and slowly walked to the door of the byre. The gray of dawn had spread over the bleak winter landscape. She looked about her. All was still and quiet.

Slowly from the depths of Jamie's dawning adulthood arose a sense of resolution. She had always possessed a strength and determination. It had been that determination which always found the lost sheep, which had learned the ways of Donachie as thoroughly as her mentor himself knew them, which had begun to learn to read. But now something even greater was calling her. And with boldness and resolve she would meet the challenge.

She *would* learn to read! She would read her mama's book!

And she *would* go to Aberdeen, and learn to be a lady!

She wiped the remaining tears from her eyes—there was no time for that now. A task lay before her—a task at which she could not fail.

For the sake of her father, she *would* not fail!

By midmorning Jamie was ready to bid farewell to Finlay's old cottage, her home of ten years. What lay ahead she had no idea. But she did know that what she must do could not be done upon the beloved heights of Donachie.

She packed her few belongings in an old rucksack, taking her mother's book and the strange bauble her father had given her the night he had died. With space only for what was necessary, she left the dresses which had so stirred her emotions. But as she laid them into the trunk after one final look, she softly declared, "I'll come back fer ye."

She filled the animals' feeding troughs. It would be enough until she reached the factor's and he sent someone up to care for them. She patted the thick woolen bodies of the sheep, then walked inside the byre one last time and ran her hand along Missy's sleek flank.

Thick clouds had begun amassing in the sky toward the eastern slope of the mountain, but she took no notice. Nor did she heed the steadily increasing wind. Her mind was set, and nothing could stop her now. Pulling her coat tightly up around her neck she marched down the path toward the estate of Aviemere, where she would speak to the factor before proceeding.

As the path wound behind a group of rocks, Jamie stopped and turned back. The cottage suddenly looked so forlorn against the winter's sky and gray granite of its surroundings. Snow here and there lay in drifts, but all else was muddy and brown.

"I will come back," she said to herself. Then aloud, as if to reassure an old friend she was not deserting her home, "*I will come back!*"

She turned back and walked out of sight down the path. Her past was behind her now. The future lay ahead.

She breathed in the crisp mountain air. It felt good in her lungs—exhilarating. She refused to allow the thought to surface that perhaps she might never walk this path again, or might never again see the dell bursting with springtime. Her step remained firm. She would not be deterred from her purpose. And she *would* come back.

Preoccupied with her thoughts, Jamie took no notice of the rapid approach of the storm. It was not until she was fully in the midst of the wind and wild flurry of suddenly falling snow that she realized this was no mild inconsequential squall. Fully accustomed to the harsh and sudden weather changes of Donachie, she yet continued on. It would have been futile to turn back now, for she was already halfway down the mountain. Therefore she pressed forward toward her goal.

The winds rose, lashing at her from every side. The snow came in earnest now, making it more and more difficult to see. It had already begun to accumulate on the path. The flakes were huge and dry, and falling as in a blanket of swirling white. Within an hour the full force of the blizzard had assailed her.

Jamie tramped on, wiping the snow from her face every several minutes, now growing cold from the biting wind.

Nothing was familiar now. She had never come this far with her grandfather. And the path had grown obliterated with white.

She stopped and looked about.

Had she gotten turned around or taken a wrong fork in the path? Something didn't seem right. She knew Aviemere lay ahead of her. But—

It must be the snow that made things look so odd!

She turned and continued on.

She could now see barely two feet in front of her. Still the wind increased in its fury, and nothing could abate the rapidly falling snow. For another hour she marched stoically on, freezing now, but afraid to stop. There could be no thought of going back. Whatever path she had been following had been gone from her sight for hours. But Aviemere lay at the bottom of the mountain, and toward the downhill direction she turned whenever there was uncertainty.

Gradually the storm let up. The wind died down and all became still about her. Jamie stopped. Frantically she glanced about to get her bearings. She should have come to the valley road by now! Which way could it be? In the distance, yes!—she could just see something—lights! It must be Aviemere!

But . . . but . . . she had not come to the road!

Perhaps she had crossed it already without knowing it. She would make for the lights—she was almost there!

With renewed energy she struggled forward. Again the snow began to fall, but she steadfastly plowed through the snow—now halfway to her knees—in the direction of the estate. A huge drift across her path forced her to change directions once more, but she worked her way around it, and continued on.

Suddenly the storm seemed to redouble its ferocity. Jamie's limbs were all but frozen now. She had lost sight of the lights, but they *had* to be in this direction! How could she take another step? It was so cold! Every movement now was agony!

The shadows of descending darkness began to fall. The road—where?—oh! where were the lights? She had just seen them, but now they were gone. *Oh! Lord, help me!* Jamie thought. *I've lost my way! I will look with mine een t' the hills . . . oh, hoo does it gae . . . I've forgotten, Gran'daddy!* By now she should have been within the warmth of George Ellice's house, sipping a steaming cup of tea.

But she had to stop, just for a moment. A short rest. She would find some secluded spot, behind a drift, out of the wind. If she could just sit down for a moment—only for a moment— just to catch her breath. She was so tired . . . only for a moment!

Jamie had stumbled onto the road, but knew nothing of it. Across it she walked, her feet buried deep in the gathering snow. She sank down onto the icy earth. Still the snow and wind raged around her.

If only she could get out of the wind for a moment or two, then she'd start up again. She had to rest. Just close her eyes . . . she wouldn't be long.

In a moment she'd get up and start on her way again. But for now, she just had to sleep. Had to—*sleep* . . .

CHAPTER TWELVE

The Sailor

The road had been deserted all day, for who would have dared such a storm? Thus, as night descended—though it was barely past midafternoon—and encased the dreary spot, the lone figure walking jauntily through the storm seemed especially out of place.

The tall, powerfully built man seemed hardly aware of the raging blizzard. Warmly clad, with hands and head comfortably bound and feet enclosed in the most protective of boots, he actually gave the appearance of enjoying it. As he walked he was alternately humming and singing gaily.

"Fifteen men on a dead man's chest," he sang. "Yo-ho-ho, and a bottle of rum! Drink and the devil had done for the rest. Yo-ho-ho, and a bottle of rum!"

He paused, as if considering the consequences of his words, though he had sung them a hundred times with his shipmates. But perhaps he was only considering their fitness on a day such as this, for then he continued,

"Or perhaps you'd like it better, old Robbie Burns, for me to be saying one of your ballads to the storm! 'Blow, blow, ye winds, with heavier gust! And freeze, thou bitter-biting frost! Descend, ye chilly, smothering snows!' "

Once again he stopped. "No, that's not just right for the day either, apologies to you, Sir Burns. But what's needed on a day like this is a *song!*"

Again he broke out, this time singing loudly, in another of his favorites from the Scottish bard:

The wintry west extends his blast,
    And hail and rain does blaw;
Or the stormy north sends driving forth

The blinding sleet and snaw:
Wild-tumbling brown, the burn comes down,
  And roars frae bank to brae:
While bird and beast in covert rest,
  And pass the heartless day.

The sweeping blast, the sky o'ercast,
  The joyless winter day
Let others fear, to me more dear
  Than all the pride of May:
The tempest's howl, it soothes my soul,
  My griefs it seems to join;
The leafless trees my fancy please,
  Their fate resembles mine!

If Robbie Taggart did not enjoy the storm, an observer—if one could be found on such a day!—would never have guessed it. All his life long he had relished activity, movement, the open air, and the sheer freedom of being outdoors and under God's sky. To be under a blue sky on top of a deeper blue sea was his supreme delight. But failing that, any other sky, even one filled with swirling white snow, would do. He had been cooped up in his mother's home for three long weeks, and when the storm threatened on the morning of his departure he scoffed at it.

Nothing would deter him from his plans!

When he had heard his mother was ill, he had come immediately from Aberdeen to be at her side. But the illness was short-lived, not as serious as originally thought, and now she was back on her feet and well.

"More fit than I, I'll warrant!" he had laughed as he kissed her goodbye.

Three weeks of peace and quiet, gentle voices, and visits by matronly women who reminded him how small he had been when they had first known him, had almost been more than he could take. And he thanked both Providence and his lucky stars that her sickness had ended when it had. His constitution had not been built for quiet evenings in front of a cheery fire with no solace but a book or two. If the fire came from the hearth of his favorite Aberdeen pub, where there was a good share of raucous laughter and music in the background, that was a different matter. That was the life for him! So much the better with a pretty lass on his arm with whom to dance a rousing jig!

But three weeks in his mother's cottage in the foothills of the highlands, with no sounds but the groaning of the firs in the wind and the bleating of sheep—no thank you, if you please! Not for Robbie Taggart!

Old Mrs. Taggart knew her son too well by this time. After all, she had raised him. She had seen the wanderlust in his eyes long before it had worked its way down to his feet and sent him off to seek his fortune. She was gratified that he had come when she needed him. He would always come. But she would not dream of deterring him longer than he chose to stay. And she never expected him to stay long. Because not only did she know her son, she had lived twenty years with a man just like him— Robbie's father.

Hank Taggart had been a traveling peddler whose route spanned the whole of Scotland and even worked his way as far south into England as Manchester. Before his death two years ago, something almost of legendary stature had grown up around him. How much he himself had originated many of the tales of his derring-do might be a question to be asked. Nevertheless, his character and escapades were frequently the topic of conversation among the housewives he served. His oversized horse-cart, with its clattering and clanging assortment of goods from tin pans to farm pails to brushes and ropes and various articles of clothing, as well as so-called "imported" porcelain vases, was always a welcome sight as it jostled down the country roads and lanes. Whether the wives looked forward to his coming for the sake of his merchandise or for the chance to visit again with Hank and his wife, and catch up on whatever new gossip and trivia was working its way from village to village, was a question Hank never bothered himself with. They bought enough to keep him and his family fed and happy. And who could ask for anything more? Hank was a family man, and therefore his wife and young son accompanied him wherever he went.

Thus the conventional meaning of the word "home" was singularly unknown to the boy Robbie Taggart. Home to him was a bouncy wooden wagon and a campfire under a starlit sky. In the winter months they worked their way farther to the south and stayed alternately with Hank's three brothers. The life could not have suited Robbie better—he loved the movement, the changing scenery, the new faces to meet almost daily. He had indeed been cut out of the same cloth as his father—"a chip off the old block," as Hank was fond of saying when he introduced his son to his friends. And therefore no one, least of all Hank, thought any the less of the boy when at fifteen he decided to strike out on his own. It was just the sort of thing he himself had done at eighteen. Thus old Hank was proud of his boy even as he said goodbye to him. He knew the feeling of becoming too familiar with the oft-traveled roads. He knew his son had to discover for himself what more there was to see *out there*.

Robbie spent the following three years traveling all over Britain, working at whatever odd jobs presented themselves. But his deepest love was reserved for his homeland, and northward his steps always returned eventually. While he was in Aberdeen, the great port of the north, where fishing vessels and great ships of commerce came to the colorful harbor of the River Dee, the sea stung his fancy. Why should he be bound by earth and rock? If there was more to see in the world, how much more exciting would it be to see it from the deck of a ship! And to what distant foreign lands would the seafaring life open his imagination!

Indeed, the life of the sea proved everything eighteen-year-old Robbie hoped for—new lands, exotic ports, new adventures every day!

He had been out to sea when his father had died. Deeply grieved that his mother had been forced to endure the ordeal alone, when he finally docked and went to see her, he came with genuine humility and not a little guilt. That very day he swore he would give up his wandering life to stay and take care of her.

Her only response had been a hearty laugh.

"I'd sooner die here an' noo than t' see ye wither awa t' nothin' standin' here in the same place day upo day. I ne'er held yer father back, an' certainly willna be holdin' ye back yersel'! Ye gae see the worl', Robbie Taggart! Yer daddy'd be prood o' ye. Jist remember t' say a prayer fer yer ol' mither noo an' then!"

Mrs. Taggart had settled in the little village southwest of Aviemere where her sister lived. Though she would not stand in the way of husband or son, the prospect of remaining in the same place for the rest of her days was comforting.

She had made but one request of him as he had set out again: "Jist come an' see me noo an' then, an' I'll dee a happy woman!"

"Try to keep me away!" he replied as he hugged her and gave her plump cheek a goodbye kiss.

His ship was wintering in Aberdeen and he had taken up temporary lodgings in the city there, to which—much as he loved his mother—he was now anxious to return. The storm caused him no concern for he planned to spend the first night of his walk back to the coast in a deserted cottage which was now only about thirty or forty minutes away. He had friends along the way if the weather remained foul. Indeed, Taggart's winning charm and quick smile had made him an abundance of friends scattered quite literally over the whole world. If no place was his home, he could be at home anywhere, and there were many men and women of different ages and nationalities who would have considered it an honor to share their room and humble fare with the youth. Whatever time of the day or night he might appear at their door, he would always find a glad and honest welcome. If the young women he had known were charmed by his deep-set, sea-blue eyes, thick, black wavy hair, and perfectly-sculptured masculine features, the others were no less taken in by his wit, infectious laughter, happy sanguine personality, and his strong sense of loyalty. They said about Robbie, "His feet may roam, but his heart always stays true!" His many friends across the globe were as good and true to him as he was to them, because they knew he would give his very life for them.

So the sailor plowed his way gladly through the snow and ice, whistling and singing the ballads of Burns, completely unaware that within a few steps all life for him would be changed.

When he heard the faint moaning sounds and stopped to listen more intently, he first thought some poor animal had either been hurt or trapped by the sudden snowfall.

Glancing this way and that, he attempted to follow the sound, very faint in the wind. Then he saw a piece of grayish clothing blowing in the wind from behind a small drift of snow.

CHAPTER THIRTEEN

Rescue

Quickly Robbie left the road and made an effort to run. When he reached the drift he tore at the snow, flinging it madly in all directions.

Jamie had reached the spot only moments ahead of him, but already a thin blanket of whiteness had covered her over. In five minutes more she would have been buried in a frozen wintry tomb.

In the gathering darkness it was difficult for Robbie to tell just how the figure was lying, but he soon uncovered the arms, then the head. Frantically he scraped the snow from the legs and turned the body over. He could still feel warmth; at least the poor child was still alive—barely!

"Dear Lord!" he breathed, laying eyes on the peaceful sleeping face. " 'Tis but a lad! What would he be doing out on a day like this!"

Jamie could not answer his question. Although she still clung to life with all the tenacity that was in her, she had drifted into the deepest sleep she had ever known. In the short time she had lain there, her extremities had grown numb with cold—a cold she no longer felt. Her eyes were sealed shut with ice where her tears had frozen. Just before she had lost consciousness a great peace and warmth had come over her. Now, as from some deep depth of awareness that went deeper than her sleep, she felt the strong arms lift her face from the snow, she tried to speak words of protest. "Let me stay and sleep—just a while longer," she wanted to say. But she was trying to speak, as in a dream, and no words would come.

"At least you're alive," Robbie said, "but you won't be for long if I don't get you out of this—and soon!"

He lifted her into his arms, hardly conscious of the weight of her small frame. Slinging her pack over his shoulder alongside his own, he set out again. Both the wind and the snowfall seemed to ease almost immediately, as if the storm had played out its fury against the daring young maiden but would not now waste its effort against the sailor it could never beat into submission. Robbie judged the deserted cottage some two miles ahead and he quickened his pace to the extent the drifted snow would allow. All the way he talked to Jamie, trying every now and then to shake her body awake, but still she hovered in the peaceful land between sleep and death, struggling not to return to the land of cold and wind and ice and snow. All had been so warm and cozy before those two rude arms had jostled her into half waking.

In about twenty minutes Robbie stood at the door to the cottage. Laying his burden once more in the snow, he cleared the drift from the entryway, put his shoulder to it, shoved in the door, picked up his cargo again, and walked inside.

To their good fortune the roof was still intact and had not yet collapsed like so many of the deserted shells which dotted the hills of the highlands. Though it was as cold within the walls as out in the storm, at least they were protected from the wind. Like Finlay's home, there was but a single room, and this one was nearly bare.

Laying Jamie down on the floor, Robbie set about the task of lighting a fire. He had brought matches and a few things with him, and there was sufficient peat (he had seen to that on his way from Aberdeen previously) to last the night. The hearth in the center of the room had not felt the warmth of a blaze since Robbie had passed that same way a month earlier. Within a short while the flames crackled under his skillful hand, though it would take some time before the cottage would be warm.

Jamie lay where he had deposited her, aware that things were going on around her, calling out after her grandfather occasionally, and mumbling incoherently, but still bewildered and trying both to cling to sleep and to escape it all at once.

Once the fire blazed to a healthy orange and yellow, Robbie returned to his ministrations, removing her coat and prying off her boots, which were by now soaked through from the melting snow and ice.

"A lass!" he exclaimed, suddenly grasping the truth of his charge. "A shepherd girl, no doubt, losing her way home from somewhere in the hills!"

Taking a blanket from Jamie's pack and placing it over her chest and shoulders, he moved her so that her feet—clearly the most serious threat—were in the direction of the fire, for frostbite could hardly be far away, if indeed it was not already too late. The fire itself would be too hot if he moved her closer to it. Therefore he lay down at her feet, unwrapped them completely to the skin, then thrust them inside his shirt. The cold of the tiny numbed feet made him catch his breath, but the warmth of his own body saved them in the end.

Gradually he could sense his efforts having their effect. The cottage slowly warmed, and every now and then Jamie squirmed uncomfortably. Feeling the hint of warmth returning to her feet, he began to rub them vigorously, then placed another blanket over them and left the fire to do its work. After an hour she opened her eyes hazily, looked at the stranger staring so strangely at her with an odd smile on his face, and tried to speak. No words would come out. By degrees she relaxed, drifted again to sleep, slept peacefully and soundly, and did not again awaken until morning light streamed through the one small window on the south wall of the cottage.

The light of dawn also roused Robbie from his uncertain doze. He looked quickly about and was relieved to find the lass sitting up where he had laid her, the blankets still wrapped tightly about her. She was staring at him with a mixture of wonder and curiosity. He smiled.

"I see you're still with us!" he said brightly.

"An' I'm thinkin' ye'll be the one I maun be thankin' fer it," replied Jamie, trying out her voice for the first time.

"No thanks required," he said laughing. "I'm in the habit of rescuing damsels in distress. You are a damsel, aren't you?"

Her brow wrinkled in perplexity. "I canna be sure—I'm nae understandin' yer meanin'."

"A lass! Am I right?"

" 'Course ye're right! Do ye—do ye think I'm a boy?" she returned briskly, her green eyes flashing with a hint of their old vigor.

"I meant no offense," he said, trying to subdue the laugh which insisted on remaining with him. "I'm afraid I'm not very good with children."

"Children! I'm nae child!"

"Ah, I see."

"I'm a full seventeen, I am!"

"Well, that *does* change everything," said Robbie, his patronizing tone lost on Jamie. "Well," he went on, at last getting his sense of the humor of it all under control, "whoever and whatever you are, you're no doubt hungry. I am!"

He rose, laid several fresh pieces of peat on the fire, and went outside to fill a container with snow to boil for tea.

Seeing what he was about when he returned, Jamie quickly pulled herself to her feet, saying, "Let me take care o' that!"

But in a moment she was on her back again. Having never been sick in her life, the sensation of lightheadedness and the tingling discomfort in her feet were altogether new to her. She was hardly used to lying flat while another served and waited on her. Her whole life had been spent serving others. Several more times she attempted to get to her feet, but her legs were too weak to hold her. At last she let out a long sigh and lay still.

"Don't worry," said Robbie cheerfully. "There's not so much to making a cup or warming up dried oatcakes—I'm afraid that's all I have, besides some dried herring and cheese. I wasn't expecting company!"

"I'm sorry t' impose on ye—"

"Impose! You were near dead when I stumbled on you! Don't think I'd leave you there, do you? My mother always packs me more than I could eat alone, anyway."

Suddenly Jamie sat up. "My pack!" she cried. "My things!"

" 'Tis all right here," said Robbie. "Was lying beside you in the snow."

" 'Tis all I hae in the world," said Jamie, relieved.

"Then I will guard it with my life."

Robbie turned his attentions to the water, now boiling, and the preparation of tea. In five minutes he handed a steaming cup to Jamie, along with an oatcake and piece of fish. With his own cup in his hand he sat down beside her.

"So," he said, "what's a young lass such as yourself doing alone in the middle of a storm like this?"

"I was travelin'," Jamie replied.

"To Aberdeen?"

Jamie's forehead wrinkled. "What makes ye say that?" she asked. "Why would ye be thinkin' I'm boun' fer Aberdeen?"

"You mumbled something about it in your sleep."

"In my sleep! So's ye cud hear me?"

"Aye. People do that, you know. I see it all the time onboard the ships." Robbie paused, eyeing her intently. "I suppose you weren't really asleep," he went on. " 'Twas almost like you were half dead—and so you were!"

"An' I said I was goin' t' Aberdeen?"

"Have you run away from home?"

"Nae, nae!" she said quickly. "Weel, maybe I have," she added. "That is, if ye can call it home now as my gran'daddy's gone."

"You live with your grandfather?"

"Fer ten years. But he's dead noo. An' I'm headed fer Aberdeen, jist like ye said."

"Relatives there?" asked Robbie, taking a bite of the dried oat biscuit.

"I hae nae people o' my own—not on Donachie, not in Aberdeen. My ain daddy's been gane mony a year, an' noo Gran'daddy's gane too."

"I'm sorry," said Robbie. "But you must have friends somewhere!"

"No one, that is unless ye call the factor a frien' 'cause he knew my gran'daddy. I was tryin' t' find his hoose in the storm."

"The factor of Aviemere?"

"Aye. George Ellice."

"That's miles from here, lass! You came down clear on the wrong slope of the mountain to find Aviemere! And you're clean past it by now."

Jamie sighed. "Then perhaps I hae nae frien's at all."

Robbie was silent a moment. He was touched by her words, which, for all their sorrowfulness, contained not a hint of self-pity. For one such as he, with more friends and acquaintances than he could well remember, the thought that anyone could be so alone, so without *anyone*, was unthinkable. He set his cup down on the hard-packed floor and thrust his hand toward her with a smile.

"Then, miss, I'd be honored to be one of your first friends. My name's Robbie Taggart!"

He took up her hand and wrapped his own—so much larger and warmer—firmly around it and shook it vigorously.

"Thank ye," replied Jamie, her lip quivering imperceptibly. "I'm Jamie MacLeod. My gran'daddy was shepherd on Donachie, shepherd fer the laird at Aviemere. An' I'm grateful fer what ye hae done fer me. But I dinna like keepin' ye frae—"

"You're keeping me from nothing, Jamie MacLeod! 'Tis months before my ship sets sail. Now, let me get you another cup of tea. You need all the warming inside you can get!" He rose and refilled her cup, humming a little tune, while Jamie sat deep in thought.

It was then Jamie first realized that it was quiet outside. The winds no longer swept through the winter skies with their death-chill, and the terror of the blizzard was almost forgotten in the warmth of the cottage. If she closed her eyes she could almost imagine herself back on the mountain, cozy and warm inside their home with her grandfather.

But no. She was not on Donachie. Her grandfather was gone, and she had left. And she had not forgotten why she had left, nor the purpose that had steadily been rising within her. She had left to find—to find—

What was it?

Suddenly new words came into her mind, words from the distant past that she had completely forgotten. Yet all at once here they were, ringing as if she had heard them only yesterday: *"Aberdeen is where we should have gone long ago. I'll find what I'm looking for there . . ."*

Gilbert MacLeod had said them so very long ago, and the little child who had listened had not understood. But she had tucked them away in that most hidden back corner of her mind, not even realizing she had done so until, lying at the door of death, they had emerged from their sleeping cocoon to give that child, now nearly a woman, the confirmation of direction she unknowingly sought.

"So 'tis Aberdeen you'll be seeking, is it?" said Robbie. "And you know the way there?"

"I was plannin' t' seek the factor's help aboot that," Jamie replied.

"Well, you'd have had a difficult time of that, where you were headed! But have no fear. 'Tis there my feet are taking me, too!"

"Aberdeen?"

"Aye, 'tis where I'm bound."

"Would ye be mindin' if I came wi' ye? Or ye cud jist give me directions."

Robbie smiled broadly. "Mind? We're friends now! I'll be giving you no directions—I'll take you there myself!"

For the remainder of the day the talk flowed more easily. Jamie was anxious to learn all she could of the great city on the sea where her future seemed to lie. And Robbie was willing to tell all he knew, even though the base of his familiarity with the city was undoubtedly different than what Gilbert MacLeod would have had in mind. He recounted countless stories of the bustling port and its people, and when he ran out of these, he told of the other ports where he had traveled. And to it all Jamie listened in awe.

In the midst of one tale, with Jamie's eyes grown so large with wonder that they could open no farther, Robbie burst into a merry laugh. "Don't worry, child," he said. "I'll hold your hand all the way. I'll show you everything you need to know. The city is nothing to fear!"

"I'm sure I'll become familiar wi' it all," she said, embarrassed by the spell she had been under.

"No doubt! no doubt!" he replied, still laughing.

"I maun get t' know the city," she went on, this time more firmly. "I'm goin' to be a lady," she declared.

"You don't say," he chuckled.

"I *do* say!"

"Well, that is something I will want to see. The gentry of Aberdeen will have their hands full with you."

"Ye're makin' sport o' me."

"I'm sorry. It's just that there's a lot you have to learn, about—things, that's all. Gentlemen and ladies aren't so likely to open their arms and homes to a poor shepherd girl. Being a lady's more than learning to talk and act like one. There's a lot for you to learn in the city, Jamie. It's not the simple life you knew with your grandfather."

"Ye said ye'd teach me."

"Aye. And that I will," he replied, again with a merry laugh. "But though I know Aberdeen, I know precious little about being a *lady*. Somebody else will have to teach you that!"

He laughed again.

Sometimes Jamie could not quite tell if he was laughing at a joke—or if the joke was her! But his mirth was infectious. Therefore she found herself joining in the fun.

Perhaps it didn't matter what was the reason for the laughter. The anticipation of a new adventure was growing within her. Whatever happened, this was the beginning of the fulfillment of her dream, and perhaps her father's too.

This was the beginning of a new life for Jamie MacLeod.

PART III

Aberdeen

CHAPTER FOURTEEN

Sadie Malone

Night had fallen when they first came within sight of the city. As they entered, the streets were quiet and dark. It was strange and eerie to Jamie, whose imagination would never have been able to dream up such a place. The quiet here was vastly different than the quiet of the mountain—a strange, inhabited silence, seemingly waiting for something to happen. With each step toward the heart of the metropolis of 65,000, she became more apprehensive—had coming here been a mistake? What would she do? This was like a foreign land!

"Seems the storm's forced everyone to their beds early," laughed Robbie.

Jamie tried to gather courage from his bravado. Everywhere she looked everything was new and unusual to her. She took in as much as the occasional candle or street lamp would allow. There were more buildings and houses and shops and carriages than she would have thought possible.

As they turned a corner, the stillness was suddenly interrupted by a sudden shriek. A volley of shouts followed, and all at once a figure shot past them. He would have knocked Jamie off her feet had Robbie not reacted quickly and pulled her out of the way. Two more figures ran past in obvious pursuit, and Jamie stared after them with more curiosity than fear.

"Well, the city's not so sound asleep as I thought," Robbie said as they continued on.

Jamie remained silent, with each step confronting new sights, smells, and sounds—and new emotions within herself. Half terrified, half excited at the prospect of the unknown, she was thankful for Robbie's strong, confident presence at her side. The blizzard had proved a blessing in disguise—she would never

103

have been able to come into this awesome place alone. What would she possibly have done?

Then the words she had spoken over her grandfather's grave returned to her—the words he himself had spoken many times: "The Lord sall preser yer gaein' an' yer comin' frae noo till all time, an' fe e'ermore."

It was true! The Lord had provided Robbie just at the precise moment of her greatest need. The Lord would never leave her alone! Perhaps the city need not overwhelm her, young and inexperienced and ignorant though she was.

Gradually the night sounds of the city increased. With the sounds came a peculiar something Jamie began to notice in the air—a tangy, pungent, unfamiliar odor. She wrinkled her nose, and Robbie laughed.

" 'Tis the sea," he said. "We're drawin' near the harbor. Won't be much longer now, Jamie. Don't you love the smell of the brine and fish and ships?"

"It might take me a spell t' learn. But whaur are we gaein'?"

"I've a friend I'm taking you to. She'll be glad to put you up."

Within ten minutes more the quiet of the city's outskirts had been altogether overcome by a host of new sights and sounds as they reached the docks. The low drone of a foghorn sounded in the distance. The creaking of wooden ships and the constant tugging of miles of rope came from the water's edge. Nearer at hand were the noises of boisterous laughter and singing from a row of dockside public houses. To a carefree spirit like Robbie Taggart, the notion never entered his mind that such a place was hardly suitable for a young lass, a mere child, like Jamie. The docks of Aberdeen were his home, and he thought no more of bringing a friend to this particular home as a gentleman would of inviting a visitor into his parlor. Besides, where else was he to take her?

At length he came to a stop before a corner building, set apart from the rest of the inns and pubs they had passed. It seemed slightly more well kept than most, though the sounds filtering through the closed portal were just as loud. On a sign above the door were the words *The Golden Doubloon*, and a treasure chest filled with colorful pirate's booty was painted below the name.

Robbie gave the door a shove and stepped in.

Jamie hesitated. Robbie turned and motioned her to follow. With cautious step she put her foot up onto the threshold, and was inside.

She squinted to take in the scene. Tables were all about, filled with men drinking ale, playing cards. Others stood. A fire blazed in the huge fireplace in the far wall. A thin cloud of blue-gray smoke hung in the air, and the volume of talk and commotion was high. Her senses had only begun to adjust to the scene when an ear-piercing shriek split the air. Unconsciously her hands sought Robbie's arm and her fingers dug into the skin. She recovered herself and stepped back just as the owner of both the yell and the establishment hurried toward them.

"Why it *is* Robbie Taggart!" exclaimed the voice. "You old sea dog! I was wondering when we'd ever lay eyes on you again!"

The hardy, buxom woman who greeted them could have been anywhere from twenty-five to forty in age, especially to Jamie's unpracticed eye. She was attractive in a harsh and rugged way, and might have been even more so were it not for the heavily applied lip rouge and face powder. Her bright green dress accented the ample curves of her figure, and she bustled toward Robbie and threw her arms around him.

"Good evening, Sadie, my darling!" he laughed. "But you don't think I'd go off forever and leave you without a word. What kind of bloke do you take me for?"

"Don't get me wrong, love," she replied. "I'd never hold it against you—'tis the nature of the beast!"

As she spoke her eyes turned toward Jamie. "And what's this you've got in tow? Picking up strays, are you, Robbie Taggart?"

" 'Tis no stray! This here's my friend Jamie MacLeod."

Sadie looked Jamie up and down, then shook her head. "And what are you going to do with him? He hardly looks fit for the sea! Too scrawny, Taggart, you should know that!"

Laughing, Robbie struggled to reply. "The joke's on you, Sadie. My friend's a her, not a him! She'll not be looking for a life on the sea."

"Hmm," said Sadie, looking over his thin companion again. "Well, well, well," she added with renewed interest and a slightly cocked eyebrow.

"And as for what I'm going to do with her," Robbie continued, "I was hoping you would help me there. This is her first time in the city."

"Me!" Sadie exclaimed with a hint of the same shrieking tone with which she had greeted her favorite sailor. "And what would

I do with a child? I'm not the mothering type, as you know full well, Robbie Taggart. Besides, I have a business to run, not a home for runaways!"

"She'll need no mothering, Sadie, only a place to stay. And maybe some small work."

"And what, pray tell, Robbie, would the likes of her know about a place like this!"

"You could teach her, Sadie. I know there's a soft spot down in that hard heart of yours. She needs the guiding hand of a woman, and I can think of none better suited for the challenge than you yourself, Sadie."

"Humph!" said Sadie, remaining silent and looking Jamie over with a critical eye once again. "Doubt I'd get much work outta her," she muttered almost to herself. "Such a scraggly little spindle of a thing!"

As they spoke, Jamie stood dumbly at Robbie's side, staring from one speaker to the other, wanting to cry, run away, and curl up and go to sleep all at the same time. This was terrible, being talked about like a sheep at the auction!

"Well, you're no doubt cold and hungry," said Sadie at last. "We can talk about all that later." She prodded Robbie toward a chair by the fire, and took no further notice of Jamie.

Jamie slid quietly into a chair next to Robbie, and for the following hour was little more than an inconspicuous shadow amid the activity around her. Robbie's attentions were distracted as now one, now another of the patrons of the place made their way over to greet and chat with him. There was no doubt that his nature and easy manner had won him a large following in the city—wherever he went he was a favorite.

Almost distractedly she listened as her future was discussed. She was too tired and too overwhelmed to say much of anything, and made no protest as Sadie agreed to let her stay on as a maid in exchange for her board and one farthing a week. Her eyes began to droop from the warmth of the fire and she hardly heard Robbie as he took up her cause and was able to extract from Sadie the promise of three farthings a week in addition to board. She had drifted asleep and was slumped over in the wooden chair before Robbie again took notice of his charge.

By then Jamie was too sound asleep even to care what happened to her as Robbie lifted her tenderly and carried her in his arms up the narrow wooden stairway to a tiny room at the back of the inn where Sadie had made a bed for her.

Depositing her gently on the bed, Robbie followed Sadie from the room. As he reached the door he stopped, turned around, and returned momentarily to the bedside.

"Sleep well, and happy dreams, shepherd lass," he whispered, pulling a blanket up and settling it around her shoulders.

He gazed for one moment more upon the peaceful sleeping face of the girl he hardly knew, then turned again and hurried downstairs, where Sadie, his friends, cold ale, and a warm fire were awaiting his company.

CHAPTER FIFTEEN

First Days in the City

The wedge of light forcing its way through the narrow window above Jamie's head awakened her the following morning.

She rubbed her eyes, stared blankly about, and tried to call to mind where she was; then all at once she remembered the events of the previous evening, which had ended in a blur in front of a roaring fire.

She lay still, recalling the past four days with Robbie Taggart, the people of his acquaintance she had met along the way, and wondering if she would ever see Donachie again, with its crisp, bubbling burns and bright broom and rich meadows. What would become of Missy and the sheep? Would George Ellice discover she was gone before next spring? He had been due up that very week, but then the storm could have changed everything.

But she had made the decision to come to the city.

For now at least, *this* was her home. Was this the life her father had been seeking when he dreamed of Aberdeen? With a sigh she thought, *Working for Sadie Malone can hardly compare with herding the sheep over the dear green hills of Donachie!*

She crawled from her bed and, standing on tiptoe, tried to look out the only window of the room. It was so smudged with coal-soot she could barely make out the wall of a high building next to Sadie's, separated from it only by a narrow, dirty close. She could see nothing else. It was certainly not Donachie!

Well, this is where my new life begins, she thought to herself. *This is what Papa would have wanted!*

Jamie pulled on her boots, which had been set carefully by her bedside, and opened the door with a loud creak. Glancing tentatively this way and that, she walked slowly down the hallway until she heard the rattle of pots and pans. Following the sounds, she made her way downstairs to Sadie Malone's kitchen.

The place was dimly lit, and especially cheerless since the overcast winter's sky permitted little sunshine to enter the small, high windows. This seemed like a room where necessary work was carried out but void of all enjoyment.

To her patrons, Sadie was perfectly suited to her innkeeper's calling. She was friendly to all and a stranger to none. She could charm even the drunkest sailor to set down his glass and lay aside his temper when angered to a row by some fellow roughneck. She was beguiler and seductress alike to boys at sixteen who considered Sadie their first love and to men at sixty who considered her their last. Diplomatic when necessary, she had put a stop to many potentially ugly situations with her own two hands. Shrewd in business, downright surly when it was demanded of her, Sadie Malone was nobody's fool. Her customers, largely sailors and dock-workers, would have given their lives for the woman. Those who crossed her quickly learned to watch their step, for even the most hardened mariner had a fearful respect for Sadie Malone. She was the mother and wife they had left behind when they had taken to the sea. Those who came regularly, therefore, loved Sadie with a strange mixture of sentiments—but they all loved her.

Sadie considered herself merely marking time as mistress of The Golden Doubloon. She had inherited the place from her father, and because she needed to survive, she ran it. But she had always harbored different notions about where her future lay. She never spoke of these things. Though friendly to all, she opened the depths of her heart to no one, man or woman. She had few of what could be considered *real* friends despite the abundance of friendships which came her way. Though Robbie might be counted one of the few friends she did have, she had her own reasons for telling him nothing of the dreams which went through her head in the loneliness of the night after everyone had left. Though many had fancied her, and had dreamed of her face during their long months at sea, Sadie had never been truly in love. Her youth lay closed in behind the necessary armor she wore.

As Jamie peered through the doorway of the kitchen, Sadie was pouring oats from a burlap bag into a large bubbling kettle over the hearth. She was simply clad in a plain brown linen work frock.

"I hope you're not accustomed to sleeping late every morning," said Sadie over her shoulder, without preamble or greeting.

"Oh, no, mem!" Jamie answered quickly. " 'Tisna often the sun beats me oot o' my bed."

"Well, let's hope not! Three farthings a week's a steep sum to pay for a sluggard."

"I'm a good worker, mem! I promise I'll ne'er sleep so lang again!"

"Don't waste any more time jibbering over it. There's plenty of work to do. There aren't many customers in the morning, but what there is will be here soon."

Leaving the kettle for a moment, Sadie took a broom from a corner and thrust it into Jamie's hands. "The front room needs to be swept up, and the tables must be scrubbed."

Clutching the broom, Jamie hurried out to the main room of the inn, asking neither about Robbie or her own breakfast, both of which were on her mind. Though there was a gnawing in her stomach as she swept, she could not keep her thoughts from turning to the puzzling sailor who had rescued her from death and had brought her to this place. Would she ever see him again? He had said they were friends. But suddenly everything around her was so new! Did she even know what a friend in the city was supposed to be? Did she know what *anything* was supposed to be? She didn't even know what a farthing was. Robbie had argued in behalf of three instead of one. Did that mean she might be sooner able to—

Be able to do what?

What exactly would become of her in Aberdeen?

Her father wanted her to be a lady. Was Sadie Malone a lady? Was she now a lady sweeping Sadie Malone's floor? If this wasn't it, then what was she to do now? Perhaps Sadie would know. Surely Sadie was a lady and knew all about such things, whatever might be the maid that swept her floors.

She swept until the floor was cleaner than even Sadie had seen it, at least within memory. Then she set about scrubbing the tables with a vigor that would have worn out ten strong men. So deep was she in concentration that she had not noticed anyone else had come into the room. When she glanced up, there stood Robbie leaning against the doorjamb. A momentary thrill coursed through Jamie. She smiled, and looked down, not understanding the strange feeling of embarrassment she felt.

"You're going to wear those tables right through if you keep that up," he said with a grin.

"I didna want t' shame ye before yer friend."

"I doubt you'd ever do that! Besides, it won't do her, or me, or you any good if you wear out on your first day."

Jamie said nothing, but moderated her pace slightly.

"It was real kind o' ye," she said after a moment, "t' speak o' me t' Mistress Malone."

"Robbie just can't help himself when it comes to good deeds!" replied Sadie, walking toward them as she emerged from the kitchen. "And a good morning to you, Robbie, my love," she added with a broad smile. "What calls you out so early on such a chilly morn? After last night, I thought you'd sleep till midafternoon!"

"I had to come by to see how my friend was getting on," he said.

"She'll be getting along fine as long as she learns to sleep a little less."

"Give her time, Sadie," said Robbie. "And I also came for another taste of your wonderful cooking!"

Sadie smiled. "Well, be quick about it, child," she said to Jamie. "Clear a table for my guest!" Casting another smile in Robbie's direction, she disappeared again into the kitchen.

As Robbie took a seat, he continued to eye Jamie with keen interest while she slowly made her way from table to table, scrubbing them first with a moist cloth, then with a dry.

"Ye'll nae doobt be leavin' fer somewhere in yer ship soon?" she asked at length.

"I doubt the weather will permit it for a few months yet," Robbie replied. "There's a heap of work to do though, painting and scrubbing and patching and mending rope and cleaning. And a rumor's about that the mate's left and isn't coming back."

"What's a mate?"

"He's the captain's second in command—you *do* know what a captain is?"

" 'Course I do!"

"Well, the captain's fond of me. He's always kinda takin' a likin' to me since I was a kid, and talk has it I might be up for ship's mate."

"That's somethin' ye been wantin', is it?"

"Who wouldn't! Maybe 'tis a bit like you becoming a lady."

He paused. "No, on second thought," he went on, "I guess

being captain would be like being a lady—just as farfetched, you might say. But getting to be mate is as close as the likes of me'll ever see."

"An' are ye sayin' the same o' me, then?" asked Jamie, stopping for a moment with her work and looking toward him.

" 'Tis right to dream, Jamie. I have my share of dreams, no doubt. But you must realize that the common working man has his place—just like maids and shepherds. And not many of us get to be captains or ladies. Just doesn't happen, that's all. You've got to be born and bred to it."

"My papa owned land."

"Did he now?" Robbie replied, showing a hint of surprise. "Then perhaps you are already a lady, Jamie."

"I dinna think so. But he said I'd be a lady someday—that is, if he hadna died."

They both fell silent for a moment.

"But it canna do nae harm t' try, cud it?"

"Not at all," answered Robbie enthusiastically. "But for now, why don't you just show me what a grand maid you are and fetch my breakfast."

"I'm owin' ye, fer helpin' me like this," said Jamie as she left the room.

"Nonsense! But when you become a lady, you can hire me to skipper your private yacht. That will be repayment in plenty!"

She laughed, then disappeared into the kitchen.

Later that night, bone-tired, Jamie crept up to her cubicle of a room. Sadie had dismissed her a few minutes past ten. The place was still full of rowdy men, but there were no more meals to be served, and Sadie could handle the ale.

The work had hardly let up a moment since she first applied the broom to the floor, although she had managed to get enough to eat. She could hardly imagine how Sadie herself, in the kitchen while Jamie still slept, and facing several more hours until the final customer was gone, held up day after day. She had not observed her daily habit of a brief afternoon nap, and on this day Jamie felt only sympathy with her employer as the first one up and the last to bed.

Jamie pulled off her boots and the smock Sadie had given her. Having no nightclothes, she had become accustomed to sleeping in her tunic and breeches. She dropped onto the bed, then realized she had not even unpacked the few belongings she was able to call her own. She sat up, set her pack on the bed, and opened it. But she never got beyond the first item. It was her grandfather's worn, old Bible. A knot rose in her throat at the sight; she was surprised to find the tears rising so quickly to her eyes.

How distant life with her grandfather already seemed! Alone in that cold, second-floor room above a dockside Aberdeen pub, how she longed for his gentle voice and warm reassuring presence. It ached to think of it, but she had not since his death felt *any* love like his. He had told her many times of the Heavenly Father whose love was always with them. But it was hard to sense that sort of love in surroundings such as these. She yearned at that moment, her body so weary, her heart so sad, to *feel* that ever-present love. Just to know it was there was somehow not enough. There had to be something more to it.

She glanced down at the black book in her hands.

Surely the answer to such questions was there. But how could she know where to look? And reading was so difficult—she could barely make out what few words she did know. Perhaps tomorrow she would stay up a little longer and try to read. Tomorrow she would be used to the long hours; tomorrow it would all come a little easier.

As she lay down and fell quickly asleep, the book slipped from her hands and fell unnoticed to the floor.

So the days passed. Gradually Jamie became more acclimated to the ways of the city.

As she found herself pining for Donachie, it could hardly be helped that something of her past inherent enthusiasm for life faded a bit. The city did not call out life to her spirit as the mountain had done.

But she carried out her tasks vigorously and with dedication. Therefore Sadie never noticed when her new maid from the hills began to lose the lively sparkle in her eyes which had always given her grandfather such joy. If the long sighs came for no apparent reason, Sadie concluded she was simply tired; if Jamie ate meagerly, how was Sadie to know she had ever done otherwise? She was a small enough girl, after all. And if Jamie did little other than sleep when she was not working, it was no doubt simply because she was too weary to do otherwise.

But the subtle change could not escape Robbie's notice.

"The city's not agreeing with you, Jamie," he said one evening, half as question, half as observation.

"Oh, no. I'm jist fine!" she answered quickly, though even as she did so she could feel the falseness of her words.

"Come now! Are you not thinking of your home?"

"Weel," she added sheepishly, "I might be missin' the mountain a wee bit."

"Do you want to go back?"

"No," she answered firmly. How could she go back? Even though she missed the life she had left, that life was gone. Returning to Donachie could never recapture it. Too much was wrapped up on her coming to Aberdeen, things even Jamie was not fully aware of.

"Well, lass," Robbie began, with all the sage wisdom of his twenty-one years, "if you're here to stay, you'll be happier all the sooner if you leave off your longing after the mountains and settle down to the business of getting used to Aberdeen."

He was right. She knew it. Comparing the city streets to Donachie only made things worse. She had to stop wondering if the factor had found the sheep, or if there were yet any signs of spring on the mountain. Spring on Donachie! She thought of the green blades of grass which would begin peeking through the snow, and of the bright faces of the flowers that would gradually dot the fellsides, and of the rush of the little burn through the meadow.

Ah, the meadow, with all its—

But she was doing it again!

She must give up her dreaming of the past! She must learn to like the city. Robbie and Sadie loved Aberdeen like she loved Donachie. There must be many wonderful things about city life too. She would look for them and grow to love them like Robbie and Sadie did.

Over the ensuing weeks Jamie made a more concerted attempt to think of herself as belonging in the city. But in her effort to forget Donachie, the face of her grandfather faded somewhat too, and as it did, she turned less and less to his dear old Bible. The treasured book, the words of the Psalms, the sound of her grandfather's voice as he read his favorite passages to her and tried to teach her to read them for herself—so much was wrapped up in the painful and confused reminders of Donachie. Perhaps these memories must be forgotten along with everything else.

At her tender age, with a faith still tenuously bound more to the memory of her grandfather than the Source of his own faith, she could not see that life in the city would have been much easier to face by strengthening such memories instead of erasing them.

But as in the blizzard, Jamie was never alone.

CHAPTER SIXTEEN

A Row on Hogmanay

Jamie could feel the excitement in the air despite knowing nothing about what festivals were like.

The day had begun early, with Sadie immediately commandeering Jamie's help in the kitchen. Not only would there be more visitors on this day, this was one of the few times of the year when Sadie prepared many special foods. She appeared for once to genuinely enjoy herself in the kitchen with all the extra baking there was to be done. Over the past several years she had become widely known for her superb haggis, that peculiarly Scottish meaty fare prepared in a sheep's bag, and she basked in the praise it brought her.

Jamie was set to work kneading dough for bread. While it was rising she swept the floors and served the few breakfast patrons. Washing up after breakfast, she noticed Sadie's unusually cheerful mood.

"Tonight'll be a special night," she said brightly. "Hogmanay, it is—the eve o' the new year! I expect half of the Aberdeen docks will come through my place. We'll be wanting to put on our best face, you know. So this afternoon, once the rooms are swept and the glasses shined, you take yourself a bit of time to take a bath and get cleaned up."

"Thank ye, mem."

The bath that afternoon was delightful, though hardly to be compared with a summer afternoon's dip in the burn that ran down Donachie, pooling here and there in wide still channels. When Jamie was finished she slipped back into her clothes. As she was putting away the soap and towels, Sadie walked by.

" 'Tis getting late, child," she said. "You'd best be getting yourself ready."

"I am, mem. I jist had my bath."

"And you have no other clothes to wear?"

"No, mem."

"You can't dress like *that* on Hogmanay day," said Sadie. "You have nothing else?"

"No, mem."

Sadie sighed. "Well," she said after a thoughtful pause, "that just won't do. Perhaps Robbie was right; you do need a woman's hand. Come along with me—there must be something we can do."

She took Jamie's arm and led her through the kitchen and up the stairs to her own small apartment of two rooms at the front of the building.

As they walked through the door, Jamie's eyes took in the sight with unabashed awe. Never had she seen anything so fine. The large bed was canopied and flounced with Queen Anne lace and pink ruffled dusters. A dressing table was similarly flounced and the windows were hung with lace. A china lamp painted with pink roses stood on the bedside table. An imitation Persian rug covered the floor. Jamie's feet had never felt such softness beneath them; she thought she could have stood there forever. But Sadie was already urging her forward in the direction of the double-door oak wardrobe.

"Now," said her employer, "there must be something here, though it's going to be impossible to find anything to fit your spindly figure. Hmmm . . ."

As she spoke she began sorting through the many dresses. There was one of every color imaginable, each brighter, if not gaudier, than the next. Sadie pulled several out, looked them over, but after each she shook her head and muttered comments to herself: "This color will never do," or, "She's much too young for this one," or, "She'd swim in this."

At last she drew out a simple gray muslin dress, its high collar trimmed with lace to match the cuffs. How a dress with such disarming simplicity had found its way into Sadie Malone's wardrobe remained a mystery, but it proved the best selection for Jamie.

"Let's get you into this and see what needs to be done."

But Jamie's attention had already been diverted to the dressing table on which stood a kaleidoscopic variety of bottles, jars, and vials. Her eyes were particularly drawn to a small lovely bottle of purple crystal. As if Sadie were reading her mind, she said, "We can get to that later. First let's see about this dress."

Requesting Jamie to remove her worn-out frock, Sadie carefully drew the muslin over her head. It hung limply on Jamie's slight frame, but Sadie reached for a pin cushion from a drawer and began pinning and tucking where necessary. She had nearly finished raising up the hem with pins when a man's voice called out from below.

"That'll be the fish monger," said Sadie, standing up. "And late—today of all days! See what you can do to finish up while I'm gone."

She hurried out, leaving Jamie, still a bit bewildered, standing before the mirror.

As Jamie studied the strange image of herself before her in the glass, she wasn't quite sure she liked what she saw. Her skin was so pale compared to Sadie's pink cheeks and high color. And her dark hair just hung shapelessly around her shoulders. She tried to twist it and stick it to the top of her head as she had often seen Sadie do, but it fell back to its original state.

With a sigh Jamie turned and again studied the items on the dressing table. She reached toward the crystal bottle, took it in her hand, sniffed at it, and realized this was the very smell she always noted about Sadie. With a feeling of trepidation she poured a little on her hands and then rubbed it on her hair and face. This seemed to give her more courage, and she investigated some of the other containers. She discovered that a small jar of pink cream when applied to her cheeks gave her the same color as Sadie's. A vial with something red in it was just the color of Sadie's lips and Jamie lost no time in rubbing some on her own. She was engrossed in a box of powder when Sadie returned.

Sadie burst into a laugh when she saw Jamie's reflection in the mirror. "What have we here?" she said. "Seems I once saw a clown in a circus that looked just like that!"

The laugh was good-natured, but Jamie could not help feeling embarrassed at being discovered in the act.

"I'm sorry, mem," she said, her lower lip trembling slightly. "I was jist hopin' t' look like ye do yersel'. But I guess 'tis nae use."

"You're still a baby," Sadie replied. "Give it time."

The comforting intent of her words was somewhat lost, coming between fresh outbreaks of giggles. "You'd best do without all that for the time being." She stepped closer, then stopped suddenly. "Whew!" she exclaimed. "Do I have any perfume left!"

"I . . . I—"

"Don't worry, child! We can wash everything else off, but it would take another bath to get rid of the perfume. So we'll just live with it until it wears off on its own."

By the time the guests started arriving later that evening, Jamie still felt rather out of place in Sadie's altered dress. Even with its tucks and hems it was still a poor fit. Notwithstanding the awkwardness she felt on account of the dress and the lingering fragrance of perfume about her, she could not help being disappointed when Robbie made no appearance as he had promised he would. Nor did it help that as she was threading her way through the jostling and rowdy crowd, a man backed into her and knocked the tray of full glasses of ale from her hand. Cursing her vigorously, Sadie's manner was strangely foreign to the budding gaiety that had been present between them in her room earlier in the day. Kneeling on the floor to wipe up the mess at the feet of so many large and clumsy boots, Jamie could feel the hot tears of disappointment and embarrassment coming to her eyes. She wanted to run away and hide!

Then she stood up, bit her lip, and tried to brush off how foolish she felt in this strange place. She would never be at home here, nor would she ever be a lady! She was out of place, and the looks she received from all the gawking men only confirmed that fact. She straightened the dress and began elbowing her way through the crowd once more to get another tray of drinks from the kitchen. In a couple of minutes she emerged again.

As she made her way toward the back of the crowded room, a large muscular hand grasped her arm, pulling her in its direction. The next moment she found herself face-to-face with a thickset bearded sailor. His face was already red from too much drink and his lopsided smile revealed a missing tooth as he leered disconcertingly at the helpless barmaid.

"My cup's dry, lassie!" he barked.

Hoping to place some distance between them, Jamie thrust her tray in front of him. "I hae some fresh ones fer ye," she said.

Until this night Sadie had served most of her patrons, and the few Jamie had encountered were regulars and for the most part a congenial lot. But the festival brought in many new faces. It was a considerably more rowdy and drunken assembly than usual, and for the past hour the atmosphere had grown increasingly tense—a powder keg ready to explode with the least spark to ignite it.

Unsatisfied with Jamie's offer, the sailor grabbed the tray and set it roughly on the table in front of him.

"Ye're new aroun' here, ain't ye? Sure ye are! Fresh oot o' the country, I'll warrant. Ain't that right, lassie?" He let out a coarse laugh and pinched Jamie's arm.

Jamie tried to back away.

"I—I got t' be servin' these drinks," she faltered.

"This is a holiday, lass—plenty o' time fer work later." He grabbed her by the waist. "Come on, ye pretty yoong thing. The pipes is playin' us a jig!"

Indeed, as he spoke, the pipes Sadie had hired for the evening had begun a rousing pilbroch and several others had taken up the tune. The sailor crushed Jamie to him and pirated her into the center of the floor where a few were dancing as best they might under the influence of a good deal of Sadie's darkest ale.

"Please!" Jamie protested. "I got me work t' do."

"Aw, Jerry ain't gonna hurt ye none," he said, clamping his hands tighter about her squirming body.

He bent over and tried to kiss her, but his hot breath sent awful shivers through Jamie's spine.

"Please!" Jamie cried, but the pipes were so loud no one noticed her predicament.

"That's it! Play the hard t' get, lass. Jerry likes that!"

She could say nothing further, pressed so tightly against the sailor's offensive chest. He laughed with gusto and pretended to dance, all the while holding Jamie tightly to him. She pushed with all her strength to get away, but every movement brought greater pain. Tears streamed down her face. Not since the blizzard had she felt so helpless! There were so many people so close by, but no one paid her the slightest attention. Even Sadie, her only hope, had disappeared.

"Please!" she sobbed again, but she felt as though her lips were merely mouthing the useless words.

Suddenly Jerry stumbled back and lurched violently away from her. Jamie, too, stumbled backward into the other dancers, not seeing at first what had separated them. Instantly the crowd forgot their dancing in favor of new and far more exciting entertainment. Even the pipes stopped, and all became deathly still as the crowd spread apart to reveal two combatants left in the middle of the floor.

Robbie had been detained on his ship, seeing to the repair of

a faulty bulkhead. The job had taken longer than expected because the one shop with the missing part had closed early for
the holiday and the proprietor had been located only after a
search of several Aberdeen public houses. Robbie had entered
The Golden Doubloon only a moment before Jamie's last helpless
protest. In three strides he had cut a path through the throng
and grabbed Jerry's shoulders to thrust him away from Jamie.

Recovering his initial shock, Jerry turned with a look of fury
on his face, and charged at Robbie like the bull of a man he was.
Already tipsy, Jerry was hardly a match for Robbie's still-sober
presence. Robbie stepped to one side and threw the charging
oaf across a vacant table. His anger roused to fever pitch, Jerry
turned with a loud oath and charged again, this time catching
his prey between his arms and slamming him to the floor under
the weight of his own body. By this time two of Jerry's shipmates
had approached to help give the upstart Taggart the thrashing
he deserved for meddling where he didn't belong. In a fair fight,
none of them would have worried about Robbie's safety, but
many of his friends who were present could not sit idly by watching a three-against-one contest. Several sprang to their feet and
approached, and before five minutes had past most of the men
in the room had joined in the row.

Sadie ran into the very center of the fray, screaming angrily
and fearfully for them to stop. She grabbed one after another by
the collar trying to pull them away, but she was able to accom-
plish little, her voice scarcely heard above the din. Jamie looked
on helplessly as Sadie ran frantically about trying to keep her
place from being wrecked beyond hope. By this time Robbie's
nose was bleeding and Jerry had nasty cuts about one eye which
would probably be black before morning. Nor were they the only
two from whom the blood flowed.

What the final damage might have been had the fight continued unchecked would be difficult to tell. But in a few moments
five constables—put on extra watch throughout the harbor area
that night—stormed through the doors. It was not until several
deft blows from their nightsticks had been administered that
some order returned. Seeing their presence, most of the rousters
simply fled before the law could lay hold on them. Jerry and his
shipmates were among the first to take to the streets as fast as
their wobbly legs would carry them. Robbie and a half-dozen
others, however, held their ground.

Jamie hurried to him the moment she spotted him leaning

heavily against one of the solid wood pillars toward the back of the room.

"What hae I done t' ye!" she cried, gently reaching toward his swollen eye.

He tried to smile, but a cut in his lip prevented more than a pathetic attempt. "None of that, lass. I'll be fine. All part of the sailor's life."

"Weel, let me get somethin' fer that eye, an' t' clean up the blood on yer nose." She hurried into the kitchen.

As they spoke Sadie was carrying on her own discourse with the chief constable, making tactful maneuvers of explanation to avoid a stiff fine on the grounds that her place was a center for trouble.

"Well, I'll be watching you, Sadie Malone," said the constable at last. "I'll let you off this time. I know that Jerry and his rowdy lot have caused trouble more than once. But you and I both know this isn't the first time it's happened here at the Doubloon!"

"Humph!" she muttered. Then quickly recovering her composure, perhaps aware that a smiling face would prove better insurance with the law than an angry one, she said, "Well, then, would you care for a drink—on me, of course?"

"What!" returned the chief, "you would attempt to bribe an officer of the Crown? No thank you, mem! You'll be making even more trouble for yourself!"

He turned and strode from the room, his men following behind him. "Remember," he called back to Sadie, "I'll be watching you!"

Furious, Sadie followed them with a glare in her eye, then turned and stalked toward Robbie with her angry eyes flashing.

"What were you thinking of, Robbie Taggart!" she exploded. "I ought to throw you out on your ear! After all I give to—"

"What are you talking about, Sadie!" Robbie retorted vehemently. "I didn't come in till after the trouble had started!"

"You're the one that started the row in the first place!"

"And what about yourself! How could you let such low-life trash treat Jamie so? What did you expect me to do?"

"So that's what this is all about?" For in truth, Sadie had been too preoccupied at the time and had not seen Jamie's predicament with the drunken sailor.

"Aye!" returned Robbie. "And I trusted you to take care of her."

"I'm sure the bloke meant no harm. Besides, the girl's going to have to learn to take care of herself sooner or later."

"She's but a child!"

"And bound to remain so with the likes of you hovering over her!"

"If you can't watch over her any better than that, Sadie, I'll take both her and my business elsewhere!"

"I told you I was running no home for strays! She's none of my concern!"

"You make her your concern, or you'll answer to me!"

"Humph!" she sputtered, eyes flashing. "Humph!"

"I'll not see her abused, I tell you!" concluded Robbie angrily.

What's come over him so suddenly? Sadie wondered. *He's as much as accusing me of abusing the girl! Nothing but a stray at that! And after all I've done for her!*

With a shrewd eye she observed Jamie as she emerged from the kitchen with a warm wet towel.

Perhaps she was not so much a child at that. Could Robbie's outburst mean more than a mere concern for the girl's welfare? Could he—?

No! she thought, quickly dismissing the idea. It was impossible Robbie could have anything but a brotherly interest in the bedraggled waif. After all, she and Robbie had long shared an unspoken understanding between them. He would never trade her for such a—a ragamuffin!

"Ye're hurtin'," Jamie said, rushing forward. "Sit ye doon."

She prodded him into one of the few undamaged chairs and began cleaning his wounds with the damp cloth.

"I'm fine," Robbie protested. "But what about you? I only wish I had come sooner."

"Oh, he didna hurt me. He jist—"

But Sadie broke in with a disgusted snort.

"Well, ain't this sweet! And what about me, I'd like to know! No one gives a fig that my place is in shambles and I was nearly arrested for the troubles the two of you brought on me! Look at this!" She grabbed up a broken chair and waved it in their faces. "And all for the questionable virtue of this—this—"

Quickly Robbie was back on his feet, glowering menacingly at her.

"All right! all right!" Sadie relented. "I'll see to the kettle. That's what we need, a nice hot cup of tea."

Jamie sighed as Sadie left for the kitchen.

"I never meant t' cause ye sich trouble," she said.

"You did nothing of the sort! Sometimes Sadie can think only of herself. She'll get over it."

He paused thoughtfully.

"If the truth be known," he went on at length, more serious in his tone, "the fault is all mine. And not because I started the row. I should never have brought you into a place like this. I don't know how I could have been so stupid."

"An' where would I be if ye hadna?" Jamie said. "I hae a roof o'er my head, an' food t' eat, and e'en a wee bit o' siller in my pocket—who kens where I be wi'oot ye?"

"Jamie, you are such a dear girl." He took her hand gently in his own. "I believe your father was right. You *were* meant for something special. Not a place like the Doubloon. This is no place for you to become the lady your father wanted you to be."

"But Sadie's a fine lady, she is."

"I think your father meant something a little more. And I'm going to do something about it, I will!"

"I dinna care where I be, Robbie, as long as ye'll always stay my frien'."

"You need never worry about that!"

He leaned forward and kissed her lightly on the forehead.

"Friends forever!" he said, then stood up. "And now I best go and see about my friendship with Sadie!"

Jamie had hardly heard his final words. She still tingled from the touch of his lips. It was a sensation far different from the awful kisses of the drunken sailor. She had been kissed by her grandfather many times. But this was something altogether new. There was something down inside her, she could not exactly tell where, a faint fluttering somewhere inside her chest.

All she could tell was that she lay down in her bed later that night with a smile on her lips.

CHAPTER SEVENTEEN

Broken Dreams

It was several days before Jamie saw Robbie again. But she unconsciously found her thoughts returning to him time and again. She wore Sadie's dress every day, absent-mindedly thinking that somehow the change in clothes had inspired Robbie's kiss.

"You ailing, lass?" said Sadie one day, walking in on Jamie languidly mopping the kitchen floor, looking as if her thoughts were hundreds of miles away.

"No, mem," was Jamie's only reply.

"Your work's been none too snappy these last few days."

"I'm sorry, mem," replied Jamie, pushing the mop more vigorously across the floor.

"Now listen here, lass," said Sadie, taking Jamie's arm to stop her activity. "I'm a woman of the world. And it seems if I'm to be in charge of you, you'd be better off confiding in me. I know more about a young girl's problems than you might think."

"Thank ye, mem. But I hae nae problems. I jist been feelin' a little different than I've felt before. 'Tis nothin'."

"It's lovesickness, isn't it, child?"

Jamie stared at her with a confused expression. "I don't feel sick at all, mem," she said.

Sadie shook her head and sighed. "You don't know anything, do you, lass? You're just an innocent babe. Well, I know all the symptoms, and you may as well not deny it. You're smitten with Robbie Taggart, aren't you?"

"I dinna ken, mem," replied Jamie, her face reddening. "He's been some awful good t' me, an'—"

"And you think you're in love with him, do you?"

"I dinna ken, mem. I dinna ken hoo love's supposed t' feel. I do like him a lot. An' he's so kind t' me."

"Well, take it from me, child, what you're feeling is nothing like love. *Smitten* is what you are, and you'll get over it when you grow up."

"Then what is real love, mem?"

"You are lucky to have me around, lass!" Sadie led Jamie to a table. They sat down and Sadie drew close to Jamie as if in a confidential manner. "Love," she began, as with great importance, "is when you want to spend the rest of your life with someone. It's when you're ready not to look at another man, and to, well, to give everything just to him. To follow him wherever he goes. It's—"

"Luv baireth a' things, believeth a' things, hoops a' things, endureth a' things," said Jamie suddenly.

Sadie looked up surprised.

" 'Twas somethin' my gran'daddy used t' read t' me," Jamie explained.

" 'Tis kind of a fancy, old-language way of putting it, but I suppose there's some truth in the words," said Sadie, then paused and rubbed her chin thoughtfully.

"Mem," said Jamie after a moment. "I'm thinkin' I feel that way aboot Robbie."

"Listen to you!" she said, laughing loudly, unsuccessfully attempting to repress her mirth. "Let me tell you, when it's the real thing, you won't just *think*, you'll *know*!"

Embarrassed, Jamie said self-consciously, "Ye won't breathe a word o' this t' Robbie, will ye, mem?"

"Oh, I'll be as quiet as a church mouse, you can count on me."

That evening a remarkably good-natured Robbie Taggart again returned to The Golden Doubloon. Signalling everyone present to fill their glasses on his tab, he threw his arm around Sadie and planted an affectionate kiss on her glowing cheek.

"I tell you, Sadie," he said jubilantly, "I really never imagined it would happen so soon!"

"What's your good fortune?" she asked. "Did you discover the lost treasure of the *Speedy Return*?"

"That old Darien schooner! Heaven knows we'd all like to know where Drummond buried her, and plenty have tried to find out. But no, that's not it!"

"What then?"

"First mate, Sadie! I've been made first mate!"

"Well, I always told you you were lucky to have Sadie around! I never once doubted you! And you'll make captain, too! Mark my words!"

Robbie laughed.

"I'm satisfied with the way it is for now," he said. "And I know I'm lucky to have you for a friend, Sadie Malone!"

Sadie's confidence was greatly bolstered by Robbie's words. Slightly ruffled by her conversation earlier in the day with Jamie, she thought that perhaps the time had come to elicit from Robbie a more positive commitment before she let him slip through her fingers. They had never spoken of marriage in a definite way, but it had been on Sadie's mind.

"And we've been friends a long time," she said, drawing close to him.

"A long time," Robbie agreed.

"I would say we were even *fond* of one another," Sadie added. "You do know my heart is yours, Robbie?"

"Of course! And you're my one and only!" he returned, grinning lightheartedly.

Growing more self-assured by the moment, Sadie, in her overconfidence, did not note the mischievous twinkle in Robbie's eye as he spoke. Heartened by his words, she gave little thought to what she said next.

"Well," she laughed, "I'm afraid that's going to be quite a blow to my little maid."

"Your little maid? You mean Jamie?"

"Aye. The poor child's smitten with you, Robbie."

"With me! Don't be ridiculous."

" 'Tis true. Ain't it the craziest thing you ever heard?" replied Sadie, still laughing.

"I don't know that I see the humor in it, Sadie." Robbie's brow knit together, the twinkle in his eye giving way to a far-off, pensive look.

"Imagine such a baby entertaining an idea like that." Sadie dabbed her eyes. Observing Robbie's seriousness, she tried to curb her amusement. "In love, of all things!"

"The idea may be ridiculous," said Robbie slowly, "but then again it may not be quite so—"

Looking up he saw Jamie in the doorway to the kitchen. Her

miserable countenance was proof that she had heard at least a portion of the conversation.

He rose and took a step toward her, but she shot across the floor and up the narrow stairs to her room. Repressing the tears threatening to spill from her eyes, she yanked Sadie's dress off and tossed it in a corner.

She was stupid to think it had made any difference! She was nothing but a coarse, country waif! She would never be anything else.

She slipped into her old tunic and breeches and dropped onto the bed, where the tears began to flow unchecked.

A few minutes later she heard a gentle knock on the door. Instinctively she knew it was Robbie. She sniffed twice and wiped a sleeve across her eyes—the last thing she wanted was for him to know she'd been crying. But her voice betrayed her.

"Yes?" she said thickly.

"Jamie, I want to talk to you," replied Robbie.

"I dinna see the need fer it."

"I deserve at least one chance, don't I?"

Jamie was silent a long while. She knew he was right; he had done so much for her, he deserved his say.

"What d' ye want t' talk aboot?" she asked at length.

"It would be easier without the door against my face."

A smile tugged at the corners of Jamie's lips. "It isna locked."

Slowly the door opened and Robbie stepped in. He remained standing, not particularly comfortable himself with the turn of events. He cleared his throat several times. Now that he was here he did not know quite what to say.

"I been sich a fool," Jamie said instead, breaking the awkward silence as she sat up.

"No. No, you haven't," Robbie answered quickly. "It's just been a misunderstanding, that's all."

"That's all, then," said Jamie, looking down at her hands in her lap. "I thought . . . I mean, I hoped—weel, it was foolish of me to . . ."

Robbie dropped down on the floor before her and took her hands in his. Had he stopped to consider how such an action was bound to raise her hopes, he might not have done so. But he was only thinking about how to keep from hurting this innocent child any further.

"Jamie," he said, "you are a sweet girl—and bonnie, too."

He reached up and touched her smudged cheek.

"Why, one of these days, when you're a mite older, you'll meet someone just as special as you are yourself, and he'll love you and want to protect you—and that's what you deserve, Jamie MacLeod! You know I care for you, and always will. I'll always be a big brother to you . . . that's not so bad, is it?"

Jamie nodded her assent, but inside she could never agree.

"Brothers and sisters love each other, Jamie," Robbie continued; " 'tis just a different kind of love. I hope you'll always be my little sister, Jamie. I couldn't bear it if that changed."

Jamie sniffed and looked away. "Ye're right," she said, trying to sound convincing. "I've ne'er had a big brother, an' it seems I'm needin' one noo."

"We need each other," he said, rising and laying his hand on her shoulder. "Now, how about if you come down and celebrate with me?"

"What are ye celebratin'?"

"I've just been made first mate of my ship."

"That's grand, Robbie."

"Now, come with me." He took her hand and led her back downstairs.

For a youngster enduring her first experience of unrequited love, Jamie managed to put up quite an accomplished front to hide her broken heart. She did not even know it was her heart that was breaking. She only knew that a rock lay in the pit of her stomach, and if she did not hold it back, a certain undefined lump in her throat would rise and bring tears to her eyes. And every time she looked at Sadie openly lavishing her affection on Robbie, she wanted to turn away. But it would be some years before she would fully understand what had taken place that day and why it had affected her so.

'Tis Sadie he loves, thought Jamie as she watched them. *An' no wonder! She's a lady! He'd be prood t' hae her at his side. I'm nae fit t' be a lady!*

For the first time in a long while Jamie's thought returned to Donachie. She had placed such high hopes on her coming to the city. But she didn't fit here. Yet there was nothing on the mountain to go back to. Where could she turn? In what direction *did* her future life lay?

Still, she did not think of her grandfather, whose memory might have brought new hope to her troubled spirit. Nor did she think of his old Bible, whose words might have brought comfort to her confused mind. Instead, she looked longingly toward Robbie who was at that moment dancing with Sadie. Though she had known him but a few weeks, whatever answers there were seemed to lie only with him, and in her pain she did not have the heart to look elsewhere.

The first moment she thought she could slip away unnoticed, she crept unobtrusively up the stairs. Once in her room she lay down and fell quickly asleep, hoping the dawn of morning would bring promise of new direction.

CHAPTER EIGHTEEN

The Vicar's Wife

The next morning brought nothing to Jamie but a new storm. Icy rain and intermittent snow pelted the coastline for several days. The forty-mile-per-hour winds threatened to dislodge several of the harbor's smaller vessels from their moorings. Robbie was shipbound, supervising frantic repairs necessitated by the turn in the weather, and no one in the Doubloon saw him throughout the duration of the storm.

Jamie had been so preoccupied with her own troubles and adjustments that she had scarcely noticed Sadie's changed disposition, which had taken a distinct turn for the worse. Robbie's concern over Jamie had taken him out of the proper frame of mind into which Sadie had thought to lead him. Now with his imminent departure looming closer as soon as the weather cleared, she knew there would undoubtedly be no opportunity to beguile him into talk of marriage this season. And who could tell what the next winter would bring? He would be visiting many distant ports, meeting foreign maidens younger and more attractive than herself . . . she didn't even want to think of it!

Thus with such thoughts and insecurities circling through her mind, Sadie's sour mood vented itself most directly upon Jamie, whom she subconsciously blamed for her failure to further her designs with Robbie.

To Jamie, however, the added load of work came almost as a relief, as healthy labor always is to a distressed mind and heart. She scrubbed and scoured and washed, and then did it all over again when muddy, rain-soaked patrons tracked in new filth on Sadie's hard-polished floor.

After many days came a break in the weather. Occasional showers and overcast skies continued intermittently, but the severe winds died and within another week and a half it appeared as if the first hints of spring were in the air.

Longing for the toss and pitch of the open sea and the prospect of new adventures, and altogether unaware of the emotions being silently harbored by the two women, Robbie came to the Doubloon to bid his farewells. In an especially exuberant mood at the challenges lying ahead, he explained that he would be off on the next morning's tide. He could not understand the sulky countenances his news seemed to bring. Goodbyes were never final for Robbie. He would see them both again soon, in the meantime they ought to enjoy what came their way, not drag with long faces.

But Jamie was still so innocent of life that he did feel a bit guilty for not finding another situation better suited to her. He could sympathize with her. However, Sadie had never acted this way before.

"Perk up, Sadie, my love," he said. "I'll be tracking mud through your door again before you know it!"

With that, and a final kiss for each of his two friends in Aberdeen, he took his leave, oblivious to the wasted hearts he was leaving behind.

After that, day followed dreary day, indistinguishable one from the other. In the emptiness of having lost her only friend, the drudgery of everyday work obscured the sight of any possible meaning in life. Jamie's father had loved her, and he had been taken away. Her grandfather had loved her, and he too had been taken from her. Then Robbie had been a friend who cared about her, and now he too was gone. In all the world, there was only Sadie. And Sadie hardly seemed to care that she existed. In the drab, colorless boredom of her daily toil, she forgot her grand purpose in coming to the city. She forgot her father's dream, her grandfather's faith, and her desire to learn to read.

From the moment Jamie awoke each morning, Sadie loaded her with work. And if things were slow at the Doubloon, Sadie hired her out to other public houses along the quay that were themselves in the midst of spring cleaning, retaining for herself the lion's share of whatever payment was received. When Jamie's day ended several hours after the guests were served their dinner, she had little strength other than what was necessary to climb to her room and drop into bed until a small glimmer of light penetrated her sooty window the following morning, wakening her to a new day on the gloomy treadmill.

The thought occasionally flitted through her mind that she might leave. She had a few shillings saved by this time. But where would she go? Would there now be anything to return to on the mountain? How could she survive there alone? And had not Aberdeen always been her goal? The future looked dismal.

One morning in early spring, Sadie handed Jamie a small pouch with several coins inside and sent her to the fish market with thorough instructions. This was an altogether new assignment, for ordinarily Sadie had not trusted Jamie with such tasks. But with a willing servant like Jamie about, why, thought Sadie, should she work herself into an early grave?

With such a rare opportunity to get out and see something of the city, Jamie eagerly accepted the assignment. The day was crisp and cold, and the sky threatened rain. She fetched a basket and her coat, then tucked the money pouch into her pocket and was off.

Walking down the winding road through the Inches, she took in the wide assortment of Aberdeen's more common elements. Crammed together in dismal and reckless fashion, taverns and shops, whose wares might have greatly interested the legal authorities, stood next to filthy and ramshackle tenement buildings—all situated against the gray backdrop of stone and timber yards with the dirty channel of the Dee at its feet. Children darted in and out from some of the tenements, and one bedraggled little boy of about eight, looking behind him as he emerged from the shadows, collided with Jamie and fell to the ground. Picking himself up, he stood dead still for a moment, perhaps thinking he was in for it. But the moment he saw Jamie's smile, he turned and darted off again into one of the dingy closes.

The fish market was about a half mile away, but Jamie took her time as she walked past the shipyards. She knew she was nearing her destination first by the permeating odor of fish in the air, and then by the loud din of voices of fishmongers and customers engaged in the age-old and heated process of barter. The open-air stalls of the market were crowded with people, barrels, tables, carts. Everywhere were heaps and piles of haddock, herring, kippers, and every other variety of fish imaginable.

Locating a herring dealer, Jamie took a deep breath—a fishy one to be sure!—and nudged her way through the crowd, at last taking her place behind the others at the stall, waiting patiently while those in front carried on the inevitable process of haggling with the dealer. It seemed that the major prerequisite for success in this form of bargaining was simple volume. And when each sale had been consummated, Jamie was never quite certain who had gotten the best of it, nor what price had been settled on. Then came her turn to be served.

She stepped forward, cleared her throat, and spoke as loudly as she could, "I'd be wantin' sum o' yer herrin'," she said, though her voice could hardly be heard in the tumult.

"Aye!" said the dealer, nudging his companion with a knowing grin. "Where ye be from, lassie? We dinna get many the likes o' you around here! Hey, Johnny, ye hear that? She says she's wantin' some herrin'!"

"Fancy that!" rejoined Johnny. "Herrin'! Do ye suppose we hae ony left? Ha, ha, ha!"

Jamie's face reddened as she realized they were mocking her.

"Well, I'm thinkin' I maun gae t' the next man, then," she said, trying to pluck up her courage.

"How many are ye wantin', miss?" asked the dealer, still laughing.

"I'm lookin' fer four dozen," Jamie replied, "if the price be right."

Here the dealer coughed momentarily, immediately modifying his demeanor. "We're only havin' a bit o' fun. Now, what can I do fer ye?"

"What price are ye askin'?"

"Well, for a lass like yersel', an' because o' the trouble I hae caused ye, I'll give ye a right good bargain at eight pence a dozen."

"Eight pence, a bargain?" said Jamie. Sadie had given her strict instructions to pay no more than six pence a dozen.

"An' only because I don't like a dissatisfied customer."

"But I haena sae mich," Jamie sputtered, by now having forgotten all about the undelicate art of wrangling over the price.

She felt a shove from behind and someone called out, "Hey, ye maunna tak all day wi' yer argle-barglin'!"

"Weel," said the dealer with a cunning look in his eyes, which Jamie was unable to discern, "how much do ye have?"

Jamie took out her pouch and counted the coins to be sure, then answered, "Thirty pence."

"Well, miss. 'Cause I like ye, an' am feelin' particular generous t'day, I'm goin' t' sell ye all four dozen fer jist thirty pence!"

Hardly awaiting her reply, the man reached out his hand

toward the coins while his companion immediately began count-
ing the fish into her basket. It was all over before Jamie could
take stock of the situation, but she thought she had come away
saving Sadie some money, although she wasn't quite sure. She
turned away with a half-bewildered expression on her face and
began making her way back through the crowd, anxious to get
away from the smelly place. But by the time she had made it to
the fringes of the throng, having been turned around several
times, she found herself at the opposite end of the market from
where she had entered. Not the least inclined to try to work her
way back through the fish market, she turned into a nearby
street, hopeful of working her way back around it to Market
Street on the other side. She tried several back streets, but each
seemed to lead in the wrong direction. She wandered about,
gradually getting farther and farther from her goal, each street
seeming to turn in confusing and patternless directions, in a
hopeless array of twists and angles that led nowhere. All was
gray and colorless, and Jamie began to grow frightened.

She walked into a street, but almost immediately realized it
was but a dead-end alley. She turned quickly to exit, but as she
did she saw two imposing figures who had stepped in behind
her and now stood blocking the way. They were two youths of
about her own age, one quite tall, the other muscular. Trying to
convince herself they meant no harm, she walked straight toward them, but they would not part to let her pass.

The taller of the two spoke. "Willie here says ye're but a
scrawny lad, but I says ye're a lass. We'd like ye t' settle oor bet
fer us."

"Willie's wrang," she answered bluntly. "Noo, if ye'd let me
pass."

"The lass wants t' be passin', Willie. What do ye think?"

"I'm thinkin' I dinna like t' lose a bet."

His tall companion laughed.

"Maybe we ought t' make her pay."

Willie brightened at the prospect. "What ye got in yer basket
there?"

"Only sum fish fer my mistress."

"Get it, Willie," said the other. "Let's see."

Jamie stepped back, clutching the basket to her.

"Please," she implored. "My mistress'd be sum awful angered if anythin'—"

But before she could finish, Willie lurched toward her. But Jamie jumped to one side.

Willie slipped and sprawled to his knees and his cohort laughed uproariously. Willie snarled and made for another attack.

"Jist a minute, Willie," said his companion. "Ain't no fair fight wi' a wee lassie the likes o' this. We ought t' let her pass."

Willie shot him a rabid glance. But the other youth caught his arm and pulled him back toward the alley entrance. "Come on, lad, like gent'men."

Still hesitant, Willie complied, perhaps because he sensed some deceptive ulterior motive in his friend's sudden turnabout.

Jamie relaxed for a moment. Perhaps they were only a couple of pranksters having some innocent fun after all. She started to walk forward, and as she did they removed their caps and swept them forward in a deep bow. Quickening her pace, Jamie broke into a run. But as she shot between the two, one of them stuck out his foot at precisely the right moment. Jamie sprawled on her face, the basket flew from her hands, and the contents went flying in every direction over the grimy street.

Recovering themselves from their laughter, Willie and his companion approached, aimed several punishing kicks at Jamie where she lay on the street, then hurriedly gathered up the fish and disappeared.

Jamie rolled over, but only in time to see their retreating heels fly around the brick corner of the alley. She tried to stand but her head was dizzy. Her hands and knees were badly scraped; a deep cut from a piece of broken glass was bleeding rather freely; and her ribs and legs ached with dull pain from the boys' boots.

Fearing the two thieves would return, Jamie forced herself to her feet, gripping a wall to steady herself. She hardly knew what to do now. Not only was she still lost, now she was empty-handed, and the thought of facing Sadie with neither money nor fish was almost as distressing as another beating at the hands of the young thugs.

By the time she limped out of the alley, tears were streaming down her face.

"Maybe she'd beleif me if I promise t' pay her frae my siller," she sniffed to herself, hardly thinking that it would take over a hundred of the farthings she worked so hard for to repay the thirty pence. And in the meantime Sadie would still be without her fish!

She walked slowly and aimlessly down the street, hardly noticing the approaching carriage. It stopped and a lady emerged, just as a wave of faintness came upon Jamie and she leaned against the wall of a building to steady herself.

"My dear! My dear!" cried the lady, hurrying toward her. "What is it?"

Jamie looked up, but could not immediately find her voice. Just as the lady reached her, Jamie's knees buckled under her. She grasped for support, clutching the lady's dress, smearing blood from the cut on her hand onto the fine white fabric.

"Oh, my dear!" cried the lady again. "Walter, she's hurt!" she called out behind her.

Coming to herself and seeing what she had done, Jamie at last found her tongue. "Oh, mem! I'm sorry! I didna mean t'— oh, yer fine dress—!"

She could say no more, finally breaking into uncontrolled weeping.

"Think nothing of the dress," returned the lady, enclosing her arms around Jamie's shoulders. "There, there . . . everything will be fine!"

"Oh, I made a mess o' everythin'!" sobbed Jamie.

"No, no," the woman comforted, still holding Jamie in her loving arms. Her voice was soft and soothing. "The dress is of no concern—but look at you! You're hurt. Can you tell me what happened?"

"I had bocht sumdeal o' herrin' fer Sadie," sobbed Jamie, "when twa cursed blaggards beat me an' staelt my fish."

"Come, my carriage is right here. You must sit down."

"Oh, no, mem. I couldna put ye oot! I done enough hairm already."

"You've been hurt, my dear. I won't take no for an answer."

She led Jamie firmly to her carriage, which was only a few feet away. The driver jumped down to help Jamie in.

"Walter," the lady said, "bring me the flask of water you keep in the boot."

The driver complied, and soon the lady was cleaning Jamie's forehead with a soft cloth.

"We must get that hand of yours bandaged!" she said. "It's really worse than I thought. Where do you live? We must get you home!"

"Oh, no, mem!" Jamie exclaimed. "I canna . . . my mistress'd be sore put oot wi' me, comin' home in a carriage an' wi'oot her fish!"

"Surely she would understand!"

"I lost thirty pence o' fish, mem!" Jamie said, wiping her tear-filled eyes and running nose with the back of her dirty hand.

"Walter," the lady called up to the driver with resolution in her voice, "take us home, please." Then to Jamie, "No need to cry. We'll get you cleaned up and work something out with your mistress. I'm sure she'll understand."

The carriage jerked into movement, and suddenly Jamie found herself being carried away—whence, she had no idea. But she was too weary to argue. It could be no worse than the Doubloon.

Although much too exhausted both physically and emotionally to pay much attention to her surroundings, Jamie was able to tell that her genteel rescuer was a far different breed of lady than her employer. Her voice was soft and pleasing. Her flaxen hair, pulled up on her head with curls peeking out from under a lovely blue velvet hat, framed a round but sensitive face. There was a pink glow about her creamy skin, but Jamie could tell immediately that it did not come from a powder box as had Sadie's. She was in her early thirties and very pretty, though perhaps not quite beautiful. Her long-lashed eyes were blue and warm, and in certain surroundings might have been just a bit shy. She was but a few inches taller than Jamie, yet maintained a daintily feminine aura about her. The dress, by now splotched with blood and dirt, was of soft blue and white cotton, trimmed with lace at the neck and cuffs and around the hem.

The lady, as Jamie would ultimately discover, was Emily Gilchrist, the wife of the vicar William Gilchrist. What such a woman in such a carriage was doing within a few blocks of the Aberdeen fish market, and on such a sleazy back street, is a question many might have asked. But none who knew Mrs. Gilchrist would have asked it. She was often to be found in such places, for she had made the poor folk of Aberdeen her special province. She was to be found wherever a gentle hand or kind word was needed, often bringing baskets of food or medical supplies. Her husband had long since ceased taking her to task for her unseemly and unceremonious, if not outright dangerous, habit. In fact, as he had accustomed himself to her peculiar ways, he had grown to greatly admire and respect his wife, not merely for her ethics, but for her pluck. As vicar of a prosperous parish, he had been in danger of growing content with his lot in life. But now his heart often went with her, and even his person upon rare occasion, and he was growing once again—down toward the poor, and up toward the kingdom of heaven.

He was therefore not surprised in the least when Emily walked into their stately home in Cornhill with a young waif in tow.

He was at that moment entertaining Lord Farquhar, one of his most influential parishioners. Farquhar cocked an eyebrow at the appearance of the ragged girl, but Gilchrist smiled warmly, if not a bit awkwardly. Emily greeted her husband and his guest, then ushered her charge past the parlor and into the kitchen where she knew everyone, especially Jamie, would be most comfortable to have her carry out her ministrations.

Jamie remained speechless throughout the proceeding. She had never been inside such a house, had never even seen one, and felt as if she were an orphan walking inside a palace—as indeed she was. But then she would have expected such a lady to live in nothing less.

CHAPTER NINETEEN

Lessons

Sadie was understandably aggrieved, if for all the wrong reasons, when she received word that Jamie would be taking up residence with the vicar William Gilchrist. Walter, the coachman, delivered the message along with a five-pound note to compensate for any losses incurred. He then gathered up Jamie's things and drove away.

It took very little time, after Jamie had poured out her whole story, for Mrs. Gilchrist to reach her decision. At first Jamie protested, thinking that she could hardly take what she did not earn. But with four children in the household, Emily had little trouble persuading Jamie that she would indeed earn her keep. Moreover, Emily felt Jamie would be a perfect companion to take with her on her visitations. For these "services" Jamie would receive her keep, and lessons.

But from almost the moment she saw her, Emily Gilchrist sensed in this young lost, homeless, confused little lamb, a tender spirit into which she longed to pour herself. She saw her not as a wandering waif on the streets, but as a developing woman waiting to be loved and nurtured. The blossoming of the beauty that lay dormant within her was to Emily Gilchrist as strong a reality as Jamie's ragged clothes, if only it could be discovered and then given room to grow. Jamie became to Emily as a daughter, a rough-hewn offspring, no doubt, whose speech and manner and whole carriage required the most basic instruction and training, but whose heart was already in the right direction. The lessons in which Jamie participated, therefore, were of a deeper and more life-changing sort than either she or the tutor imagined. Emily gave herself wholeheartedly to the strengthening and nourishment of Jamie's whole personhood. And she was not to be disappointed. For it did not take many weeks before the change began to be apparent. From the outward changes in apparel and etiquette and social behavior, over the months a radiance emerged in Jamie's eyes that told of far more than mere physical maturation. A flowering of perfect womanhood, which at Sadie's would have died a closed bud on the vine, was at hand.

Jamie's room on the second floor was fit for a princess. Its huge bay window looked out onto the broad lawns and lovely gardens of the manse, and allowed warm streams of light to bathe the place all day long. To Jamie it was all so unlike anything she had seen that a certain numbness followed her for several days. She walked about as one in a dream. Her life since her grandfather's death had been so full of change that by now she was scarcely surprised. It seemed as though the footsteps of her life were not her own to order but were being guided by an unseen hand, toward she knew not what. Therefore, she took everything as it came, if not without a little bewilderment at first, with nonetheless delight at the enchantment of the fairy tale into which she seemed to have landed.

The spacious beauty of the vicar's fine home offered a physical reflection of the sweet and peaceful spirit that dwelt there. Immediately Jamie was openly welcomed as one of the family, and it was this love, rather than the soft sheets and warm bath and clean clothes, which watered the seed lying fallow in her own heart, causing it to sprout and begin sending down roots into the eternal. She was made to feel as though she were an individual, significant to these people who scarcely knew her; and she observed the free flow of love between William and Emily Gilchrist, and among them and their four children. She and her grandfather had loved one another. But something more far-reaching was here—or perhaps in the cottage on Donachie, she had been too young to sense it. Now she was ready to receive the love they offered as a gift from on high.

Benjamin, eleven, was the eldest of the Gilchrist children, followed by his two sisters, Caroline, nine, and Cecilia, eight. These three were typical children, occasionally loud, full of play, and exuberant with life; yet they were full of respect and highly fond of Jamie. The youngest, four-year-old Kenneth, was of another breed than his siblings—far more lively, and to some more critical observers, downright spoiled. But though he was always up to his three-foot-high neck in some sort of trouble, he maintained such a cherubic smile and tender heart that he had not a single enemy among relatives or acquaintances. He had, in fact, not been spoiled by his parents at all; they simply did their best to channel the extra activity and energy he seemed to have been blessed with at birth. Young Kenneth adored Jamie from the moment he saw her.

The small staff of servants about the manse was comprised of Mrs. Wainwright the governess, Sarah the cook, and Walter the coachman, who also acted as groundskeeper. Jamie saw Mr. Avery the most—the older children's tutor, a middle-aged man of slight frame, and extremely nearsighted. In his youth he had aspired to the clergy, but his quiet, shy, self-effacing nature proved a drawback in that profession. He found himself more effective in shaping the minds of children than of his peers, and practice demonstrated him indeed more gifted in that regard.

Between Mr. Avery coaxing Jamie's mind into new avenues of activity, and Mrs. Gilchrist accomplishing the same for her spirit, changes became evident about her more quickly than she herself realized. She had been a bud waiting to open, a beautiful butterfly trapped in the chrysalis of its surroundings, struggling to break its shell that it might soar forth.

Jamie took lessons daily with the three older children in the third-floor room, once a large attic used for storage, but now converted into a schoolroom. An eager student, applying the rudiments she had learned from her grandfather and the new principles given her by Mr. Avery, she soon mastered the first primer. But learning to read was merely a gateway into further worlds of knowledge for Jamie. Science, history, and mathematics—with which she found she had to struggle; music and literature all followed in their due course. Skilled in both insight into human nature and methods of teaching, Mr. Avery led her on gradually, giving her only sufficient bites to thoroughly whet her appetite for more. He saw in his new student just the germ of the truth-loving spirit that Mrs. Gilchrist saw, and did not want to crush the bud while it was still struggling to open. But his instincts were rewarded, and before many months he found he was kept in a constant state of blessed perplexity trying to keep up with her insatiable appetite for learning. For such is the product of a mind nurtured to learn on its own rather than force-fed through what is erroneously termed the educational system.

Of all Jamie's new experiences, few could compare with the delightful times when Mrs. Gilchrist would wander into her room. They often talked for hours, seemingly spontaneously, about a host of different things. But these discussions and visits were purposefully designed by Mrs. Gilchrist to draw Jamie out as a way of subtly sharing a new way of life with her.

Frequently the topic of conversation would be the object of their visitation that day, for Jamie had begun to accompany Mrs. Gilchrist on her rounds. Jamie's genuine compassion was gratifying to the older woman, as was her openness to speak of her own thoughts and feelings when their talk turned in that direction.

"Do ye think poor Mrs. Ehlers will be able t' do somethin' fer her boy?" Jamie would ask.

"It is hard to say, Jamie," Emily might reply. "The lad has become involved in a bad crowd. But he refuses to see where it is leading him."

"Ye'd think his own mither'd be able t' influence him."

"Perhaps if she had begun to train him in his early years; but he was allowed to run free in his childhood. And now it is much more difficult to bring him back into the fold."

"Jist like the sheep," Jamie offered. "There's always a rowdy ane whas got t' gang his ane way."

"But the Good Shepherd will not rest until he's brought back—and neither will his servants."

"Is that why ye keep visitin' them folks doon in the Inches an' round aboot?" Jamie asked.

"Yes, that's certainly part of it, Jamie. Though it's not only the people in the Inches who need to hear about God's love, for there is great need in that respect, even here in Cornhill. But the servants who would go to the Inches are fewer than those who might be comfortable talking to people in Cornhill. Why, most of those poor people there would not even be welcome in my husband's own parish, though he has often tried to encourage such openness between the classes!"

"But isn't that what the church's fer, mem?"

"Yes. But sadly it is not always perceived in that way. We become so accustomed to our own little worlds that it is difficult to open them up to people who may be different and make us feel uncomfortable. Most of the people in our churches are not actually trying to be cruel or heartless in their biases toward the lower classes—though some are. But most are merely afraid."

"Afraid o' doin' guid, Mrs. Gilchrist?" asked Jamie, surprised.

Emily smiled in answer, then said, "I suppose it does seem a bit ridiculous. If only they could see it that way. But I decided long ago not to be ruled by my fears. The Bible says, 'For God hath not given us the spirit of fear: but of power, and of love, and of a sound mind.' ''

"Are ye not jist a wee bit afraid when ye gang there—I mean, t' the Inches? I was the first time I went alone, especially when them boys started teasin' me."

"I have been afraid also," Emily replied. "I remember the first time I went to visit the sister of a servant of one of our parishioners. She was in the later stages of pregnancy and having a difficult time. As I climbed those rickety stairs, I could not believe the poverty. My heart was pounding and my hands were trembling so, I wondered if I would last through the morning. But I did."

"Because ye are a strong an' courageous woman," Jamie put in, with something like awe in her voice.

"No, hardly that!" laughed Emily. "I was able to endure the sights and smells of the poverty by realizing that there was no way I *could* make it in my own strength. Only as I began to rely on God's power, to remind myself continually of His mission of love which had brought me to that place to begin with did I find I could go on. You see, Jamie, I was afraid. But I knew I could not allow myself to be *ruled* by that fear. For then that spirit of fear would have prevented me from being ruled by *God's Spirit*."

"Then it's all right t' be afraid, jist so long as—"

Jamie hesitated, not quite sure how to put this new thought into words.

"Weel," she finally went on, "as long as we dinna forgit aboot God."

"Yes," Emily answered. "He wants us to trust even our fears to Him."

"It sounds easy, Mrs. Gilchrist. But I canna think it truly is."

"In one sense, it is the most difficult thing a person will ever do. Yet, in another sense, what could be simpler? For whom are we asked to trust? The God of the universe, the Creator, the One who gave himself for us. I only pray that one day Mrs. Ehlers' son might see all this. It is simple, Jamie, but sometimes difficult to *do*—life's greatest challenge!"

"There's got t' be a chance for him because look at me!" Jamie declared.

Emily reached over and placed her arms around the young

girl's shoulders. But soon Jamie grew pensive.

"What is it?" Emily asked.

"I was jist thinkin'," Jamie replied.

"Want to tell me about it?"

"Weel," Jamie began slowly, "one thing's been troublin' me."

"What's that?"

"My gran'daddy tried t' teach me aboot God, like I'm sure Mrs. Ehlers tried t' teach her boy. But when my gran'daddy died, weel, I guess that wi'oot anyone around t' remind me, I jist began t' forgit."

"And now, are you recalling the things you learned as a child and the way of life your grandfather demonstrated to you?"

"Thanks t' you an' Mr. Gilchrist, 'deed, mem, I think I am!"

"It is the Lord who causes the seeds of teaching to grow."

"But I'm thinkin' He's usin' yersel' a lot."

Emily Gilchrist smiled. "But the seeds had long been planted in you, Jamie. You may not see that. But it is as clear to me as the sunshine and rain. I am almost coming to know your grandfather himself, just from you. I can see influences that he no doubt planted in you long ago. And that very thing gives me hope for the Ehlers' boy, too. A seed, even a tiny invisible seed, *can* grow. And prayer can many times be the water that causes it to sprout."

"But I canna help wonderin' what would hae happened if ye hadna found me."

"God has His ways," Emily answered. "And I believe if you have a truly seeking heart, you will come to God. He never leaves the honest, searching, humble, open heart alone. He will always fill it with himself."

"But it worries me t' think," Jamie went on, "that if I'm off by mysel' again, that maybe I'll forget jist like I did before."

Emily placed her arm around Jamie and drew her close. "If your roots are deep enough, that won't happen. Keep your heart open to Him, Jamie, and obey Him and do as His Word tells you. And in the meantime, with God's help, we will be sure to do a proper job of gardening! Oh, Lord," she prayed, "we thank you for your great and personal love for us! Never let us turn our backs on you. Keep us always close to your heart. Keep our minds on you, keep our hearts in love with you, and keep our actions in obedience to you. Help us, Lord, to be your children and to live as you would have us live. We are so weak and we need your help so badly. Draw near us, Lord, and purify our hearts in service and love and obedience to you."

Jamie sat in silence, Emily's arms wrapped tightly around her. Tears of peace streamed down her cheek. It was the first time she could remember the love of a woman, the love of a mother, surrounding her and giving the little girl in her heart the only home an orphan ever truly longs for. And wrapped around them both were the invisible arms of a loving Father, in whose love none are orphans but all are dearly loved children and heirs of the eternal.

Thus Jamie grew—in mind, and body, and spirit. What Finlay had begun in that old stone cottage in the heart of Donachie was now finding its completion in the stately manse in Aberdeen. Each day Jamie grew to know Finlay's God and Emily's God more personally. He was now becoming *her* God also. What she had accepted mentally from Finlay's lips on Donachie, she now received in the stillness of her heart. The words spoken by a grandfather were quickened into her spirit by the one Father. She began to read the old Bible again. But now the words spoke directly to her. And when she prayed, she spoke not to some unknowable and infinite deity, but to her very own Father. She had loved her daddy; she loved her grandfather even more; and no one could replace the mother she had found in Emily Gilchrist. But the one relationship all men and women long for at the root of all others is this Father. And that at last Jamie had begun to find.

Questions of the heart she directed to Emily. But to Mr. Avery she often went with theological queries.

"I dinna see how God can be three folks all wrapped up in one," she said one morning during catechism lessons.

Now Mr. Avery's genius for teaching was largely comprised of this: that when a question arose which he had not anticipated, he did not squelch it or give it a pat answer, but used it as a springboard for further discussion and learning. He was as ready to lay aside his planned lessons as to pursue them, taking whichever direction he felt could yield most learning of the best kind. If his students learned less of their memorized responses to the shorter catechism, they learned more of something far more valuable—the practical lessons of life, upon which the development and maturation of character are based.

"It's called the Trinity," he replied patiently; "three persons in one."

"Weel, it seems t' me that three persons must be three persons."

"Take Mr. Gilchrist as an example," replied the tutor. "He is three persons in one."

"Like God?" exclaimed Jamie.

"Not exactly," laughed Mr. Avery. "But looking at him might make it easier for you to understand what I mean. To his mother he is a son, to his parishioners he is a vicar, and to his children he is a father. See, three persons in one—three different aspects to his overall character."

"But he has only one body," said Jamie. "When Jesus was on earth, He was *here*, an' God was in heaven—an' then the Holy Spirit . . . weel, I jist dinna understand Him at all!"

Mr. Avery said nothing for a moment, pondering how to make it clear. Suddenly he had an idea.

"Come with me to the kitchen for a moment," he said.

Puzzled, Jamie followed, wondering what spiritual lessons could be had there. Sarah must have wondered also, for she gave the tutor and his youthful entourage a most peculiar look as they entered.

Mr. Avery took a chunk of ice from the counter where Sarah had been thawing a fish, and proceeded to demonstrate how the substance contained three elements in one: water, ice, and steam.

At last Jamie understood. But the greatest lesson of the day was the confirmation that the things of the spiritual world can be found in every aspect of life. She happily shared this realization, to the extreme pleasure of her tutor. They then returned to the schoolroom and the tedious subject of grammar, of which, along with pronunciation, Jamie stood in sore need.

Knowing that the heart was of ultimate importance, Emily nevertheless added to Jamie's curriculum lessons the first rudiments of social graces. Practicality considered, she knew Jamie would before long have to make her own way in the world. Even if her heart was pure gold, if she spoke like a shepherd girl from the hills and did not know how to behave with decorum in society, she would never be able to obtain a position as a maid or a governess or a cook or even a housekeeper. Thus Emily took it upon herself to make a presentable woman of her.

Tedious and frustrating as Jamie found it, she worked hard because she wanted to please Emily. And in addition, she knew it would please her father. For she still clung to the desire to validate her father's dying hope that she might one day be a lady.

"I canna haud the fork richt!" she exclaimed in frustration during one exercise on table etiquette. "It picks up the food jist as weel no maitter hoo I'm hauding it!"

But day after day the lessons progressed and Jamie tackled each obstacle with a determination which was inherent in her nature. Before summer was past, neither Sadie nor Robbie, nor indeed even old Finlay, would have recognized her. Her ragged clothing had long since been replaced with two or three lovely dresses purchased especially for her by Emily. Her shiny dark hair had grown until it fell in lustrous waves well past her shoulders; Emily suggested that nothing be done to it, for it looked most elegant just like that. Her movements had taken on a sort of unaffected grace, though there were times, especially while she was playing with young Kenny, that she forgot everything she had learned and tumbled like a boy over the carpet.

Mr. Gilchrist commented proudly on her progress: "I'd like to see Lord Farquhar's face now," he said with a warm smile.

She did meet Farquhar again, and his wife, and many other visitors from time to time. Most found her refreshing, although there were those who wondered why the vicar's wife continued to mix with such "common" elements. For her part, Jamie preferred to remain about the manse and its grounds. She was too absorbed in her studies, and too content in her friendship with the Gilchrist family, to have much chance or desire to socialize beyond those visitors who came to the manse to see her guardians.

Reading in Finlay's Bible one day, as had become her daily custom, her mind wandered to the other book that had remained tucked away among her possessions. She had continued to think of it from time to time, but had not yet opened it since her arrival in Aberdeen. She had thought of it upon occasion, but as her reading skills had increased, something within her seemed consciously to avoid a confrontation with the words she had once so desperately wanted to understand. For nearly a year now the goal of reading that book and its inscription had been her passion. Yet there had remained a fear, a fear of the unknown past, a fear of what emotions the words might raise in her, a fear that reading it might somehow cause this new peaceful life she had found to crumble.

But on this particular day, as she again thought of the book, the fears were gone. Something within her seemed to be saying that the time was right, that the moment had come, like the silent nod of approval old Finlay had given in her dream—approval which had led her down the mountain, to Robbie, to Sadie, and finally to the Gilchrists.

She rose slowly from where she sat and walked toward her bureau. Opening the second drawer, she withdrew the book, her heart pounding. In that moment she knew she must read it, but she also knew she did not want to be alone when she did. She sought out Emily, and at last found her reading in the rose garden.

"Mrs. Gilchrist," she called, timidly approaching the secluded bench where Emily sat.

"Hello, Jamie."

"Am I disturbing you?"

"Not at all. Come and sit down."

Jamie sat down on the stone bench, finding herself now unsure of how to express the strange mixture of feelings she had about the book.

"Is something troubling you, dear?" asked Emily.

"This," Jamie replied, holding up the volume, "is the book I told ye aboot, the one that belonged t' my mother."

Emily nodded and smiled encouragingly.

"I think 'tis time I read it. But I'm a little fearsome. 'Tis a mite silly, I know."

"It's easy to be afraid of the most joyous moment of our lives—there's nothing at all silly about that, Jamie."

"I didn't want t' be alone when I read it, mem."

"I'm honored that you felt you could come to me for this special moment. Go ahead," she prompted. "Read it aloud if you like . . . or to yourself."

"My reading's still a mite poor, mem, though Mr. Avery says I'm doin' right weel. So I think I'll read it t' myself, an' then ye can read it when I'm done."

The volume was a small collection of poetry by Wordsworth. Slowly Jamie opened the cover to the title page, opposite which the handwriting appeared in fine old script. Tears had already begun to gather in her eyes, but as she read, they overflowed their bounds and streamed down her face.

My dearest daughter Jamie,

I am writing this to you because I will soon be leaving this world. There were so many gifts I wanted to give you, so much love I wanted to share with you, but this book will be the only one I will have time to impart. It was given me by my own mother, so it is fitting that you should have it now. This book speaks of some of the gifts I want you to have—love, kindness, honesty, and faith. Your father is a good man; he will teach you these things. He has many grand dreams, but remember, my dear daughter, if you find love you will have attained the greatest dream of all. Whatever in life you become, never forget that the person you are will be determined by the character you allow to grow within you, not by what others, or by what the world may think.

> Your Loving Mother,
> Alice MacLeod

Jamie did not speak for some time and silently handed the book to Emily, who read it, not without shedding tears also. She put her arm around Jamie and the two sat silently for some time.

"I wonder what might hae been different had I read this sooner," said Jamie at length.

"God has His perfect timing in everything, Jamie."

"But—" she began, hesitated, then continued, "—but what about my father? What about—he had such dreams . . . his last words . . . sometimes I get so confused wonderin' what I'm supposed t' be!"

"Let God make of your father's words and dreams what He will. Who knows what might come of them, and what is in God's greater plan? Since the moment I saw you I sensed that there was something special in you. Your father must have known this, too. Who knows what he might have actually meant by those last words?"

"Do ye think, Mrs. Gilchrist, that in some way he might have been speakin' God's plan?"

"No one will be able to answer that until it comes to pass, Jamie," answered Emily, giving Jamie a tight hug.

"I guess the one thing I can be sure of is that 'tis best t' try t' live accordin' t' God's ways."

"And let the rest of life's questions fall in line behind that," concluded Emily with a smile. "You're right, Jamie. That *is* one thing we can be sure of."

In that single moment Jamie took a great stride toward maturity, perhaps a greater stride than in all the preceding years of her life. She clutched the book to her heart and knew with the faith that was growing inside her that somehow her mother's words and her father's dream would intertwine, harmonizing together into God's perfect plan for her life.

CHAPTER TWENTY

Another Change

Dora Campbell set down her china cup on the fine walnut table, taking care to use the saucer which had been provided.

The Gilchrists' parlor is elegant, she thought, *tastefully decorated but warm and cozy. Not unlike its mistress.* Dora was perhaps more attuned to such things than most persons. She was a housekeeper and could not keep from scrutinizing her surroundings. Although she was in most matters an equitable sort who sincerely tried not to judge others except by compassionate standards, she did possess a weakness where the mechanics of another's household was concerned, no less than a groom would be interested in a man's horses, or a lawyer in his portfolio.

She was a short, round, florid woman with brown, kinky hair which she tried to control by pinning it into a bun on the top of her head. She had been endowed with boundless energy, at this moment most readily evident in the movements of her quick dark eyes which never missed even a carelessly overlooked speck of dust. She would have traded a portion of this nature for a temperament which could have disregarded such things, particularly in other people's homes, but it was simply not to be. Some called her compulsive, and she had to agree. Yet that very trait, so disturbing as she now sat in the Gilchrist home, was precisely what made her so invaluable to her employer, and was the reason behind the great responsibility he gave her. Though technically a servant, she was now in fact acting on his behalf, as his emissary with full power of decision in a matter about which the laird himself did not want to have to think.

Emily refilled the delicate teacup, and Dora could not help but note the loveliness of her hostess. *What it would be like to serve in such a house!* she thought. She had heard that Mrs. Gilchrist

152

was the daughter of a baron but had married beneath her station for love and devotion. It was a sweet story, certainly one that seemed perfectly suited to the character of the gracious woman. Dora thought fleetingly of her own unhappy and cheerless household, and reflected whether such a sunny, zestful atmosphere might someday be in store for her employer and his home again. She doubted it, for one must sow the seeds of such things before reaping the rewards of them. And for two years nothing but grief had been sowed at Aviemere.

"I'm so glad you decided to pay us a visit while you were in Aberdeen," Emily was saying.

"My pleasure completely," Dora replied in her rather high-pitched tone, which always seemed somewhat breathless, as if she had just flown up a flight of stairs. "You've been so kind to my sister since her illness."

"She is one of our flock and we love her. You don't know what a relief it is to hear she is growing stronger every day."

Emily offered her guest a dish of scones as she spoke.

Dora accepted one and began to spread it with a thick slab of butter. She was as energetic about eating as she was about everything else.

"Well, it was a comfort to know someone was looking out for her, since I couldn't be here myself," Dora said, then bit into the tender scone. "It was impossible to get away until now, for almost immediately after I received word of Clair's illness, we lost three servants."

"Dead!" said Emily with some shock. "All three?"

"No, no!" Dora laughed. "Just up and quit, they did. The groom and the parlormaid—rumor has it they ran off to be married—and then the nurse. We were finally able to fill the first two positions with local folks, though I'm not sure the new parlormaid is going to work out. You know how it is with a place like Aviemere. The estate so dominates the minds of the local people that it's all but impossible to find qualified help from the village or surrounding country. And we still are in desperate need of a nurse, and that's why I was able to come to Aberdeen. The laird gave me leave to come visit Clair and to look for someone here."

"It must be difficult to care for the child without a nurse—how old is he now?"

"Almost two, he is."

"It was dreadful about his mother."

"And just as bad about the lad's father." Dora uttered a long drawn-out sigh, as if the problem was not even one to be discussed with words. "Why, in all this time," she continued, "he is still no closer to accepting her death than the week after she left us. I begin to wonder if he ever will."

"At least he has his child to console him."

"That's the worst of it! He will have nothing to do with the child. Days on end pass before he even sets eyes on the little fellow. I have never once seen him pick up the child and hold him, even for just a moment. It just breaks my heart, Mrs. Gilchrist. The two of them together, father and son, are going to pine away to nothing if something isn't done!"

Emily shook her head sadly, the dismay she felt in her compassionate heart mirrored in her soft eyes.

"That's why the first nurse left," Dora continued. "She couldn't take the dispiriting silence around the place and the mournful look in the baby's eyes. It's as if the child can *feel* what's happening around him, Mrs. Gilchrist, even though he is too young to understand it."

"I don't doubt it," returned Emily. "God has endowed children with extra senses we know nothing of. I'm sure the poor young fellow feels perfectly well the loss of his mother and his father's depression."

"Well, we've been through three nurses already. The second took the laird to task about spending more time with the lad. He flew into such a rage that he fired her on the spot. But it hardly mattered. She was about to give notice anyway. She had as much as told me so herself. But poor Mrs. Gordon—she's the one who just left, as sweet and soft-spoken a woman as you'd hope to find. She was moving things about in the nursery—she had purchased a larger wardrobe, you know, and was having the old one removed. The laird came upon the commotion and fairly exploded. You see, everything in the room had been just as Lady Graystone had planned it, and I suppose he was incensed at seeing it tampered with.

"She was all atremble when she packed her bags and walked out—hardly knowing whether to give way to her anger or her terror of the man. Left without even waiting for severance pay."

"I shall remember to keep Aviemere in my prayers," said Emily.

"Of course that is greatly appreciated," Dora returned, helping herself to another of the sweet scones. "But I was hoping you might be able to do something else for us besides."

"Whatever is in my power to do," Emily replied solemnly.

"As I said," Dora proceeded, "I came to Aberdeen in hopes of locating someone who might fill the position of nurse at Avie- mere. My sister mentioned in passing that you had a young girl staying with you who—well, who might possibly be suitable."

"You mean our Jamie?" said Emily, not a little stunned. "I— I don't hardly know what to say—she's never had experience in that sort—I mean, she's but a child and we only just recently—"

"Experience is not the first necessity," broke in Miss Camp- bell. "How old is the girl?"

"Just eighteen."

"A trifle young, perhaps . . ." mused the housekeeper.

"And but a child herself," added Mrs. Gilchrist. "Why we've only just begun to—"

" . . .but not necessarily a disqualifying attribute," her guest went on as if she had not even heard. "I have known cases where an inexperienced young maid, for instance, works out better in the long run than an older woman with many references."

"To speak truthfully, Miss Campbell," said Emily, "I had not even begun to think of Jamie's leaving us."

"Oh, perhaps I misunderstood. I thought you were looking— so you are close to the young girl then, is that it?"

"Very close. She has been as one of the family."

"Hmm," reflected Dora. "Then it seems I could hardly think of splitting you up."

"On the other hand," said Emily, as if reasoning with herself rather than discussing the question with her guest, "what else have we been grooming her for, except to find some way in the world, or rather to find God's way for her? I would enjoy keeping her here forever, but that would not be in her best interests. Perhaps this is God's way of opening a door into her future that would make a life possible for her which I could never provide her."

"Are you saying, then, that you would consider it?"

"It would be a painful parting for me. But in the end it would, of course, be up to her."

"Might I meet the girl?"

"She is out with the children at the moment. Perhaps if you could stay for luncheon, you could see her then."

Dora accepted the invitation gladly, hardly cognizant of Em- ily's subdued mood throughout the remainder of the morning, and in an hour and a half found herself seated in the Gilchrists' parlor once more. This time the slender figure of the dark-haired Jamie rescued from the backstreets of Aberdeen, sat before her.

She is young, Dora thought, *and rather rough around the edges.* After hearing her speech she wondered how she could ever have even considered the idea. Dora herself would certainly never have held the girl's mountain brogue against her, but she was, after all, hiring for one of the most prestigious families in all of Aberdeenshire. The boy would inherit the vast estate and the earldom besides. He would have to be prepared for a society that was obviously foreign to this rough-hewn country girl.

If she could only have known how much improved Jamie's tongue already was, her initial thoughts might have centered more about the girl's quick receptivity and ability to learn. And as she accustomed herself to the sound of the girl's voice, there wasn't such a vast distinction, after all.

She observed as the girl reached over to help cut young Kenny's bread and dried fish into manageable-sized pieces. There was a tenderness in her movements, and it was clear the boy was much taken with her. She got on with each of the other children equally well.

She is sincere and genuine with them, Dora thought. *She loves them, that much is obvious. If only she can learn to be firm when it is demanded of her, too.* Her thoughts strayed back to the lonely little boy at Aviemere who had no one to love him or even care for him. She cared, of course, but she had so many other duties she could not devote to him a fraction of the time he needed.

Someone who cares, who can love him, that's what he needs, thought Dora. And from what she had heard about the orphaned background of this girl at the table with her, she might be just the person who could understand the plight of a lonely two-year-old child. Her heart might be able to reach out to him, from her own experience of pain and loneliness, and give him what no one else—with all the experience anyone might ask for—would be able to. *Yes,* Dora concluded, *she just might be perfect.* Notwithstanding her unpolished mannerisms and the twang of her speech, if she could arrange it satisfactorily with Mrs. Gilchrist, this young Jamie MacLeod would be her new nurse!

Painful partings by now seemed a way of life for Jamie. For the first time in her life, she had found a friendship that went beyond the bounds of blood and kinship. These were, therefore, in certain ways among the most grievous days of her life. But it was a pain not inflicted by death as in times past, but by deep bonds of love, and thus a pain from which growth would emerge.

She had been on the verge of turning down Dora Campbell's offer when young Kenny had burst into the room, all smiles at his latest accomplishment and eager to show it to her. What child could possibly know as much love as he, with such attentive parents and brothers and sisters? What a contrast he made with the lonely baby Miss Campbell had described, the son of an earl! Was it possible she could do something for such a child? Certainly she could care for him and love him as she did Kenny. Might not that be what he needed most, even as she had needed love so desperately when Mrs. Gilchrist found her? Might not this be the Lord's way of allowing her to pass that love on to another?

If Jamie therefore felt led by an invisible hand to accept the position, it was at the same time with a mixture of anticipation and fear, and great regret that she must leave her new friendships. But she was at least able to comfort herself that the parting was not permanent, and that she would be able to see Emily and her family again.

There were a good many tears shed when the day finally came.

"Aberdeen's not so far," said Jamie of the city which had once seemed to her at the end of the rainbow.

"And we often like a visit to the country—" said Emily, but before she could finish her voice caught on a new rush of tears.

She took Jamie's hands in her own.

"I shall miss you so! In my position it is not always easy to have friends, for if the vicar's wife becomes too intimate with one parishioner, another might become jealous. So, Jamie, your friendship has meant more to me than you can know."

"Oh, Emily! You have done so much for me. Just listen to me talk now!"

Both women laughed.

"But we each know God is calling you. I believe He has prepared you for this moment. I have merely been His tool to help get you ready. As much as I hate to see you go, I am convinced that child needs you far more than we do."

"Thank you, Emily. For everything!"

"And you will be seeing your mountain again!"

"Yes," sighed Jamie, "Donachie!"

"It will be like going home for you."

"Perhaps. But without Gran'daddy there . . ."

Her voice trailed off as she fell to musing.

"Who can tell?" she resumed after a moment. "No, I really think this has been more a home to me this past year than—but I don't know. I did love my gran'daddy's cottage. But now that he is gone, I think this is my home now."

They embraced and stood several moments in each other's arms.

At last Jamie stepped back, wiped her eyes again, and turned to climb into the coach that would bear her northwest past Kintore and Inverurie, and then south to Aviemere.

In all their discussions about the change of environment for Jamie, both she and Emily had thought only of the Graystone child and his lonely need. But now as she sat silently on her way out of Aberdeen, Jamie's thoughts turned at last to the enigmatic laird of Aviemere. Perhaps if the specter of his unknown face had come to mind earlier, her thoughts might have been far different.

But it is doubtful she would have, even then, done other than she was doing, for she was set on a course not of her own design. And recognizing the hand of the Designer, she could not have refused.

PART IV

Aviemere

CHAPTER TWENTY-ONE

A New Home

Jamie breathed in a sharp breath at the sight before her. Her eyes had never beheld such a place! It seemed like a castle from one of the fairy tales she had often read to the Gilchrist children.

Constructed in the late 16th century, its Tudor design reflected the grace and elegance that had by that time begun to replace the grim, stone defensive towers of earlier centuries. Built in the shape of an upper case *E* as was so common in those Elizabethan times, it boasted large windows, a many-gabled roof, and expansive green lawns. At that moment, of course, Jamie was unable to see the three wings of the *E* as they spread out behind the impressive face of the mansion, but between each wing were some of the finest flowered courtyards in all of Scotland—rivaling the gardens of Pitmedden and the grounds of Castle Crathes.

Dora, who had accompanied Jamie from Aberdeen, led the way boldly to the door, recessed in an arched entryway, intricately carved with Dutch scrolls and what Jamie took for the Graystone coat of arms: a rising falcon bearing in its deadly talon a single olive branch with the words engraved above it—*Aut pax aut bellum*.

It was an imposing first impression, and Jamie swallowed hard. There was certainly very little about the place that seemed cheery. How appropriate the name *Graystone* seemed for the family above whose granite lintel loomed the words, "Either peace or war." Thoughts of her new employer, which she had tried to push from her mind, now crowded in with full force. She could only hope he was not as uncompromising as his ancestors. Yet nothing she had heard thus far tended to give her much expectation to the contrary.

Dora beckoned her to follow, and she stepped resolutely forward behind the housekeeper. *Now is no time to weaken*, she told herself. The decision had been made, and it would remain the right decision no matter what she encountered behind that massive oak door!

While Dora led the way, Jamie made her own quick appraisal of her new surroundings. Molded ceilings and carved woodwork enriched every room, most of which, especially those facing the side of the courtyard, tended to be light and colorful. The furnishings were a mixture of Queen Anne and later Tudor—a few originals, many replicas—and it was obvious that an experienced hand had set it all in place. Jamie wondered if this had been the work of the late Lady Olivia Graystone, of whom Miss Campbell had told her a little. Surely all this was here before her time! Yet a woman whose death had so shaken her husband must have left an indelible mark in many ways, whether the furnishings and decor were original to her or not.

All at once Jamie's thoughts turned to the baby, Master Andrew Graystone, and she knew what she must do before anything else.

"Miss Campbell," she said, her voice ringing unnaturally in the great hall through which they were passing, "when will I be able to see the baby?"

"Let's get you settled in your room first," the housekeeper replied. "I hope you won't mind the old nurse's. It's near the nursery and is quite comfortable, really, and has something of a view."

"Whatever you think is best, mem."

"And then I suppose Lord Graystone will want an interview with you."

Jamie did not reply, but Dora noted the draining of color from her face.

"Now, now, Jamie, dear," she said, "you've nothing to worry about. He's—"

She paused to clear her throat. "Well," she went on, "he generally puts faith in my expertise where household matters are concerned."

Jamie smiled wanly.

"When will I see him?" she asked.

"Generally the laird consults with the staff just before dinner, so I expect it will be then, unless he sends for you earlier."

"That's some time away, isn't it?"

Dora smiled. "You're anxious to see the child, aren't you? I can tell."

Jamie nodded.

"Then come along. I see no harm in it. And by the time we finish in the nursery, your things will have been deposited in your room and then you can rest before dinner."

Jamie's anticipation mounted as they climbed the wide stairway. When they reached the nursery, Dora opened the door without hesitation. A housemaid stood and greeted them when they entered.

"Welcome back, Miss Campbell!" she said, grasping the housekeeper's hand warmly.

"I'm happy to be back," replied Dora. "But it looks as if we weren't expected. No one met us at the village. I hope the laird received my letter."

"He did. And I'm sure Sid was planning to meet you, but he's been doubling up on his work since the new groom quit."

"No matter!" Dora replied in her perpetually breathless tone. "Let me introduce our new nurse."

Jamie was hardly concentrating on the conversation, for her eyes had been focused on the yellow-haired child sitting on a silken coverlet playing with some brightly colored blocks in the center of the room. His blue eyes turned toward her as she drew nearer. With no change in his expression, he held out a block to her. She stooped down and took it from his hand.

"Thank you," she said quietly.

"Tank you," he replied in a babyish mimicking of her words.

Jamie laughed, and he handed her another and the same ritual was repeated. The desire was nearly overpowering to take him, then and there, into her arms, but she held back, not wanting to frighten him.

"That's our new nurse," said Dora with a laugh. "Already absorbed in her duties."

Jamie turned toward the older women. "He's wonderful!" she exclaimed.

"That he is," agreed the maid proudly.

"This is Jamie MacLeod, Bea."

Jamie stood and shook the maid's hand.

"Bea is our upstairs maid," Dora explained. "She's been helping with the boy since the last nurse left."

"I'm glad to meet you, Jamie," said Bea. "My old bones aren't much up to chasing around such a little ball of fire."

She paused a moment, then added thoughtfully, "MacLeod? The name sounds familiar."

"She grew up on Donachie," Dora answered for her.

"Ah . . ." was the maid's only further response. The way her voice trailed away inquisitively, she seemed hardly satisfied, but willing for the moment to leave it at that.

"It's about time for Andrew's nap, isn't it?" asked Dora.

"Aye."

"May I put him to bed?" asked Jamie.

"He's your charge now, Jamie!" replied Bea. "He'll want the blue knitted blanket, not the silky one, and the stuffed toy. I'll bring him up a bottle of warm milk."

"I'll be back to take you to your room in a few minutes," said Dora as she and the maid made their departures.

At last Jamie was alone with Andrew. She stood bewildered for a moment wondering what to do first. The youngster seemed perfectly at ease among so many different sets of hands trying to care for him. What would he think now that she was in charge of feeding him, bathing him, walking with him, playing with him, loving him? Would he even understand the change?

Just as Jamie stooped down again, little Andrew decided to stand. Once on his feet he scurried over to the side of the room where a rocking chair held his special toy animal. He pulled it from its perch and into his arms.

"Baba!" he said with an impish smile.

"Is that your baby?" Jamie asked. "He's a fine looking fellow. What's his name?"

"Baba."

"I see. My name's Jamie."

"Mamie," repeated the toddler.

Jamie laughed. "You talk very well, Andrew. Much better than I did a year ago!"

She reached out to touch the soft toy, but Andrew pulled back sharply, and his angelic face immediately turned sour.

"Baba mine!" he informed her with all the uncompromising force of his ancestors who, as their coat of arms informed all guests, would stand for nothing but peace or war.

Almost the same minute Bea returned with the warmed bottle of milk.

"Time for *night-night*," she said cheerfully.

"Ni-ni," Andrew copied.

"Well, go ahead, lass," said Bea, turning to Jamie.

Jamie bent over to take hold of him, but she barely had her hands around his chubby waist when he wriggled free and ran to Bea. He held his arms up over his head saying, "Ni-ni, Bee-bee."

She gave a half smile in Jamie's direction. "I'm sorry, miss. I suppose these things take a day or two. He'll be used to you in no time, I'm sure."

"I understand," replied Jamie, concealing whatever disappointment she felt at the rebuff.

By evening the relationship with the child had made what Jamie considered fine progress. Bea had not been back, and Jamie had occupied Andrew after his nap and had fed him his dinner. When bedtime came, she rocked him to sleep with his Baba clutched tightly in his arms. As she laid the sleeping boy in his bed, she watched him for several long moments. In one arm he still held his Baba, and in the other his fuzzy blue blanket pulled high up against his sleeping face. He looked contented enough, she thought, hardly like the sad and lonely child she was led to believe she would find. Had the trouble here been exaggerated? Perhaps she would know more about the child after meeting his father.

Which reminded her—the interview with Lord Graystone could come at any moment!

She left the nursery immediately for her own room, there to await her summons from the laird of Aviemere.

Once there she roamed aimlessly about, rearranging some of the things she had earlier unpacked. Her few belongings filled only two drawers in the spacious dresser. Another chest stood on the opposite side of the room alongside a wardrobe which held her three dresses—all gifts from Emily. It was a nice room, she supposed, every bit as nice as hers at the Gilchrists—though a little colder. Perhaps that was simply because she was not yet at home here. Had she seen any of the guest rooms in the mansion, she would have realized just how simple her living accommodations really were. But Jamie was used to humble surroundings. This was luxury indeed alongside Sadie Malone's second-floor room where she had spent her first days in Aberdeen.

She sighed. In time she would no doubt feel the same about this room in Aviemere as she had come to feel about her home in Aberdeen at the Gilchrists.

But first she must meet the master of this estate. And she

could not quite help trembling a bit at the thought.

She walked slowly over to the large multi-paned window overlooking one of the lovely gardens in the courtyard below. The sky was still as light as midafternoon, though the day's activities had begun to draw to a close. A great lawn stretched out beyond the courtyard, and beyond it she thought she could just make out a low dark line that must be a wood, or perhaps an orchard. She strained to see the dim outline of Donachie, but the wings of the mansion blocked a clear view. She did not know in which direction George Ellice's home lay; she had heard no mention of him. He was the one person who could tell her what had befallen her former home and her grandfather's animals. She must see him one day soon.

She walked idly about, sat down and tried to concentrate on a book, but with no success.

Still no summons came.

At length, exhausted from traveling and the attempt to adjust to the newness of her surroundings, Jamie fell asleep, and remained so until Miss Campbell had to rouse her for supper in the servants' quarters. After a rather hurried meal, she returned to her room and again fell asleep, and slept until morning.

The master's summons did not come until she had been at Aviemere for three days.

CHAPTER TWENTY-TWO

The Master of Aviemere

Jamie was to meet Edward Graystone in the library at precisely seven o'clock.

As she approached the richly carved double walnut doors, her thudding heart seemed to roar in her ears and she could not stop her hands from trembling slightly. She tried clutching them tightly together, but there was nothing she could do about her racing heart. Her timid knock seemed to fall dead on the thick wood and she doubted the sound had even penetrated into the room. But just as she reached up to try again the door was opened by the tall, lean figure of the head butler, Cameron Reily. As she stepped meekly into the room, she saw immediately that she would apparently not be alone for the interview. Reily stood aside, expressionless, holding the door as she entered but allowing no eye contact to betray the slightest hint of what she should expect.

Standing in a semicircle around a massive wood desk were several other of the household staff. In addition to the dour-faced old butler, there was Sid MacKay, the stableman whom Jamie had had occasion to meet the previous day. Middle-aged and stockily built, his chief feature seemed to be a great supply of reddish facial hair—thick eyebrows, a long heavy moustache, and sideburns that extended down his cheek to meet the edges of the moustache, covering half his face. Next to MacKay stood a man Jamie immediately recognized as the factor, but his glance toward her told Jamie that Ellice did not recognize her. Completing the small assemblage was Dora Campbell. She smiled in Jamie's direction, helping somewhat to soothe the young girl's apprehension. Jamie walked slowly forward and took her place beside the housekeeper. The laird made no acknowledgment of her arrival.

"Continue with your report, Sid," said the man behind the desk in a deep though somewhat forced voice that gave the impression he would rather not be talking at all.

"Weel, ye lai—weel, sir," answered the stableman, "I suppose the lad were jist too young t' be oot on's ain. He jist didna want t' work, that's a', an' whan I ast him t' muck oot the stalls he . . ."

Jamie paid little heed to MacKay's monotone recital of his problems with the stable help. Instead, she was absorbed in the presence of the man of whom she had been living in fear for three days. He stood, rather than sat, with his feet firmly planted on the floor and his hands grasped behind his back. His stance was nearly as rigid as that of the servants before him. Easily the tallest man in the room, his broad shoulders completed the figure which was imposing indeed. Dressed in a tweed riding habit with tall brown leather boots, he looked as if he would be more comfortable upon his sorrel stallion than in this elegant Tudor library addressing his household staff. Yet his clothes and boots were spotless, unlike those of Ellice and MacKay.

This is Andrew's father, Jamie thought. The impish, round face of the child who had already begun to become her friend came into her mind, with its crop of curly yellow hair, and she tried to detect the similarities between father and son. There were none that she could readily ascertain—at least on the surface. The father's hair was auburn, rather straight, and showing signs that within a few years it might begin to thin on top. In contrast to the clean boots, his face seemed to indicate much time spent out-of-doors, for it was tanned. The expression bore none of the simplicity of the son's, but perhaps in time the child's, too, might harden into the granite-like austerity of the father's. His brow seemed chiseled into a perpetual scowl, and the dark eyes seemed to defy penetration. His look and bearing were the very personification of his name, and Jamie could not keep from wondering if in some mystical way he had not assumed the character of the very stones of granite out of which his home was made, and for which his ancestors had named their estate. From the inanimate strength of his passive bearing, he looked to be between thirty-five and forty, but his troubles had aged him; he was in reality much younger than he appeared, not yet thirty.

Jamie's initial reaction was fear, but it was quickly and unaccountably replaced by something akin to pity welling up in her heart. She could tell the man before her had borne much in his life. Intuitively she sensed that the granite features which tried to turn a brave face toward life's heartaches must one day give way and crumble beneath his feet. And that would indeed be a terrible day for one such as this, whose emotions were hidden so far in the depths of his being.

Her thoughts had no liberty to progress further, however, for the moment she heard the deep voice speak her own name, the initial dread returned tenfold upon her.

"Are you ready with your report, Miss MacLeod?" boomed the voice of Edward Graystone. There were no words of introduction or welcome.

Her voice trembled as she spoke.

"Aye . . . I mean, yes, sir—that is, your Lordship . . ."

She stopped, feeling the redness flood her face.

"Continue," he said, taking no note of her discomfiture.

"Master Andrew is doin' weel," Jamie went on nervously, trying to force calmness into her tone. "He seems t' be adjustin' t' the change in nurses. He's eatin' jist fine; he has been a wee bit fussy today, but that's nae doobt frae—"

"Has he any needs?" the laird cut in gruffly.

"Needs?"

"Yes," he answered a little impatiently. "The factor and I shall be going into Aberdeen tomorrow, and it is customary for the senior staff to give me lists of purchases to be made. As I am accompanying the factor on this occasion, I will see to it personally. You are in charge of the nursery. Therefore, it is your responsibility to assess the boy's needs and make me aware of them."

"I will tend to it this evening," Jamie replied, her nerves as well as her tongue calming somewhat. "I'll give it to Miss Campbell in the morning."

"I shall be leaving well before that. Leave the list with Miss Campbell tonight and she will see that it gets to me."

"Yes, your Lordship."

His eyes narrowed slightly at her words. She had not yet noticed that rarely did anyone address him by his title, and when they did the words usually met with a similarly odd reaction in his face.

He then turned his gaze in turn upon each of the others who had not yet been questioned, and Jamie breathed an inward sigh of relief. It did not strike Jamie as curious that the man seemed to care nothing about her background, although he was entrusting his very son to her care. For the present she had too many other things on her mind. But such questions would eventually come to her, giving her cause to wonder just what this man felt for his own son—if anything, for he seemed to treat his son's care with the same emotionless concern for mere business that he did his horses.

Suddenly Jamie realized they were being dismissed. Coming to herself, she also realized her cheeks were still burning. With a flicker of fear, she hoped the man had not noticed. He said not another word to her, and soon she found herself standing out in the hall with the others. The library doors swung closed, and MacKay and George Ellice immediately turned down the corridor without a word.

Staring at the closed library doors, Jamie could not keep her mind from wondering what a man like the laird was doing now that he was alone. Perhaps he had dropped limply back into the great leather chair, at last relaxing the tough exterior stance of the powerful laird. Or had he walked around his desk to the adjacent wall lined with bookshelves, there to choose a book to read before dinner—perhaps *Ivanhoe* or *A Midsummer Night's Dream* or a selection from Burns?

Yet as much as she tried to picture the taut, uncompromising figure as turning toward some more relaxed and human pursuit, the image remained in her mind of the only posture she had seen him in. For all she knew he still stood planted firmly behind that desk, hands gripped at his back, dark gaze fixed forward. What was he seeing now? Now that the faces before him were gone, upon what distant images were those penetrating eyes focused?

No, she thought, *he does not look like his son*. But there was something she had seen in him, something she could not quite identify, something—

Suddenly she remembered whom the man *did* look like!

She had forgotten until now. There had been a black-cloaked man, an awesome presence, stepping from a gleaming black carriage drawn by two lively chestnuts . . .

With a shudder at the remembrance of that childhood memory, she forced herself back to the present and sought out Dora's friendly company as they returned to their quarters.

Chapter Twenty-three

An Afternoon's Excursion

Several days later Jamie found an opportunity to renew her acquaintance with George Ellice when the factor had returned from Aberdeen and was again at the house.

"I thought I saw something in your eyes I knew!" he said upon discovering that the new nurse was none other than Finlay MacLeod's own granddaughter. "But I swear, I never would have known you!"

The change was indeed an astounding one, for all George Ellice could recall from his past visits up the mountain was a smudge-faced little girl who had often served him tea in the old stone cottage. And now here stood facing him, if not a full-grown woman, certainly very nearly one. *Why, she even speaks with a degree of refinement!* he said to himself.

Most anxious to learn what had become of her in the time since her departure from the region, he asked if she could come for a visit. "And I, or rather my wife, will serve *you* tea this time."

"I will look forward to that," replied Jamie.

It came, therefore, as no surprise when she received an invitation three days later. She bundled up little Andrew, sought out Sid, who was harnessing the horses to the wagon for a ride into the village, asked if she might have a ride to the factor's cottage with him. Soon she was seated beside the tight-lipped groom bouncing down the road away from the mansion.

The ride from the house to the factor's cottage was lovely, especially in the afternoon summer sun. The road that wound toward the village was lined with tall birch trees, whose leaves were just beginning to show signs of approaching autumn. The drive through the immediate grounds of the estate was about three-quarters of a mile long. At that distance stood a massive

iron gate and a small gate house. Beyond the gate ran the chief
road connecting Aboyne and Rhynie. MacKay would take this
road to the right to reach the village. But before he did, some
200 yards before reaching the gate house, he led his team off the
tree-lined estate drive to the right where, a short distance away,
was located the factor's home. Stretching out on either side of
them Jamie could see gentle green hillsides, and beyond them
vast acres of wheat and barley and oats.

In less than ten minutes they were pulling up before the Ellice
cottage, a gray stone affair with a slate roof and a neatly clipped,
fenced yard. George was just coming from the small equipment
shed to the side of the house as they approached, and walked
forward to greet Jamie.

"Welcome to you, lass!" he called.

Returning the greeting, Jamie stepped down from the wagon
and let Sid hand Andrew down to her. Thanking him, he turned
his team around and then urged them on down the road.

"Come in, come in!" said Ellice as Jamie stepped onto the
porch. He seemed very enthusiastic about their visitor. "Mrs.
Ellice," he called inside, "our guest is here!"

His words were hardly necessary, for she was already less
than a pace from the door herself.

"Glad to have you, Jamie," she replied. "It is all right with
you if I call you Jamie, isn't it? We're rather informal in our
home."

"Oh, yes, of course," Jamie replied. "I am so glad to meet
you at last, Mrs. Ellice."

The factor's wife was short like her husband, but a good deal
rounder. Her gray hair was braided and wrapped around her
head, framing a round, deeply creased face.

"And you brought the bairn, too!" exclaimed Mrs. Ellice,
whom Jamie soon found to be delightfully animated and ex-
pressive. "I must hold him! Oh! but there's the kettle. Let me
get tea ready first!" She bustled to the stove but continued to
chatter away.

At length the three were sitting around the table partaking
of tea and oatcakes, and a special shortbread Mrs. Ellice had
prepared for the occasion. Andrew tried to grab at everything in
sight and quickly lost interest in his oatcake for the greater fascination of flatware and china. Finally Mrs. Ellice took him in
her eager arms.

With his wife's attention thus diverted, the quieter George

seemed to decide he could join the conversation.

"You caused a bit of a stir up here last winter, you know," he said. "I had given you up for dead."

"I didn't know anyone paid much attention to us up on the mountain."

"Well, that may have been true to a degree. Still, when everyone was missing there was considerable speculation about what had happened. We all just assumed you'd somehow been lost in the storm."

"I nearly was," said Jamie.

"When your grandfather didn't come down at his usual time for supplies, and after the weather had cleared a bit, I sent two of the younger fellows up and they found not a soul. We thought the worst, of course, but could do nothing till the snow melted. When spring came we found not a trace, except what we thought might have been a grave. What actually happened?"

Jamie proceeded to tell them of her grandfather's death, of her decision to leave Donachie, and her eventual rescue by Robbie Taggart.

"I was on my way here, to your house," Jamie explained. "I had planned to come and tell you everything. But I wasn't quite sure of my way, and then the blizzard came up all of a sudden and I lost my bearings, and by the time Robbie found me, he said I was clear over on the wrong side of the mountain. I don't even know where I was. I'm sorry for the trouble I caused."

"Considering how severe the storm was," said Ellice, "I'm only glad you are safe. Miraculously, we only lost a few sheep. Your cow was fine. And it was probably well you left when you did, for we truly might have lost you if you had stayed, especially alone. The blizzard got worse and worse for several days after that. It was one of the worst storms in several years."

"Things seem to have turned out all right for you," said his wife.

"I should say!" said George, still astonished at the change that had come over her. "I tell you, Jamie MacLeod, I would not have recognized you had I seen you walking down the lane out in front of the house here. I did not know you when you came into the library the other day, though there was something curious about you I couldn't put my finger on. Even when I heard the name it didn't register! You've really changed, grown."

Jamie laughed. "Well, thank you. That's very kind of you!"

"It's more than the speech, though that's part of it. Someone must have taken great pains to help you."

"Yes. Mrs. Gilchrist in Aberdeen took me under her wing, you might say."

"Well, she did her job well. There's a certain refinement, a—"

"Now, George," interrupted Mrs. Ellice, "that's enough. You'll embarrass the poor girl!"

Jamie laughed again. "Let's just say the Lord has been with me all the way, even when I didn't know it, leading me in the ways He wanted me to go."

"Well, I'm glad He sent you back here," said Mrs. Ellice. "It is fitting that one of Aviemere's own should be caring for the boy. Does the laird know of your previous connection with the estate?"

"I don't know. I suppose not, if you didn't even know."

"It's a shame he doesn't take more interest in the lad," said the factor's wife, "although I'm sure he has his reasons."

"Does he blame the child for the mother's death?" asked Jamie. "She did die in childbirth, isn't that what Miss Campbell told me?"

"Aye. And that's what we're thinking," replied Ellice. "But who can say for sure about such things? He's very close-mouthed about himself, the laird is. Speaks of nothing but business, even to me, and there's not many closer to him than I am. Shed not a tear (at least that anyone saw) when his wife died. He was always a private person, even before her death. But afterward, he turned into himself and shut out the whole world. Been that way now for almost two years. You can just see the stiffness and the turmoil about him just to look at the man."

"The man's in pain, no doubt about that," added Mrs. Ellice. "But 'tis more than that."

"Why do you say that?" asked Jamie, her curiosity about the laird rising steadily.

"Can't put my finger on it exactly," she replied. "But I've been around stoic men before. Most men are stoic in one way or another—why, heaven knows, I'm even married to one!"

She laughed and patted her husband's shoulder affectionately.

Jamie smiled. The camaraderie between the pair was apparent, and reminded her vaguely of the loving relationships in the Gilchrist home.

"Even the most stoic of men," she went on, "manage to let it out one way or another. But not the laird—except when his wife was alive. But even then . . . well, I can't explain it. I don't even know myself. There's just more there than meets the eye, as they say. I'm sure of it."

"Let's not spread any doubts about the laird," chided her husband gently.

"I wouldn't dream of doing that!" Mrs. Ellice returned quickly. "But don't you think Jamie ought to know these things, caring for the lad and all? He's the one who suffers the most—poor thing! Why, Jamie, maybe you're the one to break through to the man."

"Oh, I doubt that!" said Jamie, shuddering as she recalled the intractable stare of the laird.

Two hours later, as Jamie walked back to the mansion with little Andrew, her mind was filled with the many thoughts and emotions the visit had evoked. As she considered the laird, she hardly knew whether to feel pity or anger. Then the words of the factor's wife came back to her, and she found herself wondering whether anyone would ever be able to break through the man's intimidating presence. *A meek girl like me . . . why, I'd be the last person to do that*, she mused with a smile.

But she *did* know who could break through! Yet since first meeting him she had not once remembered to take the laird to the One who could help him. So as she walked along, with the laird's son toddling ahead of her, she silently lifted up a prayer to the God whom she knew would somehow reach the master of Aviemere.

Her thoughts then turned to her grandfather. Speaking about him with George Ellice had not been easy. Several times her voice caught on rising tears. It had been just less than a year since her grandfather's death, but it seemed much longer. So much had happened. She had grown by years, not months. She had been but a child; now she was nearly a woman, with a child in her care—the child of the laird upon whose land she and her grandfather had toiled for so many years on Donachie! But the year had passed quickly, and she realized now that much of the old aching was still there. She had only glossed over it by not thinking of it. How she missed him!

And she missed Robbie Taggart!

If she had thought of him more frequently than her grandfather, perhaps it was because there was still a hope she might see him again. She had learned a little about love since seeing him last, especially from talks with Emily. And whether he could ever love her or not, she found herself longing for the sight of his face. But Emily had cautioned her that gratitude and friendship could occasionally get confused with love between a man and a woman.

Oh, there was so much she still had to learn! Life could be so confusing! How was one to know what true love really was? Had she loved Robbie? Could she love him again? The memory of his laughing eyes and warm voice still gave her a thrill. But he had been around the world, and she had never even set eyes on a city the size of Aberdeen! What must he have thought of her?

Yes, I have changed since then, Jamie mused. *But will that be enough? And what will it matter if we never meet again?*

So deep were her thoughts that she took no note of the woman approaching from among the trees on the side of the road.

"Jamie . . . Jamie MacLeod?" the woman called, approaching with a nervous gait, as if she did not want to be seen.

Jamie stopped and turned, puzzled. She did not recognize the woman, and her appearance told her she could have nothing to do with the estate. The woman came closer, glancing about nervously. An odd glint in her eyes put Jamie immediately on her guard, and she quickly caught Andrew up in her arms.

"Jamie MacLeod?" the woman repeated, coming now quite near. From her clothing Jamie could see she must be a poor tenant or worker in the village.

"Aye," Jamie replied hesitantly.

"Gilbert MacLeod's daughter?"

"Aye," repeated Jamie, trying to keep her voice level, though by now her heart was pounding in the presence of the mysterious woman.

"I thocht so, frae my sister's description o' ye, but I wadna o' kenned ye frae what I knew o' ye afore."

"Before?" said Jamie, curious but still hesitant.

" 'Tis ten years an' more syne I last seen ye—ye dinna remember, do ye?" She continued on without waiting for a response. " 'Course ye dinna! Ye couldna. What were ye, six or seven then?"

"You mentioned my father?"

"Aye, I did, lass! We was frien's, yer father an' me an' my husband."

"You knew him . . . well?" asked Jamie, taking a step closer and beginning to forget her previous caution of this rather fright-ful looking woman. She was eager to hear anything about her father.

"We did. An' ye yersel' supped at my ain table mony a time, though I can see ye dinna remember. The name's Iona Lundie."

She held out her hand and smiled, but it was evident that her lips were unaccustomed to the exercise.

Jamie took the hand. It was cool and limp. Jamie seized that brief moment of contact to quickly scan the face of this stranger who claimed to be an old friend. It was the face of a woman past middle age, lean and drawn—almost haggard—in appearance. The years had plainly taken their toll. Her eyes were pale gray, like the slate of George Ellice's roof, with a cavernous look en-circled by dark flesh. She looked worn. But there was another something in her eyes, the same something that had caused Jamie to hold back at first. Jamie could only describe them as eyes that, if they had once known, seemed now to have forgotten the meaning of love or happiness.

"Can I walk wi' ye part way up t' the hoose?" asked Iona Lundie, " 'cept I mustn't gae so far as t' be seen."

"Yes, of course," answered Jamie, "but why can't you be seen?"

"I came here t' catch sicht o' yersel', t' see if it was true. But the rest o' the eyes here be none too frien'ly toward Iona Lun-die!"

Jamie did not reply, and they resumed their walk toward the house, but at a slower pace. Jamie continued to hold Andrew, who no longer seemed to want to get down.

"So ye're workin' fer the laird, noo, are ye?"

Jamie nodded.

"Weel, I guess we all maun do what we can t' eat." There was definite derision in her tone, but Jamie couldn't tell whether it was aimed at her or the laird.

"I—I had so few other opportunities that I—" said Jamie, not quite knowing how to reply to the gruff woman, but she was cut off.

"An' ye think ye'll be happy here?" she said.

"I . . . I don't know. It is rather lonely, I suppose, but I only just arrived."

"Happiness!" said Mrs. Lundie, almost to herself. "It's been sae lang syne I e'en heard the word, I dinna e'en ken the meanin' o' it!"

"You're not happy here?" queried Jamie tentatively.

"Ha, ha!" barked out Lundie's widow with a laugh completely devoid of any merriment. Then her eyes narrowed, stopping Jamie in her tracks. The woman put a hand on Jamie's arm and spoke in a low tone with the same intensity in her gaze. "After what *they* did? I'll ne'er be happy until I see every mother's son o' them cold in their graves!" Her eyes dropped to the child in Jamie's arms and she pierced Andrew with such an awful stare that Jamie clutched him almost painfully to her as if to keep away a silent incantation being leveled by her evil eyes against the heir of Graystone.

"I'm—I'm sorry," faltered Jamie. "Your life must have—I'm sorry it's been so painful. But how can you speak so—"

"Do ye ken onythin' aboot the Graystones?" she asked piercingly.

"Very little, I suppose."

"Yer father told ye nothin'?"

"About the Graystones? No—I—I don't understand. What would my father have had to do with them?"

"They was yer father's neighbors! Ain't that eneuch!"

"Neighbors!" But even as she spoke the word, a dozen images flooded Jamie's mind. Bits and pieces from an early childhood that had no more coherence in her blurred memory than a shadowy dream—the hazy face of her father filled with frustration and disappointment, an impressive stone house, the swinging sign of a rearing stallion, terrible rain pelting a little girl, and over it all the spectre of a man in a black cloak whose face was obscured from her vision.

They had been landowners then! It had always been her daddy's dream! Why was there such a look of sorrow on his face—sorrow mingled with anger? But neighbors to Aviemere? It wasn't possible. Hadn't they lived on the other side of the village? But now it was all growing so confused!

"We—we did have land then . . ." was all Jamie could get past her suddenly very dry throat.

"On the veery borders o' Aviemere," said Iona. "Land which them cursed Graystones staelt frae yer father, mark my words! They forced an' feared him intil bankrupcie, an' then teuk his land whan it were dirt chepe! Staelt it frae him, they did! Yer father wudna lift sae much as a finger t' fecht 'em. But nae my Freddie! He was a bonnie fechter, he was, an' was aboot t' gie 'em what they deser'ed! But they got til him first. Killed him! Do ye unnerstan'—they killed my Freddie! Then yer ain father went recht after him. They ne'er got what they deser'ed—nae yet!"

They had drawn within sight of the house. As much as she wanted to know about her father, all Jamie could think of was getting away from this woman. She did not want to hear any more from such a chilling voice! And the woman's eyes looked at Andrew as if—

She just wanted to get away! What were those horrible things she had said? How could it—but it was all so blurry and confusing!

"I've got to go now," she said, keeping on toward the house. "It's—it's time for—"

As she spoke she turned, then said nothing more.

Iona Lundie was already yards away, disappearing through the trees that bordered the drive. She had no intention of going any nearer to the home of the lairds of Aviemere.

CHAPTER TWENTY FOUR

Edward Graystone

The croft was by all appearances one of the poorest, if not *the* poorest, on the entire Aviemere estate. The front yard, if such it could even be called, was overgrown and even more untidy than the dilapidated cottage itself. The thatch on the roof was uneven and broken, badly in need of repair; gaps could be seen in the walls where the stone had crumbled away with the passage of years and never been replaced.

The three children scampering about the yard in the rags they called clothes would have inspired pity in any man. But the two riders approaching on horseback were there on business, and by necessity of their position had to steel themselves against such reactions as compassion.

George Ellice had allowed such emotions to make him give these tenants more latitude than was prudent. So now the laird himself had found it necessary to step into the situation. Ellice was an honest factor, more scrupulous than most, and certainly more fair and considerate in his dealings with the tenants. Unfortunately, honesty and fairness were not the only attributes required in a factor, especially when they extended themselves toward the tenants to the expense of the laird. Thus Ellice had, against his basic nature perhaps, tried to balance these with an appropriate amount of firmness. All told, over the years, he had been able to extract rents from the most stubborn while still maintaining the respect and goodwill of most of the locals.

Yet his weakness was always evident in such hard-luck cases as the one they now found it necessary to confront. The MacRaes were two quarters in arrears with their rents. And the situation continued to worsen. With winter looming ahead, something had to be done quickly; there were no signs of improvement. At first Jimmy MacRae, who had come into the croft some two years earlier with the death of his father, had tried to make a go of it. If his children were fed scantily, he yet paid his rent on time. If the cottage was drafty, he was yet able to cut enough peats in the surrounding hills to make it through the winter. But his croft was situated on hard, rocky, unmanageable land on the edge of the moor. Not only did it take patience and hard work to coax any kind of profit from such ground, it took a good deal of luck besides. And luck had not gone with Jimmy MacRae. He was willing to work, but when times became hard last winter after a scant autumn's harvest, he found the laird an unbending man. As things worsened, he had lost his initial enthusiasm. His will to work followed his prudence with finances, and things went from bad to worse. He was a defeated man, knowing he had failed his family. But that knowledge only dug him deeper into the hole of his despair. Most of his time these days was spent in the village at The Ebony Stallion, and his presence on the croft was especially scarce when collection day came around.

Today the laird hoped to catch him unawares. Reliable information told him that he was sure to be home because his wife was ill with a fever. It being a week before the normal date for collections, no one would be looking for them yet. The laird had summoned the factor to the mansion, told him of his plan, and they were on the road within the hour. The fact that the wife was sick only heightened the difficulty in the factor's mind of the upcoming interview. Perhaps the more imposing stance of the laird could extract some sort of settlement of the situation, short of eviction.

The laird's sorrel stallion pranced powerfully beside the factor's plain chestnut. It seemed to give added emphasis to the strength and might represented by the Graystone name itself.

The children scattered as the horses trotted into the unkempt yard. The sound alone should have brought someone to the door of the hovel or from the byre attached to the back wall. But except for the noise of disappearing children and the snorting and pawing of the animals, all remained still and quiet.

The laird and factor exchanged glances. Then Ellice, knowing his duty as spokesman for the laird, called out.

"MacRae, are you about!"

There was no answer.

Ellice wished fervently that the man would show his face so they could have it out and get it over with. This was painful enough, without having to search for the man!

"MacRae!" Edward Graystone's deep voice cut into the silence.

Another moment passed. All the children had by now found hiding places in the byre or in the tall scraggly brush behind the cottage. All was dead still. Slowly the door of the house creaked open. At first no face could be seen, then slowly Jimmy MacRae stepped out into the morning light.

He looked sheepishly up at his two callers, but his eyes could not meet Graystone's intense gaze.

"We have business with you, MacRae," said Graystone.

"Aye, it appears t' be so," replied MacRae, a brawny young man who at that moment looked very small before the mighty sorrel and its master.

"What will be done about it?" asked Graystone, his tone even and unflinching.

"I dinna ken."

"Are you willing to do something about it?"

"I've tried, yer Lairdship." There was a tremor in his voice as he glanced hastily up at Graystone. "I honestly hae. 'Tis terrible puir lan', this, yer Lairdship."

"Either you are willing to work it, or you are not," replied Graystone dispassionately. "If you are not, I'll find new tenants."

"But we hae nae place t' gang . . ."

"I'm not in the business of handing out charity. As it is, you have been extended well beyond even the most benevolent standards. Most men would have thrown you out months ago. If you demonstrate a willingness to work the land and put your financial affairs in order, then an arrangement can be made. Otherwise, I'll want you out by the end of the month. Either way, no more extensions on mere good faith will be made. Do you understand?"

"Aye. But I dinna ken if I can do it."

"It's your decision."

MacRae stuck his hands in the pockets of his torn trousers and shuffled his feet uncomfortably. Finally, still looking at the ground, he said: "Weel, I'll gi' her anither go."

"Mr. Ellice will discuss our terms with you," Graystone said. Then without another word, and only a brief nod at Ellice, he wheeled his mount around and galloped off.

Graystone headed out to the moor.

His horse was in sore need of exercise. He had spent far too much time indoors in the past months, and the solitary stretch of heath would be the perfect place to take the stallion through his paces. And he and Olivia had never ridden here together, so at least it would carry no bittersweet memories.

He circumvented MacRae's meager fields of barley, then carefully picked his way through a rocky gorge, up the other side onto a small rise, emerging finally on the flat, gray, dreary moor. Even the heather did not seem to want to bloom this year, as if it, too, were still in mourning for the late Lady of Aviemere. He dug his heels into the stallion and rode hard for some time, relishing the chill wind of the overcast day as it whipped in his face. He sucked in great gulps of the air as he rode, the entire setting of the day suiting the caustic attitude in his heart toward life. After a steady gallop he pulled up into a slow canter and bent over and rubbed his mount's sleek reddish-brown neck.

This was what he chose to do over anything else. He should have been doing it more these days! It might have helped ease the pain. It always calmed him to ride over the moors and grassy hills and meadows of his land.

He winced suddenly at the careless thought.

His land!

Though he told them he preferred they not use the title, most of them called him the laird of Aviemere—*Lord Graystone*!

And he no longer made any protest. None but for an inward wince whenever the term was used.

It was not that he did not relish the title. Of all things, it was the thing he wanted most desperately. He cherished the very word. But he knew he was lord of not even the smallest speck of the dirt of Aviemere.

How the longing after it ached within him, for he loved this place as no true lord of it ever had. But he had known almost from the moment of his birth that it would never be his. As the younger son it was simply a fact of his existence that the Graystone heritage—the earldom, the wealth, the mansion, the land, and control of the estate and all its holdings—would one day be his brother's. He himself cared nothing about the power or the prestige, or even the wealth—only the land. And the bitter irony was that his brother cared only for the external trappings of the earldom and cared *nothing* for the land itself.

But Edward had realized that his life was apparently meant to be filled with ironies.

From an early age he had tried to school himself in the facts of his birth. *You will never have Aviemere! You will never have Aviemere!* Over and over he repeated the words to himself. But it did not make his love for the land grow less.

During his childhood and adolescent years he had often been left alone on the estate. His father had always had numerous business deals in hand, had traveled a great deal, and had frequently taken the older brother with him. Edward had at first been left behind simply because he was too young to go. But now he was never quite certain, as he reflected back upon it, whether he had not been invited to accompany them or had simply chosen to stay. Whatever the case, he *had* remained behind, and eventually had had no desire to leave the lovely lands called, some two hundred years earlier by the first earl, *Aviemere*.

He came to relish the freedom of being there alone with only the rather mild supervision of his tutor. Perhaps it was during those times when his surroundings became the sole consolation for a somewhat melancholy nature, that his attachment to the land began to extend its roots into the depths of his subconscious. By the time he was twelve he knew every rock and twig of heather on the place, had bathed or waded in every burn, had thrown rocks from the top of every cliff, and had ridden among all the lower slopes of the great mountain of Donachie which overlooked it all.

His life had been a solitary one, with his tutor and a few animals his only companions. But he had grown fond of such a life, and almost dreaded the return of father and brother. He knew the land, its delicacies, its dangers, and its needs better than either of them, and gradually those left in charge in their absence came to him for counsel and decisions. Yet his father and brother never knew how totally and how competently he managed their affairs during their frequent journeys to the south or abroad. And perhaps that was one of the reasons it galled him that they left him completely out of their discussions about the estate.

"No need to worry yourself about these things," his father would say as he attempted to be a part of decisions, which he felt he should have a voice in. "Go and amuse yourself." What had been left unsaid was the implication that, as the land would be his brother's, what weight could a younger brother's opinion have, anyway?

Thus his bitterness first began to grow. What amusement

could there be aside from the land? This was not only his home, this was his life, his dream, his heart, his desire. Yet they shut him out like a mere servant! If he occasionally felt an inward compunction at his treatment of a poor tenant such as MacRae, the hardness that had almost grown over his once tender heart would say that he was doing nothing but what his father would have done, or what his brother would do if he were here. What did it matter anyway? If his father was going to cast him adrift, why should his heart bleed for the sake of some lazy bounder who refused to work the land? In the end MacRae would be better off than he! At least he had no dreams that had been cruelly dashed on gray granite slopes of Donachie!

In the bitterness of his heart he could not see that all men have dreams—men high on the social scale like the lairds of Aviemere, *and* men at the bottom, like Jimmy MacRae and Gilbert MacLeod. Neither could he see that when, in their reckless pursuit of mammon, men in high places dash the fortunes and hopes of those under them, the accountability in which they are held is much greater. As his father would one day have to answer for his treatment of Gilbert MacLeod, so too would Edward Graystone have to one day answer for the future of Jimmy MacRae. Whether he was laird or caretaker mattered not a bit.

But fortunately for both laird and crofter, that future still hung in the balance. The shell had closed about Edward's heart, but the membrane was still pliable in places and had not yet solidified into irredeemable hardness. Even as he rode, tiny arrows of compunction were stinging him, and occasionally one was able to penetrate. He could not quite manage to get the face of MacRae out of his mind's eye. And that, of course, was the most healthy sign of all.

When Edward's father, Mackensie Graystone, died, the transfer of the property and title was no less painful for the second son than had been inevitable. But what cut the deepest was the fact that the heir, Derek Graystone, now the earl of Aviemere, was not even present to accept his prize! An officer in the 11th Cavalry Battalion, stationed in the Transvaal in South Africa, he saw no reason to leave his duties. The solicitors could handle all the legalities.

Edward still remembered verbatim the hastily scribbled note he had received from his older brother: "Could you watch over things in my absence? For your services, I've arranged for the solicitors to double the annual allowance specified by our father in his will. . . ."

Watch over things! As if he had not been doing that very thing for years! And without their even knowing . . . without so much as passing consideration by his father in the apportionment of his property!

So now he was not only to be treated like a common servant, he was being paid like one as well! His pride nearly forced him to leave then and there. But his deep attachment to the estate could not let him. He could stand being called Lord Graystone even if he knew it was an empty, meaningless epithet; he could bear the humiliation of receiving his monthly allowance as a *salary* along with all the other hired servants; he could bear the bitterness of knowing his father had loved his brother more—*as long as he was not forced from his land.*

But the circumstances of his disappointments ate away at his heart. As each day passed he wondered how long he would be able to tolerate the sham that his life had become.

Then an old family friend and her niece had come to Aviemere for a visit. She was recuperating from an illness, the doctor had suggested time in the country, and she had written; Edward, being the only Graystone on the premises, had answered, giving his consent, and they had come, the niece acting as both companion and nurse to the elderly Mrs. Lennox.

Showing them every courtesy, at first Edward had paid little attention to Olivia. Having had it bred into him almost from birth that one in his so-called "position" (whether titled or not, he *was* from an old and distinguished Scottish family) was bound to marry *well*—if not into the aristocracy itself, then certainly a *lady* of substance from a family of some renown. And even if his feigned title was but a mockery of the whole hierarchical system, still he could not shake free from the confines of his training as to the correctness of marital alliances. He would vindicate himself in his father's eyes—however his conscious mind would have scoffed at the notion that he still sought the old man's approval!— by marrying above his brother and making something of himself despite their disregard of him!

Therefore he was ripe for the love which began to blossom within him for Olivia, the niece of his father's friend. Her father was a merchant of good family. He could offer his daughter only a modest dowry, but a good name and a heart as of gold. For the man was one of God's true sons and he had taught his daughter in the ways of the Kingdom.

Thus Olivia began to show Edward that life could have another dimension when love was properly directed. The love he learned from her eased the ache of what he could not have in heritage. And she introduced him to something far more important even than the bond of love they came to share in their hearts—that was a quality of love that sprang from faith—faith in a God with whom Edward had had nothing more than a cursory acquaintance. She lived her faith so sweetly, so naturally, that he was almost able to believe it himself. But the walls of his bitterness were thick, and though his new wife and her God had begun to remove a good number of its outer layer of bricks, her death came before a significant breach could be made.

The irony of the death of Edward's wife was that she died trying to give him the one thing he lacked, just as he had begun to realize that perhaps he did not need it after all. She had been helping him to find a meaning in life outside Aviemere, and he had at last reconciled himself to Derek's position above him. That settled in his mind, he would need no heir. He and Olivia could be content as they were. But suddenly everything had changed, and his dream was within his grasp. And she had sacrificed herself to give him one who could carry it on after him. Then just as suddenly it had all turned sour on him; he ended up with the heir, but having lost everything else.

So he had an heir, an elusive link to Aviemere. But the price he had paid for that selfish desire burned tormentingly within him. He had his heir, but his wife was dead! The price had been too steep.

And now, he thought, even if some bizarre twist of fate somehow landed the estate squarely in his hands, it would be an empty prize. Yet he would never let a flicker of the self-recriminations that boiled beneath rise to the surface. He had paid dearly, with loss of wife and his worth as a man, and if this was all he was destined to have—a position little higher than a factor's and a son who would rightly hate him—then he would accept it, and give no man cause to ever pity him.

Pain in most forms is meant as an adjunct to the process of healing, but in Edward the pain sent him once again inside himself. There he was unable to turn his eyes toward those who might have been able to mend his heart and bring it a wholeness he had never known. Focused on the pain of his self, he could see neither the son who needed him, nor the loving Father whose arms of compassion were eager to wrap themselves about them both and draw them into His own heart. But God's means are never exhausted. And where one method fails to open the closed door of a man's heart, He sends another. So now Jamie, new in her own walk of faith, had unknowingly been sent to care for the son of this man as an instrument in the hands of the Almighty, in whose plan exist no secondary causes.

Graystone had traversed the moor by now and was coming upon a green knoll some two miles south of the MacRae croft. Suddenly he realized his fists were clenched so tightly about the reins that his nails had dug into his flesh, and his shoulders ached with tension.

He spurred the stallion into another gallop—it was the only sort of release he would allow himself.

CHAPTER TWENTY-FIVE

Guests

In three weeks at Aviemere Jamie had seen the laird only twice. After their first meeting in the library, she had passed him once in a corridor. Andrew had been with her at the time and she was both embarrassed and miffed by the impromptu meeting between father and son. The boy had hung back as if coming upon a stranger, and the father had given him but a quick passing glance. Not a word did he speak to Jamie.

It was much to her surprise, therefore, when two days later, in midafternoon, she received a summons from the laird.

"He said for ye t' come t' the parlor," said the maid who delivered the message. "And t' bring the child."

Nervously Jamie straightened Andrew's clothing, brushed his hair, gathered him up, and hurried from the nursery. Her own fear of the man was tempered by her excitement at the thought that the laird had at last sent for his son. She would do nothing to delay the long-awaited reunion, and she hastened along the hall and down the stairs as quickly as caution would allow.

At length she came to a breathless halt before the door of the east parlor. Lifting her hand she knocked softly, allowing the natural awe of Andrew's father to still the flurry of her emotions.

"Come in," came his voice.

She turned the handle, pushed the door open, and entered. To her surprise he was not alone.

Three other persons, finely attired, obviously of the local gentry, were in the room. An older gentleman, portly, with balding gray hair, and a pince-nez balanced precariously on his nose, stood off to Jamie's left near the hearth. The other two guests were women. One was about the man's age, tall and trim with

189

her graying black hair piled upon her head in intricate style. Her sharp-featured face seemed ever alert and on the lookout for something at hand. What, Jamie could not have guessed. She appeared to be the gentleman's wife. The younger woman was in her mid-twenties and extremely attractive. Though she was sitting, it was clear she was tall and graceful. The vanishing trace of a smile still lay upon her lips, and the line of her eyes still rested upon the laird where he stood opposite her; obviously, the last words spoken by him prior to Jamie's entrance had landed agreeably upon her admiring ears. There was a visible likeness between her and the older woman, whom Jamie took to be her mother.

Taking this all in in an instant, Jamie's initial reaction was hesitation at having stumbled unknowingly into such an encounter. No one in the room took note of the awkwardness evident upon her face, however, for the same moment the older woman rose from her chair and exclaimed delightedly, "Oh, there he is! What a beautiful child! He is the very image of you, Edward!"

"Thank you, Lady Montrose," said Graystone, proud but yet detached.

"Thank you for granting an old woman's request. We see so little of children at Montrose."

Inwardly Jamie sagged with disappointment. The summons was not at all what she had hoped it would be. No chance for the father to get to know the son; this was merely an opportunity to show the child off to neighbors. And even at that, the laird seemed to have been coerced into it. The attachment which had already grown up within her toward Andrew was possessive of such a scheme. How dare he use his son so! She wished she might whisk him away from the room where he was little more than an ornamental showpiece.

"Oh, Edward, you must let us hold him," said Lady Montrose sweetly. "Candice, dear, wouldn't you love to hold him?"

"Yes, of course, Mother," replied the lovely young woman, still seated. Notwithstanding her assent, she did not appear nearly as interested in the child as she was in the father, for her eyes continued directed toward the laird, with now and then a coquettish smile.

"By all means," answered Graystone.

If Jamie hesitated slightly letting go of Andrew's hand, she could hardly be blamed. She had been the boy's sole companion for so many days that it was difficult to relinquish control to these strangers who seemed more bent on massaging Lord Graystone's good will than anything else.

"You may go, Miss MacLeod," Graystone said, turning toward Jamie. "I'll send the maid when we are ready for you."

Jamie turned and exited. But before the doors had closed behind her she heard the words, "So that's your nurse—a bit young, isn't she?"

"Capable, nonetheless," replied Graystone.

With the words the doors struck shut and Jamie was left alone in the hallway.

But she could not easily pull herself away, and lingered. Concerned for the child, she gave little thought to the impropriety of eavesdropping.

Candice Montrose's voice caught her attention before she had a chance to move, and she remained glued to the spot.

"Well, she is rather quaint-looking at any rate. Where did you find her?"

"Aberdeen."

"Listen here, Edward," spoke Lord Montrose for the first time. "I don't know about you, but baby pandering is not quite my forte. Don't get me wrong; he's a handsome lad and all that. But—"

"I quite understand, Montrose," Graystone said. "Let me pour you a brandy."

"I'd be most gratified."

Jamie heard the clinking of crystal, then silence except for the muffled sounds of the two women cooing over Andrew.

"I say, Edward," said Lord Montrose, as the men caught up their conversation again, "do you think this weather will affect the harvest?"

"I don't expect it to, though our own crews won't enjoy harvesting in the rain."

The two men talked on of tariffs and harvest and weather, while Jamie shifted uncomfortably from one foot to the other, straining to hear conversation concerning Andrew.

"I say," said Lord Montrose. "Isn't that brother of yours off in Africa somewhere?"

"Yes," replied Graystone shortly. "The Transvaal. You know, the Dutch and their diamonds that Disraeli wants."

"Must be a bloody gruesome life down there. I shouldn't like it at all. A savage place, I don't wonder! Wasn't he wounded some time back? I recall hearing a report he had been killed. Then miraculously it turned out he had only been wounded and captured. He must have some stories to tell!"

"I expect so," said Graystone dully.

Then the feminine voice of Lady Montrose interjected itself into the dialogue. "I do believe little Andrew is getting tired. And really, we ought to be on our way also. We wouldn't want to overstay our welcome."

"Little danger of that," said Graystone.

"You are most gracious," Lady Montrose replied. "But you must allow us to entertain you soon."

"At your pleasure."

"Let us not allow such a long lapse until our next visit," came Candice Montrose's poised, melodious voice. "We will be having some friends for dinner next week and Mother and I had planned to send you an invitation. Please say you'll come!"

"I shall look forward to it," replied Graystone. "Let me get the door."

Suddenly Jamie came to herself.

In a panic she started to race away, but before she had advanced a half dozen steps down the corridor, she heard the doors open behind her. She stopped and turned, dead still, her cheeks flushed with red as if to announce her guilt. She was staring into the cold steel-eyed countenance of Edward Graystone.

"I don't believe you were called," he said sternly.

"I know—sir," she stammered. "I—weel, I didna hae onythin' t' do—that is, I thocht I'd stay close by—in case I was needed . . ."

She despised herself for the lie, and the fact that it was hardly convincing made it even worse.

"Then you may take the boy."

She quickly took Andrew from Lady Montrose and hurried away, trying not to notice the derisive stares of the two ladies, or the chilling look from Lord Graystone himself.

CHAPTER TWENTY-SIX

Two Conversations

For several days Jamie saw nothing of the laird.

He was in her thoughts, however. For Andrew's sake she wanted to find some means to break through his tough granite-like exterior. She had to open his heart to the boy—somehow! Yet she cringed at the very thought of facing him. Anger at his cold treatment of his son and apprehension at what he might do if she dared confront him intermingled obscurely in her mind.

Yet she knew the day would eventually come when she would have to speak to him. However timid she was, and no matter that she was just eighteen and he was a powerful laird, on poor Andrew's behalf she must try to soften the father toward his son.

But how?

One afternoon while Andrew was napping, Jamie was restless and unable to read. She wandered in search of Dora, hopeful for a visit, but learned the kindly housekeeper was gone for the afternoon. She shuffled toward the kitchen, lingered there in meaningless interaction with the cook for a few moments, before her hostess let it be known that she must be about her work and visitors—especially fellow servants—were not especially wanted. Jamie departed for nowhere in particular, walked aimlessly down several corridors, past the east parlor where she had seen the Montroses, and without realizing it suddenly found herself in a wing of the mansion she had never seen before.

She was in the middle of a grand ballroom, beyond which was a wide hallway where another parlor was located, and next to this, a gallery of family portraits. Fascinated, she walked slowly to the end, carefully looking at each face, and then discovered herself between two closed doors. All was quiet around her. Slowly she reached out to test the handles. The doors opened without a sound and she walked into a lovely little room whose French doors on the opposite wall opened out into one of the beautiful outside courtyards. The room was clean and inviting, awash in the afternoon sun.

Everything within sight was exquisite. A delicately carved walnut Queen Anne desk with a glass top caught Jamie's eye first, but she was quickly diverted toward two wing-back chairs upholstered in the richest colors of green, magenta, and blue. The hearth of imported marble was spotless—there had been no fire here for some time—, and on the mantel sat the most splendid figurines even an experienced eye would have found north of Edinburgh. To Jamie, who had never seen anything like them, these miniature figures were so lifelike in every detail that she stood fascinated as her eyes examined each one. Knowing better than to touch such precious heirlooms, as her eyes lit upon one figurine in particular, she could not help herself. It was of a shepherdess girl with two woolly lambs at her feet. Enchanted by the face, she slowly reached for it, picked it up, and drew it off the mantel.

After a moment or two Jamie realized that such a place could be none other than a woman's special room. She reached back toward the mantel to set the tiny figurine in place.

"What are you doing here?"

Jamie started, and the shepherdess girl slipped from her hands and fell with a sickening crash to the floor. She spun around to face Edward Graystone, but her gaze quickly dropped to the broken fragments at her feet.

"I—I . . ." Her heart was pounding and her lips were trembling so that she could not speak.

"Who gave you permission to come here?"

"No—one—I was just . . . it's such a lovely room . . . I didn't know I shouldn't—the doors weren't—"

"You clumsy lout!" he fumed. "You have no permission to roam about where you please! Do you understand?"

"I'm sorry," she said weakly, trying to bite back the tears rising in her eyes. She stooped down to retrieve what was left of the shepherdess and her lambs. "Perhaps I can—"

"Leave that alone!" he shouted, cutting her short. "Get out of here!"

Jamie made no further attempt to speak, knowing if she did she would burst into tears. She had clearly been in the wrong, and nothing she could say would change the guilt she felt over what she had done. Hastily she retreated and ran back down the hall, turning a corner before the rush of tears escaped. Even as she flew through the door, Graystone himself had slumped into one of the expensive leather chairs he and Olivia had picked out in Copenhagen, his face hidden in his hands.

Jamie made it unseen to the third floor and to her own room. She was greatly relieved to have seen no one and to find Andrew still asleep. She fell on her bed and allowed the tears to flow, trying to pray through the flood, but hardly knowing what to say. Should she pray for herself? She was making a mess of things and had not even been here a month! She was breaking things, stumbling in where she didn't belong, hearing words not meant for her ears, making the laird furious with her. Was she still just a ridiculous shepherd girl? Perhaps she didn't belong here at all! Emily had tried to make her believe in herself, believe that she could take her place alongside people with training. But she wasn't like these people. She didn't know how to be. She would never be a lady. She *could* never be a lady! Her dreams would wind up on the floor just like the shepherd girl she had dropped—broken and crumbled! She didn't know how to behave, how to speak, how to act around real ladies and gentlemen!

"It was a mistake to come here," she murmured, sobbing quietly now. "Oh, God, why did you let me come here? I don't belong with these people! I will never even be able to be a servant, much less a lady! Let me just go away somewhere!"

The sounds of Andrew stirring from his nap interrupted her thoughts.

All at once she remembered why she had come. It wasn't for herself. It wasn't because of the laird. It had nothing to do with being a lady. She and Emily had prayed for that dear, lonely child who needed someone to love him. Whatever else might come of it, she could still give herself to him. Even if he seemed to be a contented boy, oblivious to the turmoil surrounding him, she had still been sent to love him. And she could not turn her back on that.

She rose from the bed and went through the adjoining door to the nursery. Standing in his bed Andrew held out his arms to her. She smiled, as fresh tears filled her eyes.

"How about a walk outside this afternoon, Andrew!" she said. "Could you use some fresh air, too?"

She dressed him and within twenty minutes the two found themselves standing in the fragrant afternoon breeze.

Unconsciously they made their way along the tree-lined drive, and were halfway to the factor's friendly cottage before Jamie realized her unplanned intention. Andrew walked beside her, his small hand reaching above his shoulders to keep it enclosed in hers. The air was clean after two days of rain, and the smell of every plant, every tree, every blade of grass greeted their nostrils, mingling delightfully with the soil and the aroma of distant fields of grain, covered over with the mystery carried from the high regions of Donachie down into the valley on the gentle mountain breeze. The sky was blue, with abundant patches of billowing whiteness and not quite yet willing to relinquish the stormy control they had enjoyed in the earlier part of the week. Soon Jamie's head was clear and her good spirits restored, and she and Andrew chatted merrily as they walked along.

They had just made the turn off the main drive toward the factor's when in the distance, standing on the highway beyond the gate to the estate, she saw Iona Lundie peering into the grounds toward the house. She was hardly close enough to see her expression, but she could feel, rather than see, that same cold, foreboding gaze. The woman gave no indication that she saw Jamie at all.

Jamie shuddered and quickened her pace.

Her mind was still on the unnerving woman when she came to herself and found that they were approaching the Ellices' yard. She let herself in through the gate, then knocked on the door. The factor was gone, but Mrs. Ellice greeted them warmly.

"I hope a visit is allowed without an invitation," Jamie said.

"Hoots! You're welcome anytime!" the woman laughed. "Especially if you bring the dear child with you!"

She went about setting a kettle on to boil, and soon had laid out a rather nice tea, including a freshly baked loaf of bread and a slab of butter.

"Come along," said their hostess. "You and Andrew share tea with me this afternoon. George's out in the fields. With the sun back out, they're tryin' to get at the grain."

Andrew already had a chunk of bread and was about to dig his fingers into the butter. Mrs. Ellice laughed at his antics and reached over to help him.

"Do you know Iona Lundie?" Jamie asked after a moment.

"Oh, that one!" the factor's wife replied grimly.

"What do you mean?"

"I don't want to speak unfairly of her, for the Lord knows she has had a hard life. But she does bring much of it on herself."

"She told me her husband was killed."

"Aye! It happened immediately before Mr. Ellice and I came. Frederick Lundie was the factor before my George, you know. As I heard it, he fell from his horse out on the moor and broke his neck."

"Does—does the woman blame the Graystones?"

"Could be. You see, just before the accident—if accident it was—he had been let go of his position on the estate."

"You said he was the factor?"

"Aye. And the cause must've been something serious: the laird—that would be Mackenzie Graystone—wanted him cleared off the estate as soon as he could get his family packed up. Must have been a hard blow for the man."

"Where did they go?"

"They went nowhere. The man fell from his horse before the time was out. Then the woman went to stay with her sister in the village. But her troubles were only beginning; the following summer she lost her eldest son in a drunken brawl."

"That's terrible. The poor woman!"

"Yes, I expect she blames it all on the Graystones. But it seems these were things that just couldn't be helped."

"She said she knew my father," Jamie ventured, "and that he died about the same time as her husband."

"Oh?" replied Mrs. Ellice with a raised eyebrow. "I thought you were from Aberdeen."

"Not to begin with," said Jamie, who then proceeded to relate what little she knew of her father and her own background, as well as what Iona Lundie had told her. "So now I'm wondering if it's possible my father actually had land near here at one time," she concluded.

"No doubt it's possible," said the factor's wife. "But don't take everything that woman says seriously, for she is so full of bitterness, she might say anything against the Graystones—truth or not."

"I understand. But if my father's land was somewhere close by, I suppose—I just think—well, it would be nice to see it. Somehow it might help me to feel closer to him and know him better."

"I'll tell Mr. Ellice about this if you like. Maybe he can help you find out."

"Yes, thank you . . . but—"

Jamie hesitated.

"What is it, child?"

"He wouldn't say anything to the laird, would he? I wouldn't want him to think I was of the same mind as Mrs. Lundie."

"Be assured, Mr. Ellice will use discretion in the matter."

Late that night Jamie lay wide awake in her bed. Her mind raced with thought of her father and fragmentary glimpses of a childhood she knew so little of. Sleep was impossible.

Was it true that poverty had forced him from his land?

And how did he come to hold land in the first place?

Since her instruction under Mr. Avery and Emily Gilchrist, Jamie knew more of such things than she had before. She now realized how rare, indeed, it was for one of peasant stock to rise to that position. It was happening more in the south, in England, these days Mr. Avery had told her. But in the north the stations of society remained as they had been for centuries.

If her father had come to own land, how crushing it must have been for him to lose it! But again came the question—how could he have come by it? Finlay MacLeod and his father before him had always been peasant shepherds. Could it have come from her mother's side? But she knew even less about Alice MacLeod's family than she did her father's.

Jamie sighed.

What did it all matter anyway? Would knowing the answers to all these questions actually change anything?

Perhaps not.

Except . . . except she *wanted* to know her parents! That was what she longed for most of all. What orphan does not want to know his family roots? How she longed to know the man who died in her arms wanting better things for her, to know the woman who wanted only love for her daughter!

Involuntary tears had begun streaming down her face.

Oh, Mama . . . oh, Papa! how I miss you—how I need you! she cried out the desolation of her heart. *Oh, God, I am so alone. Help me, Lord! Help me know them!*

Suddenly the words which had so long ago been planted into her heart flooded her conscious mind:

I will lift up mine eyes unto the hills from whence cometh

my help . . . The Lord is thy keeper: the Lord is thy shade upon thy right hand. The sun shall not smite thee by day, nor the moon by night. The Lord shall preserve thee. . . .

Oh, Lord, she thought, *thank you for that promise! Help me not only to know them . . . Help me to know you, Lord!*

Comforted in the peace that she was not alone, Jamie fell asleep with the precious words—strangely mingled between her grandfather's thick brogue and Mr. Avery's precise English tongue—running through her mind.

CHAPTER TWENTY-SEVEN

A Midnight Intruder

When Jamie started awake, she thought the cause had been her dream.

She had been standing on a great stretch of barren moorland searching for her father and mother. At last she had found them, but they stood in the distance, separated from her by a wide gulf which was too deep to cross. She called to them, and unlike most dream-voices, the sound from her mouth was loud and echoed across the chasm. They called back to her, reaching out their hands, imploring her to come to them. But there was no traversing the void that separated them.

Then from in the distance, on their side of the heathland, approached Iona Lundie. She had a fearsome expression on her face and walked deathlike toward them, screaming at Jamie's father, accusing him of killing her husband. She was picking up stones from the ground and hurling them toward him. They were pelting his face, and he seemed powerless to defend himself. Jamie was shouting at her to stop, but now her voice was empty and hollow and swallowed up by the wind. It began to rain, then the rain came in torrents, and now she could no longer see her mother at her father's side. Still the woman was hurling rocks at the poor man who was her father. She could see that his face was bleeding and a look of contorted agony and confusion was in his eyes. Still the rain poured down. Gradually the width of the chasm shrank and she came closer and closer, but still she could not shout or reach him. But now the woman was not Iona Lundie at all. It was not a woman but a man, standing over her father. The rocks had ceased, but still came the rain, and still his face bled, and still he looked confused and tormented. And she was no longer herself but a little girl, helplessly, frantically trying to reach her father. But it was no use. Now the man was coming closer to him. Now—yes, she could see his face! And—could she?—yes—but how was it possible? She had never seen the man before. Yet she recognized his face! She had seen it somewhere—but where? Now the face was fading. There were no rocks in the man's hand. But he clutched something—something that flashed in the black night. She looked at the man's face again. It was a blur. Still she tried to see into it, to see where she had—

Suddenly Jamie awoke trembling and cold with sweat.

A noise had awakened her!

A noise from Andrew's room. It had not been part of her dream!

In the deathly quiet of night she lay still and listened. It must have been only the child stirring in his sleep. But no! There it was again! The floorboards creaked. Someone must be walking about!

She shot upright in her bed, her heart thumping in her ears. Yes—someone was in Andrew's room!

Suddenly a picture of Iona Lundie flashed into her mind, and with it the memory of the awful glare she had given Andrew.

I'll ne'er be happy until I see every one o' them cauld in their graves!

The woman's words re-echoed in Jamie's mind and filled her with dread. That the woman could be capable of treachery there could be no doubt. But how could she have gotten into the house in the dead of night?

Jamie jumped silently from her bed, threw a wrap about her shoulders, and crept on tiptoe toward the door between the two rooms. But what could she possibly hope to do against such a large and undoubtedly powerful woman? She looked hastily about, then grabbed up the heavy iron poker from the hearth. Trembling with terror she approached the door again, gripped the handle with her shaking hand, took a deep breath, then flung open the door.

The figure she saw bathed in the moonlight streaming through the window was not Iona Lundie's at all. It was tall, broad, and masculine, and was bent over Andrew's bed, gazing upon the sleeping face.

As the door snapped open, both startled and angered by the sudden intrusion, Edward Graystone swung sharply around. The moonlight also reflected moisture in his eyes.

A tense moment of silence followed, both too surprised to speak.

The laird broke the spell, his eyes flashing darkly as if to hide their vulnerability.

"Not only an eavesdropper, but a common sneak as well!" he seethed.

"No!" she cried. "I was just—"

She stopped abruptly. It seemed she was always having to defend herself to this man. But why should she? She had done nothing he would not have wanted her to do had there indeed been an intruder. The unfairness of his accusation welled up within her.

"I believe I was hired to care for the child," she replied boldly, all the timidity gone from her voice. "And what am I to think, with someone creeping about this room in the middle of the night? What else would you expect me to—?"

"Why you insolent little hussy!" he shouted back. "I'll not be spoken to in that tone!"

When she had first seen him, the tears standing in his eyes, she had felt momentary pity for him. She had even been willing to think that his sharp tone meant nothing and was only the result of his being caught thus exposed. But that sympathy was suddenly obliterated in the frustration over his treatment of his son, a frustration that had threatened to explode the past several days.

"Ye deserve nae better!" she retorted, forgetting for the moment all the fine speech she had learned in Aberdeen. "E'en if I were a sneak, it'd be nae worse than the coward ye are yersel'! Not man enough t' show yer affections t' yer ain son when the bairn's awake an' can git the comfort frae them!"

"Shut up!" he yelled. "And get out of here! Out of this house, do you understand! I don't want to see your face around here again!"

By now the awakened Andrew was crying in his bed.

Standing stock-still, Jamie waited to see what the father might do. Surely if he could only be brought to hold the boy once in his arms, surely then the walls of his heart would soften.

But he remained where he was, his face contorted in mingled anger and self-recrimination, the tears struggling to rise once more. Still he made no move toward the child.

At last, able to stand it no longer, Jamie dropped the poker from her hand and rushed to the sobbing baby. She scooped him into her arms, kissed him, and softly crooned in his ear.

"There, there, my wee bairn! 'Tis all right. Jamie has ye noo."

She laid her cheek against his wet face, and as she spoke his cries gradually calmed. After a few moments she turned again to face the father.

But he was gone.

With Andrew still in her arms, she turned and walked to the rocking chair and sat down.

She hardly knew what to think. The pain she had observed in the laird's face was so unexpected. Would he have perhaps gone to Andrew if she had given him the chance? What if he wasn't in truth like those names she had hurled at him? She had been wrong to judge him in her heart, and especially to call him a coward to his face!

"Oh, wee Andrew," she sighed softly, "I don't know what to think of your father."

She rocked and sang softly until both she and Andrew fell asleep in the rocking chair.

She awoke to the full light of day, Andrew still asleep, snuggled in the crook of her arm. She immediately recalled the events of the night and was filled with despair. What had she done! She had spoiled everything! When she had left Aberdeen, it had been with a strong sense of purpose in her heart. God had been leading her here, she thought. But suddenly all that purpose and sense of mission was over. She had been dismissed! And she had no one to blame but herself and the foolishness of her untamed emotions and unbridled tongue!

Oh, why had she allowed her anger to get the best of her? What did she have to be angry about, anyway? What possible business was it of hers if a man she hardly knew held or did not hold his son? Who was she to think it concerned her?

She had spoken rudely and disrespectfully, lashing out at the man, without ever stopping to pray for him or consider his own personal struggles.

Oh, Lord, she prayed silently, *forgive me! Curb my tongue, Lord, and help me to get the beam out of my own eye before I try to take the sliver out of someone else's. Oh, God—please let me have another chance! If not for my sake, then for Andrew's . . . and for his father's. I know you sent me here. Please don't allow my own vanity and stupidity to get in the way of your purpose. And comfort the laird in his pain, God, and somehow draw him closer to his son.*

Andrew began to stir, turned in her lap, and looked up in

her face, his bright eyes and smile saying that for him the night had never been. Jamie wept inside, thinking that she might never see him again, just when the bond between them was beginning to extend deep into her heart.

But as she had completed her prayer, despair had been replaced by resolve. If she must leave Aviemere, there was one thing she must do first. If the laird had told her to leave, she no longer had anything to fear from him—nothing but his menacing eyes and intimidating voice. But even those she was willing to brave if she might possibly manage to reach that tender spot she had seen exposed for the briefest of moments last night. But this time she would not face him with anger, but with humility—and with God's love for the man going before her.

She dressed Andrew, then found Bea and asked if she could mind the boy for a while. She then went to her own room, washed up, and changed out of her night clothes. She took a fleeting glance about the room that had been hers for such a short time. By later this same day she might well be packing her things and leaving this place.

The thought made her sick at heart. She would not only have failed poor Andrew, but also Dora and Emily, and even Robbie Taggart who had pulled her half-dead from the snow, and had promised to be her friend at a time when she knew not a single soul on the face of the earth. In that sense she owed Robbie as much as she owed Emily Gilchrist. But she quickly shook thoughts of Robbie from her mind. It would not do to think of him just now, for that stirred another set of confusing emotions within her!

Instead, she opened her door and marched down the hall. It was well into the morning and the laird was certain to be about his day's business. She went to the dining room, but he was not breakfasting. She climbed to the second floor and sought out the library. But he was not there either.

The thought of the little sitting room where she had broken the figurine came to her. It was the last place she wanted to see again, but perhaps it was worth a try. He had obviously been attached to the place.

When his voice answered her tentative knock five minutes later, it sounded hollow and drained, as if he had not slept all night.

"Who is it?" he said.

"Miss MacLeod, your Lordship," Jamie began. "I know I

don't deserve it, but I would like, if I might, to have a word with you."

There was a long pause, as if her statement had prompted a lengthy debate inside the room. At last his sullen voice replied, "Come in."

She stepped inside and closed the door behind her. He was standing with his back to her, looking out the French doors into the courtyard. He did not turn to face her, but she could feel his icy gaze, and the tension in his body was palpable.

Her mouth suddenly went dry and the rehearsed words left her mind the moment she had stepped across the threshold into the room. But she breathed a hasty prayer and began.

"Your Lordship," she said.

"Don't call me that!" he snapped.

"I'm sorry, uh, sir," Jamie tried to go on, ruffled by his unexpected response. "Before I go, I wanted to apologize for my words last night. I was frightened for the child, and I hardly knew what I was saying—"

She stopped. "No," she went on. "I *did* know what I was saying, but I didn't mean it to sound as it did. I had had a terrifying dream and woke suddenly and heard sounds in Andrew's room. I was afraid. You see—sir—I've grown very fond of Andrew. It has been difficult—"

She paused again, trying both to say what was in her heart, but to keep from offending again. Doggedly she began once more.

"I'm an orphan, sir. I never knew my mother, and my father died when I was still very young. I can barely remember him. Sometimes I miss them so. It makes me weep to think that I have no parents. No one to go to. No one to hold me when I'm lonely or afraid. I've got no one, sir. Sometimes I even get a little angry that my own father and mother went off and left me so alone— even though I know they couldn't help it, and even though I know they loved me. But when I was little I couldn't help thinking sometimes that it was because of me they left. And I still have to remind myself that I had nothing to do with it, and that they couldn't help their dying. It comforts me some to remember that they loved me. But it doesn't take the place of having them."

She stopped and took a deep breath. Still the laird said nothing, staring off toward the mountain in the distance.

"And maybe it's that, I'm thinking, that helps me to understand little Andrew more than most," she continued. "I just can't bear the thought of him growing up and having to feel like I sometimes feel, wondering if anyone loves him. He has no mother. And as for his father, he hardly knows him, and what is he going to think but what all children think, that somehow it's because of him that his father doesn't love him? And he can't even comfort himself that he's an orphan. It just hurts me to think—"

"Are you saying he's no better off than an orphan?" asked Graystone, his eyes still boring their way through the glass.

"Maybe, sir," replied Jamie earnestly. "No—not really. I don't know. Unless he's loved, what is the difference? Why should he grow up hating himself for something that wasn't his fault, like his mother's death? He's such a sweet bairn and deserves so much better. He deserves your love, sir. How can you go on blaming him?"

"Blaming him!" said Edward, as if the idea had struck him for the first time and he found the notion hideous.

"Aye, sir. Blaming him for his mother's death."

"Blame *him*!" he repeated. "So that's what you think! But then I suppose I've let everyone think that."

He let out a dry laugh. "You were right before—last night. You said it yourself. I'm nothing but a coward! I blame but one person for that crime—myself!"

Suddenly he swung around.

Jamie gasped at what she saw. His face was white, his eyes sunken and hollow. Yet there remained a smoldering spark in them. For the first time she was not frightened to look at him, for she now realized the resentment in his eyes was not directed at her, or anyone, but at himself.

"Myself, do you hear!" he shouted. "And for that I deserve to be hanged, not blessed with a beautiful son!"

"So you punish yourself by denying your son?" asked Jamie softly, with tears rising to her eyes. "But don't you see, it's only the boy that suffers?"

"Oh, dear Lord!" he moaned. "There's no escape. I don't deserve him."

"We—none of us—deserve God's good gifts," Jamie replied, hardly knowing where the words to reply were coming from. "We can only accept them and thank Him, and then try to do good by them."

"If only it were that simple!" he said in agony, not looking at Jamie, but pacing about the room.

"I can see you've known pain," said Jamie, weeping now. "Perhaps it isn't simple. But the pain has to stop somewhere— the griefs, the hurts. They can't be passed on from generation to generation, like land and titles and money and possessions. Love has to be passed on, not pain. No matter whose fault it is—Andrew should not have to suffer for it."

"Do you think—" he said, but his voice caught and he turned once more away from her so she would not see the tears filling the eyes of such an important man. "Do you think I *want* him to suffer!"

His voice trembled over the words like a dam about to burst. But he could not continue, and his shoulders shook with the weeping he would fain keep inside.

"Leave me alone!" he cried with such finality that Jamie knew she must leave him to suffer through his agony by himself.

She turned quickly, still weeping herself, and ran from the room.

CHAPTER TWENTY-EIGHT

Father and Son

Jamie went directly to her room and began packing her belongings.

How she longed to tell little Andrew that his father loved him! But he could never understand. He would not even know yet that he had been hurt. The pain would not solidify for several more years, and by then it would be too late to turn back the tide of his father's rejection.

Neither could she face the thought of seeing Andrew for the last time. The very idea brought fresh tears to her eyes as one by one she placed her things in her carpetbag.

At last, however, she could no longer forestall the inevitable and went to the nursery door and entered.

"Jamie!" exclaimed Bea, "ye look awful! Are ye ill?"

"No, Bea. I'm—I'll be leaving Aviemere."

"Leavin'?"

"Yes. I came to say goodbye to Andrew."

"Ye don't mean t' say the laird's been at it again! Ye were good fer the bairn."

"Don't blame him, Bea. It wasn't the laird's fault. It's just that I—"

Her voice caught, and though she swallowed several times, she could not continue.

Bea placed a sympathetic arm around Jamie's shoulder. "I'm sorry, lass. Would ye like t' be alone with him?"

Jamie nodded, and Bea left.

Now she had to face Andrew, who in his innocence could understand nothing of the emotions which were swirling about with him at their very center. He looked up, smiled sweetly, and said, "Up, Mamie!"

She stooped down, picked him up, and held him close. But she could say little to him, least of all goodbye.

Thirty minutes later the two were seated on the floor rolling a ball back and forth across the floor. Jamie's tears had subsided, although the mood in the room was still somewhat somber.

When she heard the door open, she rose reluctantly, expecting news that the arrangements had been made and that the wagon was ready to take her into the village. But as she turned, Edward Graystone's once-ominous form filled the doorway.

In an instant Jamie knew the granite facade had crumbled. The hollowness of his bearing brought a fresh ache to Jamie's heart and she lamented the part she had played in bringing it about. She could not make herself look up at him.

"I—I've come to see Andrew," he said in a halting voice.

With a silent prayer of thanksgiving in her heart, Jamie went over and took Andrew's hand. She then led him over to the feet of this man who had been little more than a stranger to him.

Slowly Graystone dropped to his knees, and with trembling arms clutched the boy to his breast, weeping as Jamie had never seen a man weep before. She turned and made her way back to her own room, closing the door softly behind her, where she sat down on the bed to await whatever summons would follow.

Some thirty minutes later she heard a soft knock on her door. She rose to answer it.

There stood Graystone, composed again, but obviously with his former strength of presence altogether shattered.

"I would like to—" he began, "—that is—may I speak with you for a moment?"

Jamie nodded.

"I feel I owe you an explanation."

"You owe me nothing," said Jamie. "Don't feel you must—"

"Please," interrupted Graystone, "I *want* to tell you . . . for Andrew's sake. And perhaps for mine. I want to make a clean breast of it. And you're as good a place to start as anywhere. You have been kind . . . to us both."

"Oh, no! I spoke too hastily to you. I had no right."

"Perhaps not. But that hardly matters. Love has its own rights. And you spoke because you loved Andrew—loved him possibly more than I."

"Oh no, sir, I know you care. You just didn't know how to show it."

"Never mind, Miss—Miss MacLeod. That's all behind us

now. I simply want you to have the whole truth. I feel you deserve it."

With her heart in her throat, Jamie said nothing, and Graystone went on.

"I am not the laird of Aviemere," he began, turning back into the nursery and pacing the small room slowly, pausing in front of the window. "But I have done nothing to dispel the illusion. My brother is the true *Lord Graystone, Laird of Aviemere*. I am nothing but a paid servant. I have loved Aviemere since my earliest boyhood, perhaps more than is decent, and would have done anything to possess it. Yet all my life I knew it would never be mine.

"Perhaps I wanted a child as much as does any man, but I had no need of an heir, so I was able to accept my wife's inability. After two miscarriages she was told she could bear no children except at the peril of her life. We were in love and would have been able to live with that. We could have had a happy life without children."

He paused, obviously struggling with rising emotion at the thought of his dead wife. He drew in a deep breath then went on.

"Then came a letter that my brother had been killed in the Transvaal. And suddenly, just like that—in an instant!—it was all mine! The thing I had dreamed of all my life was mine—the land, the estate, the mountain—everything! I cared nothing for the wealth, or even the title. *But the land!* It was the land I coveted—because I knew my brother cared nothing for it or its people and would be, if not a cruel laird, at least an uncompassionate one. But even with the news, which brought both joy and sorrow, Olivia could see even before I that one thing was missing. I lacked an heir to pass on my beloved Aviemere to.

"She came to me one day, with a smile on her lips, and announced that the doctor had rescinded his previous diagnosis and had given her his consent to bear another child. My Olivia, who was the essence of virtue, never having told a lie in her life, was willing to so degrade herself—for my selfish desires!"

In anguish Graystone wiped his eyes and drew in a deep breath, struggling with each word he uttered, yet compelled to continue, compelled at last to unburden his heart, even if to a servant, a mere child of eighteen.

"And I believed her!"

"But, sir," said Jamie, seeking any way she might to speak

out for this wretched man's defense, "why should you not have believed her? You can hardly blame yourself."

"I believed her only because I *wanted* to believe her! Just as I believed Derek was dead because I wanted to believe it. I could have seen through the lies if I had chosen to, if I had let myself. Especially Olivia's! But my head was full of greed and selfish lust for the position which had all my life been denied me by my cold but powerful father. I could see nothing else! Then—but not until it was too late and Olivia was already pregnant with Andrew—came the letter with the news that my brother lived. How I despised him for that! But it was too late! And Olivia—! But I was the only one responsible—"

He stopped again, unable to continue for a moment. Then turning his hollow eyes full on Jamie, he said, "Perhaps it is out of place for me to burden you with all this, but I feel you ought to know."

"I don't need to know, unless it helps you to tell me. It only matters to me that you and Andrew are together."

"Ah yes, Andrew!" he replied.

He returned to the crib and lifted the boy into his arms.

"I want you to know," he said. "You have cared deeply for Andrew. You have given much to him. I have watched you— though I have made certain I was never seen—you have been . . . like a mother to him."

"Please," said Jamie, tears standing in her eyes, "I have not done nearly—"

"No! You have loved him, and that's what matters most. He needs you, and it was foolish of me to dismiss you. I behaved very unkindly to you."

"I was too forward! I had no right—"

"Nevertheless, I have not been pleasant to you since you first came. I want the chance to make it up to you. I'm asking you, please—won't you stay?"

"If I can be of any help—"

"You already have been, probably more than either of us can know. You'll stay on then, at Aviemere?"

"If you want me."

"Thank you, Miss MacLeod! Though words are hardly enough."

Graystone knelt down with one knee on the floor and set the boy on his other. He brushed the yellow locks of hair from the boy's eyes, and stared into his face for a long while, seeming to behold him for the first time. What was passing through his mind he did not reveal. Andrew also scrutinized his father, touched his face, and spoke several unintelligible words to him. Then he scurried down from the knee, scampered into the adjoining room and returned a moment later with his toy. He held it out for his father to see.

"Baba," said Andrew by way of introduction.

Graystone laughed, and Jamie took the moment of levity to wipe the tears of joy from her eyes with the back of her sleeve. "I know!" replied Graystone. "It was I who brought your Baba home for you, even before you were born!" His voice was husky with renewed emotion.

He rose, took Andrew by the hand, and said, "Thank you again, Miss MacLeod. And now, if you will excuse us, I think my son and I will go outside for a short walk."

CHAPTER TWENTY-NINE

The First Flowers of Spring

Throughout the coming days and weeks of autumn, Edward Graystone made attempts to see little Andrew every day. The effort was new to him and not altogether easy. Memories continued to be roused which were not pleasant to face, and he discovered getting to know a child of two more difficult than he might have imagined.

He persisted, however, and if he was not immediately a transformed man, at least he was a growing one, and the renewed atmosphere of hopeful spirits around Aviemere was something all the staff who cared about the man rejoiced quietly in.

As for Jamie, she found she had more time on her hands than before, due to Andrew's daily visits by his father. She was eventually permitted use of the library, and gradually made many new discoveries in the world of literature which only a year before were closed to her. Almost before she realized it, winter had come to Aviemere with its first snows. But the long periods indoors did not necessarily mean dull, dreary hours. Andrew's energy was just as content expending itself in the long halls and spacious rooms of the mansions as it had been on the grassy lawns outside. Before winter was over, however, Jamie found it difficult to keep up with enough games invented for his entertainment.

Jamie's faith continued to deepen slowly, as the maturity of womanhood continued to ripen upon her countenance. Those principles she had been taught in Aberdeen imperceptibly penetrated deeper and deeper into her heart as a result of her own obedience to them, and by degrees her character came to reflect something of that same distinctiveness which had first so drawn her to Emily Gilchrist—the uniqueness of a Christlike love for all God's creatures. Jamie herself was not aware of these changes. Neither could those around her have put their finger on what was *different*. But in subtle ways they found themselves following her out of the room with their eyes, wondering if this was the same raw, untamed, inexperienced girl who had come to them only months before. Her speech continued to refine itself; there were fewer lapses into the vernacular of her upbringing. A certain lithe gracefulness now accompanied her movements, and she had put on several inches during the course of the winter. The color in her cheeks took on more subtle hues, the lustre in her long hair shone, and the green of her eyes deepened.

Yet through all, and sometimes hiding these changes temporarily—but in the same way that a cloud can obscure the direct light of the sun's rays but cannot stop its effect—was an innocent and childlike exuberance, whose zest and irrepressible spirit made her the perfect companion for the animated and energetic little toddler. Just when one of her fellow servants was puzzling over the apparent transformation in her, she would scamper down the hall behind her charge, her voice ringing out in unreserved girlish laughter, causing the observer to mutter to himself, "What was I thinking? It's only our same little Jamie after all!"

Spring soon came to Aviemere. Jamie found herself aching for a tramp over the countryside. A crisp day toward the end of March dawned bright and fair, and, notwithstanding the moisture that would still be bound in the soil and grass in the lower places, she bundled up Andrew, donned her own coat, and set out upon her favorite springtime expedition—discovering the first blossoms of spring.

She had asked the cook to prepare a lunch for the two of them, and they now stopped by the kitchen, then exited through the scullery door and walked across the clipped lawn toward the north where lay low hills and meadowland. They were walking past the stables when Edward walked out into the sunlight and hailed them.

"I say, a bit chilly to be out, isn't it?" he said.

"Good morning, Mr. Graystone!" replied Jamie. "And to answer your question—perhaps, but we are well bundled, and the sun was so bright we couldn't resist."

"And Andrew! What are you up to this magnificent spring day?"

The boy raced up to his father and Edward scooped him into his arms.

"Papa," said Andrew. "Hunning fowers!"

"Oh," said the father in a long-drawn, knowing tone, casting upon Jamie a look instead that spelled confusion.

"We're out looking for the first flowers of spring," she explained.

"I see," he said, setting the boy on his feet. "Well, have a delightful time of it! By the way, there is a lovely meadow on the other side of the orchard. I used to go there all the time, but I haven't seen the place in years. I shouldn't wonder, in fact, if it's all overgrown by now."

"We shall try in that direction then, and give you a report on its condition."

"Papa, come!" urged Andrew.

"Well, I don't know . . . MacKay and I—"

"Papa, come!" insisted the boy, taking his father's hand and tugging on it as forcefully as he could.

"I wouldn't want to encroach upon your plans."

"Nonsense! You'd be most welcome," Jamie replied. "And I scarcely think Andrew will take no for an answer!"

Turning it over for a moment in his mind, Graystone came to what appeared to be a sudden resolve, told them to wait a moment, disappeared into the stable, and had a word with MacKay; he soon returned with his coat, and within five minutes the three of them were tramping across the fields toward the meadow he had spoken of. The green grasses were a refreshing sight after the stark white cover of the winter's snows. The chill in the air was a springtime chill, and thus imbued with the promise and fragrance of coming summer, altogether unlike the chill of autumn which portends snow and darkness and death.

For a time flowers were forgotten as Andrew took off wildly through the grass, climbing on every rock he could find, hiding behind clumps of gorse. It was not until she fell down breathless in the grass, sides aching with laughter, finally having caught the hysterical child in her arms, that Jamie remembered the original purpose of their outing.

"Look!" she exclaimed. "Goat's beard."

"Yes, it is," said Edward, who had just come up behind them, and now bent over to have a look.

"Fower!" chimed in Andrew.

"Come on, it's just a little farther!" said Edward excitedly.

Suddenly his mind recalled those sweet days as a boy roaming over these very fields, discovering the joys of Aviemere. "The burn's not far! As I recall there are always fine specimens over there."

He led the way, and they traipsed through the grass for another ten minutes, occasionally running to keep pace with Andrew, until they reached their destination. The burn, peat-brown and swollen with winter runoff, frothed and bubbled within its banks as it made its way to the valley and thence northward to join the Don, when its waters would then make their way east and reach the sea just north of Old Aberdeen.

Though she did not fully realize it, these amber-colored waters were from the same burn that Jamie had loved years ago upon Donachie. Yet even as she stared into its churning waters as they tumbled past, the sight infused the joyous day with a flicker of melancholy as she thought of her dear home on the grand heights of the mountain. She looked away westward and saw it now as only a dim silhouette against the sky, a cloud overhanging its uppermost reaches. Snow still clung to the mountain in most places, and even the white in the distance brought lovely images to Jamie's mind. She recalled the afternoon she had found the lovely pure white face of the starry saxifrage peering out from a mound of snow in the crevice between two rocks. As always with such memories, the face of her beloved grandfather rose in her mind's eye, beloved more and more as she now grew better able to understand the faith he had taught her before her mind and emotions had been old enough to grasp the depth of its reality. And with the thought of his face came pictures of the cottage, the sheep in the dell, the crude grave marker she had fashioned . . .

"Do you miss your home?" came Edward's voice into the midst of her reverie.

A hint of color rose in her cheeks at being caught so far from the present.

"Aye," she answered soberly. "I'll never be able to forget it."

She paused, still reflective. Then suddenly another look came over her face.

"But—how did you know?" she said. "I didn't tell you about Donachie, did I?"

"No," he laughed. "But I like to know my people. One day it dawned on me where I'd heard your name before. I had a little talk with my factor."

"Ah," smiled Jamie. "So Mr. Ellice has been giving away the secrets of my past!"

"Nothing so dark as to cause you any concern, I assure you. In fact, I would say it's a past to be proud of."

"I suppose I am, in a way. Perhaps I'm not as prepared for life as a maid or a nurse for having spent so many years doing little more than living in the hills and caring for my sheep. And I wish I had more refinement. Sometimes I feel so lost in the midst of the least hint of what you would call society."

She stopped, thought a moment, then laughed.

"What is it?"

"I was just thinking of how out of place I feel in, as I said, *society*—among real ladies and gentlemen. That first day I stumbled into the east parlor with Andrew, and you were with your friends."

"The Montroses."

"Yes. I was so mortified!"

"You had no reason to be! You had hardly been here two weeks."

"I felt so foolish, so out of place!"

"You handled yourself just fine."

"You consider my eavesdropping outside the door behaving with proper decorum!"

"Well, that is true!" Now it was his turn to laugh.

"And to be caught by—if you'll excuse me—*the laird*, so red-handed! But yes," she said, diverting the conversation back into its former path, "I am thankful for my heritage, my upbringing, even if I am now alone. Because I am *not* alone! Since I have been living life with the Lord more close to my heart, He has given me a great thankfulness for all that has happened. I see all the events of my life fitting together into His plan for me, even though the various pieces by themselves can at times be very confusing."

Graystone looked upward at the peak of Donachie shrouded in cloud and mist. "It is difficult to imagine that you were raised there. I've always thought of it as such a harsh, even wild place. As I always considered its main tenant, Finlay MacLeod—though I'm now sorry to say I never did meet him."

"Yes, there is a wildness about Donachie. It can be harsh and unforgiving, too. And some would, I suppose, say that I was no less wild. But my grandfather—I never thought of him like that. And he was everything the mountain was. Yes, I do miss it."

"Would you like to ride up to Donachie some time? I could arrange for a horse . . . and someone to accompany you."

"I don't ride," answered Jamie with a laugh. "We had no horse, and I never had occasion to learn. And if I were to try, I would never trust myself to guide a poor animal over that rough and rocky ground. Perhaps I might walk up . . ."

Then she grew pensive once more. "But I don't know if I could go back—just yet."

"I understand."

"It is a silly notion, if you think of it, to be afraid of the past. I mean, is God any the more able to lead us forward than back? I trust Him for my future; why not with my past? Is His protection going to differ depending on the direction in time in which we travel?"

"Very thought-provoking question indeed! So you're a philosopher as well as a nurse and a shepherdess!"

"Hardly that! It shouldn't take a philosopher to answer such simple questions. I'm only trying to live by the principles I was taught. There's a big difference in *knowing* spiritual things and *living* them. And for the first time in my life, I'm now trying, with God's help, to live them."

"It seems none too simple to me."

"It's not *easy*, that is true! Very difficult in fact. But *simple*—yes."

She smiled. *"The Lord shall preserve thy going out and thy coming in from this time forth, and even for evermore."*

"Is that from the Bible?"

"Yes. It just came back into my mind. My grandfather used to read to me from the Bible a great deal—although with as thick a Scots tongue as you could imagine! But those words are a promise—when I go to Donachie, and when I go forward into whatever He has for me, God will be with me."

"How can you be so certain?"

Before Jamie could answer, Andrew, who had been foraging about the field, trotted up to them. With a merry grin he held his hands out to Jamie. They were full of torn bits of flowers mixed with grass and weeds.

"Fowers for Mamie!"

"Oh, Andrew!" she cried with such effusive thanks that the bouquet might have come from one of London's finest shops. "It's beautiful! Thank you!"

Content with the end of one project, Andrew then announced that he was hungry.

His father rose, looked about for a reasonably dry location, and, when found, they spread the cloth over the grass and Jamie opened the basket.

"I'm afraid I should have gone back for more," Jamie said.

"It looks fine," said Graystone. "Cook always prepares more than is necessary."

As they ate Jamie reflected on the question which had preceded Andrew's interruption. At length she brought up the threads of the discussion again.

"You asked how I could be certain of God's provision," she said.

"Yes. How can you know it isn't all just a bunch of rubbish the priests have concocted to preserve their religious system?"

Jamie reached out and picked up Andrew's bouquet.

"This is how I can be certain," she said. Then she laid her hand on Andrew's head. "And this also. And the burn there, the mountain, these meadows, the sky, the sheep—and what I feel in my own heart. I have been in low places, Mr. Graystone, but He has never failed to bring me out and fill my life with rich blessings such as these. The evidences of His life and creation are all around us and inside us. If we just open our eyes to it, suddenly you realize one would have to be blind—physically and emotionally and spiritually—*not* to see His presence literally everywhere. And as for the confidence that He will provide, will lead me, will guide my steps? I suppose it's past experiences in my own life that verify that His promises are true and can be believed. One of my favorite proverbs goes, 'Trust in the Lord with all your heart, and do not lean upon your own understanding. In all your ways acknowledge him, *and he shall direct your paths.*' I believe that. I *really* believe it! And I'm trying to live by it, difficult as it is."

"And what if one hasn't had such past experiences as you speak of, that demonstrate God's working?"

"Everyone has had them," she replied. "The workings of God's hand are not only all about us in the world, they are all about us within the circumstances and experiences of our lives. Most people just don't have sense enough to know to whom to attribute such working. God's ways are often silent, and so huge they become invisible to our limited sight."

Here a smile played upon Graystone's lips. There was even

a hint of a twinkle in his eye. Seeing it, Jamie realized how rarely she had seen her employer smile, and decided that he would have a nice smile if he once got into the practice of using it more often. Then suddenly she realized the smile was directed at her, and at the implication of what she had said.

"Oh, Mr. Graystone! I didna—that is, I did not mean you!" she stammered.

"You need not apologize," he replied, still amused. "My good sense has never stood me in particularly good stead. So you may well be right. We both know how blind I was for so long about my son here. So there may well be other things, spiritual truths, as you say, that I have been equally blind to. I'll have to give the matter some thought."

By this time Andrew had wriggled out of Jamie's lap where he had been sitting and had again urged his two companions into activity. Edward walked to a rise on the hill, scouting the way to the meadow they had been going to seek, when he noticed that the clouds from atop Donachie had rolled toward them across the springtime sky as they had sat eating their lunch. By the time he reached Jamie and Andrew back near the edge of the burn, a definite downpour threatened.

"We had better get back," he said. "And we haven't a moment to lose. These springtime rains can come upon you suddenly. And we don't want a soaking!"

Quickly they gathered the things. Jamie picked up the basket and Edward caught up Andrew, to the boy's squeals of rapture, and hoisted him high onto his shoulders, and off they went at as rapid a pace as they could manage. However, halfway through a shortcut by way of the orchard, huge drops of the imminent downpour began to fall. Breaking into a run, Jamie was hard pressed to match the long strides of Andrew's father, even with the boy still clutched tightly on top of his head.

No speed could have avoided the predicted soaking. Dripping from head to foot, their clothes hanging from their bodies fully drenched, they burst through the front doors of the house, laughing from the exhilarating run, even Graystone himself—to the amazement of the astonished staff—lending his booming voice to the merriment.

Hardly looking beyond the foyer itself, they stood shaking the water from their clothes, still jubilant over their comically

imprudent adventure, when Jamie glanced up to see three figures approaching.

One was Janell, the parlor maid, who had received the guests
upon their arrival. The other two were Candice and Lady Montrose.

CHAPTER THIRTY

Candice Montrose

Immediately Jamie sobered, feeling unaccountably like a naughty schoolgirl caught redhanded by the headmistress.

Graystone was indeed just as surprised, but not in the least disconcerted.

"Why, Lady Montrose—Candice!" he said as graciously as the laird of a grand estate should. "What a surprise!" He laughed. "Caught by the rain, as you can see!"

"We have obviously come at a bad time," said Lady Montrose, with the merest hint of patronizing superiority in her tone, peering down her long, sharp nose at him, then glancing toward his wet entourage. Jamie's wet straight hair hung down from atop her head and ran wildly in every direction. Lady Montrose did, in fact, look the very picture of the scolding school-mother.

"Not at all!" he replied jovially, taking no note of her condescending stance which implied, *This is hardly behavior fitting for a gentleman*! "We were out flower hunting and were foiled by the downpour!"

"Flower hunting?" queried Candice Montrose, and though her nose was much shapelier than her mother's, the impact of her eyes as they stared down from behind it gave much the same effect.

"Yes, we were looking for the first flowers of spring. And we found them, didn't we, Andrew?"

Andrew's wet head nodded vigorously, "Yes, Papa. Fowers for Mamie!"

"What a quaint notion," said Candice, hesitating slightly over the choice of the word *quaint*. "I didn't think you went in for such things."

"Actually, it was Miss MacLeod's idea."

"Ah, I might have known," said Candice, casting a cool glance for the first time in Jamie's direction.

Jamie smiled wanly, her hair dripping in her face, beginning to shiver from the wet and cold.

"We really must change out of these things," said Graystone. "You will stay for tea, won't you? I will join you directly."

"Thank you," said Candice, her voice growing perceptibly sweeter. "How very kind of you, Edward."

"Janell, show our guests to the east parlor, and see that Cameron serves them tea."

An hour and a half later the Montrose carriage pulled away from the house. The two women inside had had a very interesting afternoon, even if it had not been all they had hoped for, or expected.

At twenty-five, Candice Montrose was well on her way to spinsterhood. The problem was not a lack of suitors—there had always been an abundance of those, for she was indeed an attractive young lady. The major hindrance to a successful match had been her parents, chiefly her mother. It seemed the young men Candice herself was drawn to were too far beneath the station Lady Montrose aspired for her daughter. What in Candice's nature attracted her to men of "low breeding" was a question which troubled her mother. No one at Montrose, however, dared broach the subject.

On the other hand, those young men selected by Lady Montrose, all of reputable families, cultured, educated, and of impeccable tastes, many of whom were completely smitten with Candice, were all, to the high-spirited young lady, boring, slow-witted, and hopelessly uninteresting. Candice had no taste for a man she could lead about like a dog on a leash. But her standards greatly limited the field, for there were not many men she would not be able to control either with her beauty or with her biting wit and seductive character. She desired a strong man, strong enough to be his own man, yet not so strong as to be able altogether to resist her enchantments. Few men, indeed, fit the bill.

That is, until Edward Graystone came back on the market. Now here was a man not easily cowed by her womanly wiles—frustratingly so, in fact! He was a genuine challenge! And the best part was that she had her parents' blessing in the pursuit. He was a man of means, of ancient family of reputable standing, of some power in the county—an altogether perfect match. The only hitch from the mother's standpoint was some rumor as to irregularity with respect to the title. There was reported to be a brother somewhere, off on the continent or in Asia somewhere, she couldn't remember. But how serious could it be? Graystone himself had been at Aviemere alone and in charge since they had bought the estate southeast of the village. Whatever these so-called irregularities were, they must be minor. And Candice was getting no younger.

Over the past several months Candice had been zeroing in on her target. Winter had dampened the quest. The roads had been bad and extensive socializing had been impossible. She had spent several weeks on the Continent, the guest of a French baron at his estate on the Mediterranean, a man whom her mother had long cherished hopes for. But the appearance on the scene of a distant cousin he was apparently infatuated with immediately cooled him toward Candice, and the hopes of Lady Montrose in that direction were instantly quelled. Fortunately, she had not closed the door to Aviemere.

"Imagine," Lady Montrose was saying as the carriage jostled them toward Montrose Manor, "him traipsing over the countryside with his child's nurse!"

"Mother, you can't be inferring—" Candice rolled her eyes in exaggerated disbelief. "Why, a man like Edward Graystone would not give that homely creature a second look!"

"I've seen homelier," remarked Lady Montrose.

"She's a mere child! He must be ten years older that she—perhaps twelve. It's ridiculous, mother!"

"Hmm. I suppose you're right."

"And I've heard she is nothing more than a crofter's daughter, or a shepherd girl, or something like that."

"Who would ever think of hiring such a girl for that position?"

"They've had great difficulty keeping a nurse, from what I understand," said Candice. "Perhaps he could find no one else."

"All the more reason why he needs a wife, my dear. And soon!"

Candice cast her mother a canny smile.

"But no matter how desperate I was," Lady Montrose went on, "I'd not have some poor tenant girl caring for *my* child. Just think of what filthy habits the boy could pick up! And if it was just a temporary measure, then why has she been there so long, answer me that!"

"She knows which side her bread is buttered on, that's for certain."

"Let's hope the butter is not too thick!"

"Mother! The idea's utterly preposterous!"

A week later, the vicar of the parish church and his wife came to Montrose Manor to call. When the subject of Edward Graystone came up again, no one but Candice—who knew the vicar's wife to be a fountain of willing gossip regarding the goings-on of the area—was quite sure how the conversation had come to alight on him. Now that she had the discussion in the channel she desired, Candice sat back to listen and see what might come next.

"Lord Graystone has always been a tight-lipped man where his own affairs are concerned," remarked the vicar.

"But the servants do say an astounding change has come upon him," added Mrs. McVeagh knowledgeably.

"How so?" asked Lady Montrose.

"Well—" began the other, now into the rhythm of what she enjoyed most in the world—spreading information which was half true, half false, not bothering to distinguish between the two. "You know, of course, he took his wife's death quite hard—so much so, he would have nothing to do with the child?"

"Pitiful," remarked the vicar.

"Yes, but he's made a complete turn-around, they say," continued his wife. "Simply dotes on the boy now."

"I suspect that new nurse he hired," remarked Lady Montrose.

"I hardly think so, Mother," Candice quickly put in, able to restrain herself no longer. "I told you, Mother, she's nothing but a country girl."

"The daughter of a tenant," said Mrs. McVeagh, anxious not to lose the forward edge of her lead in the conversation.

"Disgraceful!" added Lady Montrose. "To think of the son of an earl being cared for by a peasant!"

"Is Lord Graystone actually the earl?" asked the vicar. "I thought there was some confusion concerning the old man's inheritance—one brother got the title, the other the estate, something like that."

"Oh, come now," put in his wife, "you know nothing of the

kind! Besides, you know very well we heard the other brother had been killed."

"But there were reports questioning—"

"Nonetheless," said Lady Montrose decidedly. "The Graystones are one of the county's most prestigious families, and Lord Graystone should be aware of propriety."

"I hear she's a pretty wisp of a thing, though," said the vicar's wife.

"You're not suggesting that he would . . ." said Candice, allowing her raised eyebrows to complete the sentence. "He is a Graystone, after all!"

"Yes, but a peasant girl raised so quickly to such a position might well begin to entertain certain, shall we say, lofty ambitions," concluded Mrs. McVeagh.

"Whatever grand illusions a peasant girl might entertain," said Candice, trying to convince herself more than the vicar's tongue-wagging wife, "they would not have the least effect on a man like Edward Graystone."

The conversation then drifted toward other topics. But Candice remained uneasy. She did not like the thought of the man she intended to marry associating with a common peasant. More than that, however, she did not like to be reminded that the girl was, in fact, not altogether unattractive, in her own homely sort of way, and had the laird all to himself—especially now that he had suddenly taken such an interest in the child. She wanted no scandal to taint her acquisition once she finally had him.

Somehow she must get rid of her!

Thus Candice Montrose vowed to keep apprised of the situation. There should be many more invitations to Montrose Manor, and also frequent "chance" visits to Aviemere. She could not afford to wait for invitations. If she sat at home and did nothing, who could tell what inroads the young vixen might make!

But of course, she would leave nothing to chance. Finding a new nurse must be the first priority of business. Edward would have to be convinced, but she could manage that. Then she had to make sure she was close enough to him to have an instrumental hand in choosing the new candidate.

CHAPTER THIRTY-ONE

A Journey Into The Past

Happily oblivious to the maelstrom of discourse swirling around her, Jamie was as content as she had ever had reason to be, believing her life for the present had reached a most pleasant fulfillment in her custodial care of young Andrew. She had no reason to suspect the shaking about to come.

When George Ellice hailed her one morning as she was taking Andrew out for his usual morning walk, she thought it was merely a friendly greeting. But the factor had something more on his mind.

"Good morning, Jamie," he said. "I'm so glad I caught you. Have you a moment? I have something to talk over with you."

"Of course. I'm sure Andrew won't mind a slight delay to our excursion."

"Come to my office, then."

The factor's office at the main house was a small room on the lower floor, toward the back near the stables. It was neat and orderly, though the furnishings were rather worn and there was much work stacked on the desk.

"Please, have a seat," he said, offering her the only other chair in the room other than the one which stood behind the desk.

Jamie took her place, growing more curious by the moment at the formal treatment of this interview. She sat patiently as he shuffled through a few papers and slipped on his spectacles. He then cleared his throat somewhat stiffly.

"You may recall some time ago, last fall I believe," he began, "speaking to my wife regarding your father and the uncertainties you had in your mind about his past, and yours."

Jamie's heart raced. "Yes," she answered, betraying none of

the emotions which by now hung on his every word.

"She mentioned this to me, though you probably thought the matter had been forgotten entirely. And I must admit it did slip my mind for a time. But as I was doing my spring cleaning of various extraneous paperwork, it suddenly came back to me. This year I had to do a more thorough job of it because a new cabinet will soon be arriving for this office. At any rate, I was keeping my eyes open, and that was how I first ran across the papers regarding the sale of your father's land. Your father *was* Gilbert MacLeod, was he not?"

Jamie nodded.

"Then no doubt these documents would be of great interest to you, for they specify the location of the land. You said to my wife, I think, that you didn't know exactly where you and your father had lived."

For a moment Jamie sat as one stunned. "Yes—that's right—I was only seven I think—I don't think my grandfather even knew the place. Where is it?"

"It's all outlined here," said Ellice. "It is a large croft on the far border of the laird's estate. I have been there many times to collect rents, and I shouldn't wonder if it isn't just as it was when your father had it."

"Do the papers tell how he came to sell it?" Jamie asked.

"These documents give merely facts and figures. The croft was doing poorly and your father was in heavy debt. This indicates that his payment for the property was mainly the clearance of the debts, and it seems he walked away with some twenty pounds besides."

"That doesn't seem like much if it was, as you say, a sizeable croft."

"No, it wasn't much. But he had large payments on a portion of the land he had previously purchased from the laird that he was unable to meet."

"How much would the land be worth now?" asked Jamie.

"Oh, several hundred pounds to be sure! I don't know really. But the croft is doing much better now. And your father was 'strapped,' as we say. I imagine he had little other recourse to get him out from under those debts."

"Mrs. Lundie says he was cheated."

"Jamie," returned Ellice, ruffled but not angry, "I am the laird's factor."

"I'm sorry. I didn't think about what I was saying. I would

never accuse the laird. I don't care about the facts and figures anyway. All I wanted was to see the land again."

"Of course, I know you mean no ill. But, you see, even though I wasn't factor back then, the honor of the Graystone business dealings rests on me, in a manner of speaking. Granted, Mackenzie Graystone, who was laird at that time, was a shrewd character—above cheating I'm sure, though I expect he had no qualms about profiting from another's loss. Now, about your seeing the property, when will you be available for such an undertaking?"

"Anytime! Today?" said Jamie eagerly.

Ellice smiled. "Shouldn't take us more than two or three hours to get there. I'll bring the wagon around for you at half-past eleven."

"Thank you!" Jamie said, grasping the factor's hand. "Thank you!"

At eleven-thirty Jamie left Andrew in Bea's care and hurried out to meet Mr. Ellice. The wagon stood in front as the factor had promised.

On the way Ellice explained some of the interesting particulars about the croft.

"It's been fairly prosperous since the laird bought the place, but of course he had unlimited capital to pour into it. It's near the moor so there are some portions that can be downright unmanageable. I looked up a few things after you left and it seems that year and the year before were particularly bad ones for everyone. As a small landowner with nothing to fall back on, well, it's no wonder your father had to sell."

"Is someone living there now?"

"An older couple took over after your father and they were there until about a year ago when the man died. Made a decent go of it, too. But his wife moved away to live with relatives. It's been empty since then and the laird has been working it with his own men. 'Tis a big croft and the rents are high, so we've had a bit of difficulty finding new tenants. We've discussed dividing it up into smaller crofts."

As they approached, Ellice pointed out the cottage in the distance, while Jamie tried to take in every detail.

This is the place where she was born! In the distance she could see the barren moorland. Nearer at hand were fields—fallow now without the covering of rich stocks of grain—spreading away on either side of the road. Spring sowing was in full progress and Jamie saw several workers with "seed sheets" slung over their heads and strapped about their bodies, walking in a rhythmic pattern back and forth, up and down the harrows. It was a pleasant scene, and brought her father to mind even more clearly. He must have done these very things—ploughing, harrowing, sowing, and harvesting—year in and year out, a pattern as rhythmic as the scene she was now witnessing. Yet for him the pattern had finally been broken by the harsh realities of nature, ending in ultimate failure.

"Well, here we are!" Mr. Ellice called out cheerily.

Jamie looked up from her reverie to see the large stone house just off to their right, opposite the field where she had been watching the workers. It had certainly been a nice home, perhaps even imposing, at one time, possibly seventy-five years earlier, but poor landowners and struggling tenants could ill-afford to tend to its upkeep over the years. Little could Jamie know that her own mother's ancestors had built the house and worked the land for several generations before it came into her father and mother's hands, and thence into the grasping clutches of the grandfather of her beloved little Andrew.

Suddenly shy, Jamie looked all about, her mind filling with fragmentary bits and images and scenes from her distant childhood. Slowly she climbed down from the wagon, then turned and said, "I think I'd like to look at it alone. Would you mind terribly?"

"I understand, lass," Ellice replied. "I have some business to tend to with the men. I'll be back in forty or fifty minutes."

He turned the horses around, and in a few minutes disappeared down the road.

Jamie stood frozen in the middle of the yard for some time. When she and the factor had been talking about the croft and the land and her father that morning in his office, it had all seemed so distant, so dreamlike, as if they were discussing some faraway place that had been a relic from history. As the wagon had brought her nearer, that hazy unreality began to change, and seeing the workers in the field had dissolved the detachment still further. But now, standing in the yard in front of the house she and her father and mother had lived in—suddenly it was close and personal and vivid once more in her mind: she felt as if she had come home.

She had scampered across this very place as a child. It was here that her father had scooped her up into his strong arms. It was here she had milked the cow and hung out the wash to dry.

At last she forced her legs into motion and toward the house itself. She walked up the two stone steps and turned the latch on the door. It creaked open. As she stepped inside a musty, unlived-in odor assailed her. The room was bare now, except for a heavy old table in the middle of the floor, and a broken stool. The hearth was cold. She ran her hand along the rough surface of the table—was this the very table at which they used to sit and eat and talk? She could almost remember . . .

Dinner is ready fer ye, Papa . . .

Images flooded Jamie's mind now, memories that time had long ago buried, but which the heart of the child could never fully relinquish.

Would ye like to go to the city, Jamie?

What aboot oor cottage here, Papa?

Ah, the house—I just can't hang on to it anymore, not if it means starving.

I can work harder, Papa! We dinna have t' go!

No need to work in Aberdeen. Ye'll ride about in a carriage. Ye'll wear a bonny pink bonnet. I'll find what I'm looking fer there—I know it!

Were they all nothing but empty dreams—the hope of a better life? the desperate attempt of a failing man to cling to his fancies the only way he could?

She had always revered her father, in her childish way believing him incapable of failure. Yet now maturity had begun to open her eyes to the folly of his daydreams. Losing everything, up to the very moment of his death he refused to let go of the fantasy of his daughter as a high-society lady and he her gentleman father, both decked out in rich finery, riding about in an expensive carriage. Even the immediacy of death had only partially dimmed the vision.

Her grandfather had hinted to her of this many times, but she had never had ears to hear it, because she, too, still wanted to cling to the foolish dream. Over and over he had tried to tell her about the importance of being content with the lot which was given her.

She's her father's daughter, he had said once, and the mournfulness of his tone still echoed in her mind. Was that why he had kept silent about her father? Was he afraid for her, afraid that she, too, might somehow fail in the same way his own son had?

But had he really failed?

He had possessed his daughter's love and devotion. Was that not a kind of success—perhaps the best kind of all? Yet how pitiful that it had never been enough for him! He had to have more. Oh, yes, he had tried to convince himself, it was all for Jamie. But the fruitless pursuit of an elusive quarry made him miss out on the joyful relationship he had been given, and which had been in his possession all along.

He had had many grand dreams. But remember, my dear daughter, if you find love you will have attained the greatest dream of all.

Alice MacLeod knew what her husband was made of. She knew that his kind nature would always be at war with his innate restlessness and pursuit of unreasonable goals. Perhaps she, too, feared the daughter would follow that same path.

Yet despite all these new realizations that womanhood shed upon Jamie's childhood, she continued to love her father—perhaps even more. And standing in this very room where they had lived, she could almost sense the love he had had for her. It may have been misplaced, but she could not deny it, nor deny him. He was her papa!

Jamie turned and stepped outside. She had come here seeking memories, but all at once they had become almost more than she could bear.

Gray clouds had covered the morning sun and a chill north wind had sprung up, lashing her in the face. She walked into it away from the stone house, away from the turmoil of remembering. Now was the time for prayer. Papa was gone, as well as his land. But now perhaps she understood a little better the danger she herself had always been in. Now perhaps for the first time she could join into the prayers her grandfather had always prayed on her behalf.

As she drifted by degrees up the hill away from the house, a gradual sense of thanksgiving began to steal upon her. Yes, the memories of the past brought with them heartache. But there was so much to be thankful for! God's hand had been upon her; she could see evidence of His leading and protection with every turn her life had taken. Perhaps her father's last wish for her *had* been fulfilled—but in a way he wouldn't have anticipated. No, she would never be a lady. But he had wanted the best for her, and she couldn't be happier with the life the Lord had given her. Was that not all anyone could ask for?

Without realizing the direction her steps had been taking her,

Jamie found that she had come all the way to the broken old wall separating the field from the moor. The wind swirled around her and seemed to be springing up from the dreary moor itself. She shivered for the cold and the eerie spell of the place. She recalled Mrs. Ellice saying that Frederick Lundie was killed out on the moor; it was easy to imagine such a thing happening there. Then, as if her thoughts had suddenly sprung to life, she heard from behind her—

"He died oot there," said the hollow, empty voice of Iona Lundie.

Jamie could not even force herself to turn and confront the drawn, bitter countenance. Still facing the moor, she said, "How are you—why—did you follow me here? It seems I see you wherever I go."

"There's nathin' left me but t' wander aboot, lass, seeking my revenge wherever I might find it."

"But what have I to do with it? Please," Jamie implored, "leave me alone. Stop following me—please!"

An empty laugh followed. "I ain't followin' ye, lass. It's fate that draws us togither. Dinna ya see? Fate will avenge us both!"

"But I want no revenge! Please, just leave me alone!"

"So ye say noo. But ye hanna heard the story o' my Freddie an' yer ain father."

"And I don't want to hear it!"

"But ye must, lass. Ye're bound t' hear it. The moor is where it all began. They was both killed oot there."

"No, no!" shouted Jamie, facing the widow. "My father died at home—in the cottage back there—I was with him!"

"It all started on the moor, I tell ye," she replied flatly. "Ye *must* ken—an' I think ye'll listen."

"No," Jamie insisted.

"Ye'll listen—because he was yer ain father."

Jamie was silent. Iona Lundie was right. Whatever there was to know, she *had* to listen.

"My Freddie was a desperate man. When he left that last night, I told him t' do nothin' crazy. He said he had nae choice fer Graystone said he'd keep him frae workin' again—onyplace. He said he was goin' t' git what he had comin' frae the laird— he said he would leave Aviemere a rich man or the laird would come doon with him. He told me if onythin' was t' happen to him I'd know it was the fault o' them Graystones, an' t' make sure they paid. I was sore afraid, but he said Gilbert'd speak up with me if necessary. Then he left aboot whate'er business it was, an' I ne'er saw him alive again.

"The day after they brocht his body home t' me, yer ain father turns up dead. I tried t' tell them what happened, but no one would believe a word again' the laird. An' what was I but jist an' auld, bitter widow. Then the story spreads aroun' that it were yer father what killed my Freddie. Folks said they were in on some scheme what went sour an' they turned on one anither. They seen that yer father was beaten before dyin' in the cottage doon there. They said the two men fought oot on the moor here, an' that Freddie was killed an' yer father, half dead, dragged himsel' home only t' die the next day. Mighty convenient, I say! Both deaths explained sae neatly, leavin' nae need t' look elsewhere fer the true killer!"

Jamie gripped the jagged edge of the stone wall. Could she believe this woman? Did people really think her father was a murderer?

"But it was them Graystones!" the Lundie woman continued, "that did in my husband an' yer father. Not the old man hissel'. He would hae sent his son oot t' do the dirty work. The Graystones killed the both o' them!"

"No!" screamed Jamie, but the wind seemed to carry away all her intended force. "I can't believe that," she said. But as she looked into Iona Lundie's eyes, what she saw made her stop short. Even if what she said was not true, Iona Lundie passionately believed what she said. There was such certainty in her face that it defied protest.

"Ye take one look," the woman continued, her voice seething with passion, "at Edward Graystone, an' tell me he wouldna be capable of murderin' fer his precious Aviemere. An' his brother's cut frae the same dirty cloth!"

"How can you say that?" Jamie's voice shook as she spoke. "They wouldn't do such a thing!" But the words had barely parted her lips before an image rose in her mind of the man she had first seen at Aviemere—the man who had turned his back on his helpless son for two years, the man whose dark eyes at times held a smoldering fire and at others an icy hostility. But she shook the vision from her mind's eye—he had changed!

"Ye can tell yersel' what ye want," Iona said. "But I ken ye can see the trowth in my words—because ye've seen *him!*"

"Go away!" cried Jamie. "Leave me alone!"

" 'Tis noo oor chance t' see justice done," the woman went

on, ignoring Jamie's pleas. "I couldna do onythin' aboot it before alone. I asked my sister Bea—"

"Bea is your sister!" said Jamie with a shudder. How many times had she trusted Andrew into that woman's care? He was with her right now! What if something should happen!

"Aye. But when I asked her help, she refused. I thought she could find oot what Freddie discovered. But she'd hae nae part o' it. But noo ye're there. Ye could find out somethin'. If only we ken what happened, then people'd hae t' believe me."

"I would never be party to such a thing," Jamie replied. "Give up this thirst for revenge. It won't bring him back. What's done is past!"

" 'Tis nae revenge I'm wantin', 'tis *justice*. Yer father went t' his grave with people thinkin' him a killer—dinna ye think he deserves some o' the justice due him?"

"Stop!" screamed Jamie over the wind, howling now. "I won't listen to anymore!"

She rushed past the woman and ran across the field. She did not stop until she had reached the road and met Ellice as he drove the wagon back to meet her.

She climbed up silently, saying nothing, and the factor—not seeing from whence she had come, nor seeing the solitary figure standing in the distance at the edge of the field—assumed she was still overcome with the memories of the place, and asked no questions.

She spoke hardly a word all the way back to Aviemere, and Ellice did not intrude into her silence. And what could she have said? She could hardly share with this loyal man the accusations she had just heard against his employer. He would not even listen to hints of fraud, much less an accusation of murder! Especially coming as it did, he would say, from a crazy lunatic woman! She did not even believe the accusations herself. They were nothing but the ravings of a bitter old woman—best forgotten altogether! Of course! Forgotten!

But why then could she not force them from her mind?

Dear Lord, help me to forget this terrible day, she prayed inwardly.

Yet even as she prayed, Iona Lundie's searing words seemed to burn still deeper into her mind the more she tried to erase them.

The wagon pulled up in front of the house. She climbed out, thanked Mr. Ellice, then walked toward the doors over which the inflexible, belligerent, combative words still silently cried out *Aut pax aut bellum*: Either peace or war! How fitting a motto for this cold, stern family!

She had just closed the door behind her when a shout from the stairs above stopped her in her tracks.

"There you are!" cried Edward Graystone, descending the stairs. There was anger in his voice and fire in his gaze. "What have you been doing!"

"I was out with Mr. Ellice," Jamie replied, shivering at his menacing tone. Somehow she knew this was not the time to tell him *where* she had been or what had occurred there.

"Why you incompetent malingerer! Is that all you have to say for yourself!"

What was this change that had come over him? Then all at once she went cold with a different kind of fear.

"Why—what's happened?" her words came out as a bare whisper.

"While you were off—God only knows where!—Andrew was hurt."

"Oh, no!" she cried. In a panic she raced past him and flew up the stairs, all her fears and confusion lost in terror for the little one.

Edward could hardly have missed the sight of her stricken countenance as she rushed past, and perhaps he felt some remorse for his harsh words. And perhaps later Jamie would forgive him, for she could not have known that less than an hour before he had received a most disquieting visitor onto the grounds of the estate.

CHAPTER THIRTY-TWO

An Unexpected Visitor

It was later that same evening, after she had seen Andrew safely to bed and detected by his face that he was at last asleep, that Jamie left him for the first time and went to seek out her employer.

The injuries had not been serious. The boy had fallen down a short flight of steps and received a nasty cut on his forehead. Bea was so beside herself with anxiety and self-blame that Jamie instantly repented of any thought that she could have intended the boy harm. But she could hardly assauge her own guilt. What Graystone had said was right—she had been shirking her duties. And the knowledge that she must keep silent about where she had been made it all the worse. But at least Andrew was now sleeping peacefully, with his "Baba" tucked securely under his arm. She knew what she must do. She left the nursery and went straight to the library.

Graystone's voice answered her knock.

"Come in."

She entered, and he appeared surprised to see her.

"What do you want, Miss MacLeod?" he said, the harsh edge still present in his voice.

"Mr. Graystone," she said. "I'm so sorry about what happened. You were right. I wanted to apologize."

"You do not need to apologize," he replied stiffly. "Just see that such a thing does not happen again." His tone was like ice and his eyes were hard and darker than usual.

"I will see to it, sir. That is, I will do my best."

"Then you may go."

Jamie turned and was about to leave, feeling worse than

when she had come, when another voice broke through the thick silence and stopped her.

"Edward, do you plan on denying me an introduction?"

All at once Jamie realized that in her single-minded resolve to speak to Graystone himself, she had not noticed that there was someone else in the room. Unconsciously she turned toward the voice. The man was seated, or rather draped, in a chair adjacent to the desk, slightly shaded in the evening shadows. It was understandable that she might have overlooked him initially. That would have to be the only reason, for his was not a figure easily overlooked. He was of about Edward's size, and though his face bore an odd resemblance to Edward's, it was much more striking—as handsome as it was free from those hard lines of care and turmoil which had come to characterize the younger of the Graystones. His smile was quick and relaxed and would have been almost friendly save for the conflicting cynicism of his pale blue eyes. What she failed to notice was the keen look of appraisal he had cast in her direction.

Edward sighed before he spoke, as if every word was an effort. "This is my son's nurse, Miss MacLeod," he said.

The man stood and stepped toward Jamie with his hand extended. "I see my brother is not up to this introduction," he said with an amused lilt in his voice. "I am Derek Graystone, your employer's elder brother."

All at once the sudden change in the laird—the tension, the harsh words—came clear to Jamie. No doubt it was all due to the unexpected arrival of his brother!

Jamie stumbled a few feeble words of attempted greeting, then made to leave. But again Derek Graystone's voice stopped her. "I hope we will have the pleasure of your presence at dinner," he said, the broad, good-natured grin dominating his face once more.

"It is not cust—that is, I usually eat with—" Jamie began, but Derek interrupted her.

"To blazes with propriety!" he said. "Edward, surely you're not going to deny your poor brother—home from the wars after nearly ten years—the pleasure of a lovely face to cheer my first dinner back at Aviemere!"

"I have my duties," Jamie tried to explain.

"Edward, you are a tyrant! A cold-hearted tyrant! I suppose this lovely young woman must eat in the scullery with the stable hands!"

"We observe certain customs here at Aviemere," replied Edward flatly.

"Hang your customs!"

Edward's eyebrow arched ever so slightly, and the muscles in his jaw rippled. But he answered coolly, "The decision rests entirely with Miss MacLeod."

Jamie sank with almost visible dismay. She was bound to cause someone's displeasure no matter what the outcome. She could not sit at the table with these two gentlemen! She would be completely out of place!

"I really do have my duties," she said weakly.

"And I insist," Derek replied with his grin still in place.

She glanced lamely at Derek's now silent brother, hoping for some support from him, but his eyes were boring a hole through the opposite wall—there would be no help there! He wasn't even going to help her gracefully refuse. And Derek was certainly not a man to withstand once he had his mind set.

Dinner, at best, was uncomfortable and tense. Edward spoke hardly at all, and when he did his words were clipped and terse. Concentrating so hard at not making a fool of herself, Jamie was hardly the witty dining companion she was certain Derek Graystone had expected. And the taut atmosphere was made even worse by the shocked, scandalized expressions of Jamie's fellow servants.

It came as an immense relief when the last course was completed. Edward quickly excused himself, telling his brother he could join him in the parlor for coffee if he wished.

Jamie rose also, and hastened toward the dining room doors. The last thing she wanted was to be left alone with the Lord of Aviemere.

But Graystone had other ideas. In two strides he was at her side and laid a restraining hand on her arm.

"Certainly you don't mean to compound my brother's rudeness by leaving me high and dry when the evening is still so young?"

Tensing at his touch, she could hardly find her voice. "I—I really must—I have to go check on Andrew."

"A sleeping child cannot need you as much as a lonely soldier," he said, drawing uncomfortably close.

"I—I dinna ken—I mean, I don't know what you mean."

"You must think me forward," he said, still grasping her arm. "But one in my position—facing constant danger and uncertainty, never knowing what tomorrow will bring—well, I've learned I must never hesitate when something good comes my way."

"I really must go," she said uneasily.

Spurred on by the obvious discomposure of her innocence, he took her chin in his hand, gently but firmly. "Please, at least grant me a walk in the moonlight."

"I have to go . . . I must go!"

She slipped her arm from his grip and fumbled for the door handle.

"Perhaps after we become better acquainted," he persisted. "I shall be here for some time."

Without a reply, Jamie hurried out and ran all the way to her room.

CHAPTER THIRTY-THREE

Brotherly Strife

A steady drizzle during the night had left the roads muddy and slick. However, Derek had insisted on a tour of the estate, and since the weather did not seem as if it would improve over the low clouds and gusty wind of that morning, his brother made no protest. Moreover, Edward was aching to get out of the house even if it meant spending the day with his brother.

They mounted their horses, Edward on his sorrel stallion, and Derek on a lively chestnut. Edward spoke but little. Silence was the only way he could hide the emotions swirling within him. When he had answered the knock on his study door yesterday to find his brother in front of him, with that incorrigible smirk on his face, he had felt something akin to nausea. It had been ten years since Derek last set foot on Aviemere, and Edward had wishfully begun to imagine that it might last forever.

But Derek had never been one to leave his younger brother in peace. From their earliest years Edward remembered that he never missed an opportunity to goad him—to remind him who was heir and who was the apple of their father's eye. And then as if to twist the knife still further, he would demonstrate an utter disdain for the estate, considering it a great joke that the heir gave not a fig for the land. Knowing how Edward loved the estate, he derived a great morbid pleasure in throwing his own possession of it in his face.

Edward never knew what made his brother this way. By his teens he had already started hating Derek. Years of separation had somewhat muted that feeling until he was able to convince himself he felt nothing at all for his brother. But when the farce of his supposed death had turned his world upside down, bringing with it, as it did, all the accompanying tragedy in his personal life, he realized the hatred had only been lying dormant within him.

For the first time he had recently been able to look more objectively upon his feelings for his brother and Aviemere. His new relationship with Andrew had caused him to reevaluate his priorities. He had begun to think he might be able to deal with the inevitable more calmly and with less bitterness now that he had his son to share life with.

At least so he thought until the swaggering form of his brother landed square on his doorstep!

Edward was horrified at how quickly the old hatred had resurged. Derek had not changed. He had relished that first look of shock and dismay his brother displayed, and laughed right in his face.

Then came the exchange following last night's dinner. Having his coffee in the parlor, Edward had hoped desperately that his brother would choose to retire rather than join him. But Derek would never allow such a prime opportunity to pass. He came jauntily into the room and, foregoing the coffee, poured himself a large brandy.

"Edward, my dear brother," he said with a taunting glint in his eye. "You have become stiff and stodgy in your ripe old age of—what are you now, twenty-eight, thirty? I should have expected a better reception after ten years."

"I should have expected some sort of warning of your arrival," Edward returned dryly.

"I was never one to plan ahead. One never knows what kind of turn one's life may unexpectedly take."

"So you kept your options open in case a better offer came your way."

Derek laughed.

"Exactly! Perhaps there is hope for you yet. Yes, there definitely may be, especially after having a look at the servants. That nurse is certainly a tantalizing morsel, and the parlor maid is a dish equal to any man's appetite."

"Leave my servants alone, Derek."

"I see that perhaps I have been away too long. It seems you have forgotten just who the laird of Aviemere is, and who owns every scrap of land and every ounce of flesh upon it."

"You depraved—"

But Edward bit back his retort. He would not give Derek the pleasure of his wrath.

"Have you no better welcome for your dear brother after so long?"

"How long will you be staying?"

Derek laughed again. "That's what I've always liked about you—never one to mince words." But he did not answer the question.

So now Edward must show the returning lord his kingdom. The way Derek looked at the homely cottages, sickened Edward. He could see no intrinsic beauty; everything was only a means to achieve whatever calculated ends he happened to be turning over in his mind at the time. Edward hoped to get this tour over with as quickly as possible; he could hardly tolerate what was happening inside of him as a result of being near his brother. And worst of all, he knew he could not blame his brother for the bitter attitudes of his own heart. Derek's appearance only revealed his own weakness. These past months had brought the first glimpses of happiness he had experienced in a long time, and now he despised himself for capitulating so easily to his brother's spell, and his own unforgiving heart.

"Over there," he said, pointing to a field on their left where several men were busy at their task of scattering seed, "that's the last of the sowing. We should finish in a few days. The conditions have been favorable, and I expect this to be an excellent season."

"I spoke with my solicitors in Edinburgh before coming here," said Derek. "Profits were down last year."

"Only slightly. American grain has been quite competitive since their civil war."

" 'Competitive' is putting it mildly, wouldn't you say? They are flooding the market with cheap grain. We can hardly afford to use our own grain ourselves."

"You've been out of touch for ten years, Derek," Edward replied. "The reports are exaggerated and make things look worse than they actually are. If things were as bad as they say, we would have had a much worse showing last year."

"It's possible the effects are only beginning to appear."

"I doubt it."

"Nonetheless," said Derek, drawing the word out dramatically, "I feel we need to take some action."

"Action?" Unconsciously Edward reined his horse to a stop as he said the word.

Derek reined also and turned.

"Yes," he said. "I've spoken to other landowners in London and Edinburgh. I've come to the conclusion that there is but one solution to the problem, and one with sound historical precedent. The only way to avoid inevitable collapse is to convert the fields into pastureland where sheep can graze at a fraction of what the upkeep costs us now on all these small crofts. Sheep would bring in equal income at far less expense and bother."

Edward gaped at his brother. The idea was preposterous, no better than that black era in Scottish history some eighty years earlier when tens of thousands of highland tenants had been ousted from land their ancestors had occupied for generations and had been forced to migrate elsewhere or live in squalor in the cities.

"You're talking about new Clearances!"

"Don't be so naive."

"You can't just turn the people out!"

"It was a necessity back then, as it is now," Derek replied. "It's my land and I will see it turn the best profit possible."

"A necessity, you mean, to line the already fat wallets of the gentry. There's more money in wool, human lives are expendable. Is that it?"

"Your emotionalism about the estate is quite beneath your station, Edward." Derek's reply was laced with the humor he always perceived in Edward's position. "If the market crashes, Aviemere's dear tenants will suffer as much as if they had been turned out. At least my way they will have some kind of chance."

"*If* the market crashes," Edward repeated pointedly. "And the chances of such a thing happening are extremely thin. We can sustain some loss."

"We!" repeated Derek with emphasis. "You forget again, dear *younger* brother, they are *my* losses you are speaking so casually about. And I don't fancy sustaining *any* loss."

"You can't do this!"

Derek laughed.

"Be grateful for the latitude I've allowed you over the years, Edward. But I am now back and I will make the decisions. *You* will not tell me what I can or cannot do. I was even considering stocking the hilly regions and the mountain with game and renting out hunting rights to sportsmen from the south in season. There's money to be had in that business too, dear brother."

"Just how long do you intend to stay here, Derek?" Edward forced out the words despite his fear at what the answer might be. Yesterday Derek had avoided the question, and Edward knew his brother was dangling him on a string for a reason.

Derek's initial response was a merry chuckle. Then he spoke, purposefully drawing out every word. "The army has been a good life for me. But as a man begins to get on in years, it loses some of its glamor. A man begins to look more favorably on the notion of settling down, starting a family—*producing heirs*. I've given it considerable thought and the prospect of settling permanently at Aviemere is not all odious to me."

"Then this is not a mere visit? You are not simply on leave?"

"In all likelihood," replied Derek vaguely. "The longer I am here the more this place grows on me."

"You can't simply waltz in here and turn everything upside down!" said Edward, but even as the words left his mouth he despised himself for his pleading tone. But he could not help what he said—if he must be humiliated, then let it be complete.

"There you go with *can't* again," said Derek. "Remember, Aviemere is *mine* and I can do whatever I please!"

For a moment the edge of humor in his voice was replaced with venom. But he recovered quickly, and ended with a sharp, piercing laugh.

"You cur!" Edward spat, then dug his heels into his stallion's sides and galloped away.

His whole body shook with repressed fury. There was a moment—a brief split second of time, when Derek had laughed—when he could have killed him. Only his lack of a weapon stopped him.

Was that the answer? The only way he could find peace? It was always Derek who had brought turmoil into his life. Derek who had robbed him of his father's affection. Derek who had caused him to lose Olivia. Always Derek—always delighting in robbing him of things that should have been his!

It would be a simple matter to kill him! How many times had he planned just such a ploy in his youth? Of course he would never have dared to carry out any of his fantasies then. But he knew some particularly treacherous stretches on the moor. An accident would be easy to fabricate, especially to one like his brother, unfamiliar with the terrain. There had been accidents there before—none would question it.

There was the moor now off to his left. He reined his mount into a trot and gazed out upon it. He shuddered as he remembered one such accident out there—to his father's prized thoroughbred.

Yes, it was a treacherous place, one that lent itself to thoughts of murder.

With such notions further darkening his mood, he turned toward home, though even the mere word embittered him further. What a fool he had been over the years to allow himself to believe it could ever be his! He knew it was time to let go of such folly and begin to base his life on realities—hard, cold, immovable realities.

CHAPTER THIRTY-FOUR

Midnight Encounter

Jamie saw nothing of Andrew's father for two days, and began to fear that the appearance of his brother had caused him to revert to his former ways. He made no attempt to see his son, and the boy asked constantly for his papa. No more dinner invitations had come her way, much to her relief.

Gradually the house began to take on its old tensions. Desiring no mutiny, Derek kept his distance for a time from most of the staff, and Edward's presence was silent and aloof at meals. No one saw him otherwise.

Andrew's cut was healing rapidly, but since the accident Jamie had found herself sleeping much lighter, jumping to her feet and hastening into his room at the least sound. She had fallen into a rather sound sleep one night only to be awakened suddenly by a loud cry.

She sprang to her feet and ran to Andrew's side. The boy was whimpering, but she could not be sure that his cry had awakened her. All about her, however, the house was dead still. She waited at Andrew's side, trying to soothe him back into a peaceful slumber. However, sleep continued to elude him. At length Jamie decided that a small bottle of warm milk would be needed.

She wrapped Andrew in his blanket, picked him out of his bed, and carried him downstairs to the kitchen.

As she went she heard the clock strike a single chime in the dining room. Entering the kitchen carrying a candle in her hand, she saw by the flicker of a shadow on the opposite wall the movement of a silent figure inside.

"Who's there?" she breathed.

There was no answer, but as Jamie brought the light fully into the room she saw that the other midnight visitor to the kitchen was Janell, the parlor maid.

"Janell," said Jamie, relieved. "Why didn't you answer? You scared me near to death."

Still she said nothing, just standing there as if she wanted to run away.

"Janell, are you all right? You look ill. Do you know how late it is?"

"Yes—I know—the clock just struck half past eleven," the girl rasped in a bare whisper. "I'm—I'm fine . . ."

Jamie studied her for a long moment. She certainly did not look fine. The young parlor maid, about Jamie's own age, was very pretty, for it was customary for the gentry to display only their finest servants before their guests. She had large soulful brown eyes, thickly lashed and considered more than alluring by several of the laird's young field hands. Her thick yellow hair was normally pulled up into a bun on her head, revealing a long alabaster-white neck. But now her hair hung in a tangled mass about her shoulders. The simple cotton nightdress she was wearing was torn at the shoulder.

The questions had barely begun to form in Jamie's mind about Janell's odd appearance and agitated countenance, when the other girl turned to go.

"Janell," Jamie pressed, "are you sure? Something seems wrong. How long have you been here?"

"Only a few minutes," she sniffed, trying to stifle a sob.

"What's wrong, Janell?"

"Nothing . . . I'm fine," she tried to say, but even as she did she could not keep the sobs from escaping her lips.

"Did you hear something a few minutes ago? I heard a scream. I thought it was Andrew at first—but I'm not sure."

"I couldn't help it!" cried Janell, but her words were nearly drowned by several more choked sobs, followed at last by a rush of tears. Jamie rushed up to her and, setting down her candle, placed her free arm around her.

"What *is* it, Janell, dear . . . Please, tell me what's troubling you!"

"Oh, Jamie . . ." but her sobs now prevented her from speaking coherently for some time.

"It was you who screamed out?"

"I—I couldn't help it. I was so frightened!"

"Of what? Dear, what is it!"

"It was terrible—" she covered her face with her hands and it was a moment before she could continue. "He turned my head at first," she went on in gasps, trying to catch her breath. "He *is* rather handsome, and what girl wouldn't be flattered to have a laird pay her such attention—"

"The laird!"

"I knew he didn't really mean the things he said, but still—"

"Janell, what are you saying? Do you mean Lord Graystone?"

"Aye, the laird's brother."

"Derek Graystone?" asked Jamie, whose relief was almost visible when the girl nodded. "What did he do?"

"It was late, and I had just gone to bed," she began, but fresh sobs continued to interrupt her speech. "Maybe an hour ago . . . I heard a knock at my door and—when I opened it—there he was. He pushed his way in . . . He tried to talk to me for a while but then . . . he . . . then he came closer to me, and tried—oh, Jamie, I was terrified! I pushed him away, but he kept trying. I screamed out, hardly knowing what I was doing. He told me to shut up or . . . or he'd hit me. Oh, I was so scared! He came closer again, but I got free and ran to the door and managed to open it a little and scream again. He pulled at me and tore my nightdress, and—oh, Jamie, I don't know what he would have done . . . but then we heard steps coming along the corridor and Miss Campbell's voice calling to me. He swore at me and then hurried out—in the other direction. I quickly closed the door and . . . I told Miss Campbell through the door when she came . . . I told her I'd had a terrible nightmare. Oh, Jamie! I was so ter-rified!" she sobbed.

"So then you came down here?"

"I knew he wouldn't be back, at least not tonight. I had to get something to quiet myself down—I couldn't sleep! Oh, but what if he comes back again another night?"

"Oh, dear Janell," soothed Jamie, but even as she tried to calm the girl, she could not ignore the indignation rising within her at the thought of what had happened. "He won't try anything again. He can't get away with this!"

But Janell stiffened and pulled away.

"Jamie, no! Please don't tell a soul about this! I would be mortified if everyone knew!"

"But Edward Graystone must know. He can't let his brother treat his servants so."

"What could he do? What would he do? They don't care

about the likes of us. An earl can do as he pleases with his servants. But—but I'm—I'm not that kind of girl." She broke down again, this time into quiet weeping.

At length she said again, "Please, Jamie, promise me you'll say nothing. I only told you because it seemed Providence brought you here just now. And I had to tell someone. I couldn't bear it alone. But you have to promise me!"

"If it means that much to you, Janell, then, yes—I promise."

Jamie looked at Andrew, who had fallen asleep on her shoulder. Perhaps he hadn't required the warm milk after all.

"We must get to bed," she said. "Come to my room for the night. In the morning you'll be able to face things much better."

In the morning, it was true, Janell felt much better and was able to resume her duties, though waiting upon the two brothers was a painful task, however much she avoided the mingled look of fury and teasing evil humor which Derek Graystone seemed intent on boring into her face with his penetrating eyes. Jamie, furious but, also wary of the lord, said little, and for once was glad not to see Andrew's father throughout the day. For Janell she felt only heartache. Gentlemen had toyed with peasant and servant girls through the ages and had always enjoyed immunity because of these positions. But Janell was a tender and sensitive girl, and though Derek Graystone had failed to have his way with her, she had still been scarred by the terror of it. And who could say what might happen in days and weeks to come? If this cruel man was indeed the new laird of Aviemere, could Janell ever be safe? Could *she* herself be safe? It could have been Jamie just as readily as Janell!

The shadows of evening had begun to fall when Jamie stepped from Andrew's room, the boy at last asleep for the night, and walked toward the main stairway leading downstairs to the kitchen. There, rounding a corner and looming large at the end of the corridor and blocking her way to the stairs, the form of Derek Graystone came walking toward her.

"Miss MacLeod," he said with a friendly smile. "I was hoping I might find you thus unencumbered with your . . . duties, as you say."

Jamie could hardly speak for mingled revulsion and apprehension.

"What did you want, Lord Graystone?" she asked with forced calm.

"I said before that I hoped we might become better acquainted during my stay. But it would almost appear you are avoiding me."

"I cannot see how acquaintance with one such as myself could possibly interest a gentleman of your stature." Her tone remained cool despite a growing sense of dread. All the other servants would be at dinner, and she knew Miss Campbell was nowhere nearby to effect a rescue.

"On the contrary," said Graystone coolly. "When it comes to my position or standing, 'All equal,' that's my creed. I'm no snob."

"Well, then, perhaps I must be one," she said, brushing past him and quickening her step toward the stairs. But before she had taken three steps his hand caught her shoulder from behind and pinned her against the wall.

"I begin to wonder about you, *Miss* MacLeod," he said, emphasizing the designation sarcastically. "How does a peasant girl like you come to behave in such a high and mighty fashion? Is it because the supposed lord of the manor has already spoken for you?"

"No!" said Jamie, "I—don't know what you mean! Please—"

"Oh, come now, Miss MacLeod, you know how the game is played between a lord and his servants! Now let's just go to your room and talk this over calmly."

"No. I'm going—downstairs—the others are expecting me—please!"

"Miss MacLeod! Miss MacLeod! Do you yet not understand? I know my brother has had a soft spot for you—"

"No, that's not true!"

"Deny what you will! It hardly matters. But there is a new lord at Aviemere—and you will give your gratuities to me now!"

"Like you expected Janell to give them to you?" she cried, hardly realizing how much worse it could go for her once she angered the violent man.

"So the little slut has been talking, has she?" he snarled. "Well, I'm the laird, and I'll get what I want any way I please. I own this house, this land—and I own you also!"

"Don't you dare touch me!"

He laughed an evil laugh, then squeezed her tight against the wall and pressed his fervent lips against Jamie's neck.

She struggled, but his strength was much too overpowering. She tried to cry out, but he clamped his large hand over her mouth and only whimpers—now of terror, not anger—could escape.

Suddenly she heard footsteps on the stairs. Still held in a tight grip she could not turn her head to see who it might be, but the explosive shout told her it was Edward Graystone.

He was upon them in a moment and ripped his brother violently from his prey. Jamie sank to the floor.

"You miserable wretch!" he cried. "I'll kill you!"

Derek had received several punishing blows before he was able to recover from the shock of his brother's unexpected attack. But then he turned on Edward with all the superb training of a Royal officer.

"So, my brother, it comes to this! The two of us fighting over a servant girl!"

"We don't have to fight, Derek, if you'll walk away from here. Otherwise I'll have no choice but to thrash you as you deserve!"

Derek laughed with derision. "*You* thrash *me*, younger brother?" And even as he said it he lunged forward. With renewed terror Jamie watched horrified as the skill and training of the one attacked the hatred and fury of the other.

Sidestepping Derek's initial ferocious onslaught, Edward dealt his brother several punishing blows to his midsection. But like an angered bear, Derek recovered himself and came on again, this time calling upon his ten years' experience, and it was clear the younger Edward was no match for him. With three swift blows he drew blood from Edward's nose and right eye.

"Thrash me, indeed, you miserable wretch of a younger brother!" he cried. "You're nothing! Nothing, do you hear! Nothing but a paid servant to watch over my property! Ha! ha! ha!"

But the insults were unwisely delivered, for even as he laughed at what he thought had been an easy victory, he felt the full force of Edward's fist against his jaw.

Derek staggered back, almost to the very edge of the stairway. Edward came forward and tried to seize upon his momentary advantage, but again Derek's skill resurfaced. He slammed three punishing blows into Edward's chest and belly, doubling him up gasping for air, and then dealt a severe lightning-swift cross to the head which sent Edward sprawling on his back, unconscious. But even as Derek threw the punch, he took a half step backward from the recoil of the force, lost his footing on the landing, and tumbled backward halfway down the stairway before he could stop himself. He lay for a moment stunned, then crawled slowly to his feet and slunk the rest of the way down the stairs and to his room—aching and wondering if any bones had been broken. Even if he had gotten considerably the best of it, he was hardly used to any blows finding their way to his handsome head, and not knowing his brother's condition as he lay at the top of the stairs, could not help wondering where Edward had learned to fight like that.

Jamie rushed to where Edward lay, now gradually coming to. The cut above his eye was minor, but the blood still oozed from his nose. She ran back to her room, grabbed a towel, moistened one end of it, and ran back down the hall to where he lay.

"Dear God!" he moaned as she applied the wet towel to his face and tried to clean off the cuts. "Is—is Derek—"

"He's gone," said Jamie. "He fell down the stairs."

Edward pulled himself to a sitting position where he remained leaning against the wall. Jamie ran back to her room once more, quickly poured some water from her pitcher into a cup, then ran back.

"Here," she said, "drink this."

He did so.

"Thank you," he replied, then closed his eyes and laid his head back against the wall. He was clearly exhausted.

Jamie said nothing, continuing to kneel at his side.

At length Edward spoke. "I—I could have killed him . . . that is, if I could have. I *would* have, had I been powerful enough."

"I don't know what I would have done if you hadn't come along," Jamie said.

"The fury—the hatred that was inside me—"

"You were just trying to protect me. You wouldn't have really tried to hurt him."

"No! no! I would have! I wanted to hurt him. I could have killed him, I tell you! The hatred nearly consumed me! Oh, God!—what might I have done if he hadn't had the best of me? I might have killed my own brother!"

"You can't blame yourself. He was threatening me. You were only—"

"You don't understand!" he interrupted, clearly distraught beyond the mere physical pain of his bruises. "It wasn't because of you—not all of it—not the evil feelings welling up from within me as I attacked him. I've always wanted to kill him. Always! When I saw him there pushing you against the wall, I was overcome with such—such—God help me! There is such hatred inside me! I'm not a good man! For all the selfishness and blackness in my brother, there is evil, there is hatred, there is utter depravity in my own soul. However I try to put a mask over it and hide it from the world, it is there! God help me! What's happened to me? What kind of man am I?"

He bent forward and covered his face with his hands and began to weep.

Overcome at the sight, Jamie struggled for something to say.

"Let God help you, Mr. Graystone," she said.

"Teach those things to Andrew," he replied, still not daring to look up at her for the shame of his tears. "Teach him how to live. It's too late for God to help me. I have spent my life wanting all the wrong things, and now I have nothing—and I deserve no better."

"You cannot mean that! You know it can't be true!" pleaded Jamie. "And even if it is, what's to stop you wanting the *right* things now? It's never too late! Peace is always there to be found!"

"Peace!—I've never heard of it—not for the likes of me!"

"It's for everyone," said Jamie. "And it's no more than you've always wanted. You tried to get it from Aviemere, and lately you've found snatches of it in Andrew. But that's not where it can be found."

"I know that only too well!" he said, taking his hands from before his face and holding them in front of him, gazing at the bruises and blood from his own cuts.

"Then look to where it can be found!"

He looked up and faced her squarely, no longer ashamed of his red, tear-stained eyes. For the first time since she had known him, Jamie saw deeply inside—beyond the impenetrable hardness. Even in his most tender moments with Andrew she had not seen this look. Reflected in tears she could see a pure longing for something more, a longing for the liberation of his love-craving heart. They were the eyes of a child.

"If only—oh, God, help me!" he said, but the hard knot in his throat made it difficult for him to continue.

"Yes?" she encouraged gently.

"You are so right," he went on with faltering voice. "If only—yes, you must be right—but it all seems so backward. Why are we never taught these things? If only I *could* have such a thing as the peace you talk about!"

"God *will* give it to you—gladly! You need only ask Him."

"I have never asked anything of another. I was taught that to ask for help is degrading. I would not even ask Derek for Aviemere."

"But the peace of God is the one thing we *must* ask for. To come before God is the one time in life we must truly humble ourselves and admit that we *are* nothing and *have* nothing without Him. Only by our asking can God know that we truly want it."

Again he covered his face and wept.

"I do—I *do* want it!" he sobbed.

"Then tell Him so . . . in your own heart," said Jamie.

Still kneeling beside him, Jamie closed her eyes and prayed fervently in the silence of her own thoughts for this once-proud man whose own bitterness had proved too much for him. Truly broken in spirit, he sat beside her, eyes closed but the tears still flowing.

As she prayed, all at once the words came flooding into her mind that she had heard so many times. And unaccountably as she heard them, almost as if he was standing beside her, the voice that spoke was her grandfather's, though the words were the words of her grandfather's Lord: *"See, here I staun chappin at the door; gin ony man hears my voice an apens the door, I will ging in an tak my sipper wi him, an him wi me, as I will make my hame in his hert."*

CHAPTER THIRTY-FIVE

Rumors

It was not long after the fight that Derek began to tire of the sport at Aviemere. The incident was never mentioned and the servants, of course, made not the slightest reference to the battered countenances of the brothers. After lingering about the estate for another week, Derek received a letter from his regiment. Apparently having already had sufficient fill of the boorish place, the letter from his commander must have come as a welcome excuse to make his departure.

Within two days he was gone. Not another word was said about the status of the estate. A month before, his flippant assumption that Edward would carry on as before would have exasperated Edward to inward wrath. But now it had little effect on him. For the first time in his life he had truly let go of Aviemere. And if he still bore his brother no great affection, at least the heinous bond of hatred had been sundered. As never before, he was free.

Again he began to enjoy Andrew, and even Aviemere, more than before. They were no longer the source of his peace, and thus if they fell short in his expectations, he could not be devastated.

One afternoon he wandered out to the back courtyard and found Jamie and Andrew lunching.

"May I join you?" he asked.

For sole response Andrew held up a bright red and yellow ball and cried, "Papa, look!"

"That's grand, son. Is it new?"

"Mr. Els gived it me."

"Mr. Ellice brought it back from his recent trip to Aberdeen," Jamie explained further. "Do please join us," she added, "though the fare is rather simple."

"I don't mind," he said. "It's the company, not the food, I'm interested in."

They spent the next few minutes munching on the cheese, oatcakes, and apple slices, but now that his father was present, Andrew was much too excited to eat. He wanted to try out his new toy.

"Watch me, Papa!" he cried, taking up the ball and running back a few paces from the diners. He raised his hand and swung it back, trying to hurl the ball with such force that had it made its mark it would have upset the lunch basket. As it was, it barely managed to knock a few buds from a rosebush just to his right as he lost his balance and toppled to the ground. He tumbled over giggling, his audience laughing with him, and promptly jumped up, eager for more.

Before long he had both his father and nurse involved in a game of catch, though his modest skills dictated that the ball spent more time on the ground than in the air. When Andrew began to tire, Edward dropped to his hands and knees, grabbed his son, and wrestled him to the ground, to the boy's rapturous delight. Then, lying on his back, Edward raised him over his head with outstretched arms, tossing him into the air and catching him again.

Jamie was the first to see Candice Montrose approaching, let out through the French doors of the ground floor sitting room by Cameron the butler, who still stood in somber silence, looking disapprovingly on the playful affair.

Edward sensed rather than saw her, turned, pulled himself to his feet and made a half-hearted attempt to brush the grass and dust from his clothes.

"Good afternoon, Miss Montrose. What a surprise!"

"Yes, I can see it is! I do hope I haven't disturbed anything," she said.

"Not at all! Perhaps you'd like to join us."

She smiled coolly as if to say, "Surely you jest," then explained that she was in the vicinity, and since it had been so long since she had visited she had decided to stop by.

"I hope you don't mind my doing so without an invitation?"

"Of course not! We are neighbors, after all—well, nearly so. You are always welcome." He then led her to a chair at the table where they had been having luncheon.

"You've met my nurse, Miss MacLeod?" he asked.

"Indeed I have," said Candice, casting Jamie a superior glance.

"Mr. Graystone," said Jamie, "perhaps you would like me to go ask Cameron to serve tea for you and your guest?"

"Thank you, Jamie," Edward replied, not noticing how Candice bristled at the familiar use of the nurse's Christian name.

Jamie took Andrew's hand and the new red and yellow ball and exited.

Candice's plans had been delayed due to her mother's unexpected illness. But with the first tint of pink returning to her cheeks, Candice set out again after her quarry. It distressed her to learn that she had missed the visit of Edward's brother, for what an opportunity it would have provided for dinner invitations, parties, and the like! Not to mention that Derek Graystone was reportedly even more handsome than his brother.

But she had missed him, and thus, content with her original intent, she gradually accelerated the rate of interchange between the two estates. In the weeks that followed, Edward found himself deluged with invitations to Montrose Manor. Though he was unable to accept every one, he did at least feel bound by common courtesy to reciprocate those he did accept. Thus the comings and goings between Aviemere and Montrose were frequent, and talk began to spread throughout the valley that it was not at all unlikely that Candice Montrose would soon become the next Lady Graystone.

Candice was satisfied with the progress. Of course, Edward was not the ardent suitor she would have hoped for, but she had always known him to be the cool and distant type, so she was able to build many castles in the fantasies of her daydreams by even the most minor attentions he showed her.

She still was concerned about the nurse. Invariably when she came to Aviemere, especially if she had not been expected, she found Edward off somewhere with Andrew and that MacLeod girl. However the man might want to spend time with his son, it hardly seemed necessary for that little snip of a nurse to continually tag along!

"You know how I try to ignore what is nothing but gossip," she said one day, "but something has come to my attention which I simply cannot ignore, for your interests, and for those of dear little Andrew. I hate to see his future position in society jeopardized in any way."

"What is it?" asked Edward.

"It has to do with that nurse of yours," she replied. "I have heard that she is but a peasant—in fact, that until a year or two ago, she was a mere shepherdess girl—indeed, one of your own tenants. I thought you should be aware of this."

"What makes you think I am not already aware of it?"

"Come now, Edward. You are a gentleman. I know you would have someone from only the most spotless background tend your child. Your brother is a bachelor. It is not inconceivable that your son may be earl one day."

"I have always known of my employee's status," said Edward.

"And you've done nothing? Surely you can see what a detriment such an upbringing could be socially! How long do you intend to allow his training to be governed by this—this . . . I don't know what to call her!"

"Miss MacLeod has been the best thing to happen to Andrew since his birth. I know most fathers in my position care about such things as social graces. But as for my son, his social advancement pales greatly before his emotional security. And however low her background, Miss MacLeod has given him the security that comes from being loved."

Sensing that to push further in the matter would only alienate him, Candice pulled in her tentacles. "That greatly relieves me, Edward. I fully trust your discretion in the matter. I was only concerned for the boy."

But Candice was in no way relieved. She must try an alternate tact.

Two mornings later, as she was dressing, she turned to her maid and said, "You've lived in the area most of your life, Mary. You know many of its people, do you not?"

"I was born here, mem. I know my share of folks."

"How about at Aviemere?"

"We mingle some."

"Tell me, have you heard of a sheepherder from Donachie named MacLeod?"

"I never knew him, but everyone knew of him. Kept to himself on the mountain, so I heard."

"His granddaughter is now Master Andrew Graystone's nurse."

"I did hear that."

Candice walked purposefully to her wardrobe to choose her

gown for the day. She sorted through several dresses as if she was having difficulty making up her mind.

"You know nothing else about her family?" she asked.

"Why do ye think I would know anything, mem?" In truth Candice knew very well that her maid had at one time been quite friendly with Sid, the stableman at Aviemere, and she now hoped to utilize that relationship to her advantage.

Candice pulled out a lovely pink silk dress from the wardrobe. "I didn't realize I still had this old thing," she said. "I should get rid of it. But it is still too lovely just to throw out, don't you think, Mary?"

"Aye, mem, it is that."

"How would you like it, Mary?"

The maid's eyes immediately lit up. "Me, mem?" she exclaimed.

"Yes," said Candice. "And the blue one, too—I really shall never wear them again."

"That's too kind of ye, mem."

And indeed, the maid could not remember when her mistress had been so generous.

"I would be quite willing to part with them, but—I would like a little something in return."

"I have no money for such fine dresses."

"I don't mean for you to pay me, Mary. It's something else."

"Mem?"

"A simple, trifling matter really. I must just appease my curiosity. I would like you to find out—quietly, of course—what you can about this Jamie MacLeod, the nurse at Aviemere—or about her grandfather, or whatever other family she might have. Do you understand?"

Yes, the maid understood. And how could she refuse her mistress? Besides, the dresses were exquisite.

In less than three days the maid had justified her reward. And almost the same moment she had handed the dresses over to the ecstatic Mary, Candice was making preparations to be off to Aviemere. This was far better than she had expected! How could one of the man's own servants know what he apparently did not know himself? No matter. He soon *would* know. She would waste no time delivering her tidings to the laird of Aviemere.

Edward received her cordially, but received her news without so much as a twitch of an eyebrow. *A most disconcerting man,*

Candice thought. He was the first man she had never been able to read like a book, but then that had been part of her fascination with him in the first place.

"You see why I was bound to come to you," she said.

"I see," he replied. "As you had to tell me about her being a peasant."

"But this is so much more horrifying—"

She stopped short in affected dismay. "You—you didn't know of this, did you?"

"No, I did not," he replied.

Well, that's a relief, she thought. But when she spoke, her words were, "Then I am glad I can be the one to save the Graystone name from such scandal."

"We have done well enough without your help for the last two hundred years, Miss Montrose."

"Oh, well—" her voice trailed away helplessly. The man really was utterly exasperating!

"Thank you for your concern, Miss Montrose."

"I would really feel more comfortable if you called me Candice."

"That's fine. Now, if I may show you to the door . . ."

"You understand, Edward," she persisted, "I mean no ill will toward the girl. But what would become of dear little Andrew if, when he was older, it was learned that he had in fact been raised by the daughter of a murderer?"

Whether the whole matter would have rested there is questionable, for Candice Montrose would no doubt not have given up so easily. And despite his protestations of scorn for the opinions of social circles, Edward Graystone could not help turning the thing over uneasily in his mind. If Candice *was* right—and though he did not trust her further than he could throw Andrew's new red ball, he was quite sure she was careful enough not to go about spreading false rumors; no doubt the information was reliable—there could be certain adverse consequences. As much as he liked Jamie . . . well, he would have to think the matter over prudently.

Whatever conclusions Edward may have come to had he been allowed to pursue his thoughts will never be known. Nor can it be told whether Candice would have achieved her self-grasping designs through other methods had this particular scheme failed. Events were soon removed from either of their hands when Jamie learned the substance of their conversation regarding her.

Sid MacKay, despite his uncommunicative exterior, had taken a liking to Jamie MacLeod. He was intensely loyal to his laird and had seen the healthful changes in him in recent months. Attributing this brightening of the moral atmosphere around Aviemere to Jamie's coming, he could not help feeling a fondness for her in his heart, on behalf of the Graystone family.

Never prior to Mary's chance meeting with him in the village had he made the connection between Jamie and the stories that had circulated around a decade earlier about Lundie and Gilbert MacLeod. And even as he had put two and two together, he never suspected why the news that Jamie was in all probability the daughter of Lundie's murderer had roused such a light in Mary's eye. At least he did not suspect the danger he had exposed Jamie to until the next afternoon when he saw the Montrose daughter ride up in her carriage with the same gleam in her eye. Suddenly he realized his blunder, confirmed by Cameron the butler who had overheard the first of the conversation before closing the door behind him, leaving Graystone and the Montrose woman alone.

Not revealing to Cameron the reason for his inquiries regarding the interview, Sid took his way slowly back to the stables, pondering what best he could do to alleviate the effects of his horrible mistake. At length he did the only thing he could see his way clear to do: he sought Jamie out in the nursery and made a full and heartsick confession, begging her forgiveness for relating rumors which he had no way of knowing the truth for a certainty.

Jamie thanked him, then retreated to the solitude of her own room. She regretted now more than ever not having told the laird about her discoveries regarding her father. Now it would seem that she had kept the truth from him, and he would have every reason to suspect her of ulterior motives in the matter. Indeed, she had deliberately kept it a secret, but not for the reasons he was bound to suspect.

She spent the evening and a good portion of the night as well in prayer. She must face this squarely and forthrightly. She could never let herself be the cause of bringing scandal to either Andrew or Edward Graystone. By early morning she had made up her mind as to the only honorable course of action open to her. As soon as she judged prudent, she made her way to the library where she found Edward at his desk poring over the daily correspondence.

"What can I do for you, Jamie?" he asked, looking up.

"Mr. Graystone," she began with poise in her tone, "something has come to my attention about which I must be very candid with you. I wanted you to know that I never meant to lie to you. That is—"

"Are you referring to the matter of your father?" he asked.

She nodded.

His features hardened and his eyes glinted in the old manner. "Gossip!" he exploded.

Suddenly he lurched to his feet as if pacing the room might stem some of the turbulent emotions churning within him. He strode to one of the bookshelves, then said, "I dealt with the matter, Jamie. And I made it clear I didn't give a midge's eyebrow for such gossip."

"But, sir, it might not be gossip. That is, I don't believe it is true. But everyone else does. That's the way the matter was left twelve years ago."

"I don't care if it's true or not."

"But it could reflect on Andrew. I want you to know I never even considered the harm it could have done him. And I know you're wondering why I never said anything."

"As a matter-of-fact," he said, "I've never once wondered, Jamie. I've grown to trust you and to trust your love for my son. If you said nothing, I'm certain you had good reasons."

"There are reasons, sir. But I've wrestled with whether to make you aware of them or not. But if I'm going to come to you in honesty, then you deserve to be told."

She paused and took a deep breath, looking nervous now for the first time.

"What is it, Jamie?"

"There is someone," she began, "who accuses you—that is, the Graystones—of the murder my father is said to have committed as well as the murder of my father himself."

"What?" he cried, and for a moment Jamie felt a surge of her old terror of the man. But she quickly calmed.

"Her accusations are all ridiculous. She's—she's an embittered old woman. And frightful in her own way. And I don't believe her. I don't really know what to believe! To think that either my father, or your family, could have murdered—it's all just too awful even to think of."

"Jamie, I hope none of this changes your—your position with us."

"But don't you see—it must!"

"It doesn't change anything as far as I'm concerned. No, I won't hear of it!"

"There could be talk against you—against Andrew, as he grows."

"I don't care. I can handle a little scandal!"

"But, Mr. Graystone, I'm not sure I can."

The answer brought him up short, and he said nothing.

He looked at Jamie standing before him. She was so strong in many ways—in all the ways that mattered—but still so vulnerable, delicate like one of her precious spring flowers. He thought of what she might have to face because of this—the scorn of gossip, and especially seeing the name of her father, whom she was now able to love, only in memory, dragged into the dirt of public humiliation.

Yes, maybe *he* could stand a scandal, but was it fair of him to ask her to endure one?

"Blast it all!" he cried, slamming his fist on the desk.

That very afternoon Jamie wrote to Emily Gilchrist.

Not a few tears dropped on the pages of her letter. Only a year ago she had cried at the prospect of leaving Emily. Now she was crying at the thought of going back.

The bonds that had developed within her heart for this place within such a short time were all but inexplicable on the conscious level. Certainly there was little Andrew. How could she ever bear leaving him? And no doubt a good part of the sorrow of parting had to do with the roots of her very existence which had begun and been nurtured not far from where she now stood.

But there was more. Though she could not quite explain what it was, and was perhaps a little afraid to try to explain it—for it was bound up in the person of Edward Graystone.

He had frightened her, intimidated her, angered her, but then gradually warmed to her, and finally joined her in faith. She had, without realizing it, become part of this man, his son and his home.

And it was not possible that such a parting could be easy.

But hers had been a life of sad and painful partings. And she would endure this one as she had all the others.

Two weeks later Jamie boarded a carriage, headed for the

train which would take her to Aberdeen. Her heart had been drained by the emotion of the last several days, and it seemed impossible that her eyes could shed another tear. But suddenly the well was full to overflowing again, and as the carriage lurched away, more tears came and continued through half the journey.

Edward Graystone stood with his son and watched the carriage rumble away with as much dismay, though not nearly the innocent confusion as young Andrew. Why did he suddenly feel so desolate, so empty?

He knew they would never find another nurse like Jamie MacLeod.

Why had he let her go!

Yet he knew why, as did Jamie. And they both had to trust that somehow good would come of the parting as it had of the meeting.

PART V

Robbie Taggart

CHAPTER THIRTY-SIX

The Sailor Returns

It was the first warm day of spring.

There were no spring flowers to be found along the cobbled streets of Aberdeen, but the day was lovely nonetheless, and Jamie wasted no time in taking her charges out for a morning walk.

Ten-year-old Cecilia walked sedately at Jamie's side, while the younger Kenneth skipped ahead, cockily chasing a bumblebee. He was no longer a round-faced toddler, but now a rather pudgy six-year-old. He had not changed except in height and girth. Fleetingly Jamie thought how it had been dear Kenny who had at last convinced her to go to Aviemere. She wondered about Andrew, as she often did, realizing the ache of separation may have been muted by time, but could never be obliterated.

It had been a year since Jamie had left Aviemere.

It had been a good year. God had directed her tenderly and faithfully, and even brought happiness into her life to help her forget her loss. When she arrived, Emily had insisted that she stay with them, not as a mere temporary guest, but as a member of the family. Having little choice in the immediate future, Jamie was able to accept this at first. But she knew that eventually she would have to make her own way in life, though she had no idea what she actually meant by that or how it would come about. The question was resolved, at least for the foreseeable future, about two weeks after her arrival when Mrs. Wainwright, the children's governess, approached Jamie one evening.

The governess had a widowed sister in Edinburgh who had been begging Mrs. Wainwright, herself also a widow, to come live with her. The governess had wanted to make the move, for her sister was not in the best of health, but her loyalty to the

Gilchrists prevented her. The commitment she had made to the children came first: she loved them and could never leave them in the care of just anyone.

When Jamie returned, therefore, Mrs. Wainwright felt as if God had sent her just to meet her own need.

"Now that you're back, Jamie," she said, "I know they'd be in the best of hands. Why, you are just like family!"

So Jamie was now governess to her dear friend's children— a young governess, to be sure, and one without formal training. But the children loved her, did what she said, and Emily kept Jamie one step ahead of them by teaching her whatever she might have lacked regarding the children's lessons the night before. Jamie had learned quickly, Emily was delighted to have her adopted "daughter" back, and the children seemed to feel no sting at the loss of Mrs. Wainwright.

It could not have been more perfect . . . except for the vague emptiness Jamie felt in her heart whenever her thoughts strayed westward, over the hills to Aviemere.

Dora Campbell wrote often and kept her informed of doings on the estate.

Yes, Andrew was growing. There was a new nurse and, though not to be compared with Jamie, she said, the woman was adequate. Jamie could not help smiling as she read the letter. She wanted the best for Andrew of course, and she hoped the situation was not a hardship for the new nurse, but it felt good to be held in such high esteem. At least everything about the estate must be immensely easier and less tense now that Edward Graystone had accepted his son, and more than that, his God.

One especially good piece of news came when Dora answered a vague question Jamie had posed in a letter. Janell, the parlor maid, was just fine, and, contrary to Dora's initial estimation, the girl had settled into her job nicely. As she thought of the laird, Jamie could not help wondering if he had heard anything more from his brother. Of course she dared not ask Dora about that, and Dora volunteered no information. For all Jamie knew, she was the only one of the servants who knew of the tense situation between the Graystone brothers. Dora did volunteer, however, the news that Candice Montrose's visits to the estate had increased, as had the laird's to Montrose Manor. "There's something about that woman I can't abide," she had written. "But then I'm just a housekeeper and he never would ask the likes of me. If he wants to run off and marry the woman, like everyone says he's going to, and make a fool of himself, that's hardly my concern. She's just not at all like the first Lady Graystone, that's all!''

As she read the words Jamie could not keep back an involuntary twinge of her heart. She dismissed the thought as ridiculous, but could not help the pain she felt at the memory of Candice Montrose's role in forcing her away from Aviemere. The thought of such a woman becoming Andrew's mother was almost more than she could bear.

Jamie did not wonder that she heard nothing from Mr. Graystone himself. There was a new nurse now, and loyalties must be transferred to her. It would only make it more difficult for everyone if old ties were maintained. She knew that. Of course, it was the only reasonable way. And if he did marry, she sighed, then Andrew would have a new mother to fill his emotional needs. Somehow, though, she could not visualize Candice Montrose giving the boy the security he needed. But as much as she tried to convince herself of the logic of all these things, she could not keep away the faint disappointment at the silence which hung over that portion of her memory.

But she had a new family now, and that was where her future lay—in Aberdeen, where her father had always wanted her to be!

She had already learned, through painful experiences earlier in her life, that looking back, trying to hang onto the elusive past, was no way to step fully and confidently into the future God was preparing for her. She prayed often that God would somehow allow her to retain the positive memories of Aviemere while removing the longing and ache and desire to hold on to what could never be again.

At that moment Kenny had almost zeroed in on a bee on a nearby bush. The imminent danger of reaching his pudgy little hand around it roused Jamie from her reverie and she shouted, ''Kenny!''

Startled, he jumped back and the bee buzzed off.

''Kenny, don't you know what would have happened to your hand if you had grabbed that bee?'' Jamie remonstrated gently.

''Oh,'' he replied with a grin that meant he knew very well it had not been a good idea.

''He's already been stung twice,'' offered Cecilia.

''But I got one once, in a jar,'' said the boy proudly.

''Did he like being in the jar?'' asked Jamie.

"Well . . ." said Kenny, drawing out the word sheepishly. "I guess he died in two days." Now a look of genuine remorse came over his face. "Is that what killed him?"

"I don't know," Jamie answered. "But if a creature likes to fly and gather nectar, I wouldn't think he'd enjoy being bottled up in a jar, flying continually against the sides trying to get out. I suppose he could die from sheer unhappiness and frustration after a while."

"I'm sorry I did it."

"Well, you didn't know. But God's creatures are happiest when they are doing what God intended them to do."

"Like making honey?" Kenny asked.

Jamie nodded.

They proceeded on their walk, approaching the upper end of Union Street where they began to encounter some shops of the central region of the city. Kenny now absorbed himself in banging a stick against a fence as they passed. Jamie realized there was a lesson for herself in what she had just said. "True happiness comes in doing the will of God," Mr. Avery had once taught her. But now that she recalled the lesson, she also remembered he had smiled and added, "*knowing* the will of God, now that's sometimes the hard part!"

What *was* God's will for her? Was that uncertain disquiet in her soul a feeling from God telling her that she *should* have stayed at Aviemere and faced whatever rumors were flung at her? Or was it the enemy trying to make her doubt that she had indeed done the right thing? She was happy here. But how could she *know* if God meant her to be here . . . or there?

She thought of Iona Lundie with a cold shudder. She had not wanted to hear those terrible things about her father—nor the inferences about the Graystones. Had she closed her eyes to the truth? And yet, what of the effects on Andrew? His future had to be considered too.

Yes, she had made the right decision. Perhaps the only possible decision. But still that gnawing, undefined feeling remained within her. She would simply have to trust God to continue to lead her in spite of her own uncertainties.

All at once Kenny ran ahead to the end of the street, attracted by a bright blue naval uniform. Jamie hastened after him, but did not reach the boy until he had gone up to the man, who stooped down and was now talking with him. As she approached she was struck with the white trim and ornamental brass buttons which offset the deep blue—this must be a dress uniform; it was much too fancy for normal use. She wondered if the man was an officer. The visor of his hat shadowed his face as she walked toward them, but from the laughter she heard it was already clear the friendly officer was taken with the boy.

She took Kenny's hand and began to urge him away.

"I'm sorry for his disturbing you—" she began, but as the man stood up and turned toward her, she forgot everything she had intended to say and exclaimed, "Robbie Taggart!"

With his smile still on his face but a confused look of uncharacteristic hesitancy in his eyes, the man paused momentarily, then tipped his hat and slowly replied, "M-a-d-a-m-e?"

It was hardly any wonder he did not recognize the woman, or governess, or whoever she was, dressed as she was in a burgundy linen suit with fine white lace blouse and elegantly plumed hat. In fact, he took her for the boy's mother, for she looked considerably more mature than her nearly twenty-one years.

"You have me at a disadvantage," he said. "You seem to know my name, but I don't know yours." He spoke in the same friendly voice and appraised her with a hint of the same merry twinkle in his eyes.

Jamie smiled, remembering what she had looked like the last time Robbie had seen her.

"I know," he added, warming to the still somewhat mystifying but no less delightful interchange, "that if I had indeed met you someplace before, I would not have easily forgotten!"

"But we can both see, Mr. Taggart," said Jamie coyly, "that we *have* met before and you have indeed forgotten."

"Then please extend me a thousand pardons. I shall not be so stupid again."

Now Jamie laughed outright.

"Robbie, it's me—Jamie MacLeod!"

CHAPTER THIRTY-SEVEN

The Call of Love

It took some moments for Robbie to regain his composure after Jamie's name dropped like a bombshell out of his past. Then he threw out his arms and gave her a great exuberant embrace.

"Yes!" said Robbie at last. "I see it now—my dear little snow-waif!"

"I shall never forget," said Jamie.

"And neither will I. But you mustn't take me by surprise like this again!" laughed Robbie heartily. "But come, may I stroll with you? You can tell me everything!"

With the children skipping ahead, he took her arm and they walked along Union Street, much as they had more than two years ago in the dark of a winter's night. Only now they made a handsome pair, Jamie with her green eyes shining and her fine dress, and Robbie decked out gallantly as an officer in the Queen's navy. For indeed, he too had come up in the world and it did not take much prodding for Jamie to get his story from him.

"I was bound for the Cape when I last saw you," he said. "Since the Suez Canal was completed in '69 we don't often get the thrill of rounding the Cape anymore. But we had a load of supplies and a handful of miners who were to disembark in Capetown and make their way overland to the diamond mines. There we took on the illustrious Duke of Dunsleve who declared himself game for a bit of adventure when he learned we planned to round the Cape and sail for Bombay. Well, I'm afraid old Dunsleve got more adventure than he bargained for. We had smooth sailing until about a week out of Capetown, then a squall as I'd never seen hit us. Sixty-mile-an-hour winds and buckets of rain—all free hands had to bail for their lives. Of course no one expected the Duke to pitch in, for aside from his station, the man must have been sixty years old. However, the old boy came up on deck to see where he could help just as a twenty-foot wave washed over the deck. And he was washed clean overboard."

"Oh, dear!" exclaimed Jamie. "Was the poor man lost?"

"He would have been! You can never hope to retrieve someone in water as fierce as that."

"But you found him?"

"I was close by and saw him go in."

"What did you do?"

"The only thing anyone could do—I jumped in after him! Luckily I was standing near a long coil of rope. I slit the band around it and grabbed the end as I jumped, hanging on to that rope for dear life. Even so, it was a foolhardy thing to do. Our shouts couldn't begin to be heard above the storm, and it was all I could do to keep Dunsleve from going under and hang on to that thin line of a rope."

"And what happened next?"

"Eventually another of the hands spotted us bobbing up and down like corks in the waves, and threw out more ropes and hauled us in."

"Robbie, you saved the man's life!"

"That's life on the sea. You never know what you're going to have to do!"

"But that's no small thing. I'm so proud of you!"

"Old Dunsleve was pretty taken with the valor of it all, too, although any man on our ship would have done the same. But he insisted on showing his gratitude and said I could have anything within his reach. The only thing I ever wanted was to have my own ship, and that seemed out of anyone's reach, even as wealthy as Dunsleve was supposed to be. So I told him as much and said there was really nothing I needed or wanted. But he said he was going to do something for me and that was that. So some time after we reached London on the return voyage from India, I received a letter from the duke. He had purchased a commission for me in the navy! He said it wasn't my own ship, but there was no reason it couldn't lead to that and he had a brother in the Admiralty if I should need further assistance."

"I'm so happy for you, Robbie. That's just what you wanted!"

By now they had turned and were making their way back through Queen's Cross toward Cornhill.

"But here I've done all the talking!" exclaimed Robbie. "It

was your story I wanted to hear. From the looks of it, I'd say some of your dreams have come true also."

So Jamie told her own story, commencing with her misadventures in the fish market on behalf of Sadie Malone and her rescue by Emily Gilchrist, but touching only lightly on the parts involving Edward Graystone and his history, and not at all on Iona Lundie, although she did make a veiled reference to her father's past in order to explain her sudden departure from Aviemere. Why she held back, she was not sure, although it seemed to be more for her own sake than for Robbie's. He had seen the world and would certainly never be shocked at anything she could say.

"So you see," she concluded, "I haven't exactly become a lady—but I've found something far more important."

"I'm glad for you, Jamie," he said. "I've never had what you might call a strong faith myself, but it seems to have done quite well by you. I'm glad it has made you happy. But I think you're wrong about one thing—you *have* become a lady."

He took her hands in his and gazed steadily at her. "You've become a grand lady—the grandest I've ever seen."

"Now I know why I was always so taken with you, Robbie Taggart," Jamie replied, coloring slightly.

"Yes, you were taken with me. How could I have been such a fool as to walk away from you?"

"Because you had Sadie. And I was a grubby child."

"You are that no longer." He brought her hands to his lips and kissed them gently. "You have grown up, little Jamie MacLeod! You are indeed now a beautiful woman!"

"But there's more than that to being a lady, Robbie."

"Not in my book."

"But you always were a rogue!"

He laughed. "But a rogue still knows beauty when he sees it."

"And no doubt you have seen many beautiful women in your travels, haven't you, roguish *Captain* Taggart?"

"No doubt, no doubt!" he returned playfully. "But I'm still only a lieutenant."

"But growing up, having a position in a nice home, or even being beautiful, none of that makes a lady, Robbie. Surely you know that. That takes breeding! It must be in your blood, your heritage. And that I will never have, Robbie."

"And does that matter?"

"No, that no longer concerns me. To be a lady was a childhood fancy that my father instilled in me because his life was not all he had hoped it would be. But I am content with the lot the Lord has chosen to give me. More than content, I am happy and blessed. To love the Lord in my heart—as my grandfather *told* me, as Emily *taught* me, and as pain and loneliness has *made real* to me in a more personal way—is all that matters to me now. My life is fulfilled, not because of who I am on the outside, but because of who loves me and whom I serve on the inside."

By now they had reached the front steps of the Gilchrist home. The children ran on inside, but Robbie and Jamie lingered on the porch.

"Won't you come in for tea?" Jamie asked. "I would so like Mr. and Mrs. Gilchrist to meet you. When I first came to them, all I talked about was Robbie Taggart!"

"In your thick mountain dialect?"

"Nae doobt, nae doobt! Ye canna ferget that, can ye noo, Robbie!" she laughed.

"Ah, you've come a long way in a short time, Jamie MacLeod! But regretfully, I must return to my duties. I am certain I have already passed the time I was to have reported back. But I shall be in Aberdeen a month or so. May I call on you?"

"Certainly!" replied Jamie with a smile.

For the following week scarcely a day passed in which Robbie did not contrive to see her. And as the first days passed into the following weeks of his sojourn in Aberdeen's harbor, day followed day in a pleasurable succession of evening dinners, tea when Robbie could get away, walks and carriage rides and picnics and outings with the children when the weather would allow it. They were days of pure, unspotted enjoyment, for whatever else could be said about Robbie Taggart, he knew how to have fun. His humor and laughter and bright spirits and rousing stories were infectious. Unlike her previous times with him, when she had been but a child and Robbie and Sadie had seemed so much older and wiser in the ways of the world than she, now Jamie was able to enjoy his company on the equal footing of a shared relationship to which each offered a unique contribution.

For Jamie, the carefree hours spent with Robbie were somehow reminiscent of the years on Donachie. There were no cares or heartaches or confusion, but only gaiety and lightheartedness. The sorrows of Aviemere had suddenly receded far into the distant background. She gave no thought to where it all might lead. Maybe she was afraid to allow her thoughts to look in that direction, remembering how he had left so suddenly before, with scarcely a word. Nor did she stop to ask herself how she really felt about this captivating soldier of fortune, this happy-go-lucky sailor whose feet never stopped wandering over the next horizon for adventure.

Robbie, on his part, had been stunned when first he saw Jamie on Union Street. In his sleep he found himself dreaming about her—that lustrous dark hair that looked like the silk he had seen in India with the sun shimmering on it, and her bottomless rich green eyes which could beguile him simply by their innocence and their unabashed intensity. He saw her image while he tried to concentrate upon his duties, and occasionally left half his meal on his plate. Had Sadie observed his behavior, she would have said, "Hmph! Ye been smitten, man! Plain smitten!" Then she would have excused herself. For Robbie had never been one rightly to understand Sadie's tears; thus she had learned to shed them in private.

Robbie had been what he thought was *in love* many times. As he had told Jamie on the day he had met, he had friends in nearly every port in the world, and a good many of these *friends* were women who had broken their poor hearts over adventurous Robbie Taggart. He was a good man, and would hurt no one—man or woman—intentionally. He simply did not recognize the signs of fluttering hearts when they fluttered for him. So for every woman Robbie loved, there were three that loved him.

But suddenly the tables were reversed. He was now smitten with the very one who had, as an orphan waif from the mountain, first been smitten with him. He had an altogether new feeling for Jamie than he had had before, something that almost made him tremble. There was a voice, an urging within that told him he would be a fool to let her get away. He had walked away from her once, not knowing what a woman she would soon grow to become. Now fate had given him another chance.

But even as such thoughts came to him, another voice—this time one of caution—told him: "Don't you know what this means?" He had run away from it all his adult life, never allowing a relationship to become so serious that he would have to make a commitment which would hinder his restlessness. Though he might not have known how to define the word *wan-*

derlust, he nevertheless knew that he had to remain free. Free to *go*! He could not breathe without room to roam, to travel, to explore, to see the world.

Signing on as an officer in the navy was no small pledge. But it was nothing like commitment to a woman, for even as an officer he had a certain amount of freedom. Having a wife tell you what to do was far different than the orders of a superior officer! And in the navy, the world still lay at his fingertips!

But now Jamie had changed everything!

In the presence of a love like this, would not all these fears disappear? Would not a love like this supersede everything else? And every day he and Jamie were together, and he beheld the light of her smile, he loved her more and more. No one had ever been like this!

Something had to be done!

One evening he went to The Golden Doubloon. He had been going there less frequently of late. But on this night perhaps he sought a little courage, perhaps he wanted to test his resolve in the place that was most representative of his freedom.

Sadie was serving a table of thirsty dock workers when Robbie ambled in.

"Evenin' to ye, Robbie Taggart," she said, somewhat coolly, for she had seen less of him lately than she had hoped during his stay in Aberdeen.

"Ah, Sadie, darlin'! And how are you this evening?"

"I'm fine, but if you don't mind me sayin' so, you're looking a bit pale, Robbie."

Robbie sighed. "I've been sleeping none too well these past two nights."

"I thought life became easier for the highly placed," said Sadie, with the hint of a half-cynical sneer directed at Robbie's new position.

" 'Tis nothing like that."

"What, then?"

"Sadie, we've been friends for a long time. Can I confide in you?"

Sadie could hardly be blamed if a small stab of hope shot through her well-protected but not altogether hard heart. She still dreamed of Robbie, although she had all but given up on him.

"You can tell Sadie anything, you know that."

Robbie took a seat at a nearby table where, in a moment,

Sadie joined him. He leaned forward and peered thoughtfully at her. "Sadie—" he began, "I'm in love."

Sadie's first inclination was to laugh. This, from man-of-the-world Robbie Taggart! Was it a joke?

Suddenly her heart seized her! Invisibly she clutched the edges of the table to keep herself from swooning. This she had given up expecting! Could he possibly mean—? It was too much to hope for! In the mere twinkling of an eye these thoughts raced through her brain before she came to herself and surrounded herself with a protective wall of jest to keep from exposing herself to any unnecessary pain.

She let out a loud laugh. "Oh, Robbie!" she exclaimed through her feigned laughter, "I thought you had something new to tell me. Is there a lass in all Scotland, or the wide world for that matter, that you've not been in love with?"

"But it's different this time, Sadie. At last I'm ready to change, to turn over a new leaf, to settle down."

"Settle down, Robbie! Is this you I'm talking to?"

"Yes, Sadie. Settle down—get married!"

"I—I don't know what to say, Robbie." Sadie was befuddled, though she kept up her half of the conversation bravely enough. If this was a marriage proposal, it was certainly an odd one. But then, this was no time to quibble.

"Tell me I'm doing the right thing. Sadie, she's an angel! You should meet her. But I forgot—you already have!"

If the words shattered Sadie's hastily constructed tower of hope, she did not show a thing. There had already been too many disappointments, and she had learned to deal with them silently and invisibly.

"Al—already met her?" she managed to say as the bricks of her tower tumbled down about her.

"Yes! You'll never believe it, Sadie! Do you remember Jamie MacLeod?"

Sadie's mouth fell open.

Now was indeed the time for laughter, but somehow she couldn't quite manage it. "Aye. Scrawny and dirty as I recall," she said finally.

"No more, Sadie. She is a vision!"

He stopped and rubbed his chin thoughtfully, then continued. "When I was in Capetown, a miner showed me some of the diamonds he had dug out of the earth up in the mines. Ugly things, really! I would have ignorantly pitched them aside like common rocks. How anyone could have seen value in them as they were was beyond me. I did the same with Jamie. I let a little grime and dirt, along with her rough speech and untrained exterior, blind me to what was really there—beneath the surface, the *true* person, the *real* her. I dare not do that again."

"Robbie, since when would you let a pretty lass spoil the life you have made for yourself?"

"Spoil? Never!" he exclaimed. "I would kill for her! I would die for her! What a small thing it will be for me to—to, well . . . settle down."

"A small thing?" Sadie echoed. "Perhaps for some men, Robbie Taggart. But no small thing for the likes of you. You see, you could hardly bring yourself to say the very words."

"I was only joking!" He laughed to prove it. "I am ready to do anything for her!"

"Don't you know that the blood of a wanderer flows through your veins? You can't change that! Think of what it would mean," reasoned Sadie. "After marriage she'll be wanting a crop of bairns. Women always do! Then of course you'll have to have your own house with a fence and garden. And before you know it, she'll be wanting *you*—to be there all the time, day after day."

"A small price to pay."

"And how will you earn a living, Robbie Taggart, answer me that? Do you think she'll be content to let you go off to sea for eight months out of the year—and more?"

"I'll work on land. I'll hire on down here on the docks."

"You work on land! The day that happens will be the day all the pubs along the row close down because all the sailors have become Puritans!"

"Ah, yes, Sadie," Robbie reflected, sitting back in his chair. "A fire in the hearth to greet me when I come home every night, and a dear wife waiting for me. Yes—it sounds just like the life for me!"

He jumped up as if he would march directly to the Gilchrists' door that very moment, though it was past ten o'clock.

"Sadie, I can't thank you enough for your advice!" he said.

"My advice! *My advice!*" she exclaimed indignantly. "You haven't listened to a word I've been saying, Robbie Taggart, you pestiferous bloke!"

"But that's the beauty of it, Sadie darlin'! By meaning the opposite, you steered me in the right direction. You know I never listen to you. A man couldn't have a better friend, Sadie!"

Sadie merely groaned in frustration.

With mingled annoyance and heartbreak, she watched as Robbie strolled buoyantly from sight. She watched as if he were going to his doom, not into the arms of the woman he loved. But deep in her eyes was the loneliness which came from knowing Robbie Taggart would not be hers. Perhaps no man ever would be. For light-hearted, lovable Robbie was the only man who had ever shown anything resembling love to Sadie Malone.

CHAPTER THIRTY-EIGHT

Dreams

The sun sparkled on the River Dee.

The two picnickers found it a delightful setting, with the river on the one hand and the birch and alder wood on the other. At least Jamie was delighted with the view, and the blanket of flowers surrounding them and the newly green foliage sprouting from the trees. It had been a long walk out of the city and along the South Deeside Road, but well worth it. Robbie, however, was oddly detached and even—though Jamie had never seen him this way before—a bit nervous.

She wondered if he was acting strangely because his stay in Aberdeen would soon be coming to an end. These past weeks had been so carefree, so happy. She knew she would miss him when the time came for his ship to sail. But she hadn't examined her feelings beyond that.

"I remember the last time we were together by the Dee," he was saying.

Jamie smiled. "It was all snow and ice then. But even in the starlight it was beautiful. I thought it was going to lead me to the fulfillment of all my dreams."

"I had no lofty dreams back then," Robbie mused. "Except for something so far out of reach it didn't hurt to dream about it."

"I suppose my dreams were so lofty they did hurt," said Jamie. "Until I realized they were not the most important thing in life."

"But don't you still long for them at times?"

"Yes. Every now and then I hear my father's voice saying, 'Ye would hae been a gran' lady someday, Jamie. . . .' And there are times when I feel that perhaps I failed him a bit."

"I'm sure he would be proud of you if he saw you now."

"I hope so, for I think what he really wanted was my happiness."

"And Jamie," Robbie turned his sea blue eyes intently upon her. "Are you happy?"

"Well . . . yes—yes, I am," she replied. Even as she said the words, she wondered why she had hesitated. Of course she was content with her life. She was surrounded by people she loved and people who loved her. And she had Robbie's pleasant company. There was nothing she could possible want to change.

"You seem unsure?" Robbie prodded.

"Yes, I am happy," she announced more firmly. "I'd be a fool not to be. But I've always had a streak of discontent within me. Not a wanderlust like you have, Robbie. More a wondering what else there is in life for me. It used to worry my grandfather—but I won't let it spoil things. It just every now and then makes me pensive, that's all."

"Perhaps your discontent is meant to tell you that your life is not yet complete," Robbie said; then as if the words had ignited some spark within him, he suddenly jumped to his feet and paced about in front of Jamie, who still sat on the blanket they had spread out on the grass.

"Robbie, whatever is it?" asked Jamie.

"I'm no stranger to discontent myself," he answered, still pacing. "The whole wide world didn't seem big enough to appease my longing for adventure. But, Jamie, I'm ready to give all that up now."

He stopped talking, but continued to pace about.

"Give it up? Why, Robbie? Why would you give up the life you love?"

"Because, Jamie . . . because—Jamie, I—"

He stopped and turned toward her, then dropped to his knees in front of her and fervently took her hands in his.

"Jamie, I love you! I—I want to marry you!"

Perhaps Jamie should not have been so surprised at his words.

A more worldly-wise woman would have seen this moment coming. But Jamie still viewed herself as the ragged shepherdess, and despite Robbie's lavish attentions over the last weeks, she could not believe that he didn't also see her still as the same girl he had befriended two years before. In Jamie's eyes, Sadie was still Robbie's woman, and she was incapable of seeing how much, in the growth of her spirit, she had surpassed them both.

So she could not speak for a long moment. And when finally his words did penetrate her senses, she did not know how to respond.

"Robbie—"

"Before you say anything," he quickly broke in, "I know this seems sudden, and I know it may be difficult for you to picture me as the marrying kind. But I am a man of some means now. True, a military pay is not exorbitant, but it is more than that I now have—I have position, and the promise of attaining more. I can offer you a place in society one day. I can make you the lady you have always wanted to be. No one would look down on the wife of a naval officer, in *any* society."

"But Robbie, those things are no longer important to me."

"And love!" he added. "I offer you myself and my love! Forever!"

He dropped her hands and leaned toward her and touched his lips to hers in a tender kiss.

"Oh, Robbie!" she said as he leaned back and gazed into her eyes. "It is so much for me to take in so suddenly."

"Will you at least consider my proposal?" he said, jumping up to pace about again.

"Robbie, if you would just sit still, I have something to say!"

He stopped in his tracks and looked down to where she still sat peacefully.

"Come and sit down," she said. He complied.

"Dear Robbie Taggart!" She smiled warmly at him, and this time reached out to take his hands, sweaty and clammy as they were, into hers. "How could I not consider your proposal? It was not so long ago that I thought my heart would break over you, and you have never stopped being dear to me. These last weeks have been some of the happiest of my life. I know it may be stupid of me not to tell you yes this very minute, but . . ."

But what, she thought? *Why can't I answer him? What is preventing me?*

". . . but I know one thing I must do before anything. I must pray about it, Robbie. I must ask the Lord for His voice in the matter. I do care for you. So I hope you can understand—my life is no longer my own."

"Knowing you are close, I can wait," he replied.

When Robbie left her that afternoon at the Gilchrists' doorstep, Jamie did not go directly in. Instead, she walked around back and through the yard and garden for a time.

Robbie Taggart had asked her to marry him!

This was something she had longed for, dreamed about. How many times had she envisioned herself walking arm in arm with Robbie—as his lady! True, her thoughts of him had dwindled during the past two years. But that was because her mind had been filled with so many other things. But now he was back, and he loved her, and it seemed as if her old dreams were coming true.

Then why was there that nagging hesitation in the pit of her stomach? Wasn't Robbie everything a young woman could possibly want—handsome, dashing, exciting, with the promise of society and travel and adventure thrown in?

Yes, perhaps he was everything a young woman could want. But was he what *she* wanted? More importantly, was he what God wanted for her?

And what did she want? Did she even know? At Aviemere she thought she could have remained there forever. But now back at the Gilchrists', it seemed as if she belonged here, too. And now Robbie wanted her. Did she perhaps belong with him?

Where did she belong? All her life she had been jostled from one place to another, but no one place with any one person had ever been completely home. Even on Donachie with her grandfather, her occasional discontent had focused her eyes on the distant horizon as her father's words had rung in her ears. But she could not go back—not to her father's cottage, not to the simple life on Donachie, not to Aviemere. The only place she belonged, it seemed, was right here, with the Gilchrists. But she could not stay here forever. Somewhere there was a life waiting for her. And perhaps . . . a person too—a man whom she could love and who would love her in return.

"Dear Lord," she prayed, "I don't know what I want or where I belong, or even who I belong with. But you know, Lord. Do I want to marry Robbie or do I just think I want to because I thought I wanted it before? Oh, Lord, what do I want?"

The answer came quickly, waiting only for her mind to focus on God and ask for His wisdom to be revealed. Even as she asked, she knew the answer.

"I want what *you* want, Lord!"

And for now that was answer enough in her dilemma. With that simple utterance she was reminded that He would direct her path as He had throughout her life—even before she was aware He was doing so. And she need never fear His direction, for no matter what it was, it would be what she wanted *and* what He wanted for her.

She turned and entered the house in a much more peaceful frame of mind to share her exciting news with Emily. For now they could both pray together and await the Lord's sending of circumstances to direct her steps in the way she should go.

She did not have long to wait, for the answer to her prayer had been sent days before her need to pray it.

When she walked through the door Emily met her with something which momentarily forced all other thoughts and considerations from her mind.

"This came for you while you were out," Emily said, handing her a folded note. "It came by special messenger from Aviemere," she added with a concerned look.

Jamie took it, quickly opened the envelope, and scanned the few lines from Dora Campbell. When she looked up to meet Emily's eyes, all the color had drained from her face.

"Andrew's ill," was all she said. It was enough.

After that everything happened too quickly for words or thoughts. Without even reaching a formal decision, she hurried to her room and began packing. Emily hurried out to tell Walter to ready the carriage to take Jamie to the railway station.

By late afternoon Jamie was on board the Deeside Railway between Aberdeen and Ballster. She would spend the night in Banchorg and then hire a carriage to take her the rest of the way to Aviemere.

As the train picked up speed through Old Aberdeen, she beheld through the window the crown-like dome of the King's College Chapel and the twin spires of ancient St. Machar's Cathedral. Then the train wound its way into the countryside and Jamie sat back into her seat and relaxed. What a hectic afternoon it had been, getting ready and—

"Oh, dear!" she exclaimed, suddenly clasping her hand to her mouth. "I've forgotten all about Robbie!"

What would he think when he came to Gilchrists, hoping for an answer to his proposal, only to find she had left town altogether!

Well, perhaps an answer would come to her at Aviemere. Who could tell? Possibly when she next returned to Aberdeen, it would be to become Robbie Taggart's wife!

CHAPTER THIRTY-NINE

Andrew

Edward Graystone fingered the miniature figurine on the mantel. It was not the one of the shepherdess, though that was the one he was thinking of just now.

It was odd. He used to come into this lovely parlor and think of his wife, for it had been her special room. But now whenever he wandered in here, he could only think of that little statue shattering against the floor, and how terrified Jamie MacLeod had been—how frightened *he* had made her.

He hated himself back then, but for some twisted reason he had tried to make it appear as if he hated everyone else—even his own son. But he had changed, and now the memory of it made him sick. He was no saint even now. But he had learned some of what truly mattered in life. And thanks to Jamie MacLeod, he had found the next most important thing of all—his son.

Could it be possible that it would suddenly all be for naught? Would God have given him that precious relationship only to snatch it away! That hardly seemed like the kind of God in whom Jamie had taught him to believe. But if he truly did believe, was not this the time, more than ever, to trust Him—even for the life of his son? He felt certain that's what Jamie would have said.

When Andrew fell ill, his thoughts immediately turned to her. But he could hardly call for her, when there was an extremely competent woman who had replaced her as nurse now caring for the child. But she had given so much of herself in the short time she had been here that it was impossible to forget, especially with Andrew asking constantly for her for five months after her departure.

Andrew's illness had begun with a minor cold three weeks

earlier which eventually moved into his ears. The fever went on for nearly a week, during which time he neither ate nor slept with any regularity. Hopeful signs of clearing appeared, and then his chest became congested, and if his constitution had not already been weakened by the previous infection, he might have been better prepared to combat the forthcoming pneumonia. However, his condition quickly became very serious, and the doctor's expression was grimmer with each visit. Edward's young faith was stretched to the limit.

Edward turned from the mantel and rubbed his hands across his face. The doctor had just left moments ago and there had been no change except that Andrew's pulse had grown still weaker.

"Dear God!" he cried suddenly. "Please let him live! Let me have him a while longer!"

Carelessly he rubbed the fresh tears from his eyes, which had grown dark and hollow throughout the past several days.

As he walked slowly from the room, he could hear the faint sounds of commotion from the direction of the front of the house. Immediately his body stiffened in fear.

The house was always deathly quiet these days, in deference to Andrew. Something must have happened. The servants were looking for him!

"Oh, God—no!" he moaned.

He raced from the room and down the corridor. But the moment he reached the huge entryway from which the sounds had come, he stopped still in his tracks.

There stood Jamie, with a repressed smile, which even the anxiety over her face could not altogether hide.

"Miss—Miss MacLeod . . . Jamie!" he stammered. "You—you've come back!"

"Yes," she laughed and cried at once.

"But how—how did you know?" he asked stumbling over his words, amazed and bewildered all at once.

"I'm sorry," she replied with a tremble in her voice. "Please forgive me. Dora wrote, and I couldn't . . . I just couldn't—"

"Forgive you!" he interrupted. "I've prayed—"

But he caught himself. Yes, he had prayed for her without even knowing it himself, or knowing why. And suddenly he felt strangely reticent and awkward.

"I'm—I'm glad you've come," he said at last. "I would have written myself, but . . ."

"I know," she said when he paused to search for a reason he wasn't even sure he had. "May I see him?"

"Of course," Edward replied. He turned to Cameron, who had been patiently waiting as if he heard nothing, and said, "Cameron, please take Miss MacLeod's things to a guest room near the nursery. And inform Miss Campbell of her arrival."

"Yes, sir. I'll take the baggage up," said Cameron. "But Miss Campbell already knows about Miss MacLeod, and she's rushed off in a perfect dither—to find you, sir."

"Well then, tell her I'm found, Cameron. And tell her we'll be in the nursery."

Then Edward turned to Jamie and led the way up the stairs.

"Is he any better?" Jamie asked as they reached the third-floor landing.

Edward only shook his head. He could not even repeat the doctor's grim pronouncement of earlier in the day.

"Then we must pray," said Jamie.

"I have been trying."

"It's in His hands, then."

"I know," Edward said in despair. "I know," he repeated, as if he wasn't sure that was enough.

"He loves that dear little child, Lord Graystone," she said earnestly, turning and laying her hand momentarily on his arm. "We *can* trust Him!"

He nodded, but could say no more for the variety of emotions stirring within him.

They reached the nursery door and Edward opened it. A woman was seated by the bed. She appeared to be in her mid-thirties, trim, with brown hair pinned back into a neat bun. She looked up at the two as they entered and made an attempt at a smile.

"Miss Clark," Edward said to her. "This is . . . a friend of the family—Miss MacLeod. We'd like to visit with Andrew. You may go and have a cup of tea if you like."

"Thank you, sir," said the nurse as she rose and exited.

Jamie had scarcely taken any notice of the woman who had taken her place. She rushed to the bed and knelt down beside it.

"Andrew, look who's come to see you," said Edward, assuming a bright countenance and cheerful voice.

"Jamie!" said the child in a soft voice, and though he smiled, his eyes remained glassy and dull.

"Hello, my wee bairn," Jamie said, reaching out and taking his hand. What changes had come upon him in the past year! Boyhood had begun to encroach upon the babyish demeanor she had known before. There was more of his father in him now, a certain solemnness, though what she saw may have been from his illness. Perhaps there was more of his mother in him too, but it would have been difficult for one to tell who had not known her, and doubly difficult in that his face was pale and drawn from the illness, and not even a smile could light up his eyes. His hand was hot.

"I got sick, Jamie," he said weakly.

"I know, dear," she replied. "But you'll be well soon."

"Will you stay with me?"

"Oh, aye, Andrew," Jamie said, struggling to control her voice. "And when you're better we will go for a walk like we used to."

"We'll find spring flowers!"

"Yes, Andrew. Lots of flowers!" Jamie laughed, but turning her head away so he would not see her tears.

They remained by his side for some time, until he fell asleep.

Edward sat on one side of the bed and Jamie on the other. Edward felt strangely refreshed as if he had been awakened from a deep heaviness. It seemed hope had been rekindled in him. For the first time in days he could actually visualize another spring scampering with his son about the meadows for the treasures hidden in the grass.

"You must be exhausted after your trip," said Edward at last. "Come, you'll want to rest."

Jamie rose and followed him out into the hall.

"I did not mean to presume upon your hospitality," Jamie said. "I left Aberdeen without thinking. But I have been working. I have money, and I can stay in town—"

"I won't hear of it," said Edward, and in his eyes was that implacable firmness that had once so intimidated Jamie.

"But I'm afraid I spoke out of turn to Andrew about staying. I was merely trying to—"

"And you must keep your promise!" Edward broke in. "You saw how he needs hope. He would be heartbroken if you did not stay."

"I don't know what I could do."

"I've already seen what you can do . . . for all of us around here. I haven't seen the boy's eyes light up like that in days. You are welcome to stay as long as you want, or need bids you. For Andrew's sake."

She smiled. "Thank you. I only hope I can help him."

He had led her down the hall some distance until he paused by an open door. "I believe this is the room Miss Campbell has had made up for you. There are your things." He made ready to take his leave, but after he had taken three steps back down the hall, he turned and said, "You will join me for dinner this evening?"

"Oh, Mr. Graystone, you need not—"

"Jamie, you are no longer a servant here, but a guest. I insist."

"Well . . ." she seemed to hesitate. "I suppose, then, I shall be there."

CHAPTER FORTY

Thoughts

Edward Graystone sat at his desk in the library and tried to concentrate on the mounds of paperwork before him.

Since Andrew's illness he had definitely let things go. George Ellice had tried to keep the estate in order, but there were some things only Edward could do. Every day he had attempted to set his mind to the work at hand, but each day his brain quickly fled to the more immediate fear for his son.

His mind was wandering now, but the direction of his thoughts was somewhat different. In the four days since Jamie's arrival, Andrew had begun to take a decided turn for the better, although the doctor was still guarded in his prognosis. But there was visibly more color in his white cheeks and the hint of a spark in his once-lively eyes. He had also begun to eat a little.

Yes, there was good reason to hope. Thus it seemed he ought to be able to focus his attentions on the work before him. But something else had gradually begun to overtake his thoughts and distract him from his work.

Andrew was recovering. Soon there would be no reason for Jamie to stay. When she had left a year ago, he had hardly realized how greatly he had missed her. Life had settled back into its previous routine, and except for a certain hollow echo about the place, he had reaccustomed himself to how it had been before. There were a few times when he would forget himself and listen for the sounds of her laughter as she played with Andrew. But the laughter did not come. When spring had arrived that year, Andrew had asked to go hunting for flowers, and together they had made their search. But something had been missing, though neither of them had voiced their thoughts.

But then suddenly when he saw her standing inside Avie-

294

mere's front door four days ago, it was as though a light had gone on, illuminating the whole last year in all its stark emptiness!

Whatever the thing all meant he hardly dared consider. Almost to his relief, at that moment there came a knock at the door.

"Sir, you have a caller," said Cameron. "Miss Candice Montrose."

His relief was short-lived. *Why now*, he thought?

Toying with the fleeting idea of telling the butler to make some excuse for him, he looked up to see the tall, attractive figure of his caller sweep past the butler without waiting for any further word.

"Do forgive my liberty," she said rather breathlessly. "I didn't want to pull you away from your duties so I followed your man. I hadn't seen you for some time, and heard only this morning about your son. I simply had to come straightaway and offer . . . well, to tell you how sorry I am. You know how fond I am of the boy."

Edward rose from his chair. "Thank you, Candice. We appreciate your concern." *Curious*, he thought, *she has never taken the least notice of Andrew in the past.*

"I must chide you on not informing us sooner. We are neighbors, you know, and what else are neighbors for but to share in these times of distress? I know the comings and goings between Montrose Manor and Aviemere have grown rather infrequent of late, but we mustn't allow that to continue."

Though Edward had shown a mild interest in Candice, she had at last taken his lukewarm demeanor to heart and had begun expanding the vistas of her search. She had reportedly gone to the Continent during the winter where an Italian viscount was said to be courting her. However, the rumors still circulated through the village and among the staff that a marriage was, if not imminent, certainly inevitable. At any rate, she was the last person he wanted to see just now and hoped she had not come planning to be entertained for the afternoon.

"Now, how is the boy? Is there anything I can do?"

"Actually, he seems to be getting better, though our prayers have by no means ceased for him. Thank you for your offer, but we have been managing very well."

She cleared her throat daintily. "I wondered about the boy, because on my way here to the library I saw that old nurse of yours and, well, naturally I was curious, thinking what dire straits you must have been in to call upon her after being forced to let her go."

"I don't know what you are talking about, Candice," he replied tersely. "I did not let anyone go, as you say. And I did not call upon Miss MacLeod; she came of her own accord."

"I see you are in a vulnerable state just now, Edward. But you must be firm. Don't allow her to take advantage of you. Her kind always does, you know."

"Miss Montrose, I wonder that you feel at such liberty to meddle into the affairs of Aviemere. I do not recall having asked your counsel."

"Please, Edward. Surely you know that I speak only out of my deep affection for you and your son. And I can assure you, a girl like that only means to bring—"

"Have a care, Candice, at how you speak of my guest and friend!" said Edward icily.

At this Candice drew herself up haughtily. "Lord Graystone," she said, her voice matching his glare, "I have known men in your position ruined by such riffraff."

"You may be interested to know," he answered, "that I am not *Lord* Graystone. That dubious distinction belongs solely to my absentee brother. Thus I have neither estate nor position to be ruined. But had I both, I would sooner choose to take my chances with this riffraff, as you have chosen to call the best person ever to walk into this house, than with a common gossipmonger like yourself, Miss Montrose!"

Candice stood like a grim statue, looking as if the air had been struck from her by one swift blow, hardly knowing whether to humbly submit to such treatment with diffidence or to give vent to the self-righteous indignation which was already beginning to brew within her. For several moments she said not a word.

"Now, Miss Montrose," Edward continued, "as you seemed to find your way up here so easily, I will not bother calling for the butler. You can find your own way out."

She continued to stand and stare for another moment, then turned on her heel, not smartly but in still a rather dazed fashion, and left the room.

When the door closed behind her, Edward sank into his chair. He was shaking with anger. But more than that, he was trembling because the realization which had subtly been closing in on him had suddenly become brazenly clear—at last he knew what he must do.

He found Jamie walking in the garden. She did not see him approach and he paused a moment just to watch her. He recalled the times long ago when he had hidden similarly to watch her and Andrew playing on the lawns or strolling together on a warm afternoon among the roses and azaleas. A knot formed in his throat at the memory.

Now, here he was feeling quite differently than he did then. As he watched, the scales fell from his eyes and he saw clearly for the first time how lovely she was. It was the simplicity of her beauty that was so striking, how she smiled as a butterfly winged across her path. But the tilt of her nose, her delicate neck, the shimmer of her hair, the sparkle of her emerald eyes—these were but the alabaster box containing the richest, purest ointment he had ever seen.

He almost laughed aloud at his thoughts. He was ten years too old!

He had gone in search of her impulsively, but what would he say? How could he? He turned in the confusion of his thoughts and was about to leave when all at once she spied him.

"Mr. Graystone!" she called, interrupting his thoughts abruptly.

"Oh—hello, Jamie." He tried to smile, but it was difficult to assume even the most pathetic imitation of naturalness.

"Andrew is asleep," she said, "so I thought I'd come out and pick some flowers to surprise him with when he wakes up."

He noticed then that she held a basket in one hand and a pair of shears in the other.

"He'll like that," he replied. How awkward this was!

"Are you well, Mr. Graystone? You look pale," she asked.

"No—I'm . . . that is, Jamie—what I wanted—"

He stopped. What a fool he was! Fumbling about for words like a nervous schoolboy!

"It must be the strain of the past weeks," he finished lamely.

"Thank God he is finally better."

"Yes—yes, thank God! I think I would have died myself had anything happened to him."

"God would have given you the strength to bear it," she said. "But thanks be to God! It seems in this case we need only bear our joy!"

He smiled, but inside his heart still pounded. Couldn't she hear it? His pulse echoed aloud in his very ears!

"Had you come looking for me?" she then asked. "Did you want me for something?"

"No!" he answered, rather too quickly. "No . . . I mean, yes—that is—nothing specific. I only wanted to thank you for all you have done."

"I have done so little."

"Even Miss Clark has commented on the wonderful effect you have had on Andrew. God has done the healing, Jamie, but He has used you. You came back, didn't you?"

"Of course. But how could I not?"

"Then it's true. We have both taken strength from your faith—" He paused, then blurted forward, "—and from *you*, Jamie. I—"

Suddenly he grasped her hands impulsively, but then just as suddenly, once he realized what he had done, he dropped them again. "I'm just so glad you've come," he said.

"That means a great deal to me, Mr. Graystone."

"Well," he laughed nervously. "I best let you return to your flower gathering."

He turned hastily, and, almost stumbling, hurried away.

It was preposterous! The whole thing was turning him into a bumbling fool. But this was the most alive he had felt in years!

CHAPTER FORTY-ONE

A Surprise Visit

Jamie clipped several yellow roses and held each to her nose before laying it carefully into her basket. Was there something about the air at Aviemere that made these the sweetest she had ever found?

But her thoughts did not dwell long on the glories of the garden. The recent interview with her former employer was still strongly on her mind. Of all the odd interviews with Edward Graystone she had had in the past, this one had without a doubt been the most curious. She had never seen him so awkward and flustered.

But the most peculiar thing of all was that from the moment she saw him in the garden, her heart had been thudding like a hammer against an anvil in her chest. She had felt the same thing the day she arrived when he raced into the entryway to find her standing there. But she had thought little more of it. She had merely attributed it to the strong sense of . . . of—could she say it after all this time? *Coming home.*

At dinner on that first evening they had talked so easily, once she had overcome the initial discomfort she felt at sitting at the table with, if not the laird of the estate, at least the lord of the house. She told him of the Gilchrists and about her training under Mr. Avery and of what he and Emily had taught her. She spoke freely of her grandfather and Donachie and what those years had meant to her. Edward had been more taciturn, but when he did speak, his words came from the heart and touched her the more that she knew him to be a man of few words when it came to matters of the heart. While he was telling her about the days before Olivia's death, days of eager anticipation of the arrival of their child, he suddenly stopped abruptly.

"I'm so sorry," he said. "I seem to have forgotten myself. I've burdened you enough with the woes of my family."

"I feel no burden," she had replied. "I'm honored—"

But she too stopped, all at once encumbered with awkwardness. Men and women just did not speak of such personal things to one another. She and Robbie had never spoken like this. He had never bared his soul to her, nor she to him, though at times she had wished she could have shared some of her innermost thoughts. But Robbie seemed more traditionally conscious of the bonds of propriety which were supposed to exist between a man and a woman.

Such bonds seemed suddenly to have fallen away as she and her former employer spoke. It was as if age and gender and breeding and station were all forgotten and they were simply— friends.

But how could such a thing be?

He was a gentleman and she a peasant girl! How could friendship—or anything!—exist between two persons from such vastly different backgrounds?

"What am I thinking?" she murmured aloud.

She deliberately snipped off a particularly vivid yellow and orange rosebud and examined it carefully before laying it in the basket with the others. But if she hoped her concentration on her task would dissipate her thoughts, she was disappointed. A vision slowly crept into her mind of Sadie Malone laughing about her lovesickness over Robbie Taggart. *If that made her laugh,* Jamie thought, *she would have fits over this! As would no doubt, Candice Montrose.* And with the thought came a quick dampening of her spirits. He was, after all, practically engaged to her, so the servants said. And it was only fitting. He was a gentleman. His first wife had been from a very old British family of standing. They would make the perfect couple, the talk of the county, the coming together of two such prestigious estates. For the first time in a long while, Jamie found herself wishing she was a lady after all. But she quickly dismissed the thought.

Rebuking herself, she whirled around and marched from the garden. Andrew would be awake by now, and the flowers would wilt if she did not finish with her silly fancies!

She located a vase in the gardener's closet, and after arranging the flowers, she took them up to Andrew. He was just coming awake and was delighted with her gift. He looked so much better! The fever had at last broken and the glazed, sallow look had begun to disappear. He would soon be well, and then . . .

And then—what! She would leave Aviemere again, go back to Aberdeen—she did, after all, have duties with the Gilchrists. Of course. That was where her life was now. But even at the thought of leaving, her throat tightened.

"Jamie, why are you sad?" asked Andrew, startling her suddenly from her thoughts.

"I was just thinking how much I like it here, and what a nice visit we've had," she replied, "but that soon I must go?"

"But you said you were staying . . ."

"I can't stay forever, Andrew," she said as she ran her hand through his curly yellow locks.

"Then I'll stay sick."

"No, no, my bairn. That *would* make me sad."

"Will you go today?"

"No, Andrew," she smiled. "I haven't forgotten that I promised you a walk like we used to take."

"Then I must hurry and get better!"

He then requested a story from his favorite picture book. She had barely begun, however, when there came a knock at the door.

It was Dora.

"It seems you have a caller."

"A caller? For me?" Jamie asked, puzzled.

"Yes," replied the housekeeper. "A gentleman asking for you."

"A gentleman? I can't imagine!"

"Well, dear, there's but one way to get to the bottom of it," answered the practical housekeeper. "He's waiting downstairs."

"I'll finish this a little later, Andrew," she said. He nodded a bit reluctantly, and Jamie left.

In the few moments it took her to reach the main stairway, she puzzled over the identity of her mysterious caller a dozen times. When she came to the top of the stairs and looked down at the handsomely uniformed young man standing in Aviemere's entryway, she could hardly believe her eyes.

"Robbie!" she cried, and flew down the steps like one of the goats on the slopes of Donachie.

He took her in his arms and swept her off her feet.

"You can't get rid of me that easily, Jamie MacLeod!" he exclaimed with a merry chuckle.

"Oh, Robbie! I didn't mean to do that!"

"I know and I understand. Mrs. Gilchrist told me all about it." He was about to give her an unreserved kiss when she stepped away, trying to appear casual, and led him inside.

Out of the corner of her eye Jamie had caught a glimpse of Edward Graystone descending the stair.

CHAPTER FORTY-TWO

The Laird and the Sailor

Edward had viewed the entire scene from the top of the stair. At first he tried to persuade himself that this stranger was some relative of Jamie's, however unreasonable he knew the thought to be. But he knew full well that the look in the man's eye was not the look of a cousin.

He walked steadily and unflinchingly down the steps, gathering only the most fleeting hope in seeing Jamie pull away from the man's advances. It could have, after all, been nothing but modest embarrassment.

"Mr. Graystone," said Jamie. Her cheeks were tinged with pink and she seemed flustered. "I would like to present a good friend," she continued. "This is Mr.—that is, Lieutenant Robert Taggart. And, Robbie, I would like you to meet Mr. Edward Graystone."

The two men approached one another and shook hands, Edward rather stiffly, and Robbie in his usual unassuming manner, always ready to take someone new into his wide circle of friendships.

"I hope you will forgive my brashness," Robbie said, "barging into your home like this uninvited. Jamie left Aberdeen so suddenly, I was concerned."

"That's perfectly understandable."

"Not to mention our unfinished business, Jamie," Robbie added, giving her a grin and a knowing wink.

"I'm sorry to have done that to you, Robbie," Jamie replied.

Edward shuffled uncomfortably, finding himself in the midst of an exchange he was not part of.

At length he spoke, trying his best to sound casual. "Jamie, you may take your guest into the parlor if you wish some privacy."

The color rose up Jamie's neck, and Edward could almost feel the heat mounting in her face.

"Thank you, Mr. Graystone," she replied.

"If you have traveled all the way from Aberdeen," said Edward, turning to Robbie and doing his best to put on a brave front, "you must be tired. You are welcome to stay at Aviemere."

"That's kind of you, sir," replied Robbie. "But I have already taken lodgings in the village."

"As you wish, though the invitation stands."

"Well . . ." Robbie replied slowly, apparently weighing the matter further in his mind, "—if you truly mean it. And if it's no inconvenience?"

"None at all," said Edward with courageous courtesy.

"I should be grateful to see more of Jamie than the long rides back and forth would permit."

"I'll have a room prepared for you. We dine at seven o'clock."

"Thank you, sir," said Robbie, rather more formally than he had yet spoken.

Edward turned to leave, and Jamie led Robbie to the parlor. He stopped, turned again, and watched them until they were out of sight down the corridor. Even when he could no longer see them, he heard joyful sounds of laughter.

So that is that, he thought calmly.

But when he walked back upstairs to the library and sank into his chair behind the desk where little work was being done of late, he felt anything but calm. All the gentlemanly reserve he felt appropriate in such a situation fled from him.

Whatever hopes he had about Jamie were soon dashed in the realization that this man with the flashing good looks, a gallant uniform, winning smile, and merry laughter was a far more likely man for Jamie to fall in love with. Not he, with his hard features, thinning hair, gruff voice and a past which still stung him! He tried to remind himself that Olivia had loved him. But he was younger then and the hard blows of life had not yet taken their toll. And that brought home the coldest reality of all—he was a good ten years older than Jamie. This Lt. Taggart was young, full of vigor, with life still before him—everything a young girl like Jamie could want!

Did he love her? Was it possible he could love a girl who had once been his servant? If so, did he love her enough to give her up to Lt. Taggart? He was not a man to give in to schoolboy fancies. But neither did he expend his emotions lightly. Yet was not his love—if such it was at all—measured by his desire to see Jamie happy?

Edward was not a man given to asking for things. In the past year he had requested only two things of God. One had been his plea for peace in his heart; the other, his son's life. Now he covered his face and asked for one more thing. "God," he prayed, "you know my feelings. You know I am no match for this man who has come here seeking her. Help me to accept what you have chosen for her. And above all, dear God, I ask only for Jamie's happiness."

That evening at dinner Edward staunchly made an effort to be as amiable as he could, but his heart was low. Robbie—as he insisted on being called, despite the fact that he continued to call his host Mr. Graystone—was indeed a winning personality. His merry flow of conversation and unending reserve of captivating stories of adventures in exotic lands raised smiles and correspondent good cheer even from his rival. By evening's end, his infectious laughter had even drawn Edward into the relating of a few amusing anecdotes concerning Aviemere. Worst of all, Edward *liked* this Robbie Taggart! He was an interesting, genuine, and congenial man. He left the dinner table feeling that he would be doing Jamie a great injustice to attempt anything that kept him from her. He excused himself, took his leave, and went upstairs to retire, leaving "youngsters," as he grimly referred to them, alone and to themselves.

As the laird left the dining room, silence fell for a few moments.

"There's a full moon out tonight," said Robbie at length. "I hear Aviemere has some grand gardens. How about a tour?"

They rose, he offered Jamie his arm, and she took it lightly, and they went outside. Indeed, the gardens were bathed in shimmering moonlight, and a soft breeze stirred about the couple.

"It must have been quite a change coming here for the first time," said Robbie, making conversation. "It's certainly nothing like Sadie's in Aberdeen."

He laughed.

"He did shake me a bit at first."

"He?"

"Oh! I thought you meant—I guess I was thinking—the laird,

Mr. Graystone, I mean. Yes, he *was* difficult to get used to when I first came."

"I can see what you mean," said Robbie, taking little note of her agitation. "He is a bit, I don't know, stiff."

"He isn't like that at all," Jamie responded, much too quickly. "I mean, it's easy to misconstrue him. He's really—"

She stopped self-consciously. Then hoping to change the subject, she exclaimed, "Look! The rhododendrons are especially vivid this year—the moonlight makes them look like great colored lights."

Robbie stopped walking and, gently taking her shoulders, turned her toward him. "You are the only light I see, my dear Jamie."

She smiled.

"Jamie, I've waited almost as long as I can bear." He took her into his arms and kissed her. This time she did not pull away.

"Oh, Robbie! Robbie!" Her head felt light, and the garden whirled around her.

"Please tell me you'll marry me," he said, still kissing her.

"I've had so little time to think."

"What's there to think about? I love you and you love me."

With those words, confusion again surged through Jamie's mind. He sensed her hesitation in her suddenly tense and unyielding body.

"What's wrong, Jamie?" he asked, the slightest tremble in his voice.

"I—I don't know."

"You do love me, don't you?"

She turned from him and walked a few paces away, her back turned.

Did she love Robbie? It was a question she had not even tried to answer since he had proposed to her in Aberdeen. Of course she loved him! Who could not love Robbie Taggart—adventurous and exciting man of the world! But did she love him in the way she knew she must in order to marry him?

"Jamie?" he said, coming up behind her and laying a hand gently on her shoulder.

"Oh, Robbie! I'm so confused! I—I just don't know!"

She turned around, and the wounded look on Robbie's face nearly broke her heart.

There was a long silence.

"I want to ask what is confusing you," he finally said. "But

I don't think I will." He stopped, but suddenly in a torrent of words that seemed beyond his control, he added, "It's the laird, isn't it, Jamie?"

Stunned, Jamie stared at him in disbelief.

"Oh, Robbie—I don't know!"

"I've seen it, Jamie. There's been a difference since I came here. I can see that look in your eye. You're in love with him. That's why you're confused and afraid."

"What a wild imagination you have, Robbie!" she replied, her confusion giving way to a half-angry tone. "The whole thing is crazy, and I'm a fool!"

"Then say you'll marry me!"

"Robbie, I can't! Not until I *know*."

"You want to see if you can get your gentleman friend first!" he blurted out scornfully, but he regretted his words almost before they were out.

"Forgive me, Jamie! It was a stupid thing to say. I know you'd never be swayed by such a thing. That's why I love you. Please say you'll forgive me!"

"Of course I do. I know you didn't mean it. I only wish it were that simple. I only wish—"

She couldn't complete her sentence because she still didn't know what she wished. Or perhaps she did know, but was still afraid to put it into words.

"We should go in," said Robbie tenderly. "You are right. Before you make any decision, I want you to *know*. You have to be certain."

"Thank you," she replied. "You have always been wonderful to me, from the first day when you found me dying in the blizzard. I *do* love you, dear Robbie Taggart. So believe me, my decision will not be easy."

"Then I shall never give up hope!" He reached out and gently grazed her cheek with his rough hand, then turned and walked back into the house.

Jamie watched him until he had disappeared, then turned and went back out into the moonlit garden alone. She walked slowly away from the house, reflecting on the many happy days she had spent here. Scenes and images and faces from the last two years flooded her mind in endless succession.

She did not return to the house for more than two hours.

PART VI

Jamie MacLeod

CHAPTER FORTY-THREE

Pledges

Surprisingly Jamie slept soundly that night. She had fallen asleep with the words of Psalm 121 going through her mind:

> He will not suffer thy foot to be moved: he that keepeth thee will not slumber. The Lord is thy keeper: the Lord is thy shade upon thy right hand. The sun shall not smite thee by day, nor the moon by night. The Lord shall preserve thee from all evil: he shall preserve thy soul. The Lord shall preserve thy going out and thy coming in from this time forth, and even for evermore.

And thus, with the words of the unslumbering God in her heart, she did sleep, awaking cheerful and refreshed and feeling as if a weight had been lifted off her shoulders. She dressed quickly in her brightest dress, a red and green plaid, befitting her homeland, brushed her hair, and practically skipped from her room.

Her first destination was Andrew's room. She found him sitting up in bed, squirming to get out.

"The doctor says you must stay here a day or two longer," she reminded him.

"We don't have to tell him."

Jamie smiled. "That wouldn't be truthful, my bairn. Besides, he'd know!"

She read him some stories and they talked about where they would go when he was able to get up. She fed him his breakfast when the nurse brought it up, then left to have her own.

The laird usually took his breakfast alone, and when Jamie went to the kitchen she was informed that Robbie had already been up, breakfasted, and was now out somewhere with MacKay—on horseback, the cook thought. Relieved, she ate as quickly as she dared, then went back to her own room.

She did not see Robbie all morning. In early afternoon she went again for a visit with Andrew. After several stories he began to tire and she judged it wise for him to sleep. She rose from his bedside and was preparing to leave when his father walked in.

Her whole being trembled at the sight of him, and what a different trembling this was from when she had seen him that first time in the library!

"I was just leaving," she said.

"Must you?" cried Andrew. If only she could have known that the boy's father silently cried out the same words.

"Your father wants some time with you too, you know," she said.

"You needn't go on my account," said Graystone, speaking at last. His words were clipped, forced, and his voice betrayed his sleepless night.

Jamie hesitated.

Was he just being polite? Or did he really want her to stay? "I've been with him already twice today," she faltered. "You need—you deserve some time to yourselves."

Sensing the sudden rising of a very awkward lump in her throat and the accumulation in her eyes of a mist it would be very difficult to explain, Jamie turned and fled from the room.

"Please—Jamie!" he called after her, but she continued down the hall without turning back, the tears coming in earnest now.

What have I done, he thought! Was she so smitten with the sailor that she couldn't even carry on the simplest conversation with him any longer? It would have been better for him to keep to himself the whole day! Seeing her was the worst thing he could have done! But after a night spent tossing and turning with visions of the sunlight dancing off her hair and eyes, he could not keep himself from finding her, even if only to gaze upon her from afar. Even to see her in Robbie's arms would be better than not to see her at all!

At last he turned to Andrew and said, "I must go find Jamie, son, and speak with her. I'll be back."

He left the nursery and walked down the hallway in the direction Jamie had gone. He had a suspicion . . . if only he could talk to her alone! Even if just for a moment!

He descended the great stairway and turned toward the rear of the house toward the courtyard where she and Andrew had always been so fond of playing together, where he had lunched with them on the day of the bright red ball. As he approached the glass door his heart gave a great bound within him.

In the distance, partially obscured by tree roses and shrubbery, was the outline of Jamie's form. And she was alone!

He followed her with his gaze for a few moments, then slowly opened one of the doors with a trembling palm and softly made his way toward her over the grass.

Jamie sensed his approach but did not turn until he had stopped about four feet away. The few extra moments gave her time to gather in the last of her tears and take a deep breath to still her racing, tormented, overflowing heart.

At last she turned.

"I thought you might be here," he said.

"It's always been a favorite place of mine," she answered. "Andrew and I used to be fond of this courtyard especially."

"I remember."

"Ah, yes! The day you joined us for lunch."

"And we played with Andrew's new ball."

"Yes," Jamie laughed, "and Lady Montrose came to call in the midst of it."

"She wasn't particularly amused at our games," said Edward, smiling.

Jamie said nothing in reply. The subject of Candice Montrose brought to the surface the pain which had been the reason for her tears.

"Andrew is much better," she said at length.

"Yes," agreed his father. "The doctor says he will be able to come out in a couple days."

"That's wonderful," replied Jamie, then paused. "And then I shall have to return to Aberdeen," she added.

"Must you? I mean—so soon?"

"I have my duties," she said, her voice trembling a bit.

"I know—but . . . don't you think you could be persuaded?"

"Persuaded to what?"

"Well—to stay, perhaps?"

"To stay?" she repeated. "But . . . you mean . . . but why . . . you mean for a few days?"

"Yes, yes! A few days would be marvelous—No! That's not what I meant—"

He stopped, obviously flustered.

"It was so . . . ." he tried to continue, "—it was so dreary after you left."

He laughed nervously, trying to shake off the tension.

"I know," Jamie said. "It was rather dreary for me, too. And I missed Andrew—" she stopped.

"And?"

"I mean—of course, I missed all of Aviemere, all the people here, everyone that I had grown to love."

"And now you want to leave again?"

"But I must. I have the Gilchrist children to take care of."

"And you have your Lt. Taggart waiting to take you back to Aberdeen."

"Yes," she sighed. "He has asked me to marry him." As she said the words she looked away.

He mistook her. It was as though a bomb had exploded in his ears and his fleeting hopes had been splintered into a thousand pieces.

"He is a good man," said Edward, desperately struggling to control his voice and to keep the tears in their place. He must *not* lose himself now! He had prayed for her happiness, and now he must be strong to accept the Lord's decision. "His wife will be a lucky woman."

"Yes," said Jamie, still turned away. "I'm sure she will be—when he finds her."

"When do the two of you leave?" asked Edward, his mind in a fog, hardly hearing what she said. "I know the two of you— *she*?" he repeated suddenly, a flash of hope searing his heart.

"Yes. I know Robbie will be happy when he finally finds the right woman."

"But I thought you said—"

"He did ask me to be his wife," said Jamie.

"And what did you tell him?" asked Edward in the agony of joyful premonition.

"I haven't given him a final answer," said Jamie slowly. "But I can't marry him. I know that now."

Like the crashing of a great wave all around him, her words reverberated throughout his entire being, and Edward wrestled with himself to keep his voice from shouting aloud. She was still looking in the other direction and had continued talking, but he scarcely heard what she said. He strained to hear through the thundering silence of his own ears echoing with the pounding of his heart. Then he heard something about Candice Montrose.

"I'm sorry. What did you say?"

"Miss Montrose . . . I understand that the two of you are to be married?"

What? he thought. *How could she have heard such a thing? Who was spreading such rumors? The thing was patently absurd!*

"No," he said. "We have seen one another, of course. But—"

He could not go on. His voice was starting to crumble.

Sensing his emotion, Jamie slowly turned. Their eyes met.

"Jamie, Jamie—don't you know?" His voice faltered in dismay.

"Know what, Mr. Graystone? What is it? Have I done something to displease you?"

"Dear Lord, no!" he said miserably. "I'm going about this all wrong! Oh, perhaps I should keep silent, but I will have no peace until I speak. But this is so difficult to do. Yet if there is even a small glimmer of hope."

"Hope? I don't understand."

"Candice Montrose means nothing to me! Jamie, Jamie—how can I tell you? It's you I care about, Jamie."

"Me!"

"Jamie, I love you!"

The words came as a hot blast from a suddenly opened furnace and Jamie reeled where she stood. Edward reached out a hand to steady her. The moment their hands touched they both froze, but neither withdrew.

"I'm so sorry," she said weakly, referring to her faintness. But he closed his eyes in preparation for her rebuff. "I—I never dreamed . . ."

"I'm sorry, too," he replied. "But in truth I only realized it myself a day or two ago. I was afraid to tell you."

"Afraid?"

"I didn't want to place you in an awkward position."

"An awkward position? But how could it possibly do that?" she said, the color coming back into her cheeks and a great joy beginning to overflow within her.

"This could make it difficult for you to return to Aberdeen."

"Oh, Edward! Are you sure of what you said? It's so hard for me to take in the very words I longed to hear!"

"You longed to hear! Do you mean—"

"Yes, Edward! I cannot marry Robbie—because I love you!"

He took her tenderly in his arms and held her for several moments. Neither spoke for some time.

At last Jamie broke the intense silence. But now her voice was calm and peaceful.

"For so long I tried to convince myself otherwise," she said, "that I did not love you."

"And why did you do that, my dear Jamie?" said Edward softly.

"Because how could one such as I ever expect a man in your position—"

"Jamie," he interrupted, "you're not a snob when it comes to social rank, are you?" He laughed.

She smiled. "I was thinking of you. What would people think of—you know, a shepherdess and a laird?"

"You forget. I'm no laird. I'm merely a hired caretaker. There's hardly much rank in that."

"But your family . . . your name. You are, Edward, a gentleman. And gentlemen don't fall in love with shepherdesses or nurses. They marry ladies."

Edward relaxed, then turned and, with Jamie on his arm, began walking still farther from the house, through a grassy path with high hedges on either side. They walked slowly, neither speaking.

At length Edward broke the silence.

"Jamie," he said earnestly. "However I try to tell you this, the mere words will take away from the depth of meaning I feel in my heart. But can you try to trust me and believe me, as perhaps you have never trusted me for anything before?"

"I will, Edward."

"Then I have this to say to you, Jamie MacLeod, the woman I have grown to love, and—God willing—I will be allowed to love for many years to come: Jamie, you *are* a lady! Being a lady is not something you can be born with—it's something you *are*! My Olivia had the blood, the breeding, and the family. And she too was a lady. Candice Montrose has all those things, but she is *not* a lady. You, Jamie, have been bred and nurtured in life that comes from on high. You have allowed that life to grow and deepen within you. You have allowed yourself to become the woman of God's design. And that is the essence of what makes a lady—being God's lady! *You are a lady, Jamie MacLeod!* And here and now, I want to ask you: will you consent to become Lady Graystone? Whether I have a title or not, you will always be *my* lady to me!"

They had ceased walking by now and were standing hand in

hand. With tears streaming down her face, Jamie reached her arms about the man she loved and laid her head softly against his chest. At last she knew what all her years of searching the distant horizons and dreaming of far-off places had been about. All that time she had been looking for love. She had discovered the love of her God, but he had also been preparing her for this moment, so that when it came she would realize the deep sense of completion and fulfillment it gave her.

If you find love, you will have attained the greatest dream of all. Her mother's words came back to her and suddenly took on the significance she had no doubt had in mind when she had written them to her daughter. Somehow Alice MacLeod had foreseen this search of her daughter's heart and had done her best to direct her to the fulfillment of that dream.

Her tears of joy were all the answer Edward needed to complete his own bliss. When Jamie looked up at him after a few moments, she saw tears in his eyes too—eyes that had once frightened her. But they were no longer fearsome nor impenetrable. She saw clearly into them and was thus able to read his heart, perhaps even his soul, for he had opened all to her.

By unspoken consent they turned and, arm in arm, walked slowly back toward the house, neither anxious to end the rapture of being together at last, but realizing there were things they now needed to face as a result of the pledges they had made.

CHAPTER FORTY-FOUR

A Piece of the Puzzle

Later in the day Jamie went on a more difficult errand.

She had been watching for his return with MacKay, and thus found him walking back toward the house from the stables. When he saw her coming, he looked up with obvious expectation in his eyes. But closer scrutiny of her countenance drained all hope from him.

"Robbie, I—"

"Don't say another word!" he quickly said, placing a restraining finger on her lips. "I'm sure I won't be able to take it as well as you did when the tables were turned two years ago."

"I'm so sorry."

"You needn't be."

Then he laughed. "Look at you! You are trying so hard to be solemn, but I can see that you are fairly bursting with joy. You love Edward Graystone, and from the smile I can see hiding under that attempt at seriousness, I would guess that he has returned your love. Am I right?"

She only nodded. Then her control broke and she smiled sheepishly.

"You are happy, Jamie, and that's the most important thing. Don't get me wrong. I *am* miserable! But I think I'm not as miserable as I ought to be. I think I see something I tried to tell you at Sadie Malone's a long time ago. I love you and you love me. But we have both tried to mistake that affection for something it's not. We shall always be friends, and I shall always be as a brother to you—and don't you ever try to take *that* from me!" He added these last words with a grin.

"I wouldn't dare do that, my friend!"

As they embraced, Jamie cried with her happiness. He

316

laughed at her—then with her. They strolled for some time out in the meadow behind the stables—the waif and the sailor once more, grown into an officer and a lady, enjoying more than ever that friendship, begun in a blizzard, which would warm them both for years to come.

That same afternoon Robbie Taggart took his leave, for he had extended his superior officer's good graces far too long already. And if he could admit it, he was itching to strike out for a new adventure.

Jamie wandered back into the house, saddened by her parting with Robbie, yet at the same time fighting an irrepressible urge to skip and sing. A chapter in her life had been closed, even as the future had just been opened to her. What could possibly come next?

Wondering where Edward had gone and already longing to see him again, she came into the house through the kitchen, where Dora was busily packing up several crates.

"What's all this, Dora?" she asked.

"We've been gathering cast-offs for the poor box," she answered. "The laird just brought down the last load."

Jamie glanced casually at the contents of the latest addition to the pile, which consisted mostly of clothing. Off to one side, however, she spotted a small box containing several items of jewelry.

"I don't know many poor folk who would feel comfortable in such fine things," commented Jamie.

"I doubt they'll *wear* most of it," said Dora. "The better things will be sold and the money used to purchase more practical items. But I can hardly believe what the laird has done."

"What do you mean?"

"Well, some of the things he brought down are valuable. And a little while ago he took me to the room where his wife's things are stored and told me to take whatever I thought could be used. He had a most peculiar look in his eye."

Jamie smiled to herself, thinking that she probably had the same look in her eye.

"Why, I recall," Dora went on puzzled, "when he would fly into a rage if anyone so much as *thought* of touching anything that had been his wife's. Now he's telling me to take whatever I like. Just look at this jewelry he insisted I take!" She ran her hand through it and Jamie looked closer.

Suddenly she gasped and started back.

"Jamie, what is it?" asked the baffled housekeeper.

Seemingly ignoring her question, Jamie thrust her hand into the box and drew out one small item. She stared at it for a long time. Then she looked at Dora and said in a dry, lifeless voice, "May I take this for a few minutes?"

"Of course. Are you all right, Jamie?"

Without offering an answer, she fled the kitchen, almost blindly finding her way to the stairway, and ran to her room. There she found her pocketbook, and, with hands trembling, tore it open.

She always kept her father's last gift with her. She closed her eyes and remembered how it had fallen from his bleeding hand. Now she took it between her two fingers and held it up. There remained, even after all these years, faint bits of dried blood— her father's blood!—deeply encrusted into the settings of the gems where no amount of cleaning could get it out. She laid it next to the cufflink she had just now found in the box of cast-offs in the kitchen.

They were identical.

And then, as if to dispel any simple explanations, she saw something she had failed to notice before in all this time. Engraved in the gold casing around the gems was the single letter "G."

CHAPTER FORTY-FIVE

Donachie

Jamie sat, dazed and limp, trying desperately not to let the worst possess her mind.

She had not allowed herself to think of Iona Lundie for some time. And she clenched her teeth against the onslaught of such thoughts now. But the terrible, hateful words of the bitter woman could not be stopped. She had accused the Graystones of being responsible for her father's death, and now, despite Jamie's insistent denials of the past, it seemed perhaps she was right.

Why else did her father have this cufflink belonging to the Graystone family? What could he possibly have had to do with them? Perhaps he had found it upon the roadside—but why, then, would he hold it for dear life, so hard that it drew his blood even as his life was ebbing from him? And when he had finally relinquished it to her hand, had he not tried to say something about it?

"It belongs to . . . it belongs—it doesn't matter . . ."

He had tried to tell her something but had given up. *Oh, Papa,* she thought, *it does matter! I have to know!*

If the Graystones had been involved in her father's death, would that suddenly change her love for Edward Graystone?

Suddenly the horrifying thought came to her for the first time: What if *he* had been involved? Could he have been lying to her all this time? He was younger then, harder. She had seen how cold and seemingly unfeeling he could be. Was it possible? No! That possibility was too dreadful even to think of! He couldn't— he couldn't lie . . . or kill!

There had to be some other explanation!

She must forget all about it, forget she had ever seen either

319

of the cufflinks, throw them back into the poor box where they would never trouble her again!

Yet how could she marry Edward with such a gruesome, gnawing doubt hanging over her? It would eat at her and destroy whatever love had once been there. Even the ecstasy of a few hours ago had already begun to dissipate in the shadow of her dark thoughts.

She had to confront him with her discovery, although hints of the old apprehensiveness she had felt in his presence when first she came to Aviemere had already crept back into the edges of her mind.

How could she doubt him? She angrily chastised herself! She loved him. He could be no killer! She would go to him, and he would clear up the matter in an instant. He would tell her the cufflinks had belonged to his father or brother!

She found him coming out of Andrew's room.

"I must talk with you, in private," she said. The tone of her voice worried him and quickly dispelled the smile which had spread over his face on seeing her.

"Of course," he answered, fearing something had changed between them. He had not seen her again and did not know what had transpired with Robbie.

His hand was cold and damp as he took her arm and led her downstairs to the library.

She walked directly into the middle of the room, but when he closed the doors he lingered there for a moment, afraid to turn and face her. Licking his lips, he finally turned and asked with dreadful foreboding, "What is it, Jamie?"

"You know about my father," she began, hesitating over each word.

"Yes."

"The night he died, he gave me a gift. I thought it strange, but always assumed it was a gift from him to me. But I was a mere child and didn't even know what it was. He had been holding it so tightly that its sharp edges made his hand bleed. He tried to tell me something about it but couldn't. I guess with death reaching out to take him, it did not seem important at that moment. But I carried it with me, treasured it all my life, as a parting remembrance of my father. But then after I met the Lundie woman, I began to wonder where he had gotten the thing, whether he had torn it . . . it seemed there had to be more to the thing . . . was it a clue—was it his way of telling me—"

She stopped short and swallowed. She could not bring herself to say the words.

At length she held out her hand to him and said, "Do you know these?"

"Why, yes! Those are my old cufflinks. Where did you find the other one, Jamie? It's been lost for years. I only just today gave Miss Campbell—"

But the look of agonized horror on Jamie's face stopped him short. Her face had turned ghastly white.

With terror in her eyes she slowly withdrew her hand, backed up a step or two before stumbling over a chair, never taking her eyes from his.

"Jamie—dear Jamie!" said Edward, the truth of the missing cufflink slowly dawning on him. He held out his hand and walked toward her.

"No!" she shrieked. "Stay away!"

"Jamie, it's not what you think," he said with forced calm, still approaching her with outstretched hand.

"No!" she screamed again, running past him and out of the library, out of the house.

Jamie ran and ran, hardly heeding where she went. She only knew she had to get higher, she had to have air, room—room to see, to breathe, to think. She ran up . . . up . . . always higher, until she dropped with fatigue; then she pulled herself up to run again. Now she was running along the side of the burn in the meadow, following its course up the mountain. Almost before she realized her destination, hardly thinking that her steps had continually been pointed in this direction, she looked up. And there, as it had been all her life, was the place of her own beginnings, the place where her dreams had begun, the place from which she had viewed distant horizons—

Donachie!

She had lived at Aviemere for a year, always thinking of the mountain, always seeing it in the distance. She had continually put off the trek she knew she must one day make. But today she ran as if getting there were more urgent than life itself. As everything she had thought she could hold onto crumbled around her, suddenly the mountain raced back out of the subconscious of her distant past and loomed as a mighty sentinel of hope, solid and unchanging—the one, the only unchanging entity she could grasp. In the chaos of her overturned emotions, she had even forgotten the God who had made both her and Donachie.

The sun had begun its descent in the west and it was well into the gloamin' when she reached the rocky foot of the mountain itself. Here she kicked off her shoes, for it was summer, and she had never worn shoes in summer on Donachie. Suddenly she was fifteen again and she ran with unencumbered delight, forcing the pain which lay in the valley to stay behind in the low country. This was no place for sorrow, for distress, for the questions which had plagued and driven her upward toward her home.

Now the climbing had begun in earnest but the twilight served her well, and as she penetrated deeper and deeper into the still and awesome regions of the silent mountain, gradually she began to pass the old landmarks, each of which brought a cry of joy to her lips, even as it shot a stab of bittersweet longing to her throbbing heart. All the pleasant memories of her girlhood flooded upon her as she followed the course now of this path, now of that burn, past the grassy glen where they had so often grazed the sheep, by the foot of the tall tree where one day old Finlay had shown her the falcon's nest, ever higher, ever deeper into the mystique which had always been Donachie.

How simple her life had been there, and how pleasant! Why had she wanted to leave? What had she ever hoped to find as she gazed upon the distant horizons from the summit that day of the storm? All her dreams to find something *more* had, in the end, led her back to the land of her roots. There had been nothing *out there*, in the distant world, which had not been right here all the time. Even being a lady, as Edward had said, was not something to be sought in the distant cities of society of the world, but in the quiet of one's own heart.

Everything had been here all the time!

But only old Finlay had seen it. He could not tell his son. And in the end, Gilbert had lost his life in the pursuit of the hollow dream. Everything he had so yearned for could have been his had he only heeded the wisdom of his time-wise father. But he had not been able to hear. So he had gone, never to return.

She had not seen it, either. She had been too caught up in the dream her father had implanted in her to fully grasp the truths her grandfather had so desperately desired to reveal to her. She, too, had peered longingly into the distance—not merely toward Aberdeen, but toward the horizon of what she was not, hoping to become something she never could be.

But now she had returned. At last she knew there were no

reachable horizons beyond what Finlay had always told her. It had been here all along—everything she had wanted. The life she was searching for was *within* her own heart, a life with the God Finlay had taught her to believe in. It was not to be found in some distant city. She needed only to look within. Even love, if indeed she had found it, she had discovered at the very foot of Finlay's mountain. The horizon-seeker and adventurer Robbie Taggart had not brought her love, though he had tried. No, love, now about to be wrenched away, had come to Jamie through a man very much like the mountain his family owned, the mountain she had loved.

But those thoughts brought such acute panic to Jamie's heart that she began to run once again, trying to forget.

It was very late when she finally reached the clearing where the old stone cottage stood. She shivered with the chill of the night, for she had no coat. She walked slowly to the door and reached for the latch. How many hundreds of times had she come up to this door, stepping in to find the warm loving presence of her granddaddy? She prepared her heart as she pulled the latch this time, for she knew it would be cold and lifeless inside. The door swung open, and there everything stood, just as she had left it three years earlier.

She went first to her old bed, where she found a blanket waiting for her return. She took up the blanket and wrapped it around her shoulders, grateful for its warmth. Then she wandered back outside and down the path that led to Finlay's grave. The elder, so gray and barren when she had laid her grandfather beneath it, still stood protectively over the mound, its branches covered with new green foliage.

She stood there for some time thinking only of the old man. Then suddenly she wondered what he would think of Edward Graystone. In many ways they were alike: proud and stoic, holding within themselves their pain and sorrow—even their joy sometimes. Perhaps Finlay had helped Jamie to understand Edward and to love him.

At last a thought surfaced that she had never asked herself, perhaps because she had avoided facing it. What would her father think of his daughter loving a Graystone? And what if—?

There was that awful thought again! Mackenzie Graystone, Edward's father, had cheated her own father out of his land. Had Gilbert hated the Graystones? Was the Lundie woman right? Had her father been involved in some plot against them?

The possibility was too horrifying.

What if all the things that woman said were true! What if—?

No—no! she screamed, clasping her hands to her ears and breaking out in loud sobs. It could not be!

As the sobs subsided and her emotions quieted, Jamie wondered at her own rash behavior. Why hadn't she given Edward a chance to explain the cufflinks? What a fool she had been! She was no lady! She was still a little girl—still a waif who deserved nothing better than a cottage on a mountain! Wouldn't he have explained what had happened thirteen years ago? No, he would probably have wanted her to believe in him, to trust him, without proof or denials. That was the kind of man he was!

But she had failed him! When the first opportunity had arisen to demonstrate trust in the man she said she loved, she had doubted him completely, giving him no opportunity to explain.

Yes, she had to admit, she *did* love him! But was that not a betrayal of her father? Could she have a relationship with *any* Graystone? How could she fulfill his dreams for her by becoming a *lady* of the Graystone name? Would he not scoff at the very idea?

Yet, the Lord had led her to Aviemere. Yes, she had forgotten the Lord's hand in all this! Now her mind was growing clear. It was God who had instilled in her heart her love for Edward. She could trust in God. She could also trust Edward. How could she have doubted?

"Thank you, Lord," she breathed. "Forgive me for forgetting you, for doubting. Help me to believe in you, Lord. And help me to believe in Edward, and he in me."

The day had been the fullest of her life, ending with a strenuous five-or-six-mile climb up a steep mountain. She rose from under the elder where she had been sitting, the dew already beginning to gather upon the blanket, and walked back to the cottage. A renewed courage had come to her weary body. No longer were there any doubts about Edward, nor of disloyalty toward her father. *If they could meet*, she thought, *all would be understood*. God was still leading her, even when she forgot Him, and whatever the future held would be of His design.

She was stiff with the chill of the night and the thought of a crackling fire was inviting, indeed.

Inside the cottage she gathered some dried grass and several peats which still stood beside the hearth—peats she herself had no doubt cut several summers ago—and before long had a tol-

erable fire blazing away. It was a bit smoky but she soon reaccustomed herself to the homey smell and lay down on her old
bed where she soon fell asleep.

She did not stir until the light of morning awakened her almost nine hours later.

CHAPTER FORTY-SIX

The Laird of the Mountain

Jamie awoke at peace.

Sunlight streamed through the small windows of the cottage, but the fire had burned itself out. After the briefest of moments to reorient herself to her surroundings, she rose from the bed alert and set about lighting a new fire.

The confusion of the night before was gone. She loved God, she loved her father, she loved old Finlay, and she loved Edward, and there could be no disharmony in any of her loves.

But perhaps most importantly, she was content with herself. The questions and turmoil of the night before had been the birthplace of a tranquillity greater than she had ever known. God had used the cries of her heart as an opportunity to fill her with His love. And when she awoke, she felt utterly at peace with who she was, perhaps for the first time in her life. She was not the shepherd girl trying to be a lady, nor the daughter trying to give meaning to her father's life.

She was simply Jamie MacLeod, needing only to be what God wanted her to be—shepherdess, lady, duchess, governess, or nurse. It did not matter. Her contentment lay not in such externals, not in things or positions, but only in her personhood as a child of the God who made her, and had never failed her.

Two hours later, after she had returned from a walk to the summit of the mountain, the cottage door creaked open. She was not surprised when she turned and saw Edward's large frame filling the doorway. Her heart surged with joy and she jumped forward and ran to meet him.

"Oh, Edward!" she cried, "Will you forgive me? I know you had nothing to do with my father's death. I *know*! I was foolish to doubt you, even if for a moment!"

He smiled, in a simple offering of his understanding, then came fully into the cottage and embraced her.

"I do, my dear," he answered. "But it does matter. This is no trifling misunderstanding—this is murder, and you were right to care so deeply."

"But I had no cause to doubt you, Edward."

"But you did, Jamie. Of course you did. The cufflinks are mine, and your father more than likely tore the one from the person of his attacker. You only thought what anyone would think—that the man you love killed your father."

"Don't even say the words, Edward. Please!"

"You have a right to know."

"But I don't need to."

"Oh, Jamie, what a gift you are to me!" he said, then sighed. "But even if that's true, I'm afraid I would still need to know. I've asked myself a hundred times since yesterday—could someone in my family have been responsible, or was the cufflink stolen and the whole thing merely coincidental?"

He took her hand and led her closer to the hearth where he spread out the blanket and motioned for her to sit. He sat down beside her and stared into the orange flames for a time.

"We must talk," he said at length.

"Oh, Edward, how I wish we could just forget."

"But neither of us could. That's why I had to know. When you ran off yesterday, I looked everywhere for you. At last I guessed you might have come here. I was worried, but something assured me you would be all right and that you needed to be alone. So I left off my search for you and set about trying to answer the question that had battered my brain since you reached out your hand and showed me those cufflinks.

"I went first to Iona Lundie. She was none too hospitable, and welcomed me with a cold, evil stare. But who could blame her? I was away at Cambridge when all these things transpired. Perhaps if I had been here—well, I don't know what might have happened."

He shook his head dismally and covered his face with his hands for a moment.

"We Graystones," he sighed, "have never brought much honor to our station. I know what kind of man my father was, and I know something of what my brother is capable—and, God forgive me, I've seen those same things at work within myself, struggling to turn me into a replica of my father. For the past year I've been torn with guilt many times over a little incident with one of my tenants, a family by the name of MacRae—one of my brother's tenants, I should say."

"Why, what happened?"

"Oh, nothing to go into now. I threatened to evict them, spoke harshly to them—nothing that the Graystones haven't been doing for years. But how the memory of that day grieves me as I remember that poor, wretched man—with a sick wife—standing helplessly before me while I, sitting proud and mighty and well fed on my sleek stallion, told him to pay his paltry rent or get out. Oh, God, how could I be so blind to that man's needs—"

He stopped and hid his face in his hands.

Jamie placed a loving arm around his shoulder and laid her head against him.

When the storm of his emotion had passed, he drew a deep breath, and continued.

"Anyway, Mrs. Lundie told me that my father dismissed her husband over a prized thoroughbred that was injured under his supposed care. He denied fault, and I tend to believe what she said he said—he had been a faithful servant for years—more honest than many. I worked closely with him when I was a teenager and knew him well. But more than that, I had seen my brother ride that very horse upon the moor against my father's instructions. I, myself, foolishly did it on one occasion too—perhaps the only thing we ever had in common. But Derek didn't know the moor and I warned him that he was just courting trouble. Well, trouble is not a large enough word to describe what came of it in the end. Whatever actually happened to the horse, Lundie was dismissed, extremely bitter. It was then he hatched his scheme to blackmail my family. I don't know what secret he knew, but having worked here as factor for years, and knowing what kind of men the Graystones were, I imagine he didn't have to look far for something to hang over their heads. He tried to interest your father in the deal.

"Your father had just sold his land to my father at a pitifully low price—I also spoke to George Ellice yesterday and was able to obtain some of the particulars. In fact, Mrs. Lundie is probably right when she says my father stole the land from your father and was the principal cause of his bankruptcy. I haven't been able to trace the whole series of transactions back through the ledgers as yet, but I plan to. In any case, Mrs. Lundie said that your father would have nothing to do with her husband's scheme, but I think Lundie still planned to use him for protection against any possible reprisal by my family. Then suddenly, they both were dead."

"Mrs. Lundie said everyone thought they killed each other in a violent argument," said Jamie.

"Yes, she told me that too, which I had heard before. I was not altogether idle during your year's absence, you know. I had set a few inquiries afoot about your father, but little had come of it yet."

"Thank you," said Jamie. "But do you think it could be true?"

"What?"

"That Lundie and my father killed one another?"

"It would make this whole mystery simpler. But that doesn't answer the question of the cufflink. And it's just too convenient, too simple an explanation—exactly the sort of rumor someone in power would concoct to divert suspicion from himself. And if your father tore the cufflink from his assailant, what would Lundie have been doing with it? He was hardly the type. And only one cufflink! It makes little sense!"

"But you said it was yours?"

"My father gave them to me for my eighteenth birthday. I remember because his gifts to me were so few. When I went to pack them to take them with me to Cambridge, they were missing. Later the one turned up, but I gave it little thought. It kicked around all these years until Dora was gathering her collection of cast-offs. One cufflink does little good, but the gems were of some value and could be sold to use in other settings. But I had no idea why they turned up missing or why only one found its way back—well, I do know that now! Your father wound up with the other. I suppose a dozen things could have happened to them while they were missing. But if they were stolen, why would a thief return one cufflink?"

"Edward," said Jamie, "don't you think I've had similar questions? We may never know the answers. Perhaps we will just have to live with the uncertainty. Perhaps it is God's way of strengthening the bonds between us."

"I know why I love you so, Jamie!" He drew her closer to him and they sat in silence until the fire had burned so low.

"It is peaceful up here," Edward stated at last. "I can feel why you love it so, and why you had to come back."

"It was the only place I could come to think it through. Oh, there's so much I want to show you, Edward. I grew up here!"

"And I want to see every inch of it! But now we need to think about getting back down the mountain."

Vowing to make whatever repairs were necessary to the cottage and to outfit it as a summer hideaway or a winter's lodge, and then to come often to the peaceful mountain, they took their way, after a brief visit to Finlay's grave, down the hill. Not knowing the precise direction, Edward had tethered his horse about a mile away where he had encountered a particularly steep and rocky climb. Now, as Jamie led him by a more roundabout path, he could see that his journey to the cottage had been more difficult than necessary. Once on horseback the descent became easier, but when they reached the lower levels of the mountain, they found themselves in no hurry to speed their trip home. It was late afternoon by the time they came within sight of the spacious lawns of Aviemere, and both were by this time famished.

Leaving the horse with Sid, they entered the house by way of the kitchen. There Dora Campbell immediately accosted them, looking more florid and breathless than usual.

"Your Lordship," she said. "We have a guest—that is, well, not a guest exactly. It's your brother, sir."

CHAPTER FORTY SEVEN

The Unmasking

Jamie and Edward exchanged glances.

Edward's color paled perceptibly and a stunned look spread over his face. Jamie grasped his arm as if somehow she might steady him. It did appear to have some effect, for he took a deep breath, and—seeming to come to some decision within himself— he grasped the self-control which had almost fled him.

How could his brother still have this kind of effect on him even when he felt God had given him freedom at last from worldly cares and ambitions? Perhaps God was about to give another kind of freedom—a real and tangible and earthly freedom from all the bondage that Derek symbolized in his mind. *Yes! Yes!* he thought, *the time for resolution and decisiveness has come!*

"Jamie," he said, his voice hollow and forced, but nevertheless determined in a way she had never heard it before. "As soon as I go, I want you to begin packing your things. Then get Andrew's things together—only the necessities. The rest can wait . . . or we can do without them."

"Edward . . .?" A hundred questions crowded into her mind, but she could tell from the seriousness in his tone that the time for trusting obedience had come.

"Jamie, I wanted you to have so much—most of all, Avie-mere. Though it would never have truly been ours, at least we might have enjoyed it together. I have little to offer you except myself, but it appears that will have to suffice. Even the mountain is his! Perhaps—in time—we could save enough to buy your grandfather's croft back. Yet, now that I even say the words, I know he would never sell it to us knowing how important it is to me. He will no doubt turn it into a hunting lodge. He's spoken of such things already."

"You know all that's not important to me, as long as I have you."

"I know, Jamie. I'm only trying to prepare you. Perhaps, even more, I'm trying to prepare myself," he concluded with a weary sigh, his shoulders sagging. "I didn't think it would be this hard. Oh, Jamie, I love this place!"

"You don't know what he wants."

"He hasn't shown his face here in over ten years. Now suddenly he comes twice within a year."

He shook his head. "I must expect the worst. I have no reason to hope otherwise."

Then he turned to the housekeeper. "Miss Campbell, would you kindly help Jamie?"

"Of course, your Lordship," she replied.

He opened his mouth to protest her use of the title—especially now. But stopped himself. It hardly seemed to matter anymore.

He walked to the door to go, then turned back, seemingly as an afterthought.

"Miss Campbell, you've been a faithful servant these many years," he said. "If I must leave Aviemere . . ."

He paused.

Was what he had been about to request of her asking too much? He had not always been the best of masters. Why should he think that she would—?

But the housekeeper gave him no chance even to complete his thought.

"Your Lordship, if you are leaving Aviemere, I would count it not only my duty but also my honor to continue to serve you wherever you may go," said the housekeeper, though she knew nothing of what was happening or what doom might await her employer.

Edward grasped her hand gratefully.

"Thank you—thank you Miss Campbell—Dora!" he said. "We shall need you now more than ever!"

Finally he looked toward Jamie. "Tell Dora what is going on— tell her everything! Though she has probably guessed much from listening to us talk!"

Jamie laughed, breaking the tension, and the other two joined in.

"She has a right to know." Then he spun around and strode quickly from the kitchen.

He walked down the corridor to the main staircase. He tried to focus his eyes straight ahead, but he could not prevent them from wandering occasionally toward this or that room as he passed. This is where he had been raised. He knew and loved every inch of this place. This was his own personal Donachie. But he would not look upon these beloved rooms and halls and tapestries and gardens again! He had hung on for many years, hoping and dreaming. But now the time of parting had certainly come!

Yes, it was more difficult than he had thought it would be. But he wondered what it would have been like had not God's strengthening hand been there to sustain him, or had God not already given him a far more precious gift in Jamie than a dozen Aviemeres! For God, in His wisdom, had given Edward Graystone the *real* love his heart had yearned for all his life. He no longer needed to cling so desperately to Aviemere. It suddenly dawned on Edward, as he walked toward his appointed destination, that this painful era in his life was at last coming to an end. The seeds of his new life had been planted the day innocent young Jamie MacLeod had arrived, though he had hardly known that was the day of beginnings. And now the fruit of that seed of their love was about to ripen. They would leave Aviemere behind them to start their new life—together! By the time he stood to face his brother, a great inward peace had settled over his spirit, and he thought that if Derek had any other design than the immediate assumption of his rightful place as laird of Aviemere, he would be disappointed.

He mounted the steps with renewed determination. He was anxious to begin anew. His new life with his son and the woman he loved and God to guide and protect them—it was all he needed—or wanted!

He had glanced into the parlor as he passed, but somehow he had known Derek would not be there waiting like a guest for the return of his host. He was right. Derek had gone upstairs, making himself fully at home—but then, it was his home—it always had been.

He found Derek, as expected, in the library. When Edward entered, the older brother greeted him casually with a broad grin.

"I'm glad you stock a supply of good brandy," he said, holding up a glass in which he had helped himself to the amber liquid. "Thus, waiting has its rewards."

Edward could tolerate almost anything at that moment except the prospect of his brother's malicious banter and shallow quips.

"You're welcome, of course," was all Edward could say.

"Ah, Edward! Will you never cease to be so dull?"

"I'm sorry, Derek. I suppose my wit is lost in my surprise."

"I told you I intended to make Aviemere my home one day."

"Is that the purpose of this appearance?"

"Always to the point, Edward," replied Derek. "An admirable quality, I suppose. Though really, my dear brother, soon you will no longer have the pretense of land and title to rely upon, so if I were you, I'd try to polish my wit a bit more."

"Thank you for the advice."

"I give it as freely as I have given you liberty over the years with my inheritance. Not many brothers would have been as benevolent as I have been in letting you relish in a taste of glory."

"I have never looked at it in quite that way before," said Edward with the hint of a smile. "And I now realize you are absolutely right. But I think I would have been a better man if I could have long ago walked away from your—benevolence, as you call it."

"But you didn't!"

"No. But waiting, as you put it, does have its rewards. And that privilege of laying down something I love has been reserved for me for this very day."

"Bah! Did you care that much for this place that you were willing to so demean yourself all these years?"

"I never until lately thought of it as demeaning," replied Edward. "I suppose I always thought that caring gave me something of a right to it."

"Caring—rights—such noble thoughts!" Derek smirked. "In the end, it got you nothing!"

"I'm not so sure of that, Derek. I think at this moment I have more than I ever had in my life. I know I am certainly happier today than any other day since I was born."

"But you don't have Aviemere."

"It was never mine to begin with."

"Do you concede so easily?" For a moment some of the spark left Derek's eyes. "You're taking all the sport from this, you know."

"Did you expect me to rant and rave? Did you expect violence?"

"If our last meeting were any gauge of what my expectations should have been," replied Derek, "you disappoint me, Edward. You have gone weak-kneed on me. Why, we had a name for cowards like you down in Africa, but I don't want to *offend* your weak woman's ears with it!"

"I will leave as soon as my things are together," said Edward, ignoring his brother's insults. "But there is one matter I would like to discuss with you before I take my leave," he continued, gathering new resolve.

He reached into his pocket and took out the cufflinks which Jamie had shown him. "Do you recognize these?"

Derek gazed at the items with a genuine blank expression; then slowly a light began to dawn in his eyes.

"A gift from our father, I believe," he said. "A gift to you."

"They were lost some thirteen years ago—"

"Terribly careless of you," Derek interrupted with another smirk.

"One found its way back to my bureau," Edward went on, ignoring his brother's comment. "The other was found gripped in a dying man's hand. But it did not come back to me until yesterday. I have wondered since then how my cufflink came to be in this man's hand? He was no thief, though perhaps he found it lying about and chose to clutch it with his last desperate strength. Or perhaps they had been stolen from the house, and the unknown thief killed the man. But then the question becomes more complex. For why would that thief then sneak back into the house to return only one cufflink? It is puzzling, as you can tell. Look, there is still blood encrusted around the gems!" He thrust his hand toward Derek's face.

"For a man who seems to pride himself on brevity, you are being unusually loquacious, little brother," said Derek sarcastically as he stepped back from Edward's hand after only a cursory glance. "I wonder that you don't come right out and say what you are driving at. Are you looking to me for some alibi to a murder you committed!" He laughed. "Certainly you are not trying to implicate *yourself* in some heinous crime, Edward!"

"I will speak plainly then," said Edward, dropping his hand. "Did you borrow my cufflinks?"

"Upon occasion, yes, I do believe I wore them. They are a fine set, you know."

"Without informing me, or asking my permission?"

"We were not, you may recall, in the habit of observing such niceties."

"Were you then involved in the deaths thirteen years ago of Frederick Lundie and Gilbert MacLeod?"

Derek responded with a loud, outright laugh. "My, my! You are speaking plainly!" He proceeded to drain his glass of brandy, then poured another before speaking. But he made certain the silence was long enough to be agonizing.

"Are you asking if I committed murder?"

"At least one of those men was contemplating a scheme to blackmail our esteemed family—you or our father, I presume."

"Oh—you are spotless yourself!"

"I had nothing to hide."

"And so—a perfect motive for murder then, is that what you are saying?"

Edward did not answer. Derek remained silent for a moment, deep in thought. He did not appear in any sense guilt-stricken, or even nervous, but simply weighing a decision in his cunning mind. When he spoke at length, each word was drawn out with a cool and calculating deliberateness.

"Yes, Edward," he said, "I did kill Lundie—he was nothing but a dirty extortionist."

"He had been a faithful factor!" cried Edward.

"Had been, Edward. Had been! When he turned colors on me I had no choice."

"Though it was you who got him fired?"

"Bah, Edward! Don't be so naive! Low breeds like him hardly deserve to live! But I only meant to frighten the other rotter."

"Oh, my God, Derek!" Edward cried, less in shock than in sorrow. "God help us!" His whole body felt suddenly weak and he staggered backward. He caught himself against the door. But he barely stood, so limp had his legs become. "What has our family become!"

"No doubt you'll now be off to fetch the baliff," said Derek, his smug look intact. "But you needn't bother, for I'll deny it, and it'll be my word against yours. And the word of a younger brother, hungering after the estate, will not carry much weight with the law."

"Then why tell me at all?" asked Edward, his voice still choked with dismay.

"Your docility about my return and my taking the estate from out of your hands has spoiled my sport on that account. I thought this would add some zest to the day, Edward. Seeing that look on your face—that wonderful, pale, horrified look of shock and dismay and disbelief—why, Edward, it makes the whole day worth getting up for! Ha, ha! Can't you see the irony of it? You, knowing your brother, the holder of *your* precious land, is a murderer—and you can't do a thing about it! Ha, ha, ha! I can hardly believe my good fortune with the turn things have taken. It should make for some interesting family reunions through the years, wouldn't you say?"

"Do you hate me that much?"

"It has nothing to do with hate or affection. It's merely a matter of survival and of keeping some spice in life, as they say," replied Derek matter-of-factly, but with a grin still on his face, that grin which contrived to say so much while his lips remained silent. He caught up the brandy decanter rather buoyantly, like the attentive host bent on making a good impression. "Come," he said, "have a brandy. I'm sure you could use one! Let's toast the new understanding between us, dear brother!"

This man is my own brother, Edward thought, *yet I feel as if I am looking on the devil himself!* He wanted to turn and flee, but his legs were still weak. Even more, he still hoped to find at least one spark of humanity in him.

"Now, Edward," Derek continued, as if his crimes were nothing and his brother's pain was but a lark, "there is one matter of business I wish to discuss." He paused, taking a drink from his glass as if shifting the mantle of superior authority which he had just donned. "I'm still a bit new to this landlord business and thus I would appreciate as it were, the assistance of one more experienced. The present factor—what's his name?"

"Ellice."

"Ah, yes—Ellice! As I say, Mr. Ellice would do, of course, but I would like to offer you the position in his stead. You've done well by the estate in my absence. There's no reason you have to do anything hasty in leaving."

Had Derek's words held even a vague appeal for assistance, Edward might have reconsidered his former decision in hopes of yet having some positive, and possibly even redemptive, impact on his brother. But the words were not an appeal—they were a challenge. Derek well knew his brother's weak spot, and he relished the thought of keeping him in his power. He was certain it would be difficult, if not impossible, for Edward to resist the offer to stay at Aviemere.

But Derek did not know his brother as well as he thought. The shackle of Aviemere had fallen from Edward that day. Only hope for Derek's restoration could persuade him to stay. He could clearly see his brother's intent, however, and he knew that to stay might only be a further goad to his brother's crooked morality.

"Derek, that would be impossible. And George can do for you all I could."

"That old Graystone pride—"

"Perhaps," replied Edward. "But I think I would sooner take a position as a stable hand than to work in the employ of one I respected so little."

Derek smiled, but there was a hint of surprise in it.

"Then . . . I suppose this is it," he said haltingly.

"I'm afraid so."

Even as he spoke, Edward wondered if he could really walk out—leave everything in the hands of one so monstrous. "I shall take what I can carry now, and send for the rest of my personal belongings later."

Derek raised his glass in silent consent.

Woodenly, Edward slowly turned, opened the door, and walked out of the library for the last time and toward the stair. There was but one thought in his mind: *Lord, I can't do this thing alone. Continue to strengthen me!*

Two hours later Sid drove the carriage away from the door-step of the grand mansion, with George Ellice following behind with a small wagon full of the belongings they were taking. Inside the carriage its passengers were silent and subdued, but not heartbroken. There were few tears, except for Dora's and a few that Edward managed to blink back.

But the man they had called the laird of Aviemere was content. He had everything he wanted within arm's reach. What faded in the distance behind the jostling coach represented only a shallow imitation of the happiness he now knew was real in his heart.

CHAPTER FORTY-EIGHT

Family Secrets

It had been difficult to leave Jamie in Aberdeen.

Edward loathed to be separated from her even for a moment, but he had business to complete in Edinburgh. And Andrew, who had been spirited from his sickbed prematurely, needed her now more than he did.

Edward was on his way by train to Edinburgh to consult with the family lawyer, Jacob Beasely. With his fortunes so abruptly changed and the prospect of marriage before him, Edward felt it his responsibility to set a solid course for his life and his family's future security. He still had, of course, the allowance from his father's inheritance, which amounted to four hundred pounds a year. That alone, along with what he had saved and invested during his tenure at Aviemere when he had been paid double that amount, would have provided a modest but comfortable life for him and Jamie and Andrew. But he could not picture himself spending the rest of his days in idleness. Thus, with these things on his mind, he hoped Mr. Beasely could offer him some direction.

Jacob Beasely, an elderly man just a few months short of seventy, was semiretired and kept his office in his home. It was a house befitting his respected station in a row of very similar residences along Queensferry Road, all neat, trim, affluent two-story stone homes. Edward walked up the steps to the front door with some misgivings. After all, this family lawyer was by rights and custom Derek's counselor, not his. But over the years Edward, not Derek, had dealt with Beasely, and the older man had developed a fatherly attachment toward him. In fact, he often sensed that Beasely, who was well acquainted with the situation between the brothers, felt rather sympathetic toward Edward.

Edward's knock on the door was answered by a maid who knew Edward and led him immediately to the lawyer's study.

Beasely rose when Edward entered and extended his hand to his visitor. "Edward," he said. He did not exactly smile, for he was much too businesslike for that, but he did give him a friendly nod.

"I hope my coming unannounced like this is no great intrusion," Edward said, returning the handshake and gratified by the warm intensity he felt in the lawyer's hand.

"Sit down, lad." Beasely motioned Edward to a nearby chair and then returned to his own behind the mohogany desk. "Actually, I expected you would be here sooner or later."

"Then you've seen my brother?"

"I have. And I'm terribly sorry things could not have turned out—well, differently."

"It turned out only as I should have expected. And to tell the truth, Mr. Beasely, I feel almost relieved it's over."

At that moment the maid poked her head into the office.

"Sir," she said to Mr. Beasely, "would ye be wantin' some tea?"

"Yes, Molly, that would be most welcome. We will be here for some time."

The maid left, and Beasely returned his attention to Edward. "It is most comforting to hear you are taking it so well. Have you made any plans as to your future?"

"I plan to be married soon," replied Edward; the lawyer's stately features nearly broke into a smile—at least his eyes.

"Well, well," he said. "That's grand news!" But he quickly turned serious once more. "And will the turn in your fortunes—forgive me if I am becoming too personal—but does your intended—?"

"She knows," Edward finished for him. "We have no qualms about living modestly. But I do feel inclined to make some sort of living over and above my inheritance. That is why I have come to you—to seek your counsel."

Beasely appeared genuinely pleased by the confidence Edward seemed to place in him.

"You studied law at Cambridge, did you not?" he asked.

Edward nodded.

"I would be pleased to make inquiries on your behalf. I have several friends who would be gratified to have one with your qualifications employed in their firms."

"Thank you, Mr. Beasely."

The conversation waned for a few moments as Molly returned with the tea cart and served the two gentlemen. They occupied themselves in this manner for several minutes after the maid bustled from the room. Then Beasely dabbed his mouth with a linen towel and cleared his throat to resume again in a professional manner.

"There is another matter I wish to take up with you," he said.

He shuffled through a small stack of papers until he found one in particular, then spoke again. "Actually, this matter has been sitting on my desk for some two days now as I have unsuccessfully deliberated a course of action. I fully realize affairs of the estate—perhaps even the whole family, to a degree—now rest with Derek, yet he has been far removed these many years. Moreover, I felt I would rather place it under your scrutiny first. I do not know at this point whether there may be delicacies in the situation. I received this—" he held up what appeared to be a letter, written in fine script—"two days ago. It is from a Monsieur Louis Diderot, an advocate from Marseille."

As he spoke Edward looked more closely at the letter.

"The whole thing is of such an odd nature, I should have perhaps dismissed it entirely. But there remained a grain of believability in the fabric of the story that I had to give it my attention."

Beasely went on to explain that Diderot was representing a woman accused of killing a man during a row in one of Marseille's waterfront bistros. The woman claimed self-defense, but witnesses, of whom there were several, were divided as to the truth of her story. It seemed the woman had been intimate with the man for years and had been the object of frequent abuse. The prosecutor claimed premeditation, and it appeared a lengthy trial was in the offing. Diderot was writing on behalf of the woman who was in desperate need of funds for the defense of her life. It appeared the woman, whose name was Linette D'Aulnais, avowed a relationship with the Graystones of Aberdeenshire, and was appealing to them for money.

"I've never heard of her."

"Neither had I, as such."

"Does she have any possible ground for her claim?" asked Edward.

"Ah . . . yes," returned Beasely, obviously choosing his words with care. "The letter goes on to explain that. And herein lies my hesitancy, and yet . . ."

"Mr. Beasely, you may as well come right out with it and tell me. I doubt that I can hear much these days about my family that would surprise me."

"Madame D'Aulnais says she is, well—that she is the mother of your brother, Derek!" Beasely finished, leaning back heavily in his chair as if the weight of his statement had physically fatigued him.

Edward stood suddenly and paced the floor for a moment.

He had been wrong about nothing surprising him. At first he did not even question the credibility of the woman's statement, though of course he would have to do so eventually, for such claims were constantly being leveled at the families of noblemen in the Graystones' position.

He stopped his pacing and turned toward Beasely. "You believe her?"

"Before I can exactly answer that I have to reveal to you another extremely confidential matter," said the lawyer. "Thirty-four years ago—which cannot escape you as coincidental, that being your brother's age!—your father initiated what he deemed 'a business venture.' Only he and I were to be privy to it. He 'invested'—and I used the word loosely, but that was how he always insisted that I refer to the matter—two hundred pounds annually in the enterprises of one M. L. D'Aulnais. He never enlightened me as to the exact nature of these enterprises and would never give me a straight answer when I made inquiry about the lack of any visible return on his investment. There was a confidential clause in his will which stipulated that upon his death a lump sum of 2,000 pounds was to be paid to M. D'Aulnais."

Edward stared, incredulous. At length he spoke. "Did you suspect?"

"I must say I had my suspicions," replied the lawyer. "But I never dreamed your father would try to pass off an illegitimate child as his heir. All those years I believed—as his wife must have—that he had been married before but that first wife died in childbirth. He made me swear, which I did, never to tell you that you and Derek were not both sons of the same mother. But the woman, knowing that Mackenzie would never marry her, must have simply left the child with him. So to save face, he returned to Scotland and began his fabrication of a continental marriage ending in tragedy."

Edward was dumbstruck.

"Perhaps he had his reasons for his silence, but it was unconscionable, in my opinion, to treat you as he did. And as an aside, the 'liason' did not end with your father's death. That is to say, some five years ago the name D'Aulnais came to my attention again. This time it was your brother who requested a sum of one thousand pounds to be diverted to an account in D'Aulnais's name. To my knowledge that was the last mention of the name until now."

"Then my brother must have known."

"It would seem so."

Now Derek's statement about survival came unmistakably clear. The suave, confident, swaggering elder brother was also grasping for dear life to the dream of Aviemere. To keep it he had to pay extortion to his own mother. A single misplaced word, the mere loss of good faith, could have robbed him of it all. And it was not difficult to see how another blackmailer could have incited him to murder.

The most painful blow to Edward about the whole startling revelation however, was that his father had all along chosen the illegitimate child over himself. It was possible he loved Derek's mother, for Edward well knew there had never been any love between his own mother and Mackenzie Graystone. So the child of love was therefore the favored child. He wondered why his mother tolerated the sham. But propriety was everything thirty years ago, and marrying Mackenzie Graystone, laird of Aviemere, had given her a name and an estate to be proud of. It must have been enough to compensate her for her lasting silence.

"You see why," Beasely continued, "I was reluctant in presenting this matter to your brother. He has been keeping up the duplicity since your father's death, and I saw no reason why he would not continue to do so. But my conscience is still alive, Edward, and I could no longer keep you from what I had kept hidden from you all these years."

"Thank you, Mr. Beasely. I appreciate your forthrightness."

"As far as your right to the inheritance, I doubt that this woman's claim would be legally acceptable, especially should your brother deny it. Of course we could initiate legal proceedings in the court of chancery. But that would take time and would prove very costly. The thing would not only be highly disagreeable, but it would undoubtedly take more money than you have at your disposal, as, unfortunately, your brother Derek does control the purse strings. Of course, my knowledge of the former association of your father to M. L. D'Aulnais might interest the court, and even substantiate a relationship. But it would not prove that the woman was Derek's mother. Yet if we fight it, I think in the end we would win and the court would restore you to your rightful position."

Edward was silent.

For a brief instant his old longing returned. Aviemere was his! Everything was his! He *was* Lord Graystone, earl of Aviemere!

All these years Derek had known and yet had made him suffer—even gloating in his suffering. Now he could at last seek retribution. He would walk hotly to the very doors of the mansion and dispossess the baseborn snake! His pulse was racing, perspiration beaded on his forehead. His body tensed as if he would right then spring upon the invisible form of his enemy.

Then Edward sank back and slumped in his seat. The momentary frenzy of renewed turmoil within himself at last convinced him of what must be done.

"Send the woman her money," Edward said. "And burn the letter."

"What!" exclaimed the lawyer in disbelief.

"Do it—now!"

"Edward, you can fight this—and win!"

"What would I win?" Edward sighed.

"The estate, Edward! Aviemere!"

"I laid down my desire for the estate when I left it."

"Think of how he and your father have treated you!"

"I have no taste for revenge."

"Then think of your son!"

"I am thinking of him, Mr. Beasely," said Edward, his determination more firm than ever. "I am trying to protect him from the misery I knew all my life. I cannot but believe he will be happier as a simple man without the temptations of wealth and power."

"You would leave the title in the hands of the undeserving?"

"Derek has paid dearly for what he has, and I cannot believe he will ever be happy with it. The grasping hands of greed are never able to find contentment in the empty riches they seek. If he must be punished, let that be his judgment, and let it come from God's hands, not mine. I have all I want, Mr. Beasely."

With that Jacob Beasely rose from his chair, took Diderot's letter, and, with a final glance back at Edward who merely nodded decisive consent, dropped it into the hearth, where a warm blaze quickly lapped up around the sheet, curling it into a momentary red-orange flame before it darkened, shrivelled, and disintegrated into ashes.

CHAPTER FORTY-NINE

Derek Graystone

Thus the murderer retained his place in society, and justice was not to be had in the account of Derek Graystone.

As Edward predicted, he was neither happy nor content. Perhaps his one act of contrition—though he would never have seen it as such—was that he neither married nor produced heirs as he had once threatened. The more correct assumption behind his decision was, no doubt, simply that Derek was entirely a self-centered man. He cared nothing for insuring the propagation of his existence after he was gone, especially when to do so involved the extremely dissatisfying prospect of marriage. Even for the sake of goading his brother he could not accept the idea of being tied hopelessly to one woman.

In fact, Derek was able to tolerate the life of a country squire for only one year before he applied for the reactivation of his commission and was sent abroad.

Edward did not resume his place at Aviemere even then, but left it in the hands of George Ellice, who ran the estate, if not with the love and expertise of Edward, at least with a fairer hand than the pseudo earl.

A sort of justice was ultimately laid at the doorstep of Derek Graystone five years later when certain wild Arab dervishes led by a holy man they called the Mahdi revolted against their Egyptian Khedive in the province of the Sudan. In Kordofan the so-called Mahdi's forces annihilated an Egyptian force. Before reinforcements could arrive under General Gordon, thousands of Egyptians and their British officers were massacred—among them, Derek Graystone. His life, as he had lived it, tragically came to a violent, bitter and unhappy end.

CHAPTER FIFTY

The Final Return

The road had changed little since that day eight years ago when Jamie had first traveled it.

As the couple rode through the fields where in the distance the rich golden heads of oats and barley bent gently in the soft autumn breeze, it seemed as if their hearts would burst with happiness and wonder.

The carriage slowed to a stop, and Jamie turned to Edward— for he himself was driving on this most special day. But he was already engaged in conversation with a farmer along the other edge of the roadside.

"You're looking well, MacRae," he said.

"Aye, sir. Nice t' see ye again!"

"I hear good reports from Mr. Ellice about your progress. He tells me you've begun to turn a nice profit."

"Aye. An' I hae ye yersel' t' thank fer it, sir."

"If you're making a go of it, Jimmy, it's from hard work!"

"Aye, ye're right there. But 'twas you that made me git oot o' the pub an' t' work."

"Well, I'm glad it has all worked out for you, Jimmy. We'll see you again soon."

And with those words the carriage again jerked into motion.

No, the countryside hadn't changed much. Perhaps the greatest change had been in Jamie herself. She sat in the carriage now as it clattered along the road, stately and lovely, with a glow and an air of confidence that had not been present on that first day. She spoke with grace and her movements were assured and genteel. There could no longer be any doubt: here sat a lady.

But one thing had not changed, and that was the spirit of love and caring which lived in her heart. Within the stately lady, there still dwelt the heart of the shepherd girl with all her exuberance and laughter.

"Look, Dora!" she exclaimed as the carriage turned from the road and passed through the great iron gate, "there is the Ellice cottage. See, children, through the trees!"

She looked at Edward as they made their way up the estate drive through the long row of birch trees. His face held an expression of nostalgia, and she knew why. It was a time of great joy. How they had longed for the rich land of Aviemere during their years in Aberdeen! But now that the day of their return had finally come, Edward had not been able to hide the subtle reminders of the years of suffering he had spent here.

Jamie reached out her hand to him. "It will be different for us now," she encouraged.

"I know," he replied. "God would not have led us back here if it were not to be so. Yet I am thinking, too, of those who will come after us. We must prepare them for the life they will someday face."

"Then we must never cease praying for them, now perhaps more than ever," said Jamie. "They are in God's loving hands."

"Oh, Jamie, I love you so! I could not have come back here without you at my side. For I am certain it is you who will make it different—as you did when you came before!"

The carriage began to slow and finally pulled to a stop in front of the great mansion. Andrew jumped out first, a slender, handsome lad of almost ten now. He reached up and took the hand of his mother, for Jamie was that and more to him. As he helped her alight from the carriage, she smiled at him and held his hand a moment longer than was necessary, giving it an affectionate and knowing squeeze.

Meanwhile, two children had tumbled from the other side of the carriage—a boy of four, who fairly leaped out, and a girl of two, who insisted she could do it herself and repulsed her father's assistance. Dora Campbell, however, did not refuse his hand, for her limbs were not so spry as they once had been, and her hair was a good deal grayer. By the time they had stepped down, the two youngsters were on the steps trying to work the heavy iron door latch. Edward hurried after them, hoping to make a more seemly entrance for his family.

Jamie hung back a moment. She had done the same thing on that first frightful day; then it was from awe and trepidation. Now her eyes sought out the inscription over the door. "Aut pax aut bellum." The words had carried such dread when she had read them then. Yet she felt none of that at this moment, for at last the Graystone family had settled on *peace*, and thus there was no longer any fear.

Just then the door opened and Cameron Reily stepped forward to greet the family.

"Lord and Lady Graystone," he said. "Welcome home!"

ROBBIE TAGGART: HIGHLAND SAILOR,
Book 2 in *THE HIGHLAND COLLECTION,*
is now available.